Susan Andersen

Just for Kicks

MIRA®

ISBN: 978-0-7394-7240-8

JUST FOR KICKS

This is dedicated, with love,
to two special women in my life

To
Caroline Cross
For apples and cherries and friendship and
long phone conversations.
And for all the excellent suggestions
that helped improve my writing.

And to
Mimi Armitstead
For nearly thirty years of friendship.
That memorable weekend you spent drilling
intelligent answers to dumb questions into my head
was merely one shining highlight out of so many.

You guys are the best

~Susie

Dear Reader,

I'm blessed with a great family. My husband, my son, my brothers and sister-in-law and my mother are my support system. Knowing they're always behind me gives me the wings to try new things. And perhaps you've noticed that family, whether it's the one my characters were born into or the one that they've created for themselves, is an ever-present theme that runs throughout my books.

Carly Jacobsen has assembled her own clan. She's never had her mother's approval, but she has the love and adoration of her best friend and best friend's husband as well as that of a young-at-heart older couple, and together the five of them have forged a family. They're there for each other through good times and bad, and they're always looking out for one another. Between her crew's unconditional approval, her beloved pets and her dancing, she's built a life that fulfills her. She needs nothing else to complete it.

Or so she believes.

Wolfgang Jones is not a people person. He's a man with a plan for his future who doesn't see the point in cluttering up his life with personal entanglements. But his agenda goes off track when he's sucked into Carly's messy life and his troubled teenage nephew is dropped on his doorstep.

Although he puts up a decent fight, like any good hero he eventually realizes what's really important in life.

I hope that Carly and Wolf and their tribe will make you laugh out loud and maybe shed a tear or two. Happy reading.

Susan

Just for
Kicks

One

"I don't know what to do about him," Carly Jacobsen complained to her friend Michelle as they paused to accommodate a group of Japanese tourists wanting their pictures taken with real live Las Vegas showgirls. "He's stubborn, opinionated and just won't listen."

"A typical male, in other words."

She muffled a snort. "Yeah." Her feet were killing her, but she smiled prettily for the camera and tried not to feel like an Amazon as she towered above the tourists. Thank God she and Michelle were wearing the silky brunette twenties-era flapper-style wigs from the final act instead of the towering headpieces from an earlier number. That made them only a foot taller than everyone.

"Look at it this way," Michelle murmured over the shutterbugs' heads. "At least you can be grateful he's got four legs instead of two like the guy I live with."

"There is that," she agreed. "Rufus has been one tough pup to train, but at least I have some eventual hope he *is* trainable."

"Which is more than you can say for most men."

"Right." Carly had never had any interest in living with a man. And yet… "On the other hand, you get regular sex. I only have the dimmest memory of what that was like."

They struck a couple more poses before easing away from the tourists, who bowed, smiled and murmured their thanks. Carly flashed them a genuine smile in return. She really liked the Japanese. They were polite, and that was very much appreciated, because she didn't see lovely manners every day in her business. Especially among the male half of the population.

"You wanna stop for a drink?" Michelle asked as they crossed the casino a moment later.

"No, I'd better get home. I've got hungry pets to feed."

Leaving Michelle at the little lounge they often frequented, she headed toward the dressing room to change into her street clothes before going home. She'd been dancing in *la Stravaganza*, the big production show at the Italian-themed Avventurato Resort Hotel and Casino, for so long now that she rarely heard the sounds of the casino around her any longer. But she was particularly tired tonight after spending the early morning hours wrestling with the dilemma of Rufus. He was the newest of her babies, as she called her rescued pets, and fretting over how she was going to get him past his recalcitrant behavior had made it all but impossible to fall asleep. He simply refused to be trained. And thanks to her new neighbor, she was very much afraid that the clock was ticking on the mutt's fate.

So now every clang and clatter of the electronic slots, every rattle of the balls in the roulette wheels and triumphant yell or commiserating groan of the gamblers crowding the casino floor kept time with the headache beginning to throb behind her left eye. Which perhaps explained why, when a petite white-haired lady clutching a bucketful of silver dollars slammed into her with an oversize handbag, Carly, who was generally sure-footed as a mountain goat, staggered backward.

A little clumsiness would have been the end of it, except she'd just climbed the two stairs that divided the high-stakes slot machines from their humbler brethren. Her stumble back sent the heel of her right T-strap stepping off into space, and, unbalanced, she grabbed for the railing while automatically tightening her core muscles to lift her shoulders back into alignment with her hips.

Her fingers brushed the railing but it slid through her grip. And although she straightened enough to keep from back-flopping, she landed in a graceless heap on the floor, her right leg twisting beneath her.

An obscenity hissed through her teeth as pain exploded in her ankle.

There were exclamations all around and a vague sense of people crowding close. Someone bent over her. "Are you all right, miss?"

She looked up at a man with light brown hair, backlit by the garish lights of the hundred-dollar slots at the top of the stairs. When his face swam into view, she noticed in a hazy sort of way that he was extremely handsome.

He could have been a troll for all she cared, since she could barely see through the pain clouding her vision. Besides, what she did manage to focus on was enough to tell her he lacked the edginess that usually attracted her—that certain something that turned men into what her friend Treena referred to as Got Testosterone? guys.

His face was also merely one of many. Pulling her gaze away from him, she saw that several people were gathered around gawking at her. But not, she noted, the little old lady who had knocked her on her ass.

Damn fanatic gamblers.

Studying her with concerned eyes, the man who'd inquired about her well-being crouched down next to her. "Is anything broken?"

She gingerly untangled her legs until she'd freed her trapped ankle, her breath catching as the shifting weight sent a fresh shard of pain zinging around her foot. "No. At least, I don't think so. I twisted my ankle, though." And it hurt so damn bad it was all she could do not to whimper. She was never at her finest when injured.

A guy young enough to think multiple piercings and black eyeliner and lipstick were actually a fortunate fashion statement pulled his gaze away from the generous stretch of her legs long enough to nod. "Yeah. It's swelling up."

"Needs ice," someone else agreed.

"So," murmured a portly man in a pair of Sansabelt pants that were hitched well above his natural waistline, "could I get my picture taken with you?"

"What is going on here?"

Carly's blood pressure immediately spiked. *Shit.* She knew that last voice. It was deep and accented, and God knew she'd heard its disapproving timbre directed at her on more than one occasion these past few weeks. It belonged to Wolfgang Jones, second in command of the Avventurato's Security and Surveillance department.

And her recently moved-in, pain-in-the-ass, next-door neighbor.

Two

Carly peered at the approaching man through the forest of legs surrounding her and conceded that, if she had to be absolutely honest, Jones didn't have an actual accent. Still, there was something about the precision with which he formed his words that made you just know his thoughts probably didn't wind through his brain in English.

She would have snorted if she wasn't already concentrating on not mewling like a soaked-to-the-skin kitten. But, please. Like the name *Wolfgang* hadn't already given the game away?

He muscled his way through the crowd, tall and lanky, blond and built, managing to irritate her beyond measure simply by breathing the same air she did. This was the man who had her worried sick over Rufus. All too aware, however, of the public behavior the Avventurato expected from its employees whenever they were on the premises, she pressed her lips together to keep the snarl she felt forming in the back of her throat from slipping out.

Sometimes, though, representing the hotel and casino really bit.

From the expression that flashed across Jones's deep-set eyes, she was pretty sure he wasn't any happier to see her than she was to see him. Still, he waded through the crowd, then turned in front of her to face the people gathered around.

"Go about your evening, folks," he said with his habitual stern, I-am-God-therefore-you-will-obey-me haughtiness. "I will take care of this situation." Then, turning back, he squatted down in front of her in his faultlessly tailored black suit, charcoal Egyptian-cotton shirt and pearl-gray silk tie, without an apparent doubt in the world that the tourists would do exactly as he'd bid them.

Which they did, dammit. God, he was vexing.

He had a reputation around the casino for being a guy who got things done, though. Considering their recent history, she hated to admit that Jones had any redeeming qualities at all, but she had to concede that if he gave even half the attention to his work that he was currently focusing on easing off her shoe, his rep was probably well deserved.

All the same, she knew him for the dog-hating jerk he was and she didn't trust him an inch further than she could throw him. For all she knew, his gentle handling was nothing more than a ploy to make her relax her guard. Pushing up on her elbows, she monitored him closely through narrowed eyes to make sure he didn't pull anything tricky that would cause her ankle to hurt even worse than it already did.

As the young man with the Goth makeup and facial piercings had pointed out, the area surrounding the joint in question was swollen. It was also beginning to grow warm. Her injured flesh felt downright frigid, however, compared to Wolfgang's sizable hands as he slid one over her heel and up to her calf to brace her leg while he probed the puffy flesh around her ankle with the other. The hot-skinned touch shocked her. Who ever would have suspected such a grim, cold guy could radiate so much heat?

Cupping his palm over her instep, he gently rotated her foot. His gaze flashed up in time to catch her wince. "That hurt?"

"Yes, it hurts," she said testily. Then fairness forced her to add, "But I'm pretty sure it's just twisted." She'd had enough injuries to be a pretty good judge. But all she could think was that she had two days to get the swelling down and the joint back into dancing form, because she didn't want to have to call Vernetta-Grace, *la Stravaganza*'s general manager, to tell her she'd injured herself. Again.

Carly looked down at the scimitar-shaped red scar on the knuckle above her right index finger that had cost her two days' work less than a month ago.

"How did this happen?"

She looked up at Wolfgang, at his lightly tanned face beneath pale, spiky hair. "I was ambushed by a little old lady with a monster purse." Wanting his hands off her, she thrust one of her own out at him. "Help me up."

"I don't think it is broken or even badly sprained," he agreed, and slid his fingers away from her leg with an enthusiasm that seemed to match her own. He rose to his feet in a single, easy movement, then reached down and grasped her outstretched hand, hauling her upright.

She came up faster than she expected and instinctively put her injured foot down to keep from slamming into him. The flash of pain spearing her ankle made her crumple, and only Wolfgang's quick hands wrapping around her upper arms kept her from sagging against his chest. The lilac-and-gold-beaded fringe of her costume swung out, sparkling bits of confetti that slapped up against his dark shirt and slacks.

Damn, damn, damn. Of all the men in this casino, why did

he have to be the one who'd come to her aid? And what the hell was one of Security and Surveillance's higher-ups doing playing nursemaid to a dancer, anyway?

Probably grabbing yet another opportunity to rub her nose in how responsible he was. Like being anal was a *good* thing.

He helped her to a nearby chair in front of a bank of poker machines, swiveled her seat to allow her leg to extend into the aisle and turned a plastic coin bucket on end for her to prop her heel on. Then he flagged down a waitress.

"Bring some ice and a towel, please," he said. It was clear it wasn't really a request, and the woman promptly turned away to do as he'd commanded.

"I'm guessing you don't have a lot of friends," Carly said dryly.

Crouched in front of her to check her foot once again, he slowly raised his head and looked at her with expressionless eyes. "I have no need of friends," he said with apparent unconcern.

"You're kidding me!" She was genuinely taken aback. This was the most civil exchange the two of them had ever managed, since their usual interaction consisted of heated confrontations, which had started the day Jones moved into the condo complex.

Well, heated on her part, anyway. He'd pretty much been a Popsicle. Still, even though she had little use for a man so patently lacking in appreciation for animals, she'd at least assumed he was marginally human.

Apparently not. No need of friends? That was just plain barbaric. There were a lot of things she didn't need in this world—beginning with this guy as a next-door neighbor. But her friends certainly were at the top of her Must Have list. She simply couldn't imagine what she'd do without Treena and Jax or Ellen and Mack. Dog-hating, grim-faced security guys, however, were on a different list entirely.

"I do not kid," he said stiffly.

She snapped her mouth shut and looked at him, at his chilly green eyes beneath straight, thick brows, at those sharp cheekbones and that hard, unsmiling mouth. Then she blew out a breath and gave him a clipped nod. "Gotcha. No sense of humor. I've noticed that about you."

His eyebrows gathered over the prominent thrust of his nose. But before he could respond, the cocktail waitress returned with a bag of ice and a towel and Wolfgang pulled his gaze from Carly's face to accept the items with the barest acknowledgment.

"Thanks, Olivia," Carly said to make up for his brusqueness. "I appreciate you going out of your way." After the waitress squeezed her shoulder, wished her a speedy recovery and walked away, Carly turned her attention back to Jones, who was draping the towel over her foot. "I take it you have no need to get to know your fellow workers or show the least bit of civility, either?"

He slapped the ice onto her ankle.

She hissed a breath in through her teeth. When stars quit dancing in front of her eyes, she narrowed the latter on the man in front of her. "You're a real prince, Jones." Flapping the hand she hadn't used to anchor herself against the fresh onslaught of pain that threatened to shoot her straight out of her seat, she shooed him away. "You can go now." Begrudgingly she added, "Thanks for your help."

He stood and looked at her down the length of his strong, slightly hooked nose. "You'll be able to drive?"

Probably not. "I'll be fine."

"Isn't your car a standard transmission?"

"Yes," she agreed. "A cute little five-speed. But I'm sure you have better things to do than stand around talking about my car. So, please. Don't let me keep you."

He didn't budge. "How do you intend to get home? Will you call your redheaded friend, the other dancer?"

Nope. This was Treena's day off and she and Jax had left for San Francisco after last night's show. They didn't plan to be back until late tomorrow night. She gave Jones an earnest nod anyway. "Sure. That's exactly what I'll do. Bye-bye."

Wolf looked down at her and knew she was lying through her teeth. Shit. He was going to have to take her home himself.

He didn't want to spend another minute in her company, let alone the time it would take to get her to his car, drive back to their complex and help her into her condo. She was frivolous and irresponsible, and every time he came within a foot of her she got on his nerves so bad he wanted to howl and chew concrete, to commit reckless, poorly thought-out acts, many of which culminated in turning her over his knee and blistering that round ass the way someone ought to have done years ago.

This was very not like him. So the last thing he wanted was to be thrown together with her. Still, she was through work for the night, *he* was through work for the night and she lived right next door. Clearly she couldn't work the clutch in her automobile with that badly swollen foot, and it would be criminally irresponsible of him to leave her to fend for herself when they were both headed for the same destination.

Not to mention that he owed her for the pain he'd inflicted with the ice bag. That had been uncalled for, no matter how angry her smart mouth had made him.

He sighed. "Come. I will take you home."

She looked at him as if he'd offered to molest her worthless dog instead of provide her with needed transportation. "No!" It came out loud and emphatic, and she smiled weakly at a gambler at the far end of the row of machines who glanced up from pushing the buttons that selected his poker hand. She lowered her voice. "Thank you very much, but no. That's not necessary."

"You cannot drive."

"I told you I'll call Treena."

"You lied."

She gave him a cool look from killing blue eyes. "And you know this how?"

"By being good at my job. I know how to read people a hell of a lot tougher than you."

"Fine. I lied. I'll call Mack."

He shook his head in disgust. "You would disturb Mr. Brody at this time of night when I am perfectly willing to take you home? You are the most irritating, irrespon—"

"—sible woman you have ever had the misfortune to meet. Yeah, yeah. We've had this conversation before."

Color flushed her cheeks, and only then did Wolf realize how very pale they'd been just a moment ago. She probably was in a great deal of pain. Before remorse could assail him, however, she raised her fine-boned chin.

"Fine. Thank you. A ride home would be very…thoughtful." She sounded as if the words were strangling her, but he couldn't inspect her expression for she bent over just then to lift one corner of the ice bag off her foot and check her ankle.

"Can you walk?" he demanded of the crown of her glossy brown wig.

That snapped her head up in a hurry and heavy-lidded blue eyes blazed up at him. "As opposed to what—being carried by you? Oh, yeah—I can walk."

His palms started itching. Smacking her ass would be so cathartic. He'd never met anyone who needed paddling more than this woman. He jerked his chin toward the exit leading to the parking garage. "Come on, then."

She took her time removing her remaining shoe, then got up to follow him. She did manage to hobble along under her own steam, but God she was slow. More than once he was tempted to throw her over his shoulder to improve their odds of getting home sometime before the next millennium. He didn't, of course. It would be giving in to the Jones wild streak—and unlike his dad and his sister, Katarina, that was an impulse he always kept on a tight leash. So, gritting his teeth, he strode ahead of Carly, then stalked back to take baby steps by her side for a few minutes before his impatience got the better of him and he suddenly found himself several yards ahead of her and had to rein in his strides once again.

Finally they made it to his car, and he unlocked the passenger side for her.

"Wow," Carly said as she braced one hand on the automobile's roof and looked over the vehicle with patent admiration. "This is the last car I would've associated with you."

He didn't take umbrage to the implied subtext that he was a dullard. Buying something as flashy as the converted street rod had been uncharacteristic. Still, giving in to his desire for the classic muscle car was the one time he'd let the cursed family wild streak run free. He'd figured it was a safe-enough outlet—especially if it saved him from freeing other, more destructive urges as was the usual Jones way. He ran his fingers over one of the graduated-color flames that flared from burgundy to red to orange to gold across the glossy black paint job, then opened the door for her. "Get in."

Peering into its immaculate interior, she looked down at the melting ice bag in her hand and hesitated. "I'm afraid I'll muss it up."

That was the most intelligent thing he'd yet to hear her say, and for just a moment he felt almost warm toward her. He studied her closely for the first time since they'd begun their tortoise-paced trek from the casino and saw that not only was she pale again, but now sweat beaded her upper lip and brow, as well. She clearly was not feeling her best, and with unaccustomed gentleness he reiterated, "Get in."

She did and had her head braced wearily against the seat back when he got in the driver's side. She ran her hand over the gray leather of the bench seat. "What is this? A Ford?"

"Yes." Turning over the engine, he listened to its throaty growl with satisfaction. His smile lingered as he turned to look at her. "A 1940 Ford coupe."

"It's very cool." Lifting her head slowly, as if it weighed more than her slender neck could bear, she pulled off the swingy brown wig. "Oh, that's better," she murmured. Her short blond hair was matted to her head, but she ruffled it with her long fingers and soft spikes began popping up until she once again looked like what she was: a careless, carefree showgirl.

But one with shadows beneath her eyes.

They traveled the short distance to the condominium complex in surprisingly companionable silence. Wolf began to think that perhaps a miracle might occur and they'd actually end this night in a civilized manner.

Dropping Carly off in front of their building, he went to park the car in the garage he rented. She moved so slowly that she was still waiting for the elevator when he caught up with her. They'd barely stepped off it on the second floor a moment later when barking erupted from her apartment down the hall. A grunt of disgust escaped him.

Immediately, the momentary cease-fire in their adversarial relationship came to a halt. Carly turned and subjected him to a slow, unfriendly up-and-down, and he watched her grow a good inch taller as her back stretched straight. Her blue eyes grew dark with the *screw you* expression he was accustomed to seeing in them as her dog continued to yap hysterically in the background.

And his fragile hope for just one lousy night of peace turned to dust.

Three

She'd forgotten. For a few moments there, Carly had actually let down her guard and forgotten that Wolfgang Jones was nothing but a judgmental, dog-hating jerk.

Okay, sure, Rufus was a trial, more so than any other pet she'd ever owned. But if Jones would just give her some breathing room, she knew she'd find the breakthrough she was seeking in her pup's training. She always had with the other animals she'd rescued.

She was terrified, though, that she wouldn't find this one quickly enough. She'd been lucky up until now that everyone in her building had turned a blind eye to the covenant stating that each unit in the condo was only allowed one pet.

Jones could change that in the blink of an eye. He had the power of the rules on his side, and he was such an obvious letter-of-the-law freak that it wasn't even funny. All he needed was to lodge one formal complaint and she could lose not only Rufus, but two of her other babies, as well.

The idea made her sick to her soul and her hand shook

slightly as she fit her key into the lock. Furious that Mr. Grim-and-Grimmer could bring her to this, she couldn't prevent shooting him a dark look. He was so unyielding, both physically and mentally. And as much as she hated having to explain herself, she choked down her pride and did so, keeping her tone neutral when she said, "It's not Rufus's fault, you know. He's a good dog at heart. I found him abandoned on the side of I-15 and I'm guessing he had a pretty rough puppyhood, so it's taking him a little longer than usual to settle in." The tumblers disengaged and she opened the door.

As she stepped over the threshold, her dogs greeted her with a rendition of their nightly frenzied, glad-to-see-ya dance. Rufus continued barking as he leaped up on her. And while Buster was older, quieter and more restrained, he still insisted on getting close enough to lean heavily against her uninjured leg, his tail wagging enthusiastically. Her cats jumped down from their respective perches and flowed across the room to weave in and out of her feet, meowing for their dinner. It was loud and messy and her favorite part of the day.

Wolfgang clearly wasn't as enchanted. She caught the expression on his face when Rufus jumped with joyous abandon all over his beautiful suit.

Predictably, Jones was not amused.

She swallowed a snort. As if she'd ever seen that particular emotion on his face, anyway.

"*Sitz!*" Wolfgang snapped.

"Zits?" she repeated in confusion. But Rufus abruptly quit barking, and when she turned to look at her suddenly still dogs, she saw an almost human look of discombobulation on their furry faces. Then, as if it were a synchronized event, they both plopped their butts on the floor and stared up at the tall blond man with rapt attention. Even the cats paused for a nanosecond before resuming their demand for dinner.

Wolfgang turned to her, his posture erect, his face a blank canvas that somehow still managed to project disapproval. "You're right, it is not your dog's fault," he agreed. "It's yours. Exert some damn control." And picking a brown dog hair from his slacks with one hand, he reached out with his other to grasp the knob on the door. Gently he pulled it shut.

She stared at the blank panel that had been firmly closed in her face and felt her blood pressure spike from normal to stroke level in two seconds flat. If there'd been a mirror handy she wouldn't have been surprised to see steam blowing out her ears like cartoon factory whistles. Gasping for oxygen that seemed to have been sucked clean out of the foyer, she gritted her teeth against her choler.

To no avail. "You. *Fascist.* Son of a. *Bitch!*" Furiously she swung her bag of melting ice at the door.

Her animals scattered and she limped around to face the suddenly empty entryway. "Sorry, you guys," she said guiltily. "I'm sorry. But, God, have you ever *met* such a miserable human being?" What a lousy time for Treena to be gone. Ordinarily she'd be heading down to her friend's apartment to vent and spend a comforting twenty minutes assassinating Jones's character. Instead, she sucked it up, shoved down her self-pity and limped into the kitchen to start opening cans and bags.

Hearing the sound of kibble being poured and the can opener whipping lids from tins brought the babies out of their various hiding places. And the familiarity of having Buster and Rufus do their doggy dinner jig while Rags and Tripod rubbed up against every available surface as they waited for her to put their bowls on the floor soothed Carly's ragged nerves.

She got them situated, then found a corked bottle of wine in the fridge and poured herself a glass. Her ankle was throbbing again, so she tossed back a couple of aspirin. Then, noticing the trail of water where her bag of ice had sprung a leak from its unscheduled bash against the door, she grabbed a Ziploc bag and transferred the dripping contents into it. Deciding that the water on the floor would dry just fine without her help—and that she had been pushed quite far enough for one night—she hobbled into the living room.

Where she stopped dead. "Oh, crap."

Several of her throw pillows were torn apart. An explosion of feathers, foam and shredded silk festooned her furniture and covered the hardwood floor. She didn't know how she'd missed it on her way to the kitchen but could only assume her fury over Jones's behavior had temporarily blinded her. *"Rufus!"* she yelled furiously.

The dog slunk out of the kitchen and crept past her, his belly close to the floor, to huddle in the foyer. Looking over his shoulder at her with big brown eyes, he started to crouch in a way Carly was much too familiar with.

"No!" she snapped. "Dammit, Rufe, if you pee on top of this, you are a dead dog."

But when the pup got nervous, he piddled, and a puddle began to form on the Italian tile between his hind legs.

Of course. It had been that kind of night.

She clenched her teeth against her chin's sudden desire to wobble. She would not cry, dammit. She wouldn't!

But neither would she clean up the mess right now. Collapsing onto an overstuffed chair, she propped her foot on the mismatched footstool and gingerly arranged the ice over her swollen ankle. Then she knocked back her glass of wine in one long gulp.

Rags jumped up into her lap and circled twice before sprawling over her thighs in a warm bundle of long black fur. His purr kicked in with the first stroke of her hand down his back. Tripod leaped onto the arm of the chair and walked along it with surprising grace for a cat with only three legs. Sitting down close to her, he batted at a strand of beaded fringe on her costume, then ignored her in favor of licking himself clean.

His actions reminded her she was still wearing her costume. Swell. In addition to everything else, now she'd probably have the wardrobe mistress on her case. Hopefully the news of her injury would keep her off the woman's shit list. Otherwise she'd have to make a special trip back to the casino tomorrow just to return the garment and wig—and never mind that it was her day off. Not to mention that she'd have to bum a ride or call a cab just to get there, since her freaking car was still in the casino garage.

Buster came and laid his brindled head on her knee. She raised the hand she'd been stroking Rags with to scratch between the tufts of fur that stuck up atop the dog's head. Rufus remained in the entryway, but no longer did he look contrite. Instead, he was now seated in front of the door, staring at it expectantly. She realized with a sudden shock what was likely keeping him there.

"You little bugger! Are you looking for that cretin to come back?"

The dog's ears suddenly perked up and he began to wriggle on the tiles. A sound Carly knew too well rumbled threateningly in his throat.

"Please, Rufus, no more," she begged. "No more tonight, okay? Trust me on this, the last thing you want to do is to bring yourself to Jones's attention again."

But it was no use. The young dog danced in place as sharp, staccato yaps erupted from his throat like an automatic weapon laying down a line of fire.

The pain in Carly's head and ankle pounded in rhythm with Rufus's hysteria. "No speak," she whispered, giving the command they'd learned in obedience school.

Which, of course, Rufus had failed.

"Dammit, Rufe, you're going to get us all in trouble." Infuriated that she was actually intimidated by the thought, she raised her voice. "No speak!"

The pup kept right on barking.

Of course Mr. Hotshot Know It All Jones had made him shut up with a single word. "Zits!" she snapped furiously, then felt like an idiot. *Yeah, like that's gonna work for you, Jacobsen.* It was probably the deep voice that made it work in the first place.

But to her amazement the barking stopped and Rufus raced over to stare up at her eagerly.

"Oh, my God," she whispered, and a choked laugh escaped her. "Oh, my God! You respond to that, huh? I *knew* Jones spoke German! I mean, that's gotta be German, right? He can't have meant zits as in acne—that just wouldn't make sense." She gave her head an impatient shake. "Oh, who cares, who cares?" With her fingers splayed across Rags's back to keep him from tumbling to the floor, she leaned forward and scrubbed her knuckles atop Rufus's head. "Good dog! Good, *good* dog!"

Buster, whose chin had been bumped from her thigh, bumped Rufus in return and insinuated his head beneath her hand when the younger dog stumbled aside.

"Yes, you, too," she agreed, amused at his way of getting his own despite Rufus's more flamboyant attention-grabbing behavior. She scratched the older mutt between his ears. "*All* Carly's chillen are good, good boys."

She gently displaced the animals and struggled to her feet, feeling slightly rejuvenated. She could at least wipe up the piddle and pick up the worst of the pillow innards. She'd clean up the rest tomorrow.

Then a sudden thought struck her, and looking at her assemblage of pets, she laughed out loud. "Whataya know, kids? It looks like we have a breakthrough, and it's all thanks to the bastard next door. Maybe the guy isn't completely useless, after all."

The phone was ringing as Wolf let himself into his apartment. Restless, he ignored it to pace from room to room, stripping off his clothing and discarding it with none of his usual care. He shed his jacket and dropped it over the back of one of the stools at the breakfast bar separating the kitchen from the living room. He wrestled down the knot on his tie before yanking the neckpiece off through his collar and lobbing it toward the nightstand in his bedroom. When it got hung up on the reading lamp, he disregarded the possible snags to its expensive silk and strode back into the living room, pawing open the buttons on his shirt as he went. Disgruntlement rode him like a bareback rider on a trick pony. Christ, what was his problem? He didn't get it.

All right, that wasn't true. He knew exactly what the problem was. Or more accurately, who.

Carly Jacobsen.

"Dammit!" Undecided whether his outburst was intended for the menace next door or the frigging phone, which continued to ring despite the lateness of the hour or the fact that six rings ought to indicate that he had no desire to answer it, he stalked over to the breakfast bar and snatched the receiver off the hook. *"What?!"*

"Wolfgang? Is that you?"

"Mom?" She was the last person he'd expected to hear at the other end of the line. His mother wasn't a stay-up-past-midnight kind of woman—and it was even later in La Paz, Bolivia, where she and the old man were currently stationed.

The wireless receiver tucked into his shoulder, he only listened with half an ear as his mother launched into the courteous preamble with which she began all telephone conversations. Pulling his shirttails from his waistband, he shrugged out of the garment and tossed it toward the leather couch. It fluttered to the hardwood floor before it even got halfway there, but he ignored the slowly settling billow of dark cotton to scowl at the wall that connected his condo to his neighbor's.

God, she irritated him. With her complete lack of organizational skills and her promptly stated opinions, her sloppiness and long legs and that can't-be-bothered irresponsibility. He hadn't seen much of her place, but what he had glimpsed was a mess. And not one damn thing even matched. It was a profusion of colors and patterns, with debris all over the place and all those motley cats and dogs.

And red nail polish on her toes.

He snorted and went to pour himself a scant two fingers of Scotch. He tossed the drink back in one neat swallow, and *umm-hmmed* to his mother as he used the edge of his thumb to rub away an errant drop he felt trickling down his bottom lip. All right, he'd admit that perhaps that last thing was a little picky. Lots of women wore red nail polish. Not the woman he was eventually going to settle down with, though. He was close to achieving part one of the Plan—his dream of being the Security and Surveillance honcho who sent others to take care of problems rather than being the man who was constantly sent. And when he accomplished that, it would be in a real town, not fantasyland Las Vegas. Once he kicked the dust of this place from his heels he'd hit the road to his future without a backward glance.

When the career aspect was settled, he'd start to work on fulfilling part two of his agenda, finding the right woman with whom to share his success. Maybe a nice kindergarten teacher or something. You could bet the bank that a woman like that—stable, reliable, refined—would wear pale pink polish on her toes.

Then something his mother said jerked him back to the conversation. "What? Dad's retiring again?"

"For heaven's sake, Wolfgang," his mother said with brisk gruffness. "Haven't you listened to a thing I've said?" Sweetheart that she was, however, she spared him from having to admit he had not. "We'll be moving to Rothenburg, Germany, in a month's time—perhaps two—if the offer we made on a lovely little *biergarten* is accepted."

When she put his father on to enthusiastically impart the details of the establishment they expected to buy in the quaint medieval walled town, Wolf's attention drifted again. Dammit, Carly Jacobsen was breaking the covenant rules with her apartment full of pets, and he'd be well within his rights to turn her in.

It was a shame that, for all the healthy respect he had for the rules, he'd never been and didn't intend to turn into a whistle-blower. He'd simply have to do his best to stay out of her orbit and hope that one of these days she'd actually bestir herself to give her out-of-control dog some proper training.

So it was settled. He'd made a decision and was prepared to implement it. That should take care of this unusual restlessness.

It pissed him off when it didn't.

Who needed this irritation? Wasn't it enough that he dealt with problems every single moment he was at the Avventurato? He shouldn't have to cope with this shit when he came home, as well. He had decided his course of action; it was therefore time to move on.

His father put his mother back on, and with a start he suddenly realized they were calling from his sister's place in Indiana. Instead of demanding to know if Katarina was once again unloading responsibility for her son, Niklaus, onto his mother, however, he envisioned the showgirl next door. With her you-can-just-kiss-my-ass blue-eyed glare and that fuck-me body.

Then he snapped upright. "Whoa, whoa, whoa, whoa!" he said, finally giving the telephone conversation his full attention. "You want me to do *what?*"

When he hung up a short while later, he thrust both hands through his hair, stared blankly at the wall across the room and swore. If he were a superstitious man he would be invoking that ancient mantra of being careful what you wished for.

Because suddenly he had a much bigger problem on his hands than a space-cadet neighbor with dangerously compelling sex appeal.

His parents were coming to visit him. And they weren't coming alone.

Carly knocked on her second-floor neighbors' door the following morning.

Ellen answered. "Well, hello, darling," she said warmly, and stepped back, opening her door wide in welcome. "Come in."

But when she did as the petite older woman directed, Ellen's brow furrowed in concern and she reached out to cup a protective hand around Carly's elbow. "You're limping!"

"Yeah, I got knocked on my keister at the casino last night by a little old lady with a big purse."

"Is that Carly I hear?" came a gruff male voice, and Mack, Ellen's soon-to-be-husband, came into the foyer, folding the sports section of the *Review Journal* and tucking it beneath his arm. "I thought I recognized that voice. How are you, sweetheart? You've been hurt?"

Her heart warmed at the older couple's concern. Her own mother would have treated her daughter's injury as a nuisance whose sole purpose was to wreck her day. Or she'd have gotten her maid to take care of Carly. "I twisted my ankle. The swelling's already a lot better this morning and I'm hoping I'll be good to go by the time my weekend's over."

"That's right, they moved your days off to Tuesday and Wednesday, didn't they?" Mack said. "I guess if you had to get hurt, you at least had good timing."

"That was my thought, too."

"Meanwhile, I'm sure it hurts like the devil," Ellen said, and waved her into the living room. "Go in and sit down. Do you want some ice for it?"

"No, thanks. Maybe I could put it up for a few minutes, though. It feels better when it's elevated."

"Of course. Mack, help her get settled and see that she's comfortable. I'll go pour us some coffee."

The stocky, gray-haired man ushered her into a chair in the beautifully appointed living room and cleaned a stack of papers off a hassock, then dragged it over for her foot. "Do you need me to walk the dogs?" he inquired as he slid a throw pillow beneath her heel.

Delight flooded her at his thoughtfulness. "Aw, Mack. Have I told you recently how much I adore you?" she asked. "But, no, thank you. I managed to hobble out with Buster and Rufus earlier, and I'm hoping my ankle will be up for a longer walk around the grounds this evening."

"Let me get this straight." Mack gave her a speaking look over his reading glasses. "You took the dogs out with a bum foot and Rufus didn't bolt on you?"

"Here we go." Ellen entered the room with a tray that held not only three cups of coffee, but her home-baked cookies as well, beautifully arranged upon a paper doily that graced a delicate china plate.

"Carly took the dogs out for their constitutional this morning," Mack informed her.

The older woman turned to look at Carly, her eyebrows arching toward her stylish salt-and-pepper bangs. "And Rufus didn't take advantage of your bad foot and take off?"

Carly laughed. "I know—isn't it miraculous? That's really the reason I'm here." She accepted a mug of coffee and picked a sugar-dusted chocolate cookie off the plate. "He started to. He was making his usual Great Escape beeline for the parking lot, but I said *Zits!* and he came back."

"Zits?" Mack snorted. "What kind of word is that to make a dog who's never listened to a thing anyone's ever said suddenly pay attention?"

"Not zits like a pimple," Ellen said with a look of enlightenment. She turned to Carly. "*Sitz,* am I right? It's German for sit, I believe."

"Is that what it means? How cool is that? Rufus knows German." Another rolling laugh escaped her. "Not only knows it—Rufus *loves* German. He responds to it as if it's his native language and actually pays attention. Well, he didn't actually sit, but he *came back*, which is more than he would have done yesterday. So I wondered, Ellen—" she looked at her retired head-librarian neighbor "—do you think you could look up a couple of other German commands for me on your computer?"

"Oh, darling, I'd love nothing more. Unfortunately, my cable provider is in the middle of merging with another company and my computer hasn't let me connect to the Internet since last night. When I called the cable company about it this morning they admitted it was a problem at their end but couldn't give me a concrete time when they'd be back up and running. It's frustrating. But this news about Rufus is certainly an exciting breakthrough."

Carly felt as though her heart were grinning. "Isn't it great? And as much as I hate to admit it, I have Mr. Stick Up the Butt to thank."

"Who? Oh, Wolfgang, you mean?" Mack leaned forward. "So if he already came up with this, why not just ask him for more commands?"

"And admit the one he issued while he was busy insulting me worked? That'll be a frosty day in hell."

"Of course, what was I thinking?" the father of two grown daughters said with a shrug. "I forgot for a minute there that I was dealing with a female."

"That's very amusing, dear," Ellen told him dryly. But the two exchanged a glance so full of love that Carly set down her coffee cup.

"Enough about me," she said. "Do you have the photos back from your trip to Italy yet? And how are the plans going for the wedding? Pass those cookies and catch me up on the latest."

But even as she looked at vacation pictures and listened

to her friends' plans, she admitted something she'd give a bundle to ignore.

A cold day in hell had apparently arrived. Because for Rufus's sake she was probably going to swallow her pride for a second time and ask Wolfgang Jones for help, after all.

Four

Wolf paced the area outside the security checkpoint at McCarren International Airport. The plane was late—and he couldn't decide if that was a good or a bad thing.

He was anxious to see his folks, but this crazy idea of his mother's would never work. Had he been able to convince her of that over the phone, however? Hell, no.

He damn well would, though—just as soon as he had a chance to talk to her in person. Meanwhile, she and Dad were dragging his nephew Niklaus here for no good reason.

That wasn't his mother's take on the situation, of course. And Wolf did see the disadvantage of Niklaus having to pull up stakes yet one more time. The mere thought made his jaw tighten because he'd been there and done that himself. Just how many changes of address would this make for his parents, anyhow? He'd personally lost track of the number of times they'd moved by the time he was eleven. His dad, then an American G.I., had met his future wife in Stuttgart in the late sixties. He'd promptly married her, and by the time Wolf was born in Fort Benning, Georgia, four years later, his parents had already lived on two different bases. His sister, Katarina, had been born in Camp Zama, Japan, and by the middle of elementary school Wolf had also lived in Heidelberg, Germany, and Shape-Chievres, Belgium, as well as on two or three American bases, the names of which he no longer even recalled. He'd had several additional stateside bases under his belt by the time the old man finally retired from the service.

Not that the traveling had stopped then. Oh, no. His father—

"Hey, son!"

—was striding down the concourse toward him. Wrenching his thoughts out of the past, Wolf watched his dad approach and felt the same confused mixture of emotions the older man had always brought out in him: the helpless love that warmed Wolf's heart; the disquieting desire for his father's attention; the simmering resentment that never failed to churn in his gut.

Tall and loose-limbed, Rick Jones walked right up to him and looped a wiry arm around his shoulders, pulling him in for a hug and a manly slap on the back. Wolf caught a faint whiff of beer on his breath, then it was gone as his father pushed him back to hold him at arm's length.

"Look at you!" Rick said. "You look the picture of success! Are you getting everything you ever dreamed of all those years moping around the embassies?"

"I'm working on it." If his voice was a little stiff, well, blame it on the raft of memories inundating him. Memories of all the official quarters of the ambassador he'd been dragged to as a teenager, following Rick's retirement from the army. Of always being viewed as a loser from the wrong side of those embassy doors simply because his old man had been the supply officer rather than an administrative aide or an ambassador. Recollections of the desire that had been born inside of him for something more, something that would put him squarely on the right side of those doors.

He shook the memories aside. "Where's Mom and Niklaus?"

"They're coming. All the soda the kid drank on the plane caught up with him, and you know your mother. She doesn't think anyone can find their way anywhere without her help."

Or maybe she thinks that Niklaus shouldn't have to make his way alone through a strange airport.

"She's been dying to see you, you know," Rick continued. "What's it been, cub? Two years? Three?"

Cub. Images of his father flickered across his mind's screen, faded films of a much younger Rick tossing him up in the air and catching him, tossing him and catching him again while Wolf shrieked with laughter. He heard an echo of his dad's voice saying, "How's my little wolf cub? You been a good boy for your mama?"

Then the images were supplanted by the vision of Rick being gone, even when there was no reason for him to be. Of him always being absent when he was needed most. "It's been a little over two years," he said coolly. "The last time was in Santiago, when I came down to visit you and Mom."

"*Wolfgang?*"

He turned at the sound of his mother's voice, warmth washing over him at the retained accents of her native Bavaria. That hadn't changed even after years and years of stateside military postings. Plump and rosy cheeked, dressed in her usual style-free sturdy clothing, she bustled past the security checkpoint. A lanky teen he could only assume was Niklaus slouched in her wake, hands stuffed in his pockets.

Good God, had it really been that long since Wolf had last seen him? The boy he remembered had grown from a chubby-cheeked youngster into a teenager with the Joneses' long bones and skyscraper height. The only things that still looked familiar were Niklaus's shiny brown, stick-straight hair and his hazel-green eyes.

Wolf's mother shot Rick a chastising look. "You might have waited, Richard," she said with her usual brisk sternness.

But then her eyes turned softly upon her son, and dimples appeared in her cheeks when she smiled at Wolf. She held her plump hands out to him. "Hallo, *Liebling*." Stopping in front of him, she rose onto her toes to enfold him in her arms.

He hugged her tightly in return, inhaling the familiar scent of vanilla. Maria Jones may never have been as much fun as his father, but she had been the one constant in his life, a steady and reliable guiding light. "*Guten tag*, Mom. *Willkommen*." Over her shoulder he met his nephew's gaze. "Hey, Niklaus. It's good to see you."

The teen grunted.

Maria released him and stepped back, reaching to brush her hands over his lapels. "Look at you in this beautiful suit! You look so successful, so handsome." Grasping his hand, she gave it a tug. "Let's go collect our luggage. I'm anxious to see your home."

He ushered them through Baggage Claim and out to the lot where he'd left his car. Rick exclaimed over the Ford coupe and even Niklaus's eyes lit up, although he was playing it much too cool to actually say he thought the street rod was a righteous ride.

Fifteen minutes later they pulled into Wolf's garage at the condo complex and piled out of the car. Niklaus waited impatiently for Wolf to open the trunk, then dug through a large duffel bag and extracted a soccer ball. Bouncing it with casual expertise from one knee to the next, he looked over at his grandmother. "I'm gonna go check out the pool, Gram."

"There are a couple of pools on the grounds," Wolf told him then pointed out his building. "We're in that unit in 301 when you're ready to come in."

The teen shrugged and let the ball drop, then kicked it back up with the side of his foot. Snatching it out of the air, he tucked it beneath his arm and walked away without another word.

Maria watched him go, a worried pucker tugging her eyebrows together, and Rick slung his arm around her.

"He'll be fine," he said breezily.

Wolf wasn't so sure. He'd been in Nik's shoes. He, too, had been dragged from pillar to post, but at least he'd had his mother's steady presence to anchor him. The only thing he could think to say to alleviate her obvious concern was "I'll get your bags." And that was pretty damn weak.

She turned to him. "No, *Liebling*, leave them. We're staying at a hotel."

"Don't be silly, Mom. I've got room, if Niklaus doesn't mind bunking down on the couch."

"I told him we'd stay at Circus Circus," she said, and gave a helpless little shrug that wasn't at all like her. "I thought it might…help this latest upheaval when we tell him…." She trailed off, then straightened her shoulders and handed him the carry-on case she'd had with her. "I made you a kuchen."

"Aw, Mom." It was so quintessentially Maria. No bakeries for his mother. She made her cakes from scratch, and she provided one for every occasion—even if that meant packing it from one continent to another. Carrying the case with the same care she'd no doubt given it the past three thousand miles, he escorted her up to his condo.

Once inside the foyer, he paused to glance over his shoulder at his father, who was bringing up the rear. "So you're going into business as a beer garden proprietor, huh?" He carefully kept his voice neutral. "That seems appropriate."

Maria, who had already disappeared into the depths of his apartment, stepped back around the foyer wall and gave him a warning glance. "I'll not have you sassing your father, Wolfgang," she warned him austerely, then took the carry-on bag from his hands and disappeared behind the wall again, no doubt to give his kitchen a thorough inspection.

"I'm not, I'm stating a fact. It strikes me as a good fit." And it did. His dad was a party animal and always had been. Wolf's earliest truths growing up had been that when Mom said *nein*, she meant *nein*, that the army was superior to any other branch of the United States military and that if Rick wasn't out of the country on active duty, then he could usually be found at the NCO club with his fellow brothers-in-arms. After his dad's retirement from the service, the only thing that had changed about the latter was the name of the establishment and the fact that his new cronies weren't necessarily military. Every time Rick had moved the family to a new embassy, the first thing he'd done was locate a local watering hole where he could go knock back a few and socialize.

"Leave the boy alone, Maria," Rick said. "He's right, this *will* be the perfect fit for me." He turned to Wolf, all enthusiasm and charm. "Let me dig out my photos while your mom puts on the coffee, cub, and I'll show you what we're getting. Rothenburg is a fantastic town, and the Donisl is the prettiest little establishment you've ever seen."

"I'd like to see those, Dad," Wolf said. "But first we need to discuss Niklaus."

"Yeah, sure," Rick agreed. But he headed for the door with

a brisk stride. "I'll just leave you to talk that over with your mother." And he walked out of the apartment, closing the door behind him.

Wolf swallowed the bitterness that surged up his throat as he strode into the living room. "Well, that's typical," he said with what he considered admirable mildness.

His mother, who had located his coffeemaker and was busy scooping grounds into the basket, gave him a level look. "It is well past time, Wolfgang Richard, for you to—how do the Americans put it?—cut your father some slack."

"Why?" he demanded. "Has he *ever* stuck around for the tough discussions? No," he answered without awaiting her input. "He goes out and he has fun. Hell, even at work, he turned it into one big party, instead of applying himself to—" He cut himself off.

Too late, as it turned out, for Maria's eyes narrowed and she pointed an autocratic finger at one of the stools bellied-up to the breakfast bar.

Wolf sat.

She stood across the counter from him. "I am tired of you looking down your nose at your father because he wasn't some big, important executive. We're *both* sorry that you felt such pain over being on the wrong side of the social divisions that run rampant in so many of the embassies. But there is no shame in hard work, and that's what your father put into being a supply clerk. He was good at it, and God bless him if he had fun with it at the same time."

"Yeah, God bless him." Wolf swallowed the snort he felt crowding his throat. "*He* had fun. But what about you, Mom? Where were you in all this? Besides left behind all the time to be the disciplinarian and taskmaster."

"Has it never occurred to you, Wolfgang, that a woman

doesn't stay with a man for thirty-eight years without knowing what she's getting into? I liked being in charge. It's my nature to be the disciplinarian and taskmaster."

"But when do you get to have a good time?"

"What makes you think I don't? More important, when do *you* ever have fun?" Her eyes held a deep sadness as she gazed at him. "You have beautiful suits and an important career. But you're thirty-four years old and you have no wife, no *kinders*. You don't even have a pet. This course you've set for yourself doesn't seem to be making you particularly happy."

He leaned forward. "But I will be, Mom. I've got a plan, and I'm getting close to accomplishing it. It's just a matter of putting everything together. When that's done, then I'll be happy."

"Aw, *Liebling*. Happiness isn't a goal for the future. It's what should be sustaining you while you're working toward your objectives. You're half American, for the good Lord's sake. The pursuit of happiness is one of your inalienable rights."

She was wrong. Happiness was what he'd be rewarded with down the road for all the hard work he was putting in now. It was what he'd attain once he got everything right.

But Maria was his mother, and one didn't tell one's mother that she was wrong. Instead, thinking about his nephew and the insane idea she had come up with for the teen's care, he changed the subject.

"You do know that this plan of yours to have Niklaus stay with me is impossible, don't you?" he demanded gently. All right, perhaps that equated to telling her she was wrong. Still, the idea was crazy, a crippled jet foreordained to crash and burn. "I work nights, Mom—long nights. Nik's not going to be any better off in Sin City with no one to supervise him."

"He'll be much better off having the influence of a stable man in his life, even if the situation isn't ideal. Katarina can't continue shuttling him aside whenever she has a new man or some other enthusiasm-of-the-moment in her life, only to come swooping back to interrupt the new routine he's managed to make for himself once she remembers again that she is a mother. And I have no doubt that our offer for the *biergarten* in Rothenburg will be accepted. That means dragging him to Germany, Wolf. He's headed for trouble already and I'm scared to death another move—this time to a foreign country—will be the final nudge to push him right into the thick of it. We have to head that off before it's too late."

"How is he headed for trouble?"

"By—how do you say it?—suspending out with some undesirable young people."

He had to think that through for a moment. "Hanging out, you mean?"

"Yes, that is the expression. Niklaus is a good boy, but how much longer will he remain one without a strong man to help guide his life? He needs you, Wolfgang. He desperately needs a home that doesn't get uprooted every nine or ten months." Reaching across the table, she laid her manicure-free, work-worn hand over his and looked beseechingly into his eyes. "Please."

Aw, hell. His mother had provided him with the only security he'd ever known, and she had never before asked a thing from him in return. "Fine," he agreed less than graciously. "But I'm probably not going to be in Las Vegas much longer myself, so his routine is still going to be shot to kingdom come."

"But you've been in this job for two years," Maria said, her forehead furrowing. "And you just bought this beautiful condominium. That seems pretty settled to me."

"I've been in Security and Surveillance at the Avventu-rato for almost three years, but I've moved up the ladder as far as I can go there because my boss isn't planning on retiring any time soon. And although I've freelanced at a couple other casinos who like my work, I don't plan on spending the rest of my life in this town. As for the condo, I'm subletting from a guy who took a job in the Middle East. I was unhappy with my old place and this unit had sat empty for so long that he was happy to sign a contract saying I could give a month's notice at any time. Which I plan to do just as soon as my dream job comes through. So I don't see where this move will be doing Niklaus any favors."

Not that he wouldn't take the kid with him when he went, of course, but he felt no need to verbalize the fact since his mother knew him well enough to understand that that was a given without having to be told. Still, it would be yet one more case of Niklaus having to pull up stakes and move in a long succession of them. Wolf knew only too well what that was like.

He gave Maria a sober look across the table and shook his head. "I'll do it, Mom, and I'll try my damnedest to do a good job. But if I were you, I wouldn't look for Niklaus to be thanking us any time soon."

You got that right, Niklaus thought furiously, digging his tense shoulder blades into the six-paneled wood of the entry door he'd quietly shut behind him. He had stood there long enough to overhear most of the conversation, and betrayal bit like a rabid dog deep in his gut. Grandma Maria—the one person he'd always felt he could count on—had failed to mention when she'd come to collect him from his and Mom's latest home in Evansville, Indiana, that he wasn't coming home with her and Grandpa Rick. Not that he'd been all that crazy about the idea of living in Bolivia, where Grandpa was currently stationed, but at least with Grandma he felt safe.

He gripped the black-and-white soccer ball to his hip with a force that drove the blood from his fingertips. His free hand fisted tightly at his side and tears burned like acid behind his eyelids.

He squeezed his eyes tightly shut. *I am not going to cry*, he vowed with silent ferocity. *I'm seventeen years old—or near enough, anyhow—and I will not goddamn cry like a baby.*

He forced his shoulders to relax and pried his fingers loose of the fist they'd formed, shaking his hand out. What the hell. What was another fucking move? It wasn't like he and his mom hadn't been flitting from place to place, anyway, for as long as he could remember. He must have been—what?— twelve, thirteen years old when he'd first realized he was probably more mature than Katarina would ever be.

He'd known forever, though, that Grandma Maria was in his corner, that she would always be there for him when Mom got particularly flaky. He never had to be the grown-up in the group when he was with her. Yet here she was, suddenly fobbing him off on his uncle. What the hell kind of bullshit was that?

And because of his *friends?* Sure, they dressed kind of Goth, had lots of piercings and tattoos, and occasionally smoked a little weed that one of them managed to score. But they were just regular kids, and at least with them he didn't have to be the everything's-okay-so-don't-you-worry-about-me happy camper the adults liked to believe he was.

If he had known Grandma Maria was going to dump him on Wolfgang, however, he might have attempted to bridge the gap between his friends and her during the week she and

Grandpa Rick had spent with them while Mom was packing up to move in with her newest asshole boyfriend. Too late now, though. He'd expected this to be a quick stop to see his uncle Wolf and stay in a cool Las Vegas hotel for a few days before continuing on to Grandpa's La Paz embassy. Instead, he was being dumped on a guy in whose company he'd spent maybe three or four months *combined* out of his entire life-time—without so much as a single discussion or anyone asking what *he* wanted. The only thing he knew about Wolf was that he was one of those tight-assed über-authoritarian types. Hell, Mom didn't refer to him as Dr. Gloom for nothing. The guy hardly ever smiled.

For a minute, Niklaus considered grabbing his bag out of the trunk of Wolf's boss car and striking out on his own. He could take care of himself. Shit, he'd been doing the job most of his life, anyhow. But he took a couple of deep breaths and stayed put.

He had a blueprint for his future, and being a teenage runaway wasn't part of it. He'd lived hand to mouth most of his life already and he didn't intend to do so for the rest of it. A kid on his own without an education was looking for nothing better on the employment front than to say, "You want fries with that?" *He* planned to graduate frigging high school, then get himself a soccer or academic scholarship to a university so he'd have some options. That would be a big improvement over what he'd had most of his existence.

But in fucking Las Vegas? What was he likely to find in the way of a decent soccer program in a city that was a hundred frigging degrees most of the time? What if the high schools here didn't even have soccer teams? His schooling had already been screwed up so many times, it wasn't even funny. Every time he'd gotten ahead academically, Mom had either up and moved them or packed him off to wherever Grandma and Grandpa currently resided. That had meant yet another school with yet another system for him to learn.

He was so goddamn tired of it he could spit.

Feeling his shoulders starting to creep up around his ears again, he forced himself to relax. Only thirteen more months to go and he'd be eighteen. Ten months after that, he'd have his diploma and be starting university.

So he'd stay with Dr. Gloom. And if his uncle abandoned him in Las Vegas when he took off for his frigging dream job, well, he'd be just that much closer to his goal, wouldn't he?

And hopefully by then, if he wasn't quite close enough, Grandma Maria would be willing to take him back again.

Five

•

"So there I was Tuesday morning, girding my loins to swallow my pride and ask Jones for more German commands," Carly said, winding up the story of Rufus's amazing progress over the course of the past couple of days. It was Thursday night, and she and her best friend, Treena McCall, were headed to work. "And you gotta know, Treen, that this took some major attitude adjustment on my part after the way he'd talked to me Monday night." Wheeling her car into a slot in the Avventurato parking garage, she shot a glance at the redhead in the passenger seat. She cut the engine and yanked on the parking brake, then turned in her seat to meet her pal's interested gaze more fully.

"Yeah," Treena agreed. "Having seen you in action with Wolfgang, we've gotta be talking *serious* adjustment."

"As a heart attack, toots. So, anyhow, I did the girding thing—and guess what?" Indignation ruled all over again. "The bum's disappeared!"

"That rat!" Treena's tone was full of the appropriate best-friend outrage. But her tongue was firmly planted in her cheek when she demanded, "What do you bet he did it just to piss you off?"

"That was *precisely* my first thought," Carly agreed. Then she laughed. "But all right, so maybe I'm not even a blip on Jones's radar, while I continually overreact when it comes to him."

"Ya think?"

"I don't know what it is about him. I mean, it's not as if I've never run up against a disagreeable man before."

Treena's lips ticked up in her habitual barely there, one-sided smile. "Just not one with such a great butt."

She didn't even have to think twice. "Yes! His is truly world class and, omigawd, it's been forever since I've had sex. So how fair is it that a guy with *the* finest ass ever designed to spin a girl's thoughts to getting a grip on it for a little hootchie-kootch, turns out to have the personality of a gorilla accountant?"

Treena shook her head in sad commiseration. "Life's a bitch."

"Tell me about it." She was *never* attracted to men she didn't like. They could be Adonis come to life, and it didn't matter—if they were jerks they left her cold.

Wolfgang Jones wasn't even close to Adonis and he was definitely a jerk. So why the hell had she been feeling that raw edge of sexual awareness lately whenever they'd encountered each other? "Damn chemistry," she groused as she climbed out of the car.

Treena gave her a look over the top of the sporty auto's red roof. "You talking to me?"

"No. It's just…I don't understand why certain people have chemistry with each other while other guys—people—leave you cold."

"Is that what's yanking your chain with Wolfgang? You got some chemistry going with a guy you don't like?"

"Hell, no! Well…maybe." She shook her head. "No, no, of course not. It's his lack of respect for the babies, that's all." But that wasn't all, and she gave the other dancer a helpless grimace. "Oh, crap, Treena, I don't know."

A friend for ages, Treena took pity on her and changed the subject. "So, how's your ankle feeling? You sure it's going to hold up for you tonight?"

Carly shrugged. "I'm not even sure of my own name these days." She held her fist out, knuckles facing her friend. "But here's hoping."

Treena bopped it with her own. "Promise me you won't push yourself if it starts to hurt too much."

"Cross my heart, Mom." Her tone was ironic, but she gave her friend an affectionate smile. "It feels so much better than it did Monday night—or even yesterday—and I'm pretty sure I'm back up to speed. But if I feel it start to go I'll call it a night. You have my word on that." As they headed down Row E for the garage elevator, she gave her friend a friendly bump with her hip. "So San Francisco was good, huh?"

"Oh, wow." Treena's pale brown eyes grew dreamy. "It was so great. We stayed at the St. Francis and saw as many sights as we could pack into two days."

"Jax didn't play in a poker tournament, then?"

"No, and it was so smokin' not to have a single thing we *had* to do. We ate too much and maybe drank a bit too much and just played tourists. And the weather was gorgeous. So much cooler than it is here."

"Yeah, this is unseasonable for mid-October. The temps should be dropping any day now."

"I'm beyond ready. It was such a relief when the thermometer took its normal dip a couple of weeks ago. I wasn't prepared for the temperature to start soaring again."

The noise of the casino bombarded them as the elevator doors slid open into the hotel lobby, but after years of working there Carly was adept at automatically relegating the din to background noise. Dodging the tourists who didn't wait for them to exit the car before barging into it, they skirted a bellman maneuvering a rolling luggage cart across the marble lobby floor and strode into the casino proper. They passed the Italian bistro, with its smells of garlic, tomatoes and olive oil, passed their favorite little after-work open-air lounge, then took a left at the craps tables, heading for the east wall and the short hallway that led to the employees-only area backstage of the Starlight Room.

"Ms. Jacobsen."

Damn! Carly didn't need Treena's murmured, "Looks like the bum is back," to know who she'd see when she turned around. Sighing, she pivoted on her heel.

She studied Wolfgang Jones as he strode up to them. Looking at him objectively for perhaps the first time ever, she finally got a handle on part of what her problem was. It wasn't merely that he was so cool and controlled he was damn near robotic; it wasn't even that he didn't seem to like animals. It was those two elements combined with the fact that he had that edge she liked in a man. That don't-fuck-with-me-and-don't-even-*think*-you-have-a-chance-of-tying-me-down edginess that sucked her in every time.

Part of the appeal spoke directly to her own personality, since she had no desire to tie any man down. Never had, never would.

Especially not this man.

Still, there was just something that turned her on about a

guy with the confidence to stride through life with his goals firmly front and center.

Really.

Turned her.

On.

Wolfgang had that goal orientation. She didn't have the first idea what his objectives were, but she didn't doubt for a minute that he had them. He also possessed one superbly fit body. She might have a preference for men in jeans, but beautifully cut slacks did nothing to detract from the muscular swell of his butt. Neither did his pricy well-tailored jacket disguise the width of his shoulders.

No, ma'am. There wasn't a damn thing wrong with the physique beneath those upscale threads.

He stopped in front of her, standing close enough that she had to tip her head back in order to look up into his cool green eyes. She tried to assure herself that wasn't a thrill all on its own, but knew it for the lie it was. Because at more than six feet tall herself in high heels—which meant seventy-five percent of the time—looking up at any man was a treat.

"I need to talk to you about your injury the other night," he said with crisp precision. Pulling his head back, he slid his gaze slowly down her until it reached her ankle, then back up to meet her eyes once again. "You are better?"

A little curl of warmth unfurled in her stomach. "Yes, very much so, thank you."

"Good. Then you will need to fill out an incident report so I can close the event."

The warmth iced over. Yet her eyes still narrowed on his lower lip, noting that when he wasn't all stern-mouthed the way she was accustomed to seeing him, it was much fuller than she'd previously realized. Yes, indeed, he had that beckoning edge, that look she went for in a guy—not particularly handsome, perhaps, but definitely all man.

If only he would keep his mouth shut.

Still, when she raised her gaze and saw him watching her, a frisson of sexual heat curled down her spine.

Whoa. Wait a minute. That selfsame backbone snapped erect. What the hell was she thinking? She didn't *even* intend to go there with this man. "Yeah. Sure," she said. "I'll get right on that." She turned away.

He wrapped his hand around her forearm and swung her back. She gave the long fingers and broad palm grasping her flesh—and pumping heat throughout her system—a pointed look.

Wolfgang set her loose. "*Now* would be a good time."

"Not for me, it wouldn't," she disagreed coolly. "I'm on my way to work, and I don't intend to bring myself to my G.M.'s attention by being late. Trust me, Vernetta-Grace is scarier than your entire Security and Surveillance force combined. I'm sure you understand." She shot him a challenging look from beneath her lashes. "You being so big on personal responsibility and all."

"Fine." His mouth adopted the slant of grim hardness with which she was much more familiar. "Then stop by Surveillance and sign off on the report when you're done for the night."

"Absolutely. I'll be sure to do that before we go home." She turned to Treena. "Remind me, okay?"

"Sure."

She swung back to Wolfgang. "There you go. Anything else?"

"No."

"Gotta run, then. We're on the clock in about fifteen minutes and we still have to change and get into our makeup."

He stepped back with a stiff nod and she and Treena walked away.

Once they were out of earshot her friend glanced over at her. "It's going to be a cold day in hell before we stop by to sign off on Wolfgang's incident report, isn't it?"

Carly snorted. "Oh, yeah. A *very* cold day."

She was feeling surprisingly full of herself when she bopped into the backstage dressing room a few minutes later, and just for a minute she wondered if that should worry her.

As if reading her mind, Treena shot her a dry, sideways look. "You might be having just a little too much fun from your encounter with the wolfman, babe."

Even though she'd had virtually the same thought herself, her initial knee-jerk response was to deny it. But she couldn't.

"I know," she admitted in a low voice. "And I feel like that oughtta be scaring the bejesus out of me. Yet somehow it doesn't." Instincts insisting that it was wrong, wrong, wrong to be attracted on a physical level to a man she disliked on a personal one, she raised her hand to erase the admission right out of the air. Even her instincts seemed conflicted, however, for she terminated the motion with a jerky movement that gave her a flashback to her gawky pubescent days. There was an age she'd just as soon not revisit.

Blowing out a breath, she dropped her hand to her side and gave her friend a wry smile. "It was easier when he just annoyed me. But lately it's as if all my senses are in this warped heightened state whenever he's around. And I honest to God don't understand what that's all about."

"Maybe simply that there's more to him than you first thought."

"I doubt that very much." Then a beautiful arrangement

of exotic flowers on the counter at her station caught her eye. "Hey, would you look at that?" she demanded, raising her voice. She picked up her pace across the room full of dancers in various states of undress. "Somebody must love me lots."

Rude hoots greeted her statement. "Yeah, Carly," Michelle said from down the row of stools in front of the long lighted mirror. "You're off on your regular days and rumor has it that you've been laid up with a bum ankle. Yet here you are, all hale and hearty and with a rich new Stage Door Johnnie to boot from the looks of things. What's up with *that?*" Tipping up her chin, her lower lip drooping open, she leaned into the mirror to align false lashes along her natural lash line. Then pressing them in place while the adhesive dried, she swivelled to meet Carly's gaze. "He got a brother?" she asked hopefully.

"Toots, if I had a sugar daddy and he *had* a brother, you can be damn sure I'd be holding the latter in reserve. It's been a long, dry spell for me, you know? If the day ever comes when I'm faced with that scenario, I'll probably need the spare. Just in case I break the first one."

That brought a fresh spate of ribald laughter and comments, and she dropped her dance bag on the floor in front of her station to root through the blossoms.

Discovering a tiny white envelope, she pulled it out and ripped it open. She extracted the card inside. "'Hope you're back on your feet and dancing soon,'" she read aloud. There was no signature. "Huh." She looked up to find several of her sister dancers grinning at her and a lightbulb went off in her head. "Aw, you guys, these are from you, aren't they?"

Across the room, Jerrilyn paused in fitting her towering headdress over her slicked-back hair to blow a raspberry. "Yeah, right. When's the last time you remember us buying flowers for anyone in the troupe?"

"When Georgia had her baby," Carly said. "Okay, I know we don't usually. So what was all the grinning about, then?"

"Oh, honey," Michelle said. "A woman getting flowers is always a huge event. And some of us have to live vicariously." She looked at the arrangement again. Okay, that made sense. Only... "So, who are these from if they aren't from you all?"

"Did you meet a hot young M.D. in the E.R. Monday night?" Juney asked.

"Nah. I didn't even go to the E.R., just limped on home and iced it. Besides, the last time I was at the E.R. the hottest thing I saw was a nurse named Brunhilda who you wouldn't want to drop your soap in front of in the shower room."

"You are so full of it," Treena scoffed.

Jo's head popped up over the mirror that backed Carly's "Hey, maybe you've got a secret admirer."

"Yeah, maybe," she agreed doubtfully. Then she looked at the clock on the wall and headed across the room to collect her costume. "If so, I'll have to figure out who later. I don't have time to worry about it now."

The wardrobe mistress looked up as she approached. Adjusting the measuring tape draped around her neck, she pushed a frizzy strand of hair behind her ear and selected Carly's costume from the rack. "Thanks for sending your costume and wig in with Treena yesterday," she said, and handed Carly the wisp of illusion and glitter that comprised the first act's attire. She also passed over a headdress of fountaining, white-tipped gold plumes, then pushed her slipping glasses up her nose. "I like it when I'm given time to get them clean, although you are one of the neater ones."

Carly returned to her station and quickly stripped out of her street clothes and donned her own fishnet stockings before pulling on the costume. Plopping the headpiece atop a mannequin head, she quickly applied her greasepaint. It looked trashily overdone under the harsh fluorescent lighting, but features tended to disappear beneath the stage lights in ordinary street makeup.

Her friend Eve strolled into the dressing room a moment later and stopped at her station three places down the row to prop her right foot up on the stool. She smoothed her fishnets up her calf and along her thigh. Glancing up, she caught sight of Carly and smiled. "Hey, girl," she said. "How's the ankle?"

"Back to normal." *I hope, I hope.*

"It better be," Julie-Ann said in the sugary, upbeat voice she used to slice-and-dice. "I won't have you messing up my chorus line." She laughed as if it were all a big joke.

Carly gave the young dance captain a neutral look. "Yeah, I'd sure hate to have my injury ruin your night."

"Haven't you heard, Carly?" Treena asked, deadpan. "It's all about Julie-Ann. Your comfort doesn't enter into it."

"Sure, it does," Eve disagreed. "You heard her—it could mess up her line." She cocked a brow at the dance captain. "And when did this become your dance troupe again? I thought we functioned as a unit."

"Oh, for God's sake," Julie-Ann said in exasperation. "Lighten up! It was a joke."

Uh-huh. The three dancers exchanged brief gazes. Then without further comment they went back to getting ready for the show.

But Carly turned and, reaching between her shoulder blades, gave her back a pat. "Do you see a knife sticking out anywhere?" she asked Treena sotto voce over her shoulder.

The redhead gave her a crooked smile. "Amazing how she does that, isn't it?" she said equally quietly. "It will forever remain a mystery to me how one woman can smile so angelically while poking her busy little fingers into another woman's wounds."

"And if anyone would know how that feels, toots, it would be you." Treena had come under Julie-Ann's fire the past several months while she was fighting to get her dancing back up to speed so she could pass the annual audition after an absence of almost a year away from the troupe. Instead of lending support, their dance captain had undermined her friend every chance she got.

Treena's smile turned into a full-fledged grin. "She has so lost the power to bug me."

"You've definitely decided this will be your last year, then?"

"Yeah. You know it's time for me. I'm getting too old for this and it's just plain getting tougher physically. Jax and I have been talking over some of my options."

"I'll wager you have quite a few, too," Carly agreed. "And I'm happy for you, toots. For myself, though, I'm going to miss working with you. What's it been, a decade we've been dancing together?"

"Yes, can you believe it?" Propping her heel on the countertop, Treena bent over her straight leg, stretching out her hamstrings. Slowly straightening, she gave a nod to the bouquet on the counter between their stations. "So who do you think the flowers are from?"

"You got me." She paused in tucking her hair beneath the turban portion of the headpiece to look at her friend. "I might check with the hotel florist tomorrow to see if anyone remembers anything. Because I honestly don't have a clue."

"Hey, maybe it was Wolfgang."

Carly choked, then laughed so hard tears began to leak over her bottom lashes. "Oh, shit, if you made me ruin my makeup you're a dead woman." She grabbed a handful of tissues and gently pressed them beneath her eyes to catch the overflow before it could smear her mascara. Once she was certain the damage was contained, she turned to her friend. "Do you honestly see Mr. Grim and Grimmer sending flowers to someone he's not sharing the sheets with?"

"Well…no."

"Me, neither. Hell, I can't even see him loosening up enough to *do* the hootchie-kootch."

And if sometimes she jerked awake from a dream of him hanging over her in a red-hot naked lather…?

Well, that would just remain her guilty little secret.

Six

Wolf woke up the following morning to Niklaus playing music at top volume. The discordant notes and screeching guitar licks found a corresponding pulse in his left temple, which began pounding in tune with the inharmonic sounds wailing out of the living room speakers. With a groan he rolled to the side of the bed, where he sat with his elbows dug into his knees and his aching head propped in his hands.

God, he felt awful. Burning his candle at both ends didn't even begin to cover it. He'd been running his ass off the past seventy-two hours, working his shift by night and squiring his folks and Niklaus around Vegas and its environs by day. He'd eaten rich foods he was no longer accustomed to and worked like a dog to live up to his mother's expectations.

Which had meant talking. Smiling. Being frigging *pleasant.*

What he'd netted from so much unaccustomed sociability was a dangerously volatile temper. Generally a well-managed animal, it was suddenly hurling itself at its cage doors, slavering and snarling for release. Having to listen to crap music at high decibels on too little sleep verged perilously close to the key that beast was searching for.

But even if he believed in the self-indulgence of losing his temper, this wouldn't be the time for it, since it would be the height of unfairness to take it out on Niklaus. The kid was having a rough-enough time as it was. Wolf remembered too well what it was like being ordered to pack up your belongings just when you finally got yourself settled in, only to have to start the whole lousy process all over again somewhere else.

And that was on top of the guilt he felt at leaving Niklaus to fend for himself last night.

After seeing his folks off at the airport for their flight back to Bolivia, Wolf had fully intended to take the teen home, order whatever pizza Niklaus wanted and ease him into his new situation. Instead, they'd arrived home to a message on the answering machine from the Avventurato Surveillance team's number-one man, Dan McAster. "Emergency's come up in the casino," Dan's voice had snapped out in its usual gruff-spoken way. "I need you here, ASAP."

So he'd had to leave Niklaus alone in a strange condo in a strange city practically the minute the teen's grandmother— the only person to provide Niklaus with a modicum of security—had left town. As if the kid hadn't already had enough to contend with moving in with an uncle he barely knew.

All the same—Wolf dug his fingertips into his pounding temple—that music had to go before his head exploded.

Climbing to his feet, he reached for the shirt he'd draped over the desk chair last night and pulled it on. Not bothering to button it, he grabbed a pair of khaki shorts out of a drawer and yanked them up his legs, zipping the fly as he walked into the living room.

He strode straight over to the stereo and cranked down the volume.

Niklaus, slumped on his tailbone on the couch, glowered at him, and Wolf jerked his head at the wall connecting his unit to Carly's. "Show a little consideration, Nik. We've got a neighbor."

To his surprise, the boy's expression lit up. "I know, I saw her out on the balcony last night. She is *hot!* And she's got like a hundred dogs and cats. How totally great is that?"

The mention of Carly's animals made Wolf want to furrow his brow and curl his lip back from his teeth. He managed a noncommittal expression, however, because he didn't want to ruin the first sign of pleasure he'd seen on the kid's face since Niklaus had learned his grandparents were dumping him in Las Vegas.

"Yeah," he grunted. "Great. Totally." *My ass.*

God, she made him nuts. He'd cooled his heels in Surveillance last night for a good hour after the *la Stravaganza* show was over, waiting for her to show up. But had she? Hell, no. She'd blown off the one simple request he'd made of her, and he was still steamed about waiting for her to make an appearance when he should have been back home with Niklaus.

He was hardly blown away by surprise. But he was plenty steamed.

What *did* surprise him was how close he still felt to losing the tight rein he had on his temper. The need to be nice these past few days must have taken even more of a toll on him than he'd realized. All the same, he had to put it behind him. Get his head screwed on straight.

Niklaus suddenly surged to his feet. "I'm gonna go take a shower."

"Okay, good. I'll take one when you're done, then we'll go

grab some breakfast and visit a couple of schools to see if we can find one that fits."

The boy scowled at him. "I don't suppose any of the schools in this town has a decent soccer team?"

His tone was pure teenage, don't-give-a-shit boredom, but Wolf took one look at his nephew's stiff posture and intense gaze and realized the answer mattered a great deal to him.

"I don't know, but I'll see what I can find out. Your grandmother mentioned you've got a real talent for the sport."

Niklaus shrugged and slouched off toward the bathroom.

Wolf was on the phone trying to get sports information from the nearest school when hysterical barking broke out next door. It continued unabated throughout the remainder of his conversation, and his temper was straining at its leash by the time he finally slammed the phone down. "Son of a bitch!"

He looked down the hallway toward the bathroom, but the shower continued to pound unabated. With an abrupt, decisive nod, he snatched up the incident report that he'd brought home from work and strode over to pull his door open with a force that damn near removed it from its hinges.

A UPS driver who was turning away from Carly's door jumped, and Wolf wiped the scowl from his face as he approached her.

"Is that for Carly Jacobsen?" he asked, nodding at the package in the woman's hands.

The brown-uniformed woman glanced down at the name on the label, then nodded.

He reached out for it.

She took a step back. "I need a signature, and it has to come from the recipient."

"How about from the recipient's husband?" he said, and

reached for it again. "I was just visiting next door." He could hear the dogs' hysterical barking on the other side of the door, and at the end of his patience, he roared, "*Sitz*, dammit!"

Blessed silence fell.

He turned his attention back to the woman. "Look, I don't know why Carly isn't answering the door, but give me the package, will you, please? If she has to wait until tomorrow for you to attempt another delivery, she'll be hell to live with."

It was apparently a complaint with which the woman was familiar, for she handed him an electronic device and a stylus to write his signature, then passed him the package. "Have a good one," she said, and marched off down the hallway, disappearing a moment later down the stairs.

He waited long enough for her to exit the building, then whirled around and knocked on Carly's door. The dogs started barking again and he lost the last tenuous grasp he'd had on his wrath. Hammering on the door, he half expected the solid wood to give way beneath his fist at any second. "Open. The. Goddamn. Door!"

Over the thundering of his own heart and the clamoring of the dogs, he somehow heard the slap of feet against the tile foyer on the other side of the panel. Then Carly's voice snapped, "*Sitz!*" and once again the mutts fell silent.

His jaw sagged at the sound of the German command coming from within her apartment, and he barely managed to snap his mouth shut again before the door whipped open.

Then he caught his first good glimpse of her standing on the other side of the threshold, and it was all he could do not to let his jaw drop all over again.

But, holy shit. Her face was scrubbed clean and her hair was wet. She was all gold and pink as water dribbled along her temples, down her smooth throat and over her chest, soaking into a white tank top and turning the edges of the material transparent. As he watched, the transparency spread across the uppermost thrust of unbound, truly spectacular breasts. Puckered nipples that he imagined were the result of leaving a steamy bathroom for the air-conditioned chill of the rest of the apartment poked against the still-dry portion of the top's stretchy fabric. Her feet were bare, and the sun filtering into the foyer from the living room window turned her pointy-hemmed skirt translucent enough to highlight her mile-high legs. He'd take a wild stab here and guess that she'd recently climbed out of the shower.

Hands hanging limply at her sides, she, too, looked him over as if she'd never seen him before. Even as the thought crossed his mind, her slender eyebrows drew together over her nose and her gaze rose to his face. "What do you want, Jones?"

"Uh…" He couldn't remember and latched onto the first thought to waft across his mind. "You spoke German."

Color washed up her chest and climbed her throat. "So?"

"So, nothing. I just…didn't expect to hear it." He took a step closer and the shift of weight caused the sharp edge of the cardboard box under his arm to dig into his inner elbow. It jerked him back to reality. "Here." He thrust it out at her. "The damn dogs were going crazy, so I signed for your package before their noise made my head implode."

"Oh, for—" Snatching the parcel from his hands, she whirled away and stalked into the living room. "Don't even start on my pets. There's not a dog alive who doesn't bark at the UPS man."

"Woman," he corrected. But he was operating purely on autopilot, for his brain was cutting out like a combustible engine laboring on its last fume of fuel.

The hazy view of her thighs and butt beneath her gauzy skirt didn't improve matters. From what he could see, only a narrow blue thong that widened to a little butterfly above her firm cheeks stood between her and an indecency charge. Sternly pulling his gaze away, he followed her into her apartment. "You are training Doofus in German?"

"Rufus!" She whirled around, blue eyes snapping. "His name is Rufus! How would you like to be called da Wolfgangsta?"

"I wouldn't," he admitted stiffly, his head continuing to pound. "I apologize. I will remember it is Rufus."

"Oh." She blinked. "Well. All right, then." She straightened her shoulders and met his gaze squarely. "As for the German command, yes. It seemed to work for you, and contrary to what you obviously think, I've been knocking myself out trying to find a way to get through to him."

"A whip and a chair might do the trick."

He wished the words back the minute they left his mouth. But it was too late. Carly's eyes narrowed, her chin shot up and she took an incensed step forward. "Listen, you— *Buster!*"

Her older dog, the one so goofy-looking he was almost a caricature, with his springy tufts of brindled fur sticking up atop his head and poking out like ruffles around his ankles, stepped between them, seeking her attention. Wolf didn't know exactly what happened next but thought that Carly must have almost caught the mutt with her foot. It occurred so fast that all he knew for certain was that when she pulled her stride to avoid kicking the dog, she pitched forward.

Buster scrambled aside and Wolf reached out to steady her at the same time that she flung out her hands to be caught. Given their mutual athleticism, they should have been able to right her with the minimum of contact.

But somehow the outsides of her arms slid along his inner forearms, knocking his hands aside. Her hands plowed inside his unbuttoned shirt, shoving back the open sides, then skidded along the bare skin over his ribs. As he reached for her hips to brace her, she grabbed the folds of material and hung on so tightly that she jerked the shirt clear off his shoulders to well beneath his shoulder blades. Her actions yanked his arms to his sides and the reflexive step backward that he took slammed his back against the wall. Her pets scattered, yipping and hissing, and Carly and Wolf slapped together, breasts to diaphragm. Her chin bounced off his collarbone, snapping her head back.

"Ow," she said, working her jaw. "Shit."

Wolf didn't say a word. He couldn't. Every Y chromosome he possessed was aware of the scent of soap and heat and woman—not to mention the feel of that long, lush body mashed against his. He was also howlingly aware of the dampness of her thin tank top, which was all that separated her breasts from his flesh. They were real breasts, too, soft, full globes that flattened where they met corded muscle, not the artificially enhanced tits so many of the showgirls seemed to sport these days.

He noticed for the first time that Carly's eyes had little golden flecks around her pupils and a deeper hue circling the clear blue iris. And her abrupt stillness told him she was suddenly as aware of him as he was of her. Or at least that she was aware of his awareness. Of course, the latter would be damned hard to ignore when he was half erect against her stomach.

Okay, all the way erect.

He saw her pulse tripping madly in the little hollow at the base of her throat, and he reached out to peel her off of him before he did something irrevocably stupid.

Trouble was, his shirt pinned his arms, preventing their usual full range of motion. He could still move well enough to get his hands on Carly's upper arms, and he did just that, fully intending to move her away from him, if only the couple of inches his currently shackled condition would permit. At least she wouldn't be pressed right up against the evidence of his happy-to-see-you dick.

That was the plan, anyway.

But somehow his hands, which had reached out with every intention of following the exact commands his brain issued, slid right up those smooth, firm arms and onto her warm-skinned shoulders. Then, since they were already in the neighborhood, they eased up her slender throat to frame her face. With a will of their own, his thumbs gently pressed the underside of her chin, which had a shallow dimple he'd never noticed before, and his fingers tunneled into her short, damp hair. He tilted her head back and to one side while tipping his own in the opposite direction.

Then, his heart thumping against the wall of his chest in slow, hard thuds, he rocked his mouth over the soft curves of her lips.

And, ah, God. They were sweet and pliant, and he wanted them to open up and let him in.

Now.

He widened his mouth around Carly's, then dragged it closed, sipping at her with steady, demanding suction. *Let me in, let me in, let me in.*

His eyebrows furrowed when that didn't gain him the immediate entry he sought, and he raised his head, came at her from a different direction. He tickled the seam of her lips with the tip of his tongue.

She made a sound deep in her throat, and her fingers un-

pleated the shirt they gripped and shook free of its voluminous folds. A second later, her hands were splayed against his
back, bare skin to bare skin.

And her lips parted.

Yes! Wolf plunged his tongue inside.

She tasted even richer and more addictive than he'd
imagined she would and every coherent reason why this
wasn't a good idea evaporated like dew in the desert when
she kissed him back. The control he took such pride in dis-
integrated and his mouth turned rapacious.

Carly wrapped her arms around his neck and rubbed her
breasts against his chest, returning his kiss with one that was
every bit as voracious.

He stroked his hands down her soft nape, over her shoulders and down her back, following the long line of her spine
to her round, firm ass. Gripping her through the thin, silky
material, he bent his knees and yanked her to him—and his
hard-on discovered a little piece of heaven in the soft, giving
notch between her thighs.

But it wasn't enough. He wanted his hands on the bare
skin her diaphanous skirt had hinted at, and he began gathering fabric up by the handfuls, inching the garment up the
backs of her thighs. *Got to have some of this*, his out-of-control
testosterone insisted, and he wedged a thigh between hers
and widened his stance, nudging her legs farther apart.

Got to have some of this now!

Nothing else mattered at the moment. Not the fact that
she wasn't a woman who fit into his master plan. Not the fact
that they didn't even like each other. Not Niklaus waiting
for him next door. Not—

Oh, shit, Niklaus!

Damn, something did matter. The recollection of his

nephew, who could come looking for him at any minute, splashed cold water all over the hot haze of lust that had made every other consideration seem incidental. Hell, he'd left Carly's front door wide open when he'd followed her into her apartment, and it was only blind luck that no one had poked their head in to see what was going on.

Dropping her skirt back into place, he jerked his hands away from the tempting territory they'd roamed. He reached up to thread his fingers through her short hair and pull her head back.

She blinked unfocused eyes at him and licked her bottom lip. Then her lips, ruddy and swollen from his kisses, curled up in a sultry little smile and he groaned, his new resolve seriously threatened. He wanted to return that carnal smile, wanted to dive back in and pick up right where they'd left off.

But indulging the Jones wild streak wasn't in his makeup— even if he had forgotten that fact in a moment of blistering arousal. He gave her a stern look. "I can't do this."

She returned a melting, slightly dazed smile that he felt clear to the pit of his stomach and rotated her pelvis against his erection. "Oh, honey," she assured him. "You can."

His hips pushed back at her until he caught himself and forced them to still, and he slid his fingers from her hair, gripping her shoulders instead to set her back a step.

The damn shirt pulled him up short again, but he shoved away from the wall so abruptly that it did the chore for him, tumbling her back a step. While she was still off balance, he hitched the shoulder seams of his abused shirt back into place. Then, heart pounding a savage beat, he stared at her.

What the hell had he done?

"No," he finally said when she locked eyes with him. "I really can't. You're not part of my plan."

Her eyes held confusion. "You have a plan that doesn't allow for sex?"

"*No.*"

"No?" She took a tiny step forward. "Well, then…"

He put a hand up, warding her off. "I mean yes, I have a plan that doesn't include *unscheduled* sex." And it was high time he dragged it back front and center where it belonged.

"You schedule sex?" she said in disbelief. "What, between filing reports and busting card counters? My God. You are one seriously screwed-up individual."

He'd always considered himself a seriously organized individual. Still, looking at the mussed, sexy blonde he was voluntarily walking away from, he wondered if she wasn't onto something.

But, no. He knew what he wanted out of life, and this wasn't it. Well, it was, but it would be a mistake he'd regret the moment satisfaction faded. And he had no room in his agenda for mistakes.

So he managed a negligent shrug and slapped his best emotionless expression on his face. "You may be right," he said coolly as he headed for the door. "But at least I've got a plan."

As he stepped out into the hallway, he heard a sound like steam escaping an overheated teakettle.

"Yeah, well, plan *this*, you jerk!" Carly yelled.

Closing the door behind him, Wolf thought it was just as well he couldn't see the precise gesture that undoubtedly accompanied her directive.

Seven

Carly felt as if she were two seconds away from exploding. She took a jerky step to the right, then one to the left. Thrusting her hand through her damp hair, she whirled and took yet another indecisive step in the direction of the breakfast bar.

"Damn." Stopping dead, she stared out through the sliders. But the attractive landscaping of the courtyard below her small lanai barely registered. Nor did her pets make more than a fleeting impression as they slunk out of their hiding places to vie for her attention now that she was alone again and no longer making any sudden moves.

Her skin felt two sizes too small, her body throbbed with a tight, achy, unsatiated arousal, and humiliation rode her like a monkey on an addict's back. She didn't know what on earth to do with herself. She couldn't even take her contradictory jumble of emotions to Treena to sort out as she normally would. This was simply too personal, too…raw.

And that only made her feel worse, because she had no

safety valve for this god-awful head of steam that Wolf had stoked in her.

Stoked to the boiling point, damn him, before strolling away and leaving her with no means of blowing it off.

"You bastard," she whispered. It had knocked her for a loop when she'd opened the door and seen him standing there, looking completely different from the usual spit-shined, buttoned-down, pain-in-the-ass automaton she was accustomed to seeing. Gone had been the uptight, poker-faced Surveillance honcho, and in his place had stood an angry man who'd looked sort of savage and wild.

Which, of course, had called to her. Maybe her mother was right, maybe she did need therapy.

She rejected the idea out of hand. Because, please. The guy she more or less knew for his quality clothing—the same man who always looked so pulled together, right down to his coordinating ties, who she imagined must prop himself upright in a closet to sleep so as not to wrinkle his fine threads—had pulled a vanishing act.

In his place had stood a man not only sans the tie he seemed to consider de rigueur, but in a shirt he hadn't even bothered to fasten. And the glimpse of his smooth, hard chest and rigid stomach muscles through the narrow opening, the sight of those long, muscular thighs, hair-dusted calves and big, narrow, naked feet, had frozen her in place for several heart-stopping seconds.

Even then, she'd been cool. And she would have *continued* to be cool, too…if only she hadn't tripped. If only *he* hadn't kissed her.

Dammit, he should have kept his lips to himself. Or at least had the decency to be a lousy kisser.

But he had done neither of those things. Oh, he was still

a jerk, still the worst kind of control freak. *Who the hell schedules their sexual encounters, for heaven's sake?* But Wolfgang Jones could kiss like nobody's business, and no longer did she have the comfort of assuring herself he was a clueless, cold and passionless Mr. Robotics kind of guy.

She truly wished she did, because right this minute she'd rather eat grubs than admit anything good about him. And yet...

While the man definitely had some strange hang-ups, a lack of passion wasn't one of them. There had been nothing cold about his mouth on hers. Nothing remotely chilly about the body she'd been pressed against. Damn, he'd pumped out heat like a coal-burning furnace. And Lord have mercy, those hands!

His fingers had been long and firm and oh-so-hot on her butt, and they sure as hell hadn't been the least bit hesitant about rocking her against his erection—which had been even longer, firmer...hotter. It had been so long since she'd experienced any of that sweet man-woman friction, and it had felt so good. Just a couple of lousy minutes longer and she'd have been ready to screw his brains out right there against the partition wall.

An unamused laugh escaped her. Who was she kidding? She'd been *so* past primed. That was one of the reasons the manner in which he'd pulled the plug on her, the callous way he'd left her twitching with frustration, rankled so much.

Her first impression was obviously correct. Anyone who'd work a woman into a frenzy, then leave her flat because it wasn't in his frigging schedule, *was* cold—his hot hands and hotter kisses be damned.

Catching herself standing with gritted teeth and clenched fists in the middle of the floor, Carly sucked in a deep breath and blew it out. Great. She was furious all over again.

Screw it, she had things to do today. Maybe nothing earth-shattering, but a hell of a lot more important than moaning over not satisfying her treacherous libido's needs. She really did need to get her mind away from Jones's infuriating callousness and onto something else. The question was: what? Looking around, she saw a piece of paper lying on the floor next to the chintz ottoman, and she walked over and snatched it up, grateful for the distraction.

When she realized it was the incident report Wolfgang had wanted her to sign last night, however, her blood pressure skyrocketed all over again. Crumpling it up, she tossed it back on the floor and ground it beneath her bare heel. That wasn't nearly destructive enough to satisfy her urge to annihilate, so she snatched it up again and smoothed it out. Then she proceeded to rip it into the tiniest shreds she could manage. Clutching the handful of confetti in one fist, she rummaged through her little secretaire with the other until she found an envelope. She poured her opinion of Wolfgang's report into it and sealed it up.

Tripod stropped himself against her ankles, and she bent down to pick him up, cuddling the gray-and-white cat against her breasts. He purred and butted his head against her chin.

"You're right," she said decisively, scratching the feline between his ears. "Standing around steaming is counterproductive. If I let this turn me inside out, Jones wins—and that is not going to happen." She gently set Tripod down upon the hassock. "So, let's go to the hospital and brighten someone's day. I'll change into something a little more conservative, do something with my hair, and then we'll all take off. Well, except for you, Dogface." She paused on her way to the bedroom to rub Rufus's head. "You're doing worlds better, but I'm afraid you're still not quite there yet. Soon, though, little buddy.

"Soon."

She felt much better by the time she let herself back into the apartment a couple of hours later. She unhooked Buster's leash and opened the door on the travel container so Tripod and Rags, who always needed a little time to decompress after one of their trips, could let themselves out when they were ready. Rufus was sulking over by the sliding doors and wouldn't look at her, but she consoled herself with the fact that at least he hadn't torn the place apart.

Viewing that as definite progress, she refused to let his displeasure make her feel guilty. She'd been taking her babies to local hospitals as part of the pet-therapy volunteer program for a little over four years now, and Rufus wasn't ready to be turned loose upon an unsuspecting hospital. The idea wasn't to have animals running wild, but rather to utilize pets as a means to cheer up patients awaiting surgery or—the ones she had a special affinity for—long-term care patients like the kids on the oncology ward. So until she could be certain Rufus would behave himself on a consistent basis, he'd just have to stay home.

But she was accustomed to having him think she was the greatest thing since the rawhide chew bone, and getting the continued cold shoulder from him was starting to punch little holes in her resolve. In order to keep herself from rewarding his bad attitude, which would no doubt set his burgeoning training back several giant steps, she strode into her bedroom and changed into her electric-blue bikini. She was a responsible pet owner no matter what He Who Would Not Be Named liked to say. So Rufus could just sulk.

But there was no reason she had to stick around to be tortured by it. She'd go take a swim.

A teenager she'd never seen before was rocketing from one end of the pool to the other when she let herself in through the gate several moments later. His form left a lot to be desired, and he was churning up a considerable amount of water, so she decided to give him time to wear himself out before attempting to share the pool with him. As she snapped her towel over a chaise lounge beneath the shade of the palm trees and made herself comfortable on the cheery blue-and-white delft-patterned terry cloth, she observed his dogged laps. It wasn't difficult to tell that something was definitely driving him. And she had to admit that all that anger or determination or whatever it was that propelled him was pretty darn compelling. Wryly deciding it almost made up for his lack of style, she applied sunblock while she watched him hack and kick his way through lap after laborious lap.

It became almost hypnotic after a while and she found herself yawning. Another lap and her eyes drifted closed.

The next thing she knew there was a shadow blocking the dappled rays that filtered through the palms. Shading her eyes, she peered up at a tall sun-limned, featureless phantom standing at the end of her lounge chair.

"Hey," said a young male voice that sounded as if it were consciously striving to be cool. The phantom moved, dropping down onto the chaise next to her, where he turned into a long, lanky teen with slicked-back dark hair and pretty hazel-green eyes. He swiped his forearm over his dripping forehead as his gaze skittered from her breasts to her bare stomach to her legs and back up to her face.

"Hey, yourself," she said, and cast an inward sigh, waiting for the tired pickup line that was sure to come.

"Where are your dogs?" he asked, glancing around as if expecting them to pop out of the neatly maintained grounds surrounding the pool enclosure. "You shoulda brought 'em down with you."

It was the last thing she'd expected, and she flashed him a grin that was purely spontaneous. All right, a fellow dog lover—not an adolescent jerk, at all. *You gotta love a male with the good taste to be a cut above the average Joe.* "No pets allowed at the pool, I'm afraid," she said, and gave the teenager a discreet once-over.

He was going to be a big man someday, but he hadn't yet bulked up beneath his lightly tanned skin. He still had that slightly undernourished, awkward look some still-growing adolescents got. She'd bet the bank, though, that one day he'd fill out to be an all-around hunk. And given those poet's eyes, she imagined that even now he drove the little girls wild.

She stuck out her hand. "I'm Carly, by the way."

He got tangled up in the towel he'd wrapped around himself as he leaned forward to thrust out his own hand. Dull color promptly stained his cheeks, but he extricated himself with a minimum of fuss and shook her hand firmly. "Niklaus."

"Nice to meet you, Niklaus. How do you know about my dogs?"

"I saw you with them on your balcony last night."

At midnight? "From where, toots? The courtyard?"

"Nah." He jerked his chin in the general direction of her building. "I'm your new neighbor."

"No kidding?" She regarded him with interest. "I didn't realize any of the units were even on the market."

"They probably aren't. I just moved in next door with my uncle. You might know him." His voice changed, taking on a slightly resentful tone. "Wolfgang Jones."

"That's your *uncle?*" The Iceberg had a family? That was so…human. And here she'd thought he'd sprung fully grown from the loins of Medusa.

Niklaus nodded and Carly said, "When did that happen?"

"My grandma brought me to Vegas earlier this week, but we stayed at Circus Circus so I didn't move in until last night."

And Wolfgang had had the balls to accuse *her* of being irresponsible? She would never leave a kid all by himself in a strange apartment on his first night in residence. She had half a mind to hunt him down and tell him so, too.

Fortunately she still had a few working brain cells in the remaining half. But she couldn't prevent herself from asking, "Where's your uncle now?"

"Dr. Gloom?" Niklaus shrugged. "Upstairs, I guess. Probably starching his shorts."

She grinned. Oh God, she and this kid were going to get along *so* fine. It was almost too bad that he wasn't twenty years older—or that she wasn't into cradle robbing. Otherwise she might have found her soul mate.

Still, she supposed it wasn't copacetic to foment rebellion between relatives, so she reeled in her goofy grin and slapped her best I-gotta-be-the-adult-here expression in its place. "Now, now, I'm sure he's a perfectly nice person," she said, and even managed to sound as if she meant it. *If you like the I've-got-a-plan-for-everything—right-down-to-my-own-orgasm—type.*

The latter thought kicked the slats out from under her amusement, since it brought with it a much too vivid recollection of the morning's events. *That* was a memory she had no desire to revisit.

It also had nothing to do with Niklaus, who was looking at her with the sort of hesitant longing she usually associated with her rescued pets.

There was just no way she could turn her back on that. She'd never been able to with the furry contingent, and she didn't have the heart to ignore the teen's obvious need for a friend, either. The poor kid was a stranger in Las Vegas, and within the next couple of days would probably have to contend with being the new kid on the block at a new school, as well. And as if that weren't dreary enough, he was saddled with the most humorless male in the known universe as his guardian. Who on earth had thought that was a good idea?

She rose to her feet and looked down at the teen. "I'm going to go take a quick dip," she informed him. "Then if you want to, you're welcome to come upstairs to meet my babies."

"You've got kids?"

She laughed. "No. That's what I call my menagerie. And as I said, you're welcome to come on up and meet them."

A killer smile flashed across his face and he hopped to his feet with touching alacrity. "*Sweet!*"

"You think so, huh?" She smiled at his eagerness. Then a thought popped into her mind, and her smiled widened. "So, tell me. Do you happen to speak German?"

"Yeah, sure. Grandma's from Bavaria, and both Mom and Uncle Wolf speak it so I learned as a little kid. Why?"

"Because you've just been enlisted to help me train Rufus."

They looked at each other. Then, as one, they grinned and said in unison, "*Sweet!*"

Eight

Tuesday night, Wolf leaned through the open door of Dan McAster's office. "You have a minute?" he asked when his boss looked up.

"Sure." Tossing his pen on the desktop, the head of Surveillance waved him in. "In fact I was going to contact you myself when I finished here." He searched a towering pile of papers and manila folders that occupied one side of his wide polished steel desk, threatening the stack's precarious balance when he withdrew a sheet of paper. He thrust the latter out at Wolf as the younger man stepped inside the office. "You want to tell me what the hell this is?"

Wolf crossed the room in two long strides and took the form. He gave it a quick, comprehensive once-over, then handed it back. "A report for an employee injury."

"I see that. What I don't see is why Surveillance was involved."

"I was on my way home when I came across the incident, and since it involved a scantily clad showgirl a big crowd had started to gather." He shrugged. "Nobody else was diving in to help, so I did. Turns out Jacobsen, the dancer, is a neighbor of mine, so I got her on her feet, got some ice for her ankle and drove her home."

"Okay, I understand that. I even applaud your actions. But this is your signature at the bottom of the report. Why didn't Jacobsen fill it out herself?"

"Because I pissed her off and she sent back the form I'd given her in confetti format. I figured it would be more time efficient to fill out a new one myself."

Dan shook his head. "Haven't you learned yet that you can catch more flies with honey than with vinegar? Christ Almighty, boy, crank up the charm next time!"

"I'm not really the crank-up-the-charm type." And Carly would be the last person he'd want to try it on even if he were. They needed more distance between them, not less.

"No, you're not, and that's something you need to work on." Dan leaned his forearms on the desktop and the humor in his eyes morphed into dead seriousness. "I know you're chomping at the bit to step into the top-dog slot somewhere and God knows you're ready—in every aspect except your people skills."

Wolf's stomach jittered. Before he could say anything, however—and in truth he wasn't even sure what that would be—Dan continued.

"You're the best problem solver I've got," he said. "But you need to work at making connections with your co-workers that don't begin and end with them thinking you're a cold-ass son of a bitch. There have already been several instances of people bringing Surveillance concerns to me or Beck because they were too intimidated to approach you. And you know damn well tip-offs from Housekeeping, pit bosses and the like are what keep small problems from turning into large ones."

Equipment hummed softly in the main hub outside Dan's office as Wolf struggled to assimilate the soft-core reprimand. Glancing through the open blinds, he gazed blankly at the wall of screens that showed the action taking place in every venue of the establishment, from the gaming tables and machines in the casino to the hotel elevators and corridors.

"I'm not suggesting you become drinking buddies with anyone," Dan assured him dryly.

Wolf nodded. "I know. I'll work on it."

"I don't doubt that for a minute. You're one of the hardest-working men I know." He leaned back in his chair. "So I've had my say. What brings you in here?"

"What? Oh." Shoving his hands in his pockets, he put his boss's unexpected request aside to think about later. "I need to talk to you about my days off."

"What days off?" Dan's short bark of laughter bounced around the room. "In all the time you've been here, Wolf, you've taken off, what? Maybe two days a month?"

That sounded about right. It was all part of his master plan because, for all that he didn't intend to work in Las Vegas for the rest of his life, his time here had given him the best training of his career. The Avventurato combined cutting-edge technology with state-of-the-art equipment. Plus, the nightly exposure to a dozen different situations was experience he couldn't have bought anywhere else. He never knew what would come up when he clocked into work. In the almost thirty-three months he'd worked for the casino, he had covered more combinations of circumstances than most men in the industry saw in a lifetime.

"Things have changed," he said, and gave Dan a rundown of his new status as a guardian with the same succinct brevity he'd utilize to report an incident in the hotel.

"Of course you gotta spend time with the kid," Dan promptly agreed. "Teens need a lot of supervision, and frankly, bud, you're going to have a hard-enough row to hoe just working nights, without sacrificing your days off on top of it. I'm sorry. I wouldn't have called you in tonight, except you've always been so amenable to the overtime in the past. You should have said something when you first got here. Hell, you shoulda said something when I had you on the phone. I could just as easily have called in Beck."

He almost had. Niklaus hadn't said a word when Wolf's night off was canceled, and God knew the kid would probably stick needles in his eyes before he'd ever indicate a desire for Wolf's company. Still, there had been something a little lost about him. He'd probably been feeling vulnerable after his first day at a new school, and Wolf had just left him alone to stew about it.

What the hell had Mom been thinking to leave the kid in his care? Habit was a tough mother to break, and he'd already screwed up by following his usual pattern—he'd come in and handled the job he'd been summoned to do.

"Go on, get out of here," Dan said, interrupting his thoughts. "And don't come back until Friday."

His usual days off were Tuesday and Wednesday, and he bit back an automatic protest that the additional day Dan had given him was unnecessary. He had to start thinking like…like a…

Shit.

Like a parent.

He chewed on that during the short drive home. Not much shook him, but he didn't mind admitting, if only to himself, that the idea of having total responsibility for a furious youth scared the crap out of him. He didn't have the first idea how to break through Niklaus's anger. He should, considering he had been an angry teenager himself once upon a time. He knew firsthand what it felt like to lack the power to change your circumstances. But still, he didn't have a clue how to deal with Nik.

Yet he was all his nephew had at the moment, so he'd damn well better find some kind of common ground.

It was difficult to wrap his mind around. He'd been cruising along just fine. Now he was sole guardian of a pissed-off kid…and spending far too much time thinking inappropriate thoughts about a female who was the antithesis of his ideal woman.

How had his life suddenly gone from Things-are-looking-good to Too-screwed-up-to-believe?

The apartment had a still, unoccupied feeling to it when he let himself in a short while later, and he experienced a spurt of exasperation. Pushing it aside as absurd and premature, he closed the door behind him and pocketed the keys. Niklaus wasn't out roaming the Strip on his own. He was no doubt in his room. "Nik!"

There was no answer and irritation started creeping back. He'd come home specifically for Niklaus's benefit. So where the hell was he?

Willing his impatience away, he walked briskly down the short hallway. The kid was probably listening to his ubiquitous music on his headphones and simply hadn't heard him. That was something he'd taken to doing ever since Wolf had talked to him about showing a little respect for the neighbors.

Neighbor, pal. His stride faltered. *Singular.*

Right. Just one neighbor. Carly Jacobsen. Whose body he could still feel beneath his hands, whose taste his senses refused to relinquish. His edgy discomfort took on a whole new dimension.

Don't go there. Giving himself a mental shake, he got moving again, striding purposefully toward the teen's room. At the same time, he shoved every disruptive thought of the showgirl next door into the furthermost corner of his mind. Niklaus was the important thing to keep in mind here. And thinking of the music his nephew played almost nonstop, Wolf could picture the teen, his shiny brown hair flopping as he head-bopped to the beat purling out of his earphones.

Stopping in front of Niklaus's door, he gave it a peremptory rap, then immediately winced. Maybe he should try reeling in the worst of his authoritarian tendencies for a while. It probably wasn't the best tactic to take with a rebellious teen, even if it was against his nature to pussyfoot around.

As it turned out it didn't matter, for there was no response. A disquiet settling in his veins, Wolf reached out and turned the knob. He pushed the door open a crack. "Niklaus?"

There was no response, and opening the door all the way, he saw that the room was empty. Not only was Niklaus not here, his ever-present soccer ball lay in lonely splendor in the middle of his unmade bed. For the first time Wolf felt a flicker of cold uneasiness.

Where the hell could he be? Anxiety started to rise, but he firmly shoved it down and ordered himself to think. *Keep your head on straight and apply the same logic you used last year when that couple lost their seven-year-old son at the Avventurato.*

He turned on his heel and strode back toward the living room, trying to ignore the voice in his head that whispered locating that boy hadn't touched his emotions since it hadn't involved his own flesh and blood.

Hell. He'd always prided himself on not *having* emotions, but suddenly everyone was acting as if that were a bad thing. He could still see the shock on Carly's face the night she'd hurt her foot and he'd told her he didn't need friends. She'd looked at him as if he were some crazy lowlife. And tonight's lecture from Dan kept replaying in his mind. So he guessed it was acceptable to be a little freaked when a member of his own family went missing.

He didn't have to like the way it made him feel, though.

Worrying about all the ways a kid could get hurt in this city made it hard to concentrate. He couldn't seem to shake the alarm he felt knowing that he'd had a finite area of the hotel's interior and its limited grounds to search for the little boy who'd gone missing at the Avventurato.

Not all of frigging Sin City.

Then he reined himself in. It was far from a sure thing that Niklaus was lying somewhere injured or even out trying to sneak into a strip joint. There were any number of places right here in the complex where a teen could hang out. It was possible Nik had run into another kid on the condo grounds. Or he could be at one of the pools, the clubhouse or the gym.

Wolf hiked over to the sliding door that led to the balcony. He reached for the lock on the glass doors with the intention of conducting a quick survey of the courtyard below. Finding it already unlatched, he made a mental note to have a talk with Niklaus about house security when he found him and opened the slider.

"...full of a bunch of rich kids who drive cars that probably cost more than my mom makes in a year," Niklaus's voice said. "Not that *that* would be real tough to do."

Wolf's neck and shoulder muscles, which until that moment he hadn't realized were clenched into inflexible bands of stress-induced tension, abruptly relaxed. Blowing out an inaudible sigh of relief, he quietly stepped onto the balcony and peered into the shadows, wondering who his nephew was talking to.

No one was there.

"Yeah, right," a woman's voice said with sexy-voiced skepticism. "As if a handsome, interesting boy like you won't have the girls eating out of your hand within days. And rich is actually a bonus, toots—or so my mother is always telling me."

The tension in Wolf's neck came roaring back. *Shit.* He knew that voice. Easing forward silently, he looked beyond the connecting wall into the balcony next door and saw a number of candles glowing upon a low table. Two pairs of feet were propped up on the table's edge in front of them. He could only see to about mid-shin, but it was enough to notice that his nephew and Carly Jacobsen seemed to be sitting pretty damn close to each other.

Then a long, slender foot with red-painted toenails nudged one of Niklaus's feet and Wolf's temper promptly shot from quiescent straight into the stratosphere. Gritting his teeth, he barely managed to bite back a snarl, while his inner voice howled, *No touching!* Dammit, she had no business touching Niklaus. What the hell was wrong with her? More to the point, what was a woman with her kind of sexuality doing hanging out with a sixteen-year-old kid in the first place?

He watched as Carly's toe withdrew and she crossed her ankles on the tabletop. "So your uncle specifically chose this rich-kids' school for you?"

"Yeah." Niklaus's voice was glum.

Wolf held his breath, waiting for her to rip his character to shreds. That was *all* he needed in his already razor-wire-wrapped relationship with his nephew—a little biased intervention. One negative word from her and he would probably never find a level playing field on which to meet the kid.

She gave Niklaus's foot another poke with one of her red-tipped toes, and through his fury at her continued tactile teasing, Wolf realized with a spurt of satisfaction that her feet were actually kind of ugly. They were callused and slightly misshapen.

He was so busy staring at them to keep from thinking about other parts of her that he knew damn well were off-the-scale attractive, that he was caught by surprise when, instead of the character assassination he expected, she merely said, "Aren't there any redeeming qualities to the school at all?"

"Well, it's got a decent soccer team." Then enthusiasm suddenly replaced Niklaus's usual bored tones. "No, the truth is, it's got an *awesome* team—they've won the league cup four years running. And all I gotta say is the current goalie better watch his back, because I'm trying out for the position tomorrow and I plan to ace it."

"There you go, then," she said easily. A beat of silence went by, then she added, "I'm guessing that's important to you, huh?"

"Fuck, yeah. It's—"

"Whoa, whoa, whoa, *whoa!*" All the mellow humor left Carly's voice and her feet thumped to the balcony's floor. Candlelight wavered in the draft her sudden movement created, a black cat hit the deck and her funny-looking dog scampered into sight, glancing uneasily over his brindled shoulder as he huddled against the outer adobe wall of the enclosure. "You do *not* use that language around me, Niklaus, are we clear on that?"

"But you—"

"Said it under great provocation when I burned my thumb on the nacho pan. *Are we clear?*"

"Yes," Niklaus mumbled. "Sorry."

"Thank you. And I apologize as well for saying it in front of you." She swung her feet back up onto the tabletop, and her voice regained its relaxed friendliness. "So tell me why being on this soccer team is a big deal to you."

"Because I'm really good at it, and soccer is going to be my ticket to a good college."

"Is that so? Have you ever considered having your grades be your ticket instead?"

"Actually…yeah." He laughed, clearly pleased with himself. "I've more than considered—it's an important part of my plan."

Wolf smiled. It looked like he and his nephew had something in common after all.

"Oh, God deliver me from another freaking man with a plan," Carly said, her voice dropping from warmly approving to exasperated.

"Huh?"

Wolf's brows drew together because he understood the reference, even if Niklaus didn't. Before he could decide how he felt about the scorn that was so obviously directed at him, her voice continued.

"Never mind," she said. "It's not worth talking about. So, you get good grades on a regular basis, then?"

"I maintain a 3.9 grade-point average."

"Wow. Good for you! That's very impressive, Niklaus."

"Yeah, well, I figure if grades can bag you a scholarship and *sports* can bag you a scholarship, then excelling at both would be kind of like…uh, like—"

Hitting the daily double, Wolf thought, proud of the kid.

"Winning the daily double."

"Yeah!"

Wolf tried not to let Niklaus's obvious pleasure in her answer eat him alive with jealousy. Especially since he wasn't even one hundred percent certain what bothered him most, the fact that his nephew could talk so easily to her when he barely gave Wolf the time of day, or that *she* was so easy with Niklaus when she'd clearly be happy to see his guts strung from here to Hoover Dam.

Whoa. He slapped the brakes on that train of thought. Of *course* the only person he was interested in having a relationship with was Niklaus. Moving silently, he eased over to the far edge of his balcony to try to see farther into the one next door.

Carly caught a slight movement on the lanai to her left and found herself staring into the shadows as if expecting a bogeyman to materialize. When she failed to see anything at all, let alone a mythical hobgoblin, she turned her attention back to Niklaus.

"So college is your goal?" she asked him. Seeing the matching blissful expressions both he and Rufus wore as the teen stroked the pup's head, she grinned.

He grinned back at her. "Absolutely. The only one in my family who's been to university is my uncle Wolf. I plan to be the second."

Wolf. She liked that diminutive, and hearing it out of the blue caused her to straighten slightly from her indolent slouch. She had very deliberately not solicited gossip from Niklaus about his uncle, not wanting to take advantage of their budding friendship that way.

But seeing as how the teen had brought up the subject himself…

"Where did your uncle go to school?" she asked casually.

"Penn State."

"Huh. What was his major?"

"I dunno." He gave her a curious look.

Okay, Jacobsen, reel it in. What do you care, anyway? "Do you plan to attend Penn, too?"

"I'm not fixated on any particular school. I intend to keep my options open until I see who offers the best scholarship. Then I'll take it from there."

"So best-case scenario would be choosing the most comprehensive scholarship from between a number of competing universities?"

"Yeah."

Once again something caught her eye on the balcony next door, and this time she stared until her eyes adjusted to the darkness beyond the candles she'd lighted on the little mosaic coffee table. Was something actually there or was her imagination tricking her into seeing shadows within shadows? She shook her head, for all was still. Damn. She was clearly seeing things.

Then the something she thought she'd imagined shifted infinitesimally, and she didn't have a doubt in the world what it was.

Or rather who. Good God, was Wolf *spying* on them? Her temper threatened to flare, but she tamped it down, thinking furiously.

And a small smile curved her lips. Because it seemed to her that anyone who went to so much effort to snoop truly ought to receive full value for his trouble.

Only… What could she do to give Wolf the wrong impression that wouldn't also plant ideas in Niklaus's head? Ideas she was pretty sure didn't already exist, since she'd been very, very careful to be as asexual as possible around the teen.

She reached for the bottle of sparkling cider, turning the label toward her in the hopes that from a distance Wolf would assume it held wine. "You're falling behind, pal. If you're going to hang with the big kids, you gotta keep up." She topped up Niklaus's flute and set the bottle back in the ice bucket by her feet. She raised her own half-full glass toward him. "To…friends. Bottoms up."

After he obediently knocked back his cider, she set her flute down on the table and rose to her feet, extending her hand. "Let's go inside," she said softly. "I've got a special treat for you."

She barely had time to show him the plate of cookies she'd begged from Ellen before a thunderous pounding commenced at her front door. Swallowing a grin, she went to let Wolf in.

Nine

The instant Wolf laid a fist to Carly's door her dogs started barking their fool heads off. The noise faded when the door opened and they recognized him, but Rufus promptly leaped out into the hallway and jumped up on him.

Wolf barely noticed, his attention all for Carly, who stood there staring up at him all wide-eyed and innocent-looking.

As if butter wouldn't melt in that lush mouth, he thought irritably. As if seducing his nephew was the furthest thing from her mind.

"Well, hello there," she said. "Fancy seeing *you* here." She pointed at Rufus and said with abrupt sternness, *"Platz!"*

The dog immediately dropped to the ground and looked up at him with a big doggy grin, his long pink tongue lolling out the side of his mouth.

Wolf's gaze narrowed as he considered his neighbor. She looked almost demure with her face scrubbed free of makeup and that spectacular showgirl's body partially disguised by an oversize men's pin-striped shirt buttoned all the way to the hollow of her throat. Her sleeves were rolled back to expose her slender forearms, but the shirttails hung halfway down her thighs, nearly obscuring the tight pair of denim capris she wore beneath them.

"You must be looking for Niklaus," she said, breaking the silence to step back and fling the door wide. "Come in. You're just in time to join us for—" she cleared her throat with a delicate *ahem* "—cookies."

He glared at her. "Is that what you're calling it these days?"

"That's what I've always called them, toots."

Niklaus appeared in the archway to the living room, looking none too pleased to see him. "What are you doing here?" he demanded. "I thought you had to work."

"I thought it would be nice if we could spend more time together, so I cut things short and came home. Imagine my surprise when I got there and you were gone without so much as a note telling me where I could find you." Forgetting all about his newfound resolve to dial back on the authoritarian attitude with his nephew, he ordered peremptorily, "Get your stuff. We're going home."

A dull flush stained Niklaus's cheeks. "I don't think so." He glanced at Carly and crossed his arms over his chest before turning his attention back to Wolf. Stubbornness squared his jaw. "I'm not ready to leave. I haven't had my cookies yet."

Wolf's temper edged toward the red zone, but his tone dropped into the frozen tones of command he used when dealing with cheating casino patrons. "Nik, get your stuff. *Now*."

"I don't have any stuff," the teen said stubbornly.

"Good. Then let's go." He turned on his heel, expecting his nephew to fall in behind him.

"Niklaus, wait."

Slowly he turned back to stare incredulously at Carly. She

dared? She dared bring this to a showdown between the two of them, with Niklaus caught in the middle? But even as he watched through narrowed eyes, Carly strode into the other room. She returned a moment later with a plate that held a frilly paper doily and…damn—cookies.

"Here." She handed the platter to Niklaus. "Take them with you. You haven't lived until you've eaten Ellen's cookies." Reaching out, she gently brushed back a slippery hank of hair that had fallen over the boy's forehead. "Good luck with your tryout tomorrow. Let me know how it turns out."

His expression lightened. "I will—you'll be the first one I'll tell. Thanks for the great nachos and sparkling cider and stuff." He hefted the plate of fancy cookies. "And for these."

"Yeah, about those. You don't think you get 'em all, do you?" She peeled back a section of the Saran Wrap and filched a chocolate cookie and a shortbread-looking one from the plate. "Return the plate to Ellen when you're done, okay?"

"Who?"

"Oh, that's right. You haven't met Ellen and Mack yet. Just drop the plate off here, then, and if it works into everyone's schedules I'll take you down and introduce you to the woman who baked these. Not only are you going to love her, but once you're on her good side she'll see to it that you have all the cookies you can handle."

"Cool." Niklaus looked at Carly, hesitated, then bent his head and gave her a quick buss on the cheek. With a glare for Wolf, he turned and stomped, red-cheeked, out the open door.

Carly turned her attention to him, her blue eyes morphing from warm and affectionate to ice-cold. "You're an idiot," she said in a low voice that didn't carry past the two of them. "An idiot and a judgmental eavesdropper." Splaying her hand dead center in the middle of his chest, she exerted pressure until he found himself backing out into the hallway.

Then she closed the door in his face.

Well, shit. That hadn't gone the way he'd expected. Blowing out a frustrated breath, he walked back to his own apartment.

Niklaus turned on him the instant he cleared the threshold, getting in his face until they stood nose to nose. "You *ever* embarrass me like that again in front of a friend and I'm outta here," the teenager snarled. "No way am I gonna let you treat me like a snot-nosed six-year-old. Not when I've been responsible for myself since I fucking *was* that age."

It hadn't occurred to Wolf to consider Nik's upbringing in that light, but knowing his sister, the kid probably had been in charge of himself since he was a tyke. He nevertheless heard himself saying in his own defense, "Well, excuse the hell out of me. I thought I was rescuing you."

"Rescuing me?" the boy said incredulously. "From what?"

Crap. He could hardly say he'd been eavesdropping on their conversation. Carly seemed to have figured it out, but so far Niklaus apparently hadn't tumbled to the fact, and he'd just as soon keep it that way. As he racked his brain for a reasonable explanation, his grudge against Carly solidified. She'd all but taken him by the hand to usher him into this mess.

He did not like being played.

Shrugging, he said, "I thought...Carly's not exactly your contemporary. I thought you might be in over your head."

"And you got that impression based on what? The juice and cookies she was serving me?"

Carly was right. He was an idiot, Wolf thought, wondering what the hell to say now.

He was saved from having to come up with an immediate response when an arrested expression suddenly came over Niklaus's face. The boy's mouth dropped open. "What? You thought she was *hot* for me?" Then Nik's lips firmed once again. "Man, you are one seriously twisted individual. But, even if there *was* a chance in hell of that ever happening," he said flatly, "that would be between her and me. My sex life is none of your frigging business, got it?"

Okay, the kid had a point. Just as his own father hadn't known squat about Wolf's life when he was a teenager, he didn't know much about Niklaus's. And he didn't have to think twice to know how he would have felt if Rick had instigated this same conversation with him when he was Nik's age.

Even as he was opening his mouth to say, "Got it," however, Niklaus roared over his incipient agreement like a loaded locomotive with a full head of steam.

"Just for the record, *Uncle* Wolf, you're not my daddy. And even if you were, I'll be seventeen next month and I lost my virginity two goddamn years ago, so it's too late to save me from myself. I didn't let anyone make my decisions about sex then, and I sure as hell don't intend to start now. Not even so I can have a lousy roof over my head."

Wolf had let him have his say, but he didn't intend to let that last statement pass. Grasping Niklaus's shoulders, he backed him up a step and met the boy's furious gaze squarely. "The roof over your head is not now, nor ever will be, contingent on talking about your sex life. Room and board are yours for as long as you want them, Nik. But that doesn't mean there aren't rules you have to follow."

Niklaus rolled his shoulders and took a step back, breaking the physical connection between them. "Like what? Being in my jammies and tucked in bed by ten?"

Wolf laughed. "No. Your grandmother tells me you have excellent grades."

"Hey." Niklaus stared at him. "You laughed, and your face didn't break or nuthin'." Then he raised his eyebrows. "Grandma told you I make good grades?"

He could hardly tell Niklaus he'd overheard him telling Carly. "I believe *excellent* was the word I used. She's really proud of you, you know." The latter, at least, was the truth. "And as long as they remain excellent you can go to bed any time you want. But I expect you to be in the house by eleven on school nights and by 1:00 a.m. on weekends. I also expect you to leave me notes letting me know where you're going to be—and how I can reach you. I'll look into getting you a cell phone for that purpose. You'll also lock all the doors when you leave, which you failed to do tonight."

"I did so lock the doors!"

"You locked the front door. You left the slider unlatched."

"Big deal." Niklaus tossed his hair out of his eyes. "Like anyone's gonna scale the frigging wall to the third floor."

Wolf just looked at him, and the teen finally shrugged. "Okay, fine. I'll be sure to lock every door in the joint. Is that it?"

"No. You made an issue out of telling me to butt out of your sex life, and I'm inclined to agree it's none of my business. So just assure me you're practicing safe sex and we won't discuss it again."

"Jesus. Do I look stupid to you?" Niklaus shot him a how-did-you-manage-to-live-this-long look.

"No. So I'll take that as an assurance." He tipped his chin at the plate of cookies Niklaus had set on an end table just inside the living room. "If I pour us some milk, will you share some of those with me?"

"Gee, what fun." The teen heaved a put-upon sigh.

"Giving *you* half when I could have been sharing them with a built blond babe." He fell silent for a second, then shot Wolf a sidelong glance. "So, you, uh, really thought Carly might be…interested in me?"

Good going there, Jones. Put some thoughts into the kid's head that weren't already there, why don't you? "What can I say, it was a moment of insanity. I'm tired and I looked at the situation and jumped to a hasty, ill-thought-out conclusion."

"Yeah," Niklaus agreed glumly. "Like a showgirl's gonna get the hots for a high school junior."

"I wouldn't put anything past that showgirl," Wolf muttered to himself as he walked into the kitchen.

Niklaus followed with the cookie plate. "Man. You sure haven't spent any time getting to know your neighbors since you moved in, have you?"

Wolf paused in his rummage through the refrigerator to glance over his shoulder at his nephew. That question sounded awfully damn similar to a couple of others he'd fielded lately. Why was everyone suddenly so concerned with his social life—or, more accurately, his perfectly satisfying lack of one? "Why do you say that?"

"Please." The teen snorted. "I haven't seen you shoot the breeze with a single person since I got here." He gave Wolf a disgusted look. "Take Carly, for example."

An image of doing just that flashed like wildfire through Wolf's mind, threatening to burn out of control. He sternly stamped it out. "What about her?"

"You guys are employed by the same casino, and she lives right next door. That means seeing each other at work, passing in the hallway, sharing a common wall. Close proximity, you know?

"Yet have you done anything to take advantage of this

God-given situation?" The teen shook his head in disgust. "Hell, no. Anybody can see you don't know the first thing about her. And I gotta say—" he picked up a cookie and stuffed it in his mouth "—it's your loss."

When Carly arrived at work Thursday night, she found another arrangement of flowers on the countertop at her station. It was from an anonymous admirer, just like the last one. The card included in the new arrangement read, "It's a pleasure to see you dancing again."

It was an innocuous-enough sentiment, yet for some reason it gave her an uneasy feeling.

"I guess I just don't care for surprises," she said in Treena's apartment after the last show later that night.

"You love surprises," Treena said.

"Okay, mysteries, then."

Jax, the love of Treena's life, handed both women a glass of wine and sat down next to the redhead on the couch across from Carly's chair. Wrapping a possessive arm around Treena, he brushed a lock of his streaky brown hair off his forehead and looked at Carly. "What's so mysterious about it? You're a showgirl. You're hot. Some guy is smitten."

"Some *anonymous* guy is smitten. I don't like anonymous."

"Okay, I can understand that. You're the straightforward type. Still, it's just a bunch of flowers."

She took a sip of her chardonnay and nodded. She agreed—intellectually. Emotionally, however, the anonymity scratched at some deep, primal feeling of exposure. "That card gives me visions of some guy sitting in the audience watching my every move. I had planned to check with the hotel florist to see if anyone there remembers who bought the last arrangement, but it slipped my mind. I'm going to do that tomorrow, though."

Jax's dark brows drew together. "You really are freaked about this."

"Yes, I am." She pressed the wineglass to her breasts. "Look, I know it's probably stupid, but tonight's bouquet just gave me this weird vibe. A single anonymous floral arrangement is one thing. But two? In my experience guys are usually pretty straightforward. They want to get laid, they send flowers. But they make damn sure you know who they're from. Women are the ones who do the Secret Santa thing with their friends."

A crooked little smile curved Treena's lips. "So maybe that's the answer. Maybe what you've got here is a lesbian admirer."

"Hell-o." Jax sat up, blue eyes bright. "This is just my two cents' worth, of course, but if it was *Treena* being pursued by an amorous lesbian, I'd only have one thing to say."

"And that would be?"

"Can I watch?"

His breath whooshed out of his lungs when Treena and Carly, with near perfect synchronization, respectively jabbed an elbow in his side and bounced a pillow off his head. "Hey." He hugged his girl to his side and caught Carly's pillow before it fell to the floor then lobbed it back into her lap. "No need to get testy. It was just an observation."

"Men are such pervs." But Carly had to admit he'd distracted her from the disquiet tonight's flowers had generated. Before she could say so, Jax sobered.

"Look, if you're really uneasy about this, maybe you oughtta go talk to Jones."

She pffffed a breath between pursed lips. "And tell him what? That someone is sending me hundred-dollar bouquets?"

"Yeah. Then make him understand how the anonymity doesn't sit right with you."

"I can't make that man understand diddly, Jax. You know we don't deal well together."

Jax's blue-eyed gaze met hers squarely. "That habit you have of giving him your bitch look might have something to do with it. Trust me, babe, having seen it for myself, I'm here to tell you it's scarier 'n hell."

"Jackson," Treena admonished, but Carly cut her off.

"No, let him speak, Treen." She straightened in her seat, uncurling her legs and dropping her feet to the floor. "So the trouble between me and Wolfgang is all my doing? Is that what you're saying?"

"Not if I wanna live, clearly," Jax said with wry good humor. He didn't have any problem, however, meeting her gaze. "But you have to agree it probably escalates the tension between you."

"Funny, I didn't notice it stopping him from kissing me and putting his hands all over my butt." *Oh, crap.* She hadn't meant to say that. She should have grown beyond such reactionary mouthiness by now, but she never had been one to take criticism lying down.

Not after fielding eighteen years' worth in her mother's series of upwardly mobile, rules-driven houses.

"He assaulted you?" The humor dropped from Jax's eyes and he straightened from his comfortable slouch against her friend. His voice went low and menacing. "I'll beat him to a bloody pulp."

Treena stared at her, equally horrified.

"No! That is…it wasn't like that, Jax."

"What was it like?" The eyes that met hers held the blank, flat gambler's stare that Jax used to play professional poker.

She wanted his usual friendly gaze back. "Well, he didn't force himself on me or anything. It was, uh—" *shit, shit, shit!* "—consensual."

The tension left his big shoulders and he relaxed back into the couch. Treena, on the other hand, continued to study her, a faint half smile playing around her lips, replacing the concern that had burned in her tawny brown eyes seconds earlier. "Why, Carly Jacobsen. You slut. When did this happen—and how come this is the first I've heard of it?"

"Last Friday—and I didn't know quite what to say. He rousted me from my shower in order to be his usual obnoxious self about Rufus. But when I went to give him a well deserved dressing-down, I tripped over Buster and landed smack up against his chest."

Heat bloomed deep in her stomach, and she shook her head to clear away the remembered sensory impression of all that bare, hot skin. "Anyhow, the next thing I knew he was kissing the bejesus out of me." Her eyes almost crossed just thinking about it. "And I gotta admit, Treen, the man can kiss."

"Were you wearing a little towel?" Jax asked. "That maybe fell to the floor when you tripped?"

She gave him the bitch look he'd mentioned earlier. "What are we, in junior high school? And what is it with you and all these sex questions today, anyway?"

"Ignore him," Treena advised. "His accelerated schooling as a kid made him miss out on the usual sexual exploration stuff most of us go through as juvies. He's trying to make up for lost time."

"Hey," Jax said indignantly, "I'll have you know this is stunningly close to one of my favorite fantasies, except in mine the woman fresh from the shower usually runs up against the masked cat burglar."

"Yeah, we've played that one," Treena said. "But do me a favor and try not to visualize my best friend naked, okay? You don't want to piss me off."

"Nope, don't wanna do that. Not when I'm this close to getting you to marry me." Jax hugged her to his side and grinned at Carly. "So if you and Wolfgang are smooching buddies now, why the big retreat about taking your concerns to him?"

Carly's mood soured. "Our temporary detente was called off when he got me all worked up, only to kick me to the curb when he suddenly remembered I wasn't part of his plan."

"He has a plan?" Treena looked disconcerted for a moment. Then she rallied. "Okay, that's actually a good thing, right? Guys with plans make you hot."

"No, guys with *goals* make me hot."

"Is there a difference?" But Treena flapped her hand dismissively. "Never mind. So what's Wolfgang's plan?"

"Oh, he didn't share that part. But apparently unscheduled sex with me isn't one of its many components."

"He schedules *sex*?" Jax demanded incredulously. "As in makes an actual appointment?"

"Evidently."

He was silent for a moment. Then he blew out a breath. "Okay. So the guy has a few control issues. Still, you've said yourself that your love life's been in a long-time slump. Why is that, anyhow?"

"What?" She stared at him. "What does that have to do with anything?"

"Nothing. But you're always talking about how you're not getting any. The fact is, you could bag any guy you wanted. So why haven't you?"

Treena straightened. "That's true," she said thoughtfully. "You used to have a healthy sex life, but lately, for all that you say you want to get laid, you don't seem to be doing anything about it. Why is that?"

"I think it's your fault."

Treena stared at her openmouthed for a second. Then, snapping it closed, she nodded. "Sure. Okay." Her long leg flashed across the distance between couch and chair and she caught Carly's kneecap with her big toe. "What are you, crazy? How do you figure your lack of a love life is my fault?"

"I'm surrounded on all sides by all this True Love crap. Between you and Jax and Mack and Ellen, maybe I'm subconsciously thinking that I should hold out for something more." She rammed her fingers through her hair. "And is that skewed, or what? It's not like I ever pined for the fairy tale."

"What the hell is the fairy tale?" Jax asked.

"You know," Treena said. "The Prince, the castle, the kids."

"I don't need some damn man to take care of me. And frankly, the minute men get too comfortable it just means dirty socks in the bedroom, wet towels on the bathroom floor and someone constantly telling you how to behave and what to do. That's not for me."

"On behalf of my fellow man, I object to your blanket condemnation," Jax said. "But if that's how you really feel, it seems to me Jones would be right up your alley. It's an opportunity to get back to the kind of relationship you like, and, hey, good kissing is nothing to sneer at."

She gave him a look and he grimaced. "Or not," he said. Then in an obvious ploy to change the subject, he said hastily, "So, detente, huh? That's what I like about you Vegas showgirls, you're always throwing around the ten dollar words."

"Weak, Jackson," Treena scoffed. "Like she's gonna be distracted by the old look-baby-I'm-a-sensitive-guy-who-doesn't-automatically-think-all-you-showgirls-are-dumb-bimbos gambit. Besides, you know perfectly well Carly has a teaching degree from Cal State."

He turned his head to stare at her. "I do? She does?"

"Sure. I told you that."

"No, honey, you didn't." He turned back to Carly. "You were a teacher?"

"Well, not exactly. Dancing paid my way through school. Unfortunately, I didn't discover until I did my student-teaching rotation that I actually liked to dance better than I liked to teach. I got my degree anyhow in an effort to please my mom—as if *that* was even a remote possibility. But I never used it."

"Damn. I *love* hanging around you two. I learn something new every day. Still, now you've got me a little concerned, too. If you don't want to talk about the anonymous flowers with Jones, how about someone else in his department?"

"Dan McAster, maybe," Treena suggested.

"Except the same problem applies. Aside from an unspecified uneasy feeling in my gut, I don't have anything real to report at this point."

"So report that," Jax said. "Tell them you can't put your finger on the exact reason why, but not knowing who's sending you these bouquets makes you uneasy. You've got good instincts, Carly. They're not going to blow you off."

She shook her head. "I just can't—not yet. The whole thing is probably nothing and I don't want to look foolish." Especially in front of Jones.

"'Nothing' would be best-case scenario," Jax agreed. "But, babe, erring on the side of safety is never foolish."

"You might as well save your breath," Treena told him. "You're not going to win an argument with her. Carly's picture is in the dictionary next to *stubborn*."

"Aw, you sweet talker." She smiled at her friends, touched by how seriously they took her admittedly nebulous concerns.

"Just promise us that you won't let your pride keep you from getting help if you need it," Treena demanded.

"I won't. I promise. I may be stubborn, but I'm not stupid." Then in a subject change every bit as blatant as Jax's had been, she said cheerily, "So, have you guys met Wolfgang's nephew, Niklaus, yet? Despite his family affiliation, he's a really great kid."

Ten

New schools sucked.

Niklaus slung his bike-messenger style bag across his back and made his way down the hallway of Silverado High. If he had a car he could at least take off for lunch and spare himself having to walk into the crowded cafeteria where everyone was guaranteed to know everyone, except him. But he didn't, and the only fast-food places were too far away to reach on foot during the time allowed.

So he stopped at his newly assigned locker, dumped his bag inside and slammed the door shut, giving the combination lock's dial a twirl before turning away. He walked toward the cafeteria as if he knew exactly where he was going, but then ruined the effect, if anyone was even looking, by pausing just outside to take a few deep breaths and brace himself. Two no-neck jocks muscled by him and he pushed through the doors in their wake, his eyes trained on the backs of their leather-and-wool letterman jackets.

Man, those had to be stifling in this climate.

The ghosts of Meals Past assaulted his nose, voices roared and plastic trays were slammed down on long tables, making heavy crockery and silverware rattle and thump in the percussive rhythm of high school lunch hour. He dodged a football being tossed between two tables and headed for the hamburger–hot dog line with the intention of grabbing something to take outside to the shade of one of the bristlecone pine trees. It had cooled down to a reasonable eighty degrees in the past couple of days.

He had just reached the end of the line when a heavy shoulder slammed into his, shoving him several steps backward.

"Watch where the fuck you're going," snapped the refrigerator-size guy who'd rammed into him, and the pack of students surrounding him guffawed as if the jerk was some frigging stand-up comic. The boys in the group were dressed in more letterman jackets and two of the girls wore burgundy-and-white cheerleader outfits. One of them, a brunette with silky medium-length hair, hadn't laughed along with the rest of her crowd, and she glanced back at Niklaus, a little frown puckering her delicate eyebrows. For one breathless moment they made eye contact.

Then the jock who'd jostled him snapped out a name he couldn't quite catch, and she turned back to her group, taking a couple of long-legged strides to catch up.

Niklaus couldn't figure out what a girl like that was doing with Refrigerator Boy, who was clearly an—

"Asshole," he muttered under his breath, still watching her retreating back as he joined the end of the fast-food line.

"You got that right."

Jerking his gaze back front and center, Niklaus saw the boy in front of him turning in his direction and conducted a quick survey when the other teen faced him fully. The guy looked amiable enough, but there had to be a catch. In Nik's numerous and varied high school experiences, most friendly overtures came with built-in agendas.

The teen in front of him was about five-ten, and had red hair and freckles that failed to render him folksy and cute. His aw-shucks-golly coloring to the contrary, he looked pretty damn tough and competent.

He thrust a square, freckled hand at Niklaus. "Kev Fitzpatrick," he said. "My friends call me Paddy."

"Niklaus Jones." He shook Kev's hand but didn't offer carte blanche to call him Nik. He'd save that until he knew the guy one helluva lot better than a five-minute meet-and-greet in the lunch line.

"I watched you show your stuff to Coach Jarzinski the other day."

"Yeah?" He'd seen a dozen or so people in the stands after school on Wednesday, but he hadn't memorized any one face.

"Yeah. And I know Coach hasn't posted anything yet, but it was plain to see you're good. *Really* good. So I'm guessing you'll be taking my place as goalie any day now."

And there it was—the catch. *Shit.* He cast a furtive glance over his shoulder to see if Kev's friends were waiting in the wings to beat the crap out of him.

The quick, guarded check to make sure his flank wasn't exposed was purely automatic, learned through hard experience. He'd been the new kid on the block so many times he'd lost track of the actual numbers.

The lessons it had taught him, however, had not been forgotten.

He must have been too obvious about it, though, because Fitzpatrick hurried to say, "Hey, this is not a problem. I in-

herited the position the end of last season when Gene Win-
kler's dad got transferred and he had to move. Truth is, I'm a
much better striker than goalie. We *need* someone strong in
the net."

They'd reached the counter by then, and Kev turned away
to order a burger and fries. As soon as he was through, he
stepped aside and waited for Niklaus to place his order. When
their food came, he picked up his tray and jerked his chin to
indicate a table across the room. "Come on. I'll introduce you
to the guys on the team."

Niklaus followed him across the cafeteria, wondering if he
was being the world's biggest chump. For all he knew, he was
blindly setting himself up for a fall, because, face it, it was rare
that a new schoolmate was this friendly on first meeting.
Even so, he ambled in the other boy's wake, while the part
of him made suspicious by more than a few memorable disappointments hung back, waiting for the punch line and half
expecting to find himself the butt of some in joke.

But Kev merely led him to a tableful of guys and said, "This
is Nik Jones."

Before Niklaus could even decide if he should jump on him
for shortening his name, close to a dozen guys all said, "Hey."

Okay. So far, so good.

Then the redhead added, "And, I'm guessing, our new
goalie."

A cheer went up.

A blonde down the table leaned forward and said, "I hope
so. We saw you play for Coach yesterday—"

"Wednesday, you moron," someone else corrected.

"Whatever. Yesterday, day before yesterday—who gives a
shit? The point is, Jones is a helluva goalie."

There was enthusiastic agreement.

"And we need to get Paddy back to playing forward where he belongs."

"Amen, brother," Kev agreed. "Not to mention that I knew Nik here was gonna be my soul brother the minute I heard him call Rushman an asshole."

This elicited loud whooping, and Nik set his tray on the table and took a seat when Kev plopped down on the bench and waved for him to join them. Wrestling open his milk carton, he said, "So, what's the deal with that guy?"

"Hotshot football player," the blonde said, and leaned down the table to offer his hand. "I'm Josh Loran, by the way."

There turned out to be eight guys besides him and Paddy sitting at the table, and one by one the rest of them shook hands and told Niklaus their names. Only a couple of those names stuck, however: Kev's, Josh's and a light-skinned black kid named David Owens, who told him, "Rushman's captain of the football team, and football rules in this school. The team thinks their farts don't stink. And as for the rest of the student body?" He made an abrasive sound between pursed lips. "Well, I hate to be the one to break this to you, Dog, but you might as well understand up front that us soccer guys don't exist."

Niklaus stared at the teen across the table. "You're kidding me, right? I mean, I've run into that attitude at other schools, but they had pretty lousy teams. You guys have won the fricking state championship four years running!"

"Yeah, we have. And except for a coupla college scouts, our parents and our girls, no one gives a rip."

"That's seriously skewed, man."

"No shit," nine voices agreed in unison.

"Surely you are joking, madam."

Carly looked across the counter at the Avventurato florist, a tall, pale, cadaverously thin man with all the natural joie de vivre of an undertaker. A discreet pin on the breast pocket of his funereal-black suit read Mr. Belzer. Not Jim or Bobby Belzer—Mister. *O-kay,* she thought wryly. He was obviously not one of those let's-all-be-pals kind of guys. Assuming a sober mien of her own, she said calmly, "No, Mr. Belzer, I am not. I'm perfectly serious."

"Do you have any idea how many orders we fill in a given day, young lady?"

She tried to be patient, because in truth she'd expected this reaction. But his obdurate expression didn't make it easy. And *please,* he had maybe ten years on her, which hardly made him old enough to be talking to her in that condescending tone. Not to mention that the guy needed to make up his mind. Which was she—a madam or a young lady? But shoving her irritation aside, she merely said, "I imagine you fill dozens of orders. I'm just asking you to think back to yesterday's."

"I must have had fifty orders yesterday. And that's not including the floral arrangements we make up for the suites."

She bit back a sharp retort and drew a deep breath. Then, looking him in the eye, she said pleasantly, "I'm sure you're extremely busy. And I'd much rather keep this just between you and me. But if you're simply too strapped for time to help I suppose I could always ask Wolfgang Jones in Security and Surveillance to look into the matter for me." She swallowed hard to push down the snort she felt forming in her throat. Like that was ever going to happen.

Still, it worked. Wolf's take-no-prisoners reputation was obviously as widespread throughout the Avventurato holdings as she suspected, for the florist's expression suddenly turned much friendlier.

"No, no, that won't be necessary," he hastened to assure her, treating her to a rousing couple of seconds of riotous good humor when his pale lips jerked back into a frozen rictus of yellowing teeth. "But you must understand that if it was a cash transaction, you're still out of luck. However, if the buyer used a credit card we'll have some sort of record. What is your name again?"

"Carly Jacobsen. It was an arrangement of exotic flowers about yea high." She leveled her hand, palm down, about twenty inches above the countertop. "You delivered it to my station in the dressing area behind the Starlight Room."

"You're an employee?"

"Yes. I dance for *la Stravaganza.*"

He looked at her down the length of his nose for an instant, then turned away. "Lisa!" Belzer snapped his fingers, and when a twentysomething woman appeared, he said, "Give Ms. Jacobsen whatever she needs. I'll be in the back room if you find yourself in dire need of my expertise." His tone made it clear that that had better be a last resort, and he turned on his heel to stalk, back rigid, from the retail floor.

"Fun guy," she said conversationally to the young woman.

"Oh, yeah."

Lisa was much more cooperative and worlds cheerier than her boss, but in the end she still came up empty.

"I'm sorry," she said after paging through a blue spiral notebook full of handwritten notations. "I can't find an entry for an arrangement sent to the showgirls' dressing room. Not one." Her brow creased as she looked up at Carly. "Are you certain they came from this shop?"

"Yes."

"This is really weird, then. If I were searching by the buyer it wouldn't be unusual to have no record, because payment could have been made with cash. But we always have a record of deliveries. Yet there's nothing here. Not for last night and not for the other date you gave me, either."

"Well, sh—" She cut herself off before the entire curse escaped her lips.

"It," the florist finished for her and nodded. "Yeah. I'm really sorry not to be of more help."

"No, listen, I appreciate the effort you put in. Would you do me a favor, though? If you should happen to catch another order of flowers for me, would you make a note of who's doing the ordering? I'm getting a little freaked by the anonymity."

"Absolutely. And I'll spread the word to the other florists, too. I can't guarantee Belzer's cooperation, but the other two are real nice gals. And, who knows, maybe Belzer will be more accommodating than I think. After all, you must have some sort of clout to have gotten this much help out of him."

"Nah." She smiled. "I just evoked the name of someone he wants to deal with even less than me."

It wasn't what she'd hoped for, she admitted as she turned away to retrace her steps through the hotel's shopping area, but that couldn't be helped. At least she'd made an effort, and that made her feel marginally more in control of the situation. She was probably making a mountain out of a mole hill, anyhow.

All the same, it felt good to have taken steps toward finding out where the flowers had come from, even if the end result hadn't been particularly illuminating.

As she headed across the lobby toward the parking garage, a janitor remolding the ashtray sand into the stylized A that was the Avventurato's logo stopped to watch her go by. He looked vaguely familiar, and she smiled and gave him a nod. A moment later she caught a glimpse of Wolf talking to a couple of bellhops and her purposeful strides faltered. Almost as though he felt her stare, he suddenly looked up. As their eyes met, he, too, stilled.

Damn. What was it about him that made her heart pound faster every time she saw him? She was way beyond trying to fool herself into believing it was merely irritation.

His eyes were like green lasers boring into hers, and it took a concerted act of will to pull her gaze away. Wetting her lips, she continued toward the door to the garage stairwell, assuring herself that she was merely doing what she'd planned to do when she'd left the flower shop, heading for home.

She certainly wasn't running away.

Even if it sort of felt that way.

The janitor watched the sway of Carly's hips as she walked away. She'd smiled at him. That meant she remembered him from the night she'd hurt her ankle. He hadn't been sure if she would, since he'd been coming on shift at the time and had still been in his street clothes. As far as he was concerned, one of the biggest drawbacks of his job was that once in uniform people tended to act as if he was invisible. But that obviously wasn't the case with Carly. He'd clearly made an impact on the glamorous showgirl when he'd tried to help.

He would have helped her even *more* if that hot-shit security clown hadn't shown up on the scene and ordered everyone on their way, as if they were nothing and he was king of the casino.

Rage circled like a shark through his consciousness, but he took several deep breaths and sent it diving back to the depths where it belonged. What was done was done. And as Dr. Asher was fond of saying, there was no percentage in obsessing on what couldn't be changed. Besides, he'd watched that night from a distance, and it had been obvious that the pretty dancer didn't like the blond guy any more than he did.

He bet she liked the flowers he'd sent her, though. She should—they were pretty damn spectacular, if he did say so himself. Unfortunately on his salary he couldn't afford Avventurato florist prices. But he was often sent to clean up in the wake of high rollers' private parties when they demanded the service after normal housecleaning hours. And when that had happened on the night following Carly's accident, the first thing he'd noticed in the trashed suite was the complimentary arrangement of exotic flowers on the Florentine credenza. Realizing a beautiful showgirl must be accustomed to receiving extravagant gifts, he'd helped himself to the arrangement and personally delivered it to the Starlight Room's dressing area later that morning. She deserved flowers a helluva lot more than some deep-pocket gambler who likely hadn't even noticed them in the first place.

He watched now as Carly disappeared through the door to the parking garage, then turned back to his job. But he smiled as he worked because, all told, he was quite pleased with his progress. Not only had he stamped his impression on Carly at their first meeting, but he'd already given her the sort of gifts she expected.

He'd always known he was destined for the finer things in life.

And at this rate, he'd bet his next six paychecks that he'd soon secure the adoring affection of a statuesque chorus girl.

The following Friday, Niklaus came up with a plan.

He liked it here. It might not have started out that way, and he still wasn't thrilled about the way Grandma and Grandpa had dumped him on Dr. Gloom's doorstep. But his new school was pretty decent, the soccer team was stellar and he was its brand-new goalie—Coach Jarzinski had stopped him outside the gym after fourth period Monday to tell him so. He'd also made some friends already—and not with the usual group of misfits he generally fell in with simply because they were the most likely to open up to the new kid who probably wouldn't be around long enough to form lasting relationships with anyone else. Paddy, Josh and David were actually friends Grandma Maria would approve of.

And then there was Natalie Fremont.

Nik's expression grew dreamy as he thought about the cheerleader who'd looked back at him last week after Asshole Rushman had bounced him out of the burger line. Apparently she'd transferred into the same Advanced Biology class he was taking just a couple of weeks before he'd arrived, which made them the last two students to join the class.

And yesterday Mr. Burnham, a science teacher of extraordinary brilliance, had assigned them to be each other's lab partner.

Man, she was pretty—all legs and big brown eyes and shiny brown hair. And she'd smiled at him this morning, which had punched dimples in both cheeks. That had about knocked him on his butt.

Life was definitely looking up.

Hell, even Uncle Wolf was almost tolerable. He wasn't the most fun guy in the universe, but he had one attribute in common with Grandma Maria that Niklaus really appreciated—Wolf insisted on being the adult in this relationship. He had rules and shit that were kind of a pain in the ass, but Nik didn't have to worry about day-to-day stuff like paying the bills, buying the groceries or finding creative new ways to keep him and his mom from being evicted from their current lodging. So he guessed his uncle was okay—except for the older man's bogus plan to score his dream job somewhere else.

Niklaus could certainly do without that particular black cloud looming on his horizon.

He'd tried like crazy to think of a way to approach Carly about moving in with her if Uncle Wolf did end up booking out of town. But as easy as he found it to hang out with her, he couldn't quite cough up the nerve to ask if he could live with her. After all, she'd known him for all of about two weeks. And while she seemed perfectly content to ply him with food and spend time with him, he couldn't see her wanting some high school kid moving in with her on a permanent basis. She had a bunch of friends in the building already and probably all the company she'd ever need in Buster, Rufus, Rags and Tripod.

Still, that didn't mean he couldn't utilize her in a different way. It seemed to him that she might just be the perfect vehicle for enticing Wolf into staying right here in Las Vegas.

He'd bet the big bucks that his uncle hadn't gotten laid in…damn, probably forever, which might account for his generally grim demeanor. Not that Nik intended to attempt pimping Carly out or anything. It was just…

She was the coolest person he knew. She was sexy and hip and really easy to talk to and stuff. And on top of all that, she was a freakin' Las Vegas *showgirl*, which was right up there with Playmate of the Year, if you asked him. Hell, it was maybe even better, considering there was no airbrushing involved. Uncle Wolf acted like he didn't even notice those things, but since he was supposed to be some hotshot security guy, he had to have observed at least *some* of her attributes. Like, no one could tell Niklaus that his uncle hadn't made note of that no-airbrush factor.

Wolf might not be a barrel of laughs, but he wasn't dead, for crissake.

Near the top of the pro column on the why-Carly's-the-perfect-solution-for-keeping-Dr. Gloom-in-Las Vegas list was the added bonus of her living right next door, as he had pointed out to Wolf just last week. All he had to do was throw the two of them together and let nature take its course.

Granted, Uncle Wolf was no bargain. Still, he had a good job, a great car, he was taller than her and it wasn't like he was butt ugly or anything. Plus, he'd probably be so grateful at the thought of maybe having sex with Carly that he'd no doubt be extra nice to her.

Girls loved that kind of shit.

So the plan was to figure out ways to get them together long enough to set the wheels in motion.

Then maybe he'd get to stay in town long enough to find some way to woo Natalie away from Asshole Rushman.

Eleven

"Hey, Wolf, come take a look at this."

Wolf looked up from the report he was completing and saw Dave Beckinsale, more commonly known as Beck, standing in front of the screens that filled the north wall of the Security and Surveillance control center. He climbed to his feet and walked over to join his co-worker.

Beck indicated the screen he was currently watching. "What do you think?"

He monitored the play at a blackjack table on the casino floor for a couple of minutes, then glanced at Beck before turning his attention back to the action onscreen. "The woman with the brown hair, second from the end. You think she's cheating?"

"Yeah. But how?"

Wolf watched a while longer. "I don't think she's counting—she's not paying close enough attention to anyone else's cards. Could be wired."

"That was my thought, too. I had Fred crop the image

down to her ear, but it's covered up by her hair so it's impossible to know for sure one way or the other." Beck tossed back the last of his coffee, then blew out a soft breath. "I'm sure leaning in that direction, though. Yet if she is, who's her partner? If he's the card counter, he'd have to be nearby. But I've been scanning that area for the past twenty minutes, and I haven't sighted anyone acting even a little suspicious."

"I'd say one of us needs to get out on the floor to have a look around, then."

Beck stepped back from the screen and lobbed his plastic-capped cardboard cup into the nearest trash receptacle. "I'll do it. I could stand to stretch my legs, anyway."

"Okay, good—I'll get back to my paperwork. If nothing shakes loose pretty quick, though, let me know and we'll explore another avenue." He looked at his watch as Beck left and saw it was close to quitting time.

Normally he would have shrugged that aside, pumped at the prospect of ferreting out a solution to something that had all the earmarks of a brand-new scam. New swindles cropped up on a regular basis in the always popular attempt to rip off casinos, but Avventurato's Surveillance department had an excellent record of breaking the codes of the current latest and greatest. And since for every fraudulent scheme they solved, two new ones soon came along to replace it, it was a never-ending education, a fact for which he ordinarily had the greatest appreciation.

With Niklaus kicking around the apartment all on his own on a Monday night, however, Wolf found himself hoping that—just for this one evening—the current scam would turn out to be something simple that they could quickly solve.

Beck was back in less than twenty minutes. "I know she's wired," he said. "I can feel it in my gut. But I can't prove it and I can't find a single person I can tie to her."

Wolf shut down his file on the computer and leaned back in his chair. "Fred," he called over to the Surveillance team's youngest tech. "Call up all the videos covering area four that you have for the past twenty-four hours." Hearing the snap of command in his voice—and Dan McAster's demand in his head that he be more warm and fuzzy toward his fellow employees—he added in a softer tone, "Will you?"

Fred shot him a startled look, then flashed a friendly smile. "Sure thing, Mr. Jones."

Okay, that wasn't too painful. And Dan was probably right—he did need to polish up his people skills if he wanted to be boss.

It soon became apparent that looking through the videos wasn't going to be a quick process, and he excused himself to call Niklaus. He tried their home number first, but when that garnered no answer, he scowled at his watch, which read a quarter past eleven—fifteen minutes beyond the time he'd told the kid to be in the apartment—and dialed Nik's cell phone.

It was answered on the fourth ring. "Hey," Niklaus said, sounding cheerful.

"Do you know what time it is?"

"Since I don't own a watch," his nephew replied, his voice going from friendly to bored, "and I haven't looked at a clock lately—no, I don't."

"It's after eleven. I thought I told you I wanted you in the apartment by then."

"I'm in the goddamn complex as we speak." Niklaus's voice was now fuck-you sullen. "The guys came over, we went swimming and they just left. I'm on my way upstairs right now. Does that meet with your approval, Your Dictatorship?"

Dammit, why could he never do anything right with this kid? He hadn't even managed to meet "the guys" yet, so he didn't have the first idea if they were suitable friends or the exact kind of punks his mother had worried about Nik hanging out with in his last school.

Yet even knowing he'd set the stage for his nephew's response by starting their conversation with an accusatory tone, his instinctive reaction was to dig in and defend a not-worth-defending position.

With a faint sigh, he kissed his pride goodbye and said, "I'm sorry, Nik. I shouldn't have jumped to conclusions. I know you're a responsible kid." Silence greeted his admission, so he forged on. "Something came up here at work. Will you be all right if I'm late tonight?"

"No. I'm a frigging baby who can't be trusted to be left on his own."

Shit, shit, shit, shit, *shit!* "That's not what I meant." *I feel bad about not spending more time with you. Guilty, goddammit.* "I'll be home as soon as I can."

"Whatever."

The phone went dead in his ear. He snapped it closed and returned it to his jacket pocket. Running a hand through his hair, he muttered, "Well, that went just fucking swell."

"You got yourself a teenager, Mr. Jones?"

Wolf turned in his seat to see one of the custodians emptying his wastebasket. He'd never paid much attention to the janitorial staff before, but now, worried about his lousy parenting skills, he heard himself admitting, "My sixteen-year-old nephew is living with me and I can't seem to talk to him without messing it up."

The custodian nodded. "That's pretty much the lot of a teen's parent, all right," he agreed. "The good news is, they eventually grow up and are actually pleasant to be around."

He regarded the older man with interest. "You have teenagers as well, then?"

"My boys are twenty and twenty-two now, and we finally get along pretty good. But Belinda, my baby, is fifteen, and somehow my sweet little girl turned into the Bride of Satan overnight." He shook his head. "Her mama's been on the receiving end of most of her crap, but believe me, she saves enough lip for her daddy to set my teeth on edge." He grimaced. "Me and the wife just go day by day, hoping we can hang in there long enough for our sweet baby girl to come back to us."

They talked for a few moments longer, and when the janitor moved on Wolf realized that it helped to know he wasn't the only one feeling out of his depth with the teenager under his roof. Acknowledging he wasn't alone allowed him to put the argument with Niklaus out of his mind and buckle down to reviewing the videos with renewed concentration.

It was dull work keeping his attention on a screen that fast-forwarded the goings-on in the requested area with a rapidity that threatened eye strain. It was either that or watch it in real time, but while it saved him and Beck hours of viewing, it netted them no information.

Until a man wearing the black Avventurato maintenance department uniform appeared at the table they were scrutinizing. "Fred, back that up and freeze on the employee, will you?"

"Sure thing, Mr. Jones." The tech did as requested.

Wolf stared at the man's image. It wasn't a face he recognized, but then again, this was a large organization. "Zoom in on his name tag."

The screen narrowed down to a discreet sewn-on gold patch. Its black cursive embroidery read Mike Gregory.

"I'm on it," Beck said before Wolf could even request a background check.

"Okay, Mike," Wolf murmured to the frozen image. "Let's see what you're up to."

Without having to be asked, Fred zoomed out again and Wolf watched the man on-screen squat behind the blackjack table. The time on the tape read shortly after 3:00 a.m. this morning. He turned to the tech. "Do you have any imaging for the dealer's side?"

"On this particular table for this particular time frame?" Fred shrugged. "No, sir. Sorry."

"He's got to be wiring it. Five'll get you ten we find some kind of microscopic surveillance camera." He looked over his shoulder. "Beck! You got anything yet?"

"Yeah." The other man joined them, printout in hand. "Mike Gregory, thirty-seven years old, was hired three weeks ago. He came with some pretty decent references."

"He usually work the graveyard shift?"

"Yes. But, funny thing, he's off tonight. Ordinarily I'd snap up those five'll get me ten odds, but in this case I think I'll pass. I think we're gonna find a camera installed on the dealer's side of the table, too. Maybe one of those hold-card versions like the World Poker tour uses."

"Yes, it has to be something that scans the dealer's hold cards as they're dealt." He stared at the screen, his mind working furiously.

Beck nodded his agreement. "But can you visualize any way to have the dealer search for it without tipping off Gregory? I sure as shit can't."

"That's what keeps tripping me up, too. I have this sinking feeling that the range for this kind of rig has infinite possibilities for anyone who knows how to broadcast it beyond our own closed-circuit setup. We know he has to be monitoring it to tell the player how to bet, but is it from somewhere right here in the hotel or from his home—which is where, by the way?" He subjected the data sheet from Human Resources to a quick read, then called Fred over to run a check to make sure the address was a valid one.

"Hell," Beck said glumly, "for all we know he could even be in another state…although that doesn't seem very plausible if he intends to avoid arousing suspicion."

"Plus, where's the thrill in long-distance play? I don't have enough knowledge of this type of electronics to say it definitely couldn't be done, but I agree it's unlikely he'd go so far afield. Let's call in the pit boss. If he doesn't have any better ideas, then we devise a way to disconnect the player's wire before she can tip off her accomplice."

As it turned out, nothing better did occur to the pit boss. Once they'd discussed some of the possibilities and the man had left to return to the floor, Wolf stared blankly at the wall of monitors as he hashed through a number of ideas.

Unfortunately, he had to reject each one as too weak, too implausible or just plain undoable.

His attention snapped into focus when he spotted Carly and her redheaded friend Treena, still dressed in their show costumes, posing for a photo with some tourists. As he watched, they left the group who'd been gathered around them and made their way to the little open-air lounge in the center of the casino.

"Keep an eye on our player," he said to Beck, heading for the door. "I'll be back in a minute. I have an idea."

Carly was having a perfectly lovely time with some of her sister dancers when she looked up to see Wolf standing just outside the lounge. She realized he'd been waiting to catch her eye when he immediately pointed at her, then at Treena, and jerked his chin to indicate they should come to him.

When she flipped him a one-handed gesture in return, she could all but hear him grind his teeth. Apparently not many defied that my-word-is-law attitude he wore like a second skin. Or maybe they just didn't live to tell the tale.

Either way, it made her day to be one of the few, the proud, and she smiled to herself as Wolfgang strode into the lounge, his face grim.

The tableful of showgirls grew quiet when he approached them a moment later.

"Ladies." He gave them a nod, then directed his attention at her and Treena. "Ms. Jacobsen, Ms. McCall. Could I have a moment of your time?"

She opened her mouth to tell him flippantly that they *still* weren't interested in having a ménage à trois with him, so he might as well quit asking. But then she closed it again, the words left unsaid. As fun as it would be to see how he'd handle the attention such a bombshell would garner from a bunch of women in full girls-night-out mode, she was more curious about what he could possibly want from her and Treena.

With a shrug, she climbed to her feet, tossing some money on the table to cover her drink.

Treena did the same but picked up the martini glasses Carly had been ready to leave behind and handed her hers. "Waste not, want not," she murmured, and took a sip of her Lemon Drop.

Wolf turned sideways and swept an arm out to indicate they should precede him. Before they took more than a step, however, Julie-Ann stood up from her spot at the other end of the table.

"I'm the dance captain of this troupe," she informed him imperiously. "And if two of my girls are in trouble, I need to know."

Wolfgang subjected the younger woman to one of his unsmiling appraisals. "I'm not sure why you'd jump to the conclusion that anyone's in trouble, but it seems to me if you were truly concerned for…'your girls,' what you'd need to do is help, not get the dirt. Sit down." His voice went frigidly authoritative. "This doesn't concern you."

Julie-Ann sat.

Carly bit back a whoop of delight, but the moment they were out of earshot, she said, "That is possibly the smartest thing I've ever heard come out of your mouth." She laughed. "I mean, it goes a *long* way toward cleansing my palate of your imperialistic ways. Why, I almost feel…indebted."

"That's very convenient, considering I have a favor to ask you both. Just how grateful are you?"

"Well, I draw the line at murder or having your baby. But anything else—you just name it, pal, and I'm your girl."

"Lordy, yes," Treena agreed. "Me, too."

"Good. Come with me."

She exchanged a glance with her friend as they trailed Wolfgang into the employee sector. Treena essayed the tiniest of shrugs and flashed her a lopsided little smile behind Wolf's back when he paused in front of the door to Security and Surveillance. Then they grinned at each other, and in the way of close friends, Carly knew they were both reliving Wolf's cool-voiced set-down to Julie-Ann. "Beautiful," she murmured.

"Oh, yeah," Treena agreed.

Wolf turned to face them, the key card in his right hand suspended in front of the lock and his left hand sliding into his slacks pockets. "You two talking in code?"

"Sort of," she admitted agreeably. "It's girl speak."

"That would explain why I don't have a clue what you're

talking about." He slid the card into the lock and pushed the door open, standing aside so they could enter first.

Carly looked around with interest and noticed Treena doing the same. The room was large and sort of *Star Trek* space-tech looking. The decor was heavy on shiny chrome; several desks scattered around the area were made of that metal and one entire wall was composed of it, although that was broken up by floor-to-ceiling screens. She'd have liked a closer examination of the action the latter captured everywhere, from the casino floors to the hotel hallways to the employee area to the parking garage. Instead, she glanced at Wolf, wondering why on earth she and Treena were here.

He led them over to a man monitoring the wall of screens. "Ladies, this is Dave Beckinsale. Beck, this is Carly Jacobsen and Treena McCall. As you can probably tell by their costumes, they dance in *la Stravaganza*—and I think they might be able to help us get close to our player without tipping off the resourceful Mr. Gregory."

"Cool," said Beck, and a young man manning a computer across the room cleared his throat.

Wolf was busy scanning one of the screens, but he waved a hand in the technician's general direction. "That's Fred. He's one of our techs."

Carly had just enough time to watch Fred's face redden to the tips of his somewhat prominent ears before Wolf leaned into the screen that he'd been examining and said, "See the second player from the right, the woman with the brown hair?"

She and Treena leaned forward for a closer look and acknowledged that they did.

"Well, here's the deal." He succinctly explained what he and Beck suspected, then told them how he thought they might be of assistance. "We don't usually use civilians, but I think this is going to take a woman's touch to pull it off without freaking out our player's accomplice. I've told you what I need, but the truth is you'll probably have to wing it in order to get the job done. Do you think you can handle that?"

"No problem," Carly promptly asserted, thinking it sounded like fun. Sort of like playing Mata Hari, except she'd be on the side of the good guys instead of the Nazis and, of course, bypass that death-by-firing-squad thing. Oh, and there wasn't actually time for her to incorporate the courtesan part, which was almost a shame considering the state of her sex life these days. Still, it was definitely a chance for a little playacting and an opportunity for a bit of adventure without the peril.

Clearly Treena wasn't as enamored of the idea, for her delicate brows drew together. "Is this dangerous?"

Wolf didn't blow off her question. Instead, he gave her a sober look and said, "It shouldn't be. Aside from a few sensationalized robbery attempts on the casino cash rooms, I've only ever heard of one armed patron—and apparently he was drunk as a lord or it probably wouldn't have even occurred to him to bring in a gun, let alone brandish it. Table games generally draw the kind of crooks that get their kicks from putting something over on the house, rather than from violence. Then, too, the risk-to-reward ratio on robbery is a lot more acceptable than the same standards applied to armed robbery. *That* tends to get your average crook a lot longer prison sentence, which renders it too cost ineffective."

"Plus," Beck assured her, "we'll wire you and have a number of men out on the floor to come to your assistance if you need it."

The tech across the room scrambled to his feet. "I can help with the wiring."

Wolf shot him a glance that had him sitting back in his

chair. Then his gaze slipped right past Treena to Carly, and he conducted a comprehensive examination of her body beneath her skimpy costume. "I'll wire them."

She felt the touch of that gaze clear down to her bones, and before she could do something stupid like give in to it, she said firmly, "In your dreams, both of you. Treena and I will wire each other."

"It requires a professional touch," he argued coolly. But the heat that burned in his eyes suggested his motives bore little relationship to professionalism.

"Then I guess you'd better hope we do a good job, hadn't you? Because it's that or nothing."

"As you wish." His hands going up in surrender, he stepped back. "I'll go get the paraphernalia."

Treena turned her back on the remaining men in the room, fanned herself with her hand and said in a low voice, "Lordy, Lordy. I think I'm having a hot flash—and I'm not even the one he was directing all that heat at. The Cool Hand Luke facade is very misleading. Apparently when he's in the mood, the man's a freaking flamethrower."

"Tell me about it," she agreed glumly. "It's grossly unfair."

"You're having a tough time hanging on to your grudge against him, I take it?"

"Let me put it this way, I'm definitely feeling the heat." *From the inside out.* "But I'm keeping my distance, because give him two minutes and he'll freeze you in your tracks." Flicking her fingers to signify this was the least of their worries right now, she tried to focus on what they needed to do in the next half hour rather than on the effect Wolf's touch might have had on her peace of mind if she'd allowed him to wire her up. But it didn't help that on top of the sexual buzz he'd managed to generate in her, she was also impressed with the way he handled his job. Because for all that she'd always regarded him as a strictly by-the-book kind of guy, he clearly wasn't averse to thinking outside the box to get the job done.

She couldn't help but admire that.

She shoved her appreciation aside. "Just so I'm certain we're both on the same wavelength here, what's your take on what he wants us to do?"

"Expose and hopefully disable the receiver in the woman's ear."

"But in a way that she and her accomplice will buy as purely accidental, right?"

"That's how I read it."

"Yeah, me, too. And that got me thinking—remember how Jax arranged to meet you?"

"Having a tray of half-empty drinks spilled on me by the waitress he tripped up is kind of hard to forget," Treen said dryly.

"A variation of that might be our simplest, most direct method."

Treena nodded and the corner of her mouth crooked up in a little smile. "Except, being the sweet-natured optimists that we are, our glasses will be half full."

"If not entirely."

Wolf rejoined them carrying two tiny microphones. He explained how to put them on, then walked them to a rest room down the hall. After fumbling a little they eventually figured out the best way to apply the devices so they were both stable and invisible. Ten minutes later they'd tested them with the guy manning the receiver and were headed for the casino floor, Wolf's final instructions echoing in their ears.

"What do you think, do we act as if we've had a little too much to drink?" Carly asked Treena as they walked into the noise and confusion of the casino moments later.

"That would be the most believable."

"Wolfgang, if you're listening," she said in a low voice, resisting the urge to talk directly into her cleavage, "you damn well better clear this with the brass. We do *not* want to be called on the carpet tomorrow morning for doing what's needed to help you tonight."

They stopped by the bar on their way to the blackjack tables. "Hey, Tim," she greeted the bartender. "I'd like a piña colada in a hurricane glass, please."

He looked up from the limes he was quartering. "That's quite a departure from your usual cosmopolitan, Jacobsen."

"I know. But I'm in the mood for something nice and sticky."

"Make that two," Treena told the bartender. She grinned at Carly when he walked down the bar to get the ingredients. "It occurs to me that we don't know which ear this mike thingamajig is in, or even if she has one in both."

"So you're thinking we ought to double-team her?"

"Hey, if we're going to do this, do it right, I say. I vote she oughtta be one soggy little card cheat by the time we're through."

"Treena Sarkilahti McCall, you are one diabolical woman." The bartender returned with their drinks, and upon accepting hers, Carly clinked it against her friend's. "Here's to ya. I've always admired that mean streak of yours."

Taking tiny sips of their oversize drinks, they drifted up to the blackjack table and stood behind the brown-haired woman. After watching her win three hands in a row, Carly leaned into Treena. "Wouldja lookit all those chips? Nice to see *someone's* on a winning streak." She slurred her words just the tiniest bit. "Hey, speaking of which—" She gave her friend a nudge.

"Jeez, watch it, will ya?" Treena steadied her glass, which

had come close to slopping over the edge. "What the hell was that for?"

"Wha' was the deal with you interruptin' my conversation with that guy in the bar?" She slurped a little more piña colada through the straw.

"I was gettin' bored. And c'mon, it's not like it was going anywhere, anyway. It never does."

Ouch. That was a little too close to the reality of her recent love life for comfort. It didn't exactly stretch her acting ability to narrow her eyes at her redheaded friend. "Well, aren't we smug. Not everyone's lucky enough to have a guy like yours."

Treena preened.

"'Course it doesn't hurt that you refuse to allow a li'l thing like his wedding vows to innerfere with your pleasure."

Treena gave her a one-fingered jab. "Take that back, you bitch!"

"Who you callin' a bitch, bitch? I'm just sayin' it like I see it."

"Well, you're blind as a bat!" Treena drilled her finger in a little harder.

"Who you kiddin', girlfriend—this is me you're talkin' to. We both know your honey's a married man." She grabbed Treena's finger and hung on when the other woman tried to pull it out of her grasp. Both their drinks began to slosh. "And don't be pokin' at me. I'm sorry if you don't like the truth, but there's no call takin' it out on me. Jus' keep your hands to yourself and we won't have us a problem." Freeing Treena's finger, she gave her own a less-than-coordinated snap and treated her friend to a loose smile. "But I forgot for a minute who I'm talking to. Dippin' your hands in another woman's well is your stock in trade, innit, Red?"

With an enraged snarl, Treena lurched at her, and making

eye contact, they both allowed their drinks to fly from their glasses. The icy liquid hit the brown-haired woman on either side of her head.

The woman screeched and leaped off her stool, her hands going to her dripping hair.

"Now look what you did," Treena whispered.

"*Me?* I don't see any drink left in your glass, either, girl." But she whipped her attention to the woman. "I am so sorry, lady. Here, lemme clean you up." She grabbed a towel off the tray of a waitress who'd rushed up and used it to blot the woman's dripping hair, sweeping drenched strands behind her ears. She glanced at Treena when it exposed a small device tucked into the card cheat's left ear.

A fine wire leading from it disappeared down the collar of the woman's cashmere top, and Treena exclaimed, "Oh, your beautiful shrug! Here, lemme get it off you before it's ruined." She started tugging it down, exposing more of the wire for the benefit of the security cameras trained on them.

"Will you *stop?*" Slapping frantically at her hair to cover her ear once again, the woman jerked away and pulled the shrug back into place.

"We're sorry, we're sorry," Carly said, and both she and Treena stepped back, hands held up in surrender. "We didn't mean to get so carried away. Oh, perfect," she added under her breath. "Here comes Security."

The woman started, and Carly leaned forward to once again brush a drenched hank of hair behind her ear.

"Listen, please don't make a fuss about this to them," she begged in a low voice. "I know we created a hell of a mess, but my friend and I could both lose our jobs over this. If you'll just let us take you to the ladies' room to clean up, we'll make it worth your while, I promise."

"Okay," the woman agreed, and seeing that the dealer had already "colored up" her winnings, she scooped up the stack he'd made considerably more manageable by substituting a few large-denomination chips for the numerous lesser-value ones and dumped them into a huge handbag. She slid a fifty dollar chip in front of the dealer, then turned back to Carly. "Get me out of here."

Still apologizing profusely and bickering as to whose fault the dousing had been, Carly and Treena escorted the woman to the nearest ladies' room. She saw Wolf approaching as she opened the door, and for just one moment she stood poleaxed by the wide grin on his face. Then she gathered herself, discreetly flashed a spread-fingered hand at him and mouthed, *Give us five* as Treena ushered the player into the ladies' lounge.

An attendant manning a stack of towels sat at a small table by the vanity. Treena slipped her a twenty and jerked her head toward the door. The woman got up and left as Carly grabbed a towel and handed it to the brown-haired woman. "Look, I know we can't make up for wrecking yer phenom...phenomini...really big winning streak, but we do have a bunch of friends who work here."

"Yeah," Treena agreed. "So if you want free spa treatments or an appointment to get your hair done by Terrence, we can get you that."

"Uh-huh—wha' she said. We can also get you tickets to our show or even to Cirque O or Celine. Or how 'bout dinner in the Lume di Luna Room?"

"Right now I'd settle for a visit to that stall. Where it's *quiet*," the woman added significantly.

"Oh, sure, absolutely. Whatever you want," Carly said. "Mum's the word."

"Yeah. You betcha," Treena added. "Knock yourself out. We'll be real quiet. Won't make a peep."

"Take another towel," Carly urged. "Here. Have two. They're small."

The woman growled and, clutching her bag to her chest, stalked into the stall. She slammed the full-length door shut behind her.

Carly tiptoed over to it and pressed her ear to its hand-painted Italian countryside panel. She heard murmuring but could only make out a word here and there. One of them, however, was *removing*. Another was something *piece*.

Betting it was *earpiece*, she gave Treena the thumbs-up and her friend opened the door to Wolf, Beck and another man.

Carly was back sitting in one of the plush seats, her legs crossed, when the woman came out of the lavatory, blotting her hair on the little hand towel. She stopped dead when she saw the men standing there and plunged her hand into her voluminous bag, taking a hurried step backward.

Treena stuck her foot out and tripped the cheat. The woman sacrificed her grip on her bag in favor of trying to catch her balance and it tumbled to the floor.

Wolf reached it almost before its half-spilled contents had stopped skittering across the tiles. He swept up a small gadget about the size of a pack of gum. "I'll take this." Wrapping its trailing wire around the device, he then handed it over to the other men, who headed for the door.

"What do you think you're doing?" she screeched. "Give that back!" When they walked out without a backward glance, she turned her fury on Wolf. "I want your name," she snapped. "Your superior's going be hearing from me about this."

"Oooh." Carly and Treena made "big threat" noises.

Wolf, however, regarded the woman with his usual cool

lack of expression. "The name is Wolfgang Jones. And, please, do that. I always appreciate having my work brought to his attention."

Chest heaving, the woman stared from his hand manacling her wrist to Carly and Treena, murder in her eyes.

Carly swung her crossed leg and gave the woman a sweet smile in return. "Girl," she said with her usual clear diction. "You are so busted."

Twelve

The janitor frowned at the closed door of the women's rest room into which Carly, a redheaded showgirl and the woman they'd spilled their drinks on had vanished. When he thought of the three Security and Surveillance men who'd walked into the ladies' room bold as you please not five minutes later, his frown became a scowl. Two of the men had re-emerged almost as quickly as they'd entered it. The stern-faced blonde, however, whom he knew was a top Security and Surveillance honcho, was still in there.

The janitor wondered if Carly was in trouble.

He had to admit it wouldn't be entirely unjustified if she were. He was more than a little disappointed in her himself. She'd been *drunk* on the job. Not only that, but she and the redhead had made spectacles of themselves. This was not at all the kind of behavior he found acceptable, and he was frankly surprised at Carly's part in it.

He'd been willing to overlook her skimpy outfits and her sometimes garish makeup, since they were requirements of the job. There was even a certain prestige about them, for they were all part and parcel of the showgirl mystique. Public displays of drunkenness, tussles with other dancers and drenching a paying customer, on the other hand—well, that was *not* conduct becoming a woman to whom he'd tendered his heart.

He might have to rethink extending the gift of his undying affection to her. Because, in all honesty, he was no longer sure she was worthy of the honor.

There was a faint familiar buzzing in his ears as the old anger, the one Dr. Asher was so certain he'd conquered, re-appeared. Taking a tight grip on his broom, he walked away, trying to decide what he was going to do about it.

For forty-eight minutes Marcia Bowen, the brown-haired woman who had cheated the Avventurato out of $247,000, stonewalled Wolf. She sat in the interrogation room, playing the outraged victim right up until the minute he lost patience.

"Look," he finally said flatly. "I'm tired, I want to go home, and I'm through screwing around. If you're willing to take the fall and let your partner walk free, I can work with that. It's probably too long since you've checked in with Mike Gregory, anyway, so no doubt he's already fled for parts unknown and left you holding the bag. But that's fine with me, because my only responsibility is to close out the incident. I might as well quit beating the bushes for a second bird when I've already got a nice juicy one in the hand." Slapping onto the table the monitoring device that he'd taken from her, he looked her in the eye. "That would be you, lady, with your stack of unlawfully gained winnings and your two-way radio that, under these circumstances, could only be used for one purpose. Security also reported that the table where you were playing was illegally wired with a microscopic surveillance camera. That's sufficient to turn you over to the police. So if I can't make you understand that it's in your own best interest to cooperate with me, well, then, I guess I just can't." He rocked his chair back on two legs and reached over to crack open the door to the interrogation room. "Beck!"

His co-worker appeared almost before the reverberation of his name had faded, pushing the door wider to poke his head into the room. "Yeah, boss?"

Wolf felt a warm spurt of appreciation for the upgrade in status but merely said with stern command, "Call Metro and tell them we need immediate transportation for a card cheat. Explain the circumstances and tell them we're prepared to press charges."

"You got it." Beck's head withdrew.

"No, wait!"

Beck stuck his head back in and Wolf lowered the front chair legs back onto the floor. He looked across the table at the woman who had blurted out the demand. She appeared a lot less assured than she had thirty seconds ago. "Do you have something you'd like to add, Ms. Bowen?"

"I've never done anything like this before and I don't want to go to jail simply because I was stupid enough to fall for some guy's line and his skill between the sheets. So if I tell you where to find Mike and how he planned this, can you cut me a deal?"

"That's a distinct possibility," Wolf agreed, and settled in to negotiate. "Start talking."

By the time Wolf finally got home, 5:00 a.m. had come and gone. It had taken a while to take down Bowen's statement.

It had taken more time to track Gregory and his equipment, which the man had been in the midst of dismantling, to the room he'd rented within the hotel. Even more of the early morning hours had been eaten up bringing him down to Surveillance, interrogating him and then turning both Gregory and Bowen over to the police, with all the requisite paperwork that involved.

Pulling off his tie, he opened Niklaus's bedroom door a crack and glanced inside. His nephew was sprawled out on his stomach sound asleep, his blankets half kicked off the bed. Wolf closed the door and headed for the kitchen.

He poured a glass of milk and grabbed a cold piece of pizza out of a carton he found on the breakfast bar, then carried them into the living room, where he flopped into his leather chair. He took a gigantic bite out of the pizza and rested his head against the chair back while he chewed.

What a night.

He had to admit that when he moved on to greener pastures he was going to miss certain aspects of the Avventurato. Something new cropped up in this job every day, and there were times when he had to fight like a bear to avoid becoming addicted to the adrenaline rush.

This was one of them.

His eyes still closed, he gulped down half his glass of milk. A sudden memory of watching and listening to Carly and her friend con Marcia Bowen zoomed across his mental screens and he laughed out loud. If those two ever decided to give up dancing, they could make a real future for themselves in espionage.

Okay, the truth was he'd hardly noticed the redhead except to appreciate the way she'd played off Carly—and Carly off her—as if each could read the other's mind. He had to admit, though, that both women had far exceeded his expectations.

He couldn't help but marvel over the fact. It probably wasn't real PC of him, but who could have predicted the ditzy blonde, with her crazy-ass menagerie of cats and dogs, would turn out to be so quick-witted? She'd grasped the situation at a glance and molded the circumstances as if they were clay and she the master sculptor. She obviously understood something of human nature, as well, because with a few brief comments Bowen had been so much putty in her long, warm fingers.

He sure as hell wouldn't mind feeling those fingers on him.

Are you out of your mind, Jones? Administering a mental head slap, he spiked upright from his lazy slouch on his tailbone, nearly spilling the remainder of his milk. What the hell was the matter with him?

It was exhaustion, no doubt about it. It had been ages since he'd enjoyed the release of sex. And he couldn't deny Jacobsen was a physically desirable woman, so his dead-tired brain had made a quantum leap. And giving her that I'd-like-to-fuck-your-brains-out look earlier in the control center sure hadn't helped matters. What the hell had he been thinking? Stoking the fire of this unwanted attraction between them was just begging for trouble.

Clearly it was time to give his own private escort service a call. Prostitution might be illegal in Clark County—unlike most of the other counties of Nevada—but everyone turned a blind eye to the high-class call girls who worked the hotels as long as they kept their medical certificates up to date and remained discreet. Everyone, that is, except the Avventurato Surveillance team. That's how he'd met Gina, a pricy escort-for-hire he'd ushered from the premises. She'd taken her eviction with grace and good humor, flirting with him and offering to knock his socks off for free. Knowing when he was being played, he'd said a stern thanks but no thanks, put her in a cab and sent her on her way.

Then she'd called him at work the next day, told him she found him attractive and reiterated her offer. When he discovered she had no interest in a permanent relationship with him, he'd found himself taking her up on that offer. They'd settled into occasional encounters filled with good sex and a genuine mutual respect. He didn't allow himself to avail of her generosity very often, but sometimes the need simply grew stronger than he could withstand.

And with all the urges a certain blonde kept generating in him these days, he had a feeling he'd be giving Gina's service a call very soon.

Right this minute, however, all he wanted was to hit the sack. He had two days off and he planned to use them getting to know Niklaus better—and this time he would find a way to talk to the kid without pissing him off. For that he needed a fully functioning brain, which in turn called for several hours' sleep, so after a quick trip to the bathroom to brush his teeth and wash his face, he peeled out of his clothes and crashed face-first onto the mattress.

He barely had time to pull the blanket up over his shoulders against the air-conditioned chill before he sank like a stone into sleep.

The apartment was quiet when he woke later that day. Peering at the clock, he saw it was past four in the afternoon. Swearing, he rolled to sit on the side of the bed, instinctively knowing without having to check that he was alone. School had been out for more than an hour, but if Nik had been home he was gone now. And God only knew when he might be back.

Damn. So much for them spending more time together.

He shoved off the side of the bed and headed for the bathroom, scratching his chest and giving his morning erection an absentminded stroke. After relieving his bladder, he washed up and brushed his teeth, then pulled on last night's slacks and ambled into the kitchen, making a beeline for the coffeemaker.

There was already a full pot on the burner and a note propped up in front of it. He poured a cup and drank half of it in one gulp, then topped off his mug and took it and the note over to the breakfast bar. Perching one hip on a stool, he flipped open the folded-in-half piece of paper.

Uncle Wolf, he read. *Homework done—gone to pool. Come down when you wake up. Gonna BBQ. Nik.*

He smiled. That was pretty great. Maybe the kid didn't hate his guts, after all. He finished his coffee and set the mug in the sink, then headed back to the bedroom to see if he could locate a pair of swim trunks. When his search proved futile, he traded his fine-fabric slacks for a pair of cutoffs that dated back to the late eighties. He grabbed a towel out of the bathroom, found his keys and let himself out.

He was rounding the stand of trees at the back of the pool enclosure a minute later when he heard an unfamiliar male voice say, "I hear you're on the varsity soccer team, Niklaus."

Surprise ground him to a halt behind the elephantine trunks of the date palms.

The same voice asked, "Is that something you wanted for yourself, or something your dad or your uncle pushed you into?"

"Nah, I wanted it myself," Niklaus said. "Uncle Wolf's not the chatty type, unless he's layin' down the ground rules, so he hasn't said much at all about the game, except to mention that Grandma Maria told him I was real good at it. And as far as my old man goes…" Nik went quiet for so long, Wolf decided he'd probably changed his mind about sharing the saga of the sorry son of a bitch who'd knocked up Katarina, then taken off before Niklaus was even born. His nephew cleared his throat, however, and admitted, "Well, I don't know who he is. I mean, I *know* who he is—at least his name and stuff. But I've never met him, you know?"

"Trust me," the man said. "That isn't necessarily a bad thing."

"Jax, for God's sake!"

Wolf stepped between the tree trunks to see Treena give the large man at her side a poke in his muscular chest. Then she turned to Nik. "You'll have to forgive Jax," she said with a slight smile. "He had team sports forced on him by his father, and he assumes every kid is similarly mishandled."

The man called Jax shrugged. "It happens."

"Not to me, though," Niklaus said with a cheerful grin. "I *luv* soccer."

"I'm glad to hear it. So, you got a mom?"

"Yeah, in Indiana."

"How did you get clear out here when she's way back there?"

What was the guy doing, writing a damn book? That kind of nosiness was a prime example of why it was smart never to get close to people. They always wanted to hear all the embarrassing details of your life.

Niklaus apparently didn't have the same problem opening up to strangers that Wolf did, however, for he merely said, "She found another loser to hang all her hopes on, and my grandparents are moving back to Germany where my grandma's from, so they couldn't take me in this time." He hitched his wide but still bony shoulders in a who-gives-a-damn shrug. "So Uncle Wolf got stuck with me."

He jerked in shock. But before he could step forward to refute the claim, a petite older woman with stylish salt-and-pepper hair said gently, "I doubt 'stuck' with you is the way your uncle looks at it."

Yeah, you tell him, lady.

"I agree." The back of Carly's spiky-haired head came into view as she leaned forward on a chaise Wolf had looked right past in the shadow of the palms. "And what do you mean about your mother hanging her hopes on some guy?"

"You know. Obsessing over the loser du jour. Getting all hung up on him so she can guarantee getting her heart stomped to paste when he ends up treating her like sh—uh, garbage."

The older lady gave him an off-center smile. "That's pretty cynical thinking for a boy your age."

Niklaus shrugged. "It's not like it hasn't happened a hundred times before. Mom falls in love at the drop of a hat."

Wolf had to admit his nephew had his sister nailed. That was pretty much Katarina to a tee, all right. The kid must have been odd man out every damn time she'd tumbled into her version of love. It occurred to him that for all he thought *his* teen years had been dicked up, at least he'd always had the stable influence of his own mother.

"Well, that must have been hard on you," Carly said without sentimentality. "But at least your mom's picking them because she actually *likes* something about them. My mother's been married three times, and each husband was picked strictly to satisfy her never-ending quest to move up the social ladder."

Wolf looked for the downside of that scenario but couldn't quite find it. It seemed to him that choosing a man of substance for a mate was a hell of a lot more sensible than Katarina's scattershot ooh-I-love-your-tattoos style.

But he wasn't here to eavesdrop—or to socialize with a bunch of strangers, for that matter. The part of him that guided his social interactions urged him to turn around and go back to the apartment until all these people went away. He'd learned the hard way to stay aloof, thanks to those hierarchy-conscious embassy functions he'd had to endure when he was Nik's age. He'd finally wised up and started keeping to himself around the time he turned eighteen. Life was much easier that way.

In this instance, however, he gritted his teeth and kept moving. Niklaus had invited him down here and he wasn't about to slap down the first overture his nephew made. He could make nice with the neighbors if he had to. Sooner or later they were bound to go home and leave Nik to him.

His nephew was the first to spot him, and the teen's eyes actually lit up. "Hey, Uncle Wolf!" he greeted him, coming over to open the gate to the pool enclosure. "I'm glad you made it. You know Carly and Treena, right? Well, this is Treena's boyfriend, Jax, and Mack and Ellen, who live next door to them. They invited us to a barbecue."

Shit. Okay, he thought, not exactly what he'd expected, but he'd still get to spend a little time with Niklaus, who was clearly on his party manners and at least pretending they got along. Wolf shook hands with the big man he'd watched earlier, the gentle-voiced older woman who'd stuck up for him and then with a short, bulldog of an older man, a guy with watchful eyes and a grip of iron. He nodded to Treena and tried not to look at Carly at all.

That was easier said than done. Like a needle to magnetic north, his gaze kept sliding compulsively in her direction. She was wearing a halter top that looked like it had been fashioned in the forties out of some old-time floral draperies. It had one of those heart-shaped necklines that showcased her generous breasts, and the matching shorts were the kind a tap dancer of that era might have worn. Her face was bare of makeup, which he found damn near irresistible. He had a sudden, stupid urge to tell her how pretty she looked, so before he could blurt out something that would make him sound and feel like a complete idiot, he hurried to say, "I want to thank you two again for helping out last night." Although his appreciation was meant for both of them, he focused his attention strictly on Treena.

She gave him a crooked smile that popped a shallow crease in her cheek. "I was a little apprehensive at first," she admitted. "But it turned out to be a kick and a half."

"And you owe her twenty bucks for it," Carly said with no smile at all.

O-kay. She'd been a hell of a lot more congenial last night. But even as he adjusted his expression to make damn sure it didn't give away any more of his surprise than it already had, she added in a much friendlier tone, "What I mean is, Treena gave the powder room attendant twenty dollars to disappear, and it doesn't seem right that she should have to foot the expense."

"No, you're right, she shouldn't. I'll put in a request for a refund when I go back to work on Thursday."

"What'd you guys do, Carly?" Niklaus demanded, and the tiny awkward moment was smoothed over as the women relived their part in fooling Bowen with dramatic embellishments and a laughing self-deprecation that made it sound as if it was just sheer blind luck that the woman had finally shut down communications between herself and her accomplice.

"Don't let them snow you," Wolf said with a slight smile as he recalled their constant bickering chatter, which had befuddled, disarmed and, in the end, drawn Bowen along in their wake. "They were amazing." Then he surprised himself by relaxing his ironclad rule of giving out information on a need-to-know-only basis and regaled the assembled group with an abbreviated version of how the rest of the morning had gone.

He sensed the slight relaxing of the adults around him, but it was Niklaus's obvious approval that felt like his true reward. His nephew seemed to like hanging out with this mismatched group, so Wolf put some thought into how he might make himself fit in with them a little better, if only for the afternoon.

Ellen helped him out when she found him—old habits dying hard—standing by himself mere moments after he'd made his pledge to find a way to fit in. "Have a cookie?" she invited, holding out a plate.

"Thanks." He helped himself to a couple. "Did you make these yourself?"

"Yes, I did."

He tasted one, and discovering it to be among the best he'd ever had, he told her so. When Ellen's face lit up with pleasure, the tension in his shoulders relaxed and he flashed her a slight but genuine smile. "You remind me of my mother," he said, amazed at himself because, truly, with her stylish appearance and easy friendliness, she was nothing like his stolid, reticent mother.

"Do I? Why is that?"

"I'm not sure," he admitted. "You're more chic and outgoing than Mom will ever be. I suppose it's the cookies—

only with my mother, it's cakes. She makes the world's best cakes and she's got one for every occasion." Suddenly recalling that he'd eaten Ellen's baking before, he said, "I imagine you have platefuls of cookies for the same thing."

Ellen grinned up at him. "It must be a generational thing. Women of a certain age simply believe everything goes better with a little food, especially if it has sugar and fat in it." She took his hand. "Niklaus tells me your mother is from Germany. Come sit with me for a minute and tell me all about her. I'd stand here to chat, but I'm getting a crick in my neck."

The corner of his mouth ticking up, he allowed her to tug him over to the grouping of chairs and chaises beneath the palms.

Over the course of the next hour, he learned that Ellen and Mack were getting married in a month's time and listened to the women discuss an upcoming shopping trip to look for bridesmaid dresses for Carly and Treena. He listened to Nik talk sports with Mack, then discovered he knew more about the subject than Jax did and actually managed to contribute enough to the conversation to keep from embarrassing his nephew with his ignorance. When he learned that Jax had been a math prodigy who'd started MIT at fourteen, they discussed how math probabilities impacted house advantage and spawned new methods for cheating the casinos.

It took a bit of standing back and observing for him to figure out Jax's relationship with Mack. After watching them interact both down by the pool and after they'd moved the get-together up to Treena and Jax's apartment, however, he decided that even though they insulted each other with impunity, they appeared to harbor a genuine fondness for each other.

That impression was reinforced when, out on the lanai, Mack waved his spatula at the smoke billowing off the burgers on the grill, looked Jax in the eye and said, "So tell me, card bum, when are you going to make an honest woman of my Treena?"

Wolf glanced curiously from the younger to the older man. "I didn't realize you were Treena's father." They didn't look anything alike.

Treena and Carly, pulling condiments and a potato salad out of the refrigerator on the other side of the open sliding glass door, hooted with laughter.

"Did I say something amusing?"

"Nah." Mack shook his head. "I've got a couple of girls of my own, but these two are my surrogate daughters. I look out for their interests." He gave Jax a meaningful glance.

"Look all you want, old man."

"Jackson, be nice," Treena said, sticking her head out the door. "And as for you, *Dad*, this is one of my interests you no longer have to look out for. You're gonna have to find something else to beat Jax up about. Because last night I agreed to marry him."

Carly shrieked, "Oh, my God!"

Ellen said, "Oh, darling, how absolutely *fabulous*," with a reverence Wolf thought people reserved for church. Mack grumbled, "About damn time," but then smiled broadly.

Wolf could only stare, nonplussed, as everyone seemed to explode into action. Hugs and kisses were exchanged, the men shook hands and thumped each other's backs. He glanced over at Niklaus, who shrugged as if he didn't get it, either, but then grinned his appreciation of the others' obvious happiness.

Relieving Mack of the spatula, Wolf rescued the burgers

that were in peril of going up in flames. When they sat down to eat, he eyed Carly covertly as she and Ellen took turns demanding to know if Treena and Jax had set a wedding date and a host of other details he never would have dreamed people actually cared about. He was momentarily mesmerized by the way her laughter lit up her face but shook it off to try to make sense of the women's conversation. In the end he didn't know what the hell to think. They jumped from topic to topic and talked in a shorthand that bounced like a foreign language off his ability to comprehend. And he'd always prided himself on being good with languages.

As if Jax had the same problem, or was perhaps simply taking pity on the male half of the dinner party, he suddenly turned to Wolf and said, "Hey, I've caught a few glimpses of your car and I'd love to see it up close. How about showing it to Mack and me after dinner?"

"Sure," Wolf agreed, and drew a deep breath of relief when the men pushed back from the table a short while later and escaped. Talk about being tossed into the deep end of the socializing pool. "Is it always like that?" he asked as they loped down the stairs.

Reaching the ground floor first, Jax glanced over his shoulder as he pushed open the door. "Like what?"

"The women, with all that wedding talk."

"Oh, this was nothing," Mack said. "Wait until they really get going planning Jax and Treena's affair. Now, me, I was all for the package deal at the Little Chapel of the Flowers, but Ellen wants a 'real' wedding. What does that mean, do you suppose? Hell, I thought the chapel was a pretty place and they get their cakes from the Chocolate Swan. What's more real than that?"

"Maybe it means having a real church for your families to

come to," Niklaus said. "Are your families gonna be there?" He edged past the men to reach the rented garage first.

"My daughters are coming," Mack said. "Ellen never had kids, but her brother will be here."

"My family's all gone," Jax said, and stuffed his hands in his jeans pockets. "And we haven't talked to Treena's family yet, so I'm not sure about them. I can't imagine, though, that they're gonna be too thrilled to find out she's marrying a professional gambler—even one who can promise her a financially secure future."

"Why not?" Nik demanded, punching in the garage door code.

"They're steel workers in Pennsylvania. Down-to-earth, rigid-work-ethic kind of people, you know? They've never understood her desire to dance. I think Treena's folks still hope she'll come to her senses one day and marry someone with a real job who'll take her away from Sin City." He shrugged and gave them a sheepish smile. "Which is a very long way of saying I'm not sure yet if they'll be at the wedding. But for her sake I hope so."

"I met them once and they were nice people," Mack said. "Which is more than I can say of Carly's mother the one and only time I met her. Now, *there* was a piece of work."

The garage door began rumbling up toward the ceiling, but Wolf ignored it to catch the conversational thread Mack had thrown out. "What do you mean?"

"Carly's the warmest-hearted woman I know," the older man said. "But her mama treated her like she was a cross between the village idiot and the slut of Sodom and Gomorrah. I didn't like her or her la-di-dah attitude, and I— Holy shit, boy. *This* is your car? How come I've never seen it before?"

"Because it's blink and you miss it, he whips it into the garage so damn fast," Nik said in disgust. "This is probably the most righteous ride in the entire state of Nevada, but will he let anyone who really knows how to display it to its best advantage drive it? Huh-uh, no sir. No one gets to sit behind the wheel but him."

Mack snorted. "You're sixteen, boy. I wouldn't let you drive a beauty like this, either."

"Hey, I'm almost seventeen!"

"Yeah, there's a convincing argument," Jax said. "Seventeen-year-olds never drive too fast or shoot the breeze with their buds when they're supposed to be keeping their eyes on the road." He knuckled the top of Niklaus's head, then bent down to give the custom paint job a closer inspection. "That's why their insurance rates are so low."

Wolf felt a surge of appreciation for the men's defense of his decision. But it was Mack's comment about Carly and her mother that kept trying to snag his attention.

Sternly he pushed his curiosity away. What possible difference could her relationship with her mother make to him? Sure, she was hot and he'd like to tumble her into the nearest bed. But he wasn't going to. He was going to get his eye back on the damn goal where it belonged and bury this crazy attraction for a woman who painted her toenails Fuck Me Red once and for all.

And tomorrow he was calling Gina.

Thirteen

The janitor's shift was finally over and he clocked out for the evening. It had been a long day and he'd had an uncharacteristically difficult time concentrating on his duties. Pleased to be relieved of the burden, he headed straight for the employee locker room, where he changed into his street clothes. Many of his fellow custodians simply wore their uniforms to and from their homes, but his standards were higher than that. Convenience was never an acceptable excuse for sloppy habits.

He didn't intend to be a janitor his entire life. So far he'd been overlooked whenever he'd put in for in-house promotion, but that would change. The only reason it hadn't happened already was because of that damn guest who claimed he'd let himself into her room uninvited.

As if she'd been even a fraction as deserving of his regard as his Carly was.

An old familiar dissatisfaction began stirring deep inside, but he tamped it back down. He was too exhilarated to allow anything to spoil his evening.

He donned his neatly pressed navy Dockers, his pin-striped shirt and navy-and-red-striped power tie, then changed into clean socks and slid his feet into his polished loafers. Frowning at the hint of dust sprinkling their brown cordovan surface, he propped his left foot onto the bench that divided the two rows of lockers and used a small hand towel to buff first it then the right shoe back to pristine perfection. Only when both loafers once again shined to his satisfaction did he turn back to his locker and pluck his comb from its place on the shelf.

He pulled it through his light brown hair until every gleaming strand was in place. Then, restoring the grooming utensil to its exact allotted spot, he stood back and smiled at his image in the mirror hanging on the locker door.

He could honestly say with all due modesty that he was a well-favored man. His hair was thick and healthy, his teeth were even and white, and he kept himself in fighting trim. When women looked at him, he knew it was with desire, for he was handsome, gainfully employed and a man of distinction.

He, however, only had eyes for Carly Jacobsen.

He grinned rakishly into the mirror. And why shouldn't he? He was utterly happy, last night's anger no more than a dim memory. Stories had been circulating throughout the Avventurato all day long. Apparently Carly and her redheaded friend had helped Security and Surveillance catch a card cheat yesterday evening. Everywhere he'd turned, it seemed, employees had been talking about it.

She hadn't been drunk, after all. Nor had she actually been squabbling with her redheaded friend, whose name he could not recall. Not that her name mattered, for she was a nonentity, supremely unimportant in the universal scheme of things. It was Carly who counted, and she had been brave and intrepid and loyal to the casino—attributes that made her worthy once again of his affection.

He hadn't a doubt in the world, in fact, that she'd be thrilled to learn she was the absolute perfect woman for him.

Fourteen

It was Rufus's big day, his debut as an official pet-therapy volunteer. The event was a hallmark in his training, and one Carly felt they'd been working toward forever. She'd really been looking forward to it, but now that the day had actually arrived, her concentration was shot to hell, her thoughts everywhere but on the one thing she should be thinking about.

It took a concerted effort simply to focus on the traffic as she drove down West Charleston. She had to shut out the sound of Tripod and Rags moaning their usual we-hate-cars dirge in cacophonous two-part harmony from their backseat carrier. The dogs were easier since they adored the car and rode with pure delight, their heads thrust out the passenger window, Rufus's windblown ears and tongue nearly obscuring Buster's face.

Which was all pretty much business as usual. Except, rather than enjoy the mutts' antics and anticipate the next few hours, she couldn't quit wondering what on earth had prompted her to agree to have dinner at the Joneses' apartment tonight.

Well, okay, she knew what. Nik had really wanted to ac-company her to the hospital to see Rufus do his stuff. But the schedule simply wouldn't accommodate that wish, because Iago Hernandez was being sprung from the children's oncology ward today. The boy's mother planned to be there to take him home long before Nik would be released from school, and Carly had promised the little boy eons ago that the day he finally got to go home, she'd bring the babies in expressly to give him a proper send-off. So, because she felt guilty about disappointing Niklaus, she'd felt honor-bound to agree to dinner.

Big mistake. She'd known it on a bone-deep level even as she'd assured the teen she would be there. Because Niklaus's home was also Wolfgang's home, and she was far from ready to spend another evening in *his* company.

She'd barely recovered from yesterday's barbecue.

Not that she hadn't known Wolf would be attending it— Niklaus had asked if it was okay to include his uncle when they'd invited him. But she'd expected to see Spit Shine Wolfgang, not the disheveled sex god who'd shown up in his place.

It made her all sweaty just thinking about it. He'd been six feet three inches of long, lanky bone, muscle and naked skin, with only the most disreputable pair of threadbare cutoffs she'd ever seen covering him. Hell, she would have sworn the man didn't even own a pair of jeans.

She would have been wrong. Not only did he possess the raggiest pair of cutoffs Planet Earth had ever produced, but one look at him wearing them and she'd somehow turned into Desperate Barbie drooling over Bedable Ken. The sight of him, standing with the late October sun turning his thick shock of stand-up hair almost white and his wide shoulders the color of toast, had made her mouth go drier than the Mojave—while a destination farther south had gone very, very moist.

It had also made her snap out that inane command that he pay Treena back her twenty bucks. She'd recovered quickly enough, smoothing out her tone of voice enough to almost make her demand sound like a request. But Holy Mary, Mother of God—just what was it about him that reduced her to a seething puddle of rampaging hormones? Sure, he had a killer body, but so what? She was surrounded by fit, good-looking men every day at work. Not one of them, however, had ever affected her the way Wolfgang did.

When they'd all gone up to Treena's to put dinner together, Wolf had detoured by his apartment to put on a navy-blue T-shirt. It had helped a little. At least she hadn't had to stare at those bare shoulders across the dinner table.

Mostly, though, it had turned out to be a case of too little, too late, because the soft knit had bonded like a lover to the muscular planes of his chest. It had stretched thin over the roundness of his biceps. And even though the tee fit looser over his midsection, the damage was done. She'd already seen the defined bands of his abs, the sleek hollow of his spine. And unfortunately her mind's eye wasn't the least bit shy about replaying those particular visions over and over again.

Thank God for Treena and Jax's announcement. It was the only thing that had saved her butt. Until then, between Wolfgang's casual, barely there attire and the fact that he'd been behaving halfway sociable for the first time ever, she'd been teetering on the ragged edge of panic, scared to death someone was going to notice at any minute her clear desire to jump his bones and comment on it.

"Jumpin' Jones's bones," she said aloud to her oblivious pets, and shook her head. "Sounds like a rap song, doesn't it, kids?"

No one answered.

She wheeled into UMC's parking lot moments later and parked the car, then simply stared through the windshield at the modern multistoried sandstone-colored edifice. She spent a minute drawing in and exhaling breaths to steady herself, then shook out her hands, clipped on the dogs' leads and climbed out of the car. Collecting the cats' travel container, she headed for the cancer center. It was time to focus on why she was here. It was way past time to put her crazy jones for Jones on ice and concentrate on making sure Rufus performed his maiden stint admirably. This morning was about Iago, not her screwed-up libido.

The eight-year-old was waiting in his room, propped up on his adjustable bed reading a Spider-Man comic. A suitcase stood next to the door.

"Hey, Iago, is that your bag?" she said cheerfully as she breezed through the door. "I bet you can hardly wait to get home."

"Miz Jacobsen!" His dark eyes lit up. Tossing his comic book aside, he pushed himself higher against his pillows. "You came!"

"Well, of course I came. Told you I was gonna send you off in style, didn't I? You know Buster and Rags and Tripod. I'm afraid the cats are still a little freaked by the ride, so we'll just give them a minute to settle." She set the container on the floor and opened its door. "In the meantime—" she led her new recruit forward "—I'd like you to meet Rufus."

Iago was underweight and denuded of hair, but none of that mattered as his entire face lit up. "Oh, wow! He's gotta be 'bout the coolest dog I've ever seen!" He shot the older mutt a guilty look. "Sorry, Buster. You're cool, too. It's just that you're, uh—"

"A little goofy-looking." She ruffled the dog's topknot and grinned at the boy on the bed. "That's okay. Buster's not at all vain. And he's very secure in his masculinity. He knows his sweet nature makes up for a certain lack in the looks department."

Iago grinned, too, then patted the bedspread next to his hip. "C'mere, boy," he said to Rufus, his smile getting even bigger as the dog leaped up onto the bed next to him and licked his face.

It was clearly a case of love at first sight. Iago had always been thrilled to see her arrive with her animals, but he'd never reacted to the other three the way he did to Rufus. And Rufus bonded to the boy like Lassie to Timmy, curling up alongside him, his head on Iago's thigh and his eyes glued to the youngster's face in rapt adoration.

When Mrs. Hernandez arrived about twenty minutes later, all four pets were draped over Iago's bed. But it was obvious that Rufus was the star attraction for the little boy. Watching him as his mother swept a host of cards and photographs off the bulletin board and packed them with his stack of comics into the suitcase by the door, it was clear to Carly that the frail child was torn between finally getting to go home and having to tear himself away from his newfound soul mate.

A radical thought popped into her head, and she immediately shoved it away. But it popped right back front and center again. Her heart began to thump in her chest and cold sweat gathered between her breasts. She felt sort of jumpy and sick to her stomach, but after several minutes of fierce internal debate, she knew what she had to do.

Wiping her suddenly damp palms on the seat of her shorts, she walked over to Mrs. Hernandez and pulled her aside for a consultation.

* * *

When Wolf arrived home at five that afternoon, he was beat. All he wanted was a cold beer and a few minutes' peace and quiet.

"Hey." Niklaus met him at the door, bouncing on the balls of his feet. "You're late."

"Yes, I'm sorry." Guilt about going in to work on his day off jabbed his conscience as he strode toward the kitchen with his nephew dogging his footsteps. "I figured between school and soccer practice I had until four-thirty before you got home and I fully intended to be here before you. But I didn't factor in an accident on Decatur." He grabbed a Heineken out of the fridge, popped the top and took a long pull. Lowering the bottle, he looked at his nephew. "How was your day?"

"Pretty good." Niklaus gestured toward the short hall that led to the bedrooms. "You need to go change your clothes. Carly's gonna be here in about fifteen minutes."

"Carly?" He lowered the bottle he'd raised without taking another sip, unease tightening his gut. "She's coming here?"

"Yeah, I invited her for dinner. Go change. Put on what you wore yesterday. I think she liked that."

No! She couldn't come here. He needed to unwind. To chill. To decompress. What he did not need was a repeat of the nerve-screaming awareness of a certain lissome showgirl that had hallmarked the previous day's get-together.

Only…

Niklaus had a big smile of anticipation on his face. And looking around, Wolf saw that his nephew had neatened up the apartment and set the rarely used table in the little dining nook with three plates that actually matched. A full complement of cutlery was correctly arranged at each place setting, and a glass-encased candle sat in the middle of the table between the salt-and-pepper grinder and a napkin holder he hadn't even known they owned.

Blowing out a breath of defeat, he shoved his fingers through his hair. "Okay. I'll change. But I'm not putting on those ratty old cutoffs." It was bad enough that he'd shown up in them yesterday for what had turned out to be a party.

"Whatever. But you gotta lose the tie. This is supposed to be casual, and a tie doesn't say 'neighborly.'"

"I didn't even know a tie could talk. If it doesn't say 'neighborly,' what does it say?"

Nikolaus grinned. "Accountant? Undertaker? Take your pick."

"I think I'll pass." Shaking his head, he walked down the hall to his bedroom, where he kicked off his shoes, hung his jacket in the closet and removed his chatty tie. Then he dropped to sit on the bed with his back against the headboard. He stretched his legs out in front of him and took his time finishing his beer.

When the last sip was gone, he reluctantly climbed to his feet and changed into a pair of khakis. He left on his Egyptian cotton white-on-white-striped shirt, but unfastened the button at his throat and rolled his sleeves up his forearms. For about three seconds he considered shaving again, but then rolled his shoulders irritably. Screw it. This wasn't a date. Hell, if he'd been halfway smart, he would have blown off McAster when he'd called requesting an hour or two of his time and gotten in contact with Gina instead. He'd at least have been a lot more relaxed now and better able to cope with this frigging dinner. What the devil had Nik been thinking?

He rejoined the teen in the living room a minute or two

before Carly was due to arrive. Fifteen minutes later Nik started asking him the time. Ten minutes after that, his nephew started pacing the foyer and *he* started doing a slow boil, which took considerable effort to hide from the teen, which ticked him off even further.

"Where is she?" Niklaus asked anxiously after demanding to know the time yet again. "She was supposed to be here half an hour ago." He glanced uncertainly at the front door. "Maybe I oughtta go see what's holding her up."

"You check on your dinner," he said, then wondered why he didn't smell anything cooking. But he shook the thought aside. "I'll go."

Closing the door carefully behind him, he turned toward Carly's apartment. It took a mere three strides to reach her front door, and he pounded his fist against it. Damn woman, he fumed, getting the kid's hopes up, then not bothering to follow through.

There was no answer, but when one of her dogs started barking in the condo he was almost positive he heard a faint shushing sound, a conviction that grew when the dog fell silent. He pounded again "Carly! I know you're in there. Open up."

Still no answer.

He looked at the lock. He'd learned a great deal during his stint in the security department at the Avventurato, and the first thing he'd done upon moving to this complex was exchange the standard flimsy locks that came with the condos for some good solid dead bolts.

Carly had clearly never changed hers, and it took him all of forty seconds to jimmy her lock. Another second and he was on the other side of her front door, closing it quietly behind him. Then he strode into her living room.

No one was there. Nor was anyone in the kitchen or out on the lanai.

But there was a faint sound coming from her bedroom, and he headed down the hall. "Carly!"

"Go away. Just…go away."

He'd already reached the bedroom when the dull lethargy in her voice registered. The room's blinds were closed and he peered into the dimness.

A trickle of unease slid down his spine. It intensified when the funny-looking dog named Buster slunk over, pushing his nose under Wolf's hand with an anxious whimper.

Okay, this wasn't normal. Carly should be yelling at him for the breach of privacy, and in his experience her pets were never nervous. Something was clearly wrong. Unable to locate the wall switch, he walked over to the nightstand and stretched out a hand toward the bedside lamp.

"*Don't*," she said raggedly in the same instant that he clicked some illumination into the room.

Shock jolted down the nerves of his spine. She'd been crying. Her eyes were red and swollen, her fair skin was blotchy, and the tip of her nose was ruddy. She looked sodden and bereft and…vulnerable.

He'd never seen her even close to such a state, and an odd frisson of something—well, he wouldn't call it protective, and it sure as hell couldn't be termed *tender*, but something—unexpectedly powerful shivered through him. Which was patently absurd, of course. All the same, he moved her black cat aside and sat on the side of the bed. Against everything he knew to be smart, he reached out to swipe his thumb beneath her left eye, collecting a little smear of tears on its pad. Unthinkingly, he brought the anointed thumb to his mouth and sucked the salty moisture from it. "Are you all right?"

Then he shook his head. "Dumb question, obviously you're not. Are you sick? Did someone die?"

"No." But her voice wobbled. She knuckled her eyes, wiped the back of her hand beneath her nose and took a long, shuddering breath. Then she suddenly focused on him. "What are you doing here, Wolfgang? How did you get in?"

"Your door was ajar."

"It was?" She blinked uncertainly, then shook her head as if it didn't matter. "In any case, you're in, I guess. What do you want?"

Prepared to launch into a reminder of her obligation, he said, "Niklaus—"

"Oh, God!" Plainly stricken, she cut him off. "His dinner!" She picked up the three-legged cat that had been in her lap and set him on the bedspread next to her hip, where he immediately collapsed in a boneless sprawl. "I forgot all about it. Give me ten minutes. Five. I can pull myself together in five." *Somehow*, her expression seemed to say.

He almost told her to forget it. Clearly something had happened today to put her in this state, and for this one time Nik could simply live with the disappointment. Besides, he'd understand once Wolf told him Carly was upset. Like any right-thinking male, he'd most likely be grateful he didn't have to deal with a crying female.

Except...

Carly seemed to want the distraction. She could have demanded a rain check, but instead she was scrambling off the bed and striding toward the adjoining bathroom, her long legs gleaming beneath a pair of shorts whose hems actually ended at a fairly conservative mid-thigh. The next thing he knew, the door closed behind her, leaving him alone except for her pets.

Well, holy shit. Now what? With nothing better to do, he swiveled on the mattress to examine her bedroom.

It was surprisingly homey. And neater than he expected, he thought, remembering the night he'd brought her home after she'd t.visted her ankle at work. Come to think of it, though, when he'd passed through her living room and kitchen a few minutes ago they had been tidy, as well.

He shook his head impatiently. What was he, one of those old maids who swiped their white gloves across random surfaces checking for dust? Hell, no. He was decidedly more interested in the room's overall…ambiance…than in its state of cleanliness.

And its ambiance definitely said Woman.

It smelled really good, for one thing, sort of like—well, he didn't know what, because it wasn't exactly flowers or powder. Just good. Pretty.

Female.

For another, the coverlet he sat on and its matching heap of pillows were all a pale, lacy yellow. It didn't get much girlier than that. The arrangement might be a little mussed at the moment, but the deeper gold walls looked recently painted and the hardwood floor was pristine, its gleam broken only by a flower-patterned area rug. One corner of the room was taken up by a spool-backed wooden rocking chair, with a soft, fringed, emerald-green throw spilling from its seat. Bright artwork of African women in colorful, textured clothing graced two walls, and he climbed to his feet for a closer look. He was studying one when Carly walked back into the room.

He looked at her. And blinked. She was still wearing the same shorts and gauzy top, but gone were the puffy eyes, the red-tipped nose. If he hadn't seen it for himself he'd never have guessed she'd been crying. "Quite a transformation."

She shrugged. "Nothing like a little cold water, Visine and Preparation H to fix a girl up."

"Preparation—" He felt his jaw go slack and firmed it up. "I won't even ask."

She patted a gentle fingertip beneath her right eye. "Shrinks swollen tissues."

"Mein Gott."

His befuddled amazement apparently provided a little comic relief, for her lips curled up in a faint smile. Then she blew out a breath. "Let me just take care of the babies and I'll be ready."

Following her to the kitchen, he watched as she poured water into her pets' bowls. Buster happily lapped it up, but the two felines twined between her ankles, complaining loudly when they discovered it wasn't food she was dishing up.

She really did have incredible legs. Smooth, sleek and so long and limber they'd drape easily over a man's shoulders—

He slammed a door on the thought. God. What was it about her that could transform him from coolly in control to mindlessly horny by doing nothing more erotic than filling a bowl of water?

Damned if he had a clue. But it ended *now*, he told himself as he escorted her to his condo, careful to keep at arm's length.

Niklaus was at the door to greet them. "Hey," he said to Carly. "I thought maybe you weren't coming."

"I'm sorry I'm so late," she said. "I had, um, a busy afternoon and I lost track of the time."

"Uh-oh. Did Rufus screw up?"

"No, he was great." To her obvious horror, her voice cracked on the last word and fat tears rose in her eyes. She dashed them away with the side of her hand and shook her head fiercely. "I'm sorry. I gave Rufus to Iago and I'm feeling pretty raw about it."

"You gave Rufus *away?*" Niklaus stared at her as if she'd confessed to dumping the dog on the freeway.

"Who's Iago?" Wolf asked.

Nik turned to him. "He's this kid with cancer that Carly visits in the pet-therapy program."

"His cancer is in remission," Carly clarified. "And he went home today after months in the hospital."

Niklaus turned to her. "But even so, you can't just give your dog away!"

"They fell in love with each other, Nik. It was the right thing to do. Really." The unsteady wobble in her voice made her sound less than certain, however.

The teen's attention was focused on only one fact in any event. "If you wanted to get rid of him you could have given him to me!"

"That's enough," Wolf snapped. "Take a good look at her. Does she look like she wanted to get rid of him?"

Niklaus gave her a stony stare. "She looks okay to me."

"Then you're not looking closely enough. She was crying her eyes out when I went to her apartment and she's barely holding it together now."

Carly gave him an insulted look. "Do me a favor, Jones. Don't help me out."

Niklaus peered at her. "You were crying?"

"Yes!" she snapped with a resurgence of her usual, don't-mess-with-me spirit. "I was crying, so what? You can't possibly think I *wanted* to give Rufus away?" An expression of heart-breaking uncertainty crossed her face. "Do you?"

Niklaus wrapped his arms around her and gave her a big hug. Wolf watched as Carly's big, bad screw-you posture deserted her. Fisting her hands in the teen's T-shirt, she clung to him. A loud sob escaped her. "I didn't," she repeated. "But when he and Iago clapped eyes on each other, it was love at first sight. That little boy's been in and out of hospitals since he was six years old, Nik, and he's missed out on so much of the stuff that other kids take for granted. He can *use* a dog like Rufus, but it killed me to give one of my babies away. Oh God, I'm getting your shirt all wet."

She disengaged herself and took a step back, wiping both cheeks with her hands. "I'm sorry." She visibly pulled herself together. "Look, I'm nothing but a wet blanket this evening. Maybe I should just go home."

"No!" Wolf and Niklaus said together. But it was his nephew who continued, "No, you gotta eat and you probably shouldn't be alone. And dinner is just about ready. Come in here and sit down." He led them to the table in the dining area. "I'll light the candle. Do you want something to drink?" The doorbell rang. "Oh, look, there's dinner now." He loped out of the room.

"Aha." Wolf watched him go. "That would explain why I didn't smell anything cooking."

"You got some money, Uncle Wolf?" the teen called from the foyer.

"Boy," Carly said with a watery sigh, "you just got stuck all the way around, didn't you?" She finished wiping her cheeks, then gave them a pinch and ran her fingers through her hair to fluff up the soft blond spikes.

An hour ago he probably would have agreed, but somehow he didn't feel the least bit stuck at the moment. Unsure how to verbalize the sentiment, however, he simply gave her a one-sided smile and went to pay the delivery person.

"Hope you like Chinese," Niklaus said as he carried a

fragrant bag into the dining area moments later. He dropped the sack on the table and started rooting through it, dragging cartons out and arranging them in the middle of the table. "I got a mix of stuff, so there oughtta be something here you'll like."

"When it comes to food, I pretty much like everything," Carly replied. "And this smells wonderful. I just realized I haven't eaten since breakfast."

Wolf detoured by the kitchen to collect a handful of serving spoons. He looked through the opening at Carly. "What would you like to drink? We've got milk, water, beer, soda— if Nik hasn't drank it all—and, I think, a little red wine."

She chose wine and a minute later they all sat to eat. Niklaus took three bites as Wolf and Carly were dishing up their plates, then shoved back from the table. "I gotta go brush my teeth. My ride's gonna be here any minute."

Wolf narrowed his eyes at his nephew. "What ride? Where do you think you're going?"

"My lab partner's picking me up to work on a class project at the library." He backed from the room even as he explained. For the second time in fifteen minutes the doorbell rang and Nik loped down the hallway. "Get that, will you? I can't work on a biology project with garlic breath."

At least he'd finally get to meet one of "the guys," Wolf thought as he excused himself to Carly and went to answer the door. But when he opened it the person on the other side didn't turn out to be the teenage boy he'd expected. Instead, a slender, pretty girl with shiny brown hair stood in the hallway.

Wolf covered his surprise and ruthlessly suppressed the inclination of his lips to curl up so his sudden amusement wouldn't show. But, please. Biology, indeed. No wonder dental hygiene was suddenly such a priority. "Hello," he said. "You must be the lab partner."

The girl nodded. "I'm Natalie."

"Nice to meet you. I'm Wolfgang, Niklaus's uncle." He stepped back, motioning her to follow. "Come in. Nik will be out in just a second." For lack of a better idea, he led her to the dining nook. "This is our neighbor, Carly Jacobsen. Carly, this is Natalie."

"Niklaus's biology partner," Carly said with a slight smile.

"Uh-huh." He looked at the girl, who was surreptitiously studying Carly, and directed her attention to the multitude of cartons on the table. "Have you eaten? We've got more Chinese food than we can possibly eat and you're welcome to help yourself."

"Oh, no, thank you, Mr. Jones. I had dinner at home."

Niklaus skidded into the room. "Hey, Natalie. I see you've met my uncle and Carly. Well, we'd better go. See you later, Uncle Wolf. I'll be back by eleven." He ushered the girl from the room, a faint waft of aftershave trailing in his wake. Seconds later the front door banged closed.

Wolf and Carly looked at each other. One beat passed, then another. Then they both grinned.

"I think Nik has a different kind of biology in mind than just research for a class project," she said.

"What gave him away? The rubber he burned getting her out of here or the cologne?"

"That would be a toss-up." She glanced down at the food on her plate, then back up at him, her smile fading. "I should probably take this home and get out of your hair."

"No. Stay," he commanded. "This is the most relaxed you've looked all evening, and I'm not rushing you out the door simply because Niklaus forgot he had a hot date. Eat."

"Okay. Thanks." She settled back in her seat and picked up her fork. "Nice candle," she said, indicating the Glade 2 in 1 that usually sat on the toilet tank in the bathroom.

"Yeah, that Nik. He knows tricks to putting together a table that would put the Stewart woman to shame."

The rest of their conversation was surprisingly easy, and in what seemed like no time at all they'd put a sizable dent in the cartons. Despite Wolf's protests, Carly insisted on loading the dishwasher while he put the leftovers in the refrigerator. It wasn't until he walked her to her door a short while later that the sadness seeped back into her expression.

Not that she didn't try to hide it. "Thank Niklaus for dinner for me, will you?" she said with a determined smile. "And thank you. It helped."

"For what it's worth," he said, thinking of all he'd learned about her tonight, "I think the sacrifice you made was an honorable thing."

Her full lower lip trembled. "You didn't even like Rufus."

"I didn't dislike him. I didn't get to know him. Maybe that was my loss."

She made a small, wounded sound, and because his intention hadn't been to make her cry, he leaned down and stopped the little moan with his lips. It was pure impulse— one that he recognized a second too late as a major mistake.

A second after that her hands came up and twined through his hair. And abruptly he accepted that he was about to make a much bigger one.

Fifteen

Hot hands, hot lips, hot skin.

Usually when a woman said a man was a hottie, Carly thought through a haze of arousal, she was speaking metaphorically. Wolf, however, literally pumped out heat. She wouldn't be surprised if she ended up with his fingerprints scorched into her hide. Feeling her last functioning brain cell go up in flames, she rose onto her toes to press herself against the source of all that fiery energy. Her hands glided from Wolf's hair to his strong neck, and her breasts flattened against his chest.

With a low sound of approval rumbling in his throat, he moved the two of them through the front door she'd unlocked just moments earlier, then kicked it closed and locked it again behind them. The babies came running, but as quickly as their presence registered on her ordinarily pet-sensitive radar, it fell off again.

All her attention was locked on Wolf, who was plainly a man with a mission. He slow-waltzed her with a featherlight guidance straight through the minefield of furry bodies brushing against their lower legs. Leaving the foyer behind, he blazed a path across the living room and, yanking her closer yet, steered them with impatient strides down the hallway toward her bedroom.

All without once breaking their kiss. His finesse made Carly's head spin, but not as much as the heart-wrenching gentleness of his lips.

Considering the authoritative way he handled her, it both aroused and confused her. He grasped her firmly, directing her where he wanted her to go, his long, strong hands locked around her hips. Nor did his body leave her in any doubt about what he wanted from her. There was no slow build-up for Wolfgang. With a thick, solid ridge nudging her stomach, there wasn't the slightest chance of mistaking his erection for anything but what it was. Yet his lips molded hers softly, and he sipped from them as if taking sacramental wine from the most fragile of chalices.

He wasn't even using his tongue.

The thought no sooner flitted across her mind than she wondered why. Her parted lips were certainly an invitation, and Lord knew she wanted to feel his tongue on her own, wanted to taste his flavors.

So when have you ever needed an engraved invitation? The answer was an immediate *never*. She was neither shy nor miss-ish, so taking the initiative, she eased her tongue into his mouth, where she gave the well-mannered organ in question a delicate lap.

Another sound rumbled in his chest, only this one was lower in tone, a more animalistic prepare-to-mate growl. His hands tightened around her hips as his strong, supple tongue shed its polite manners quicker than a wolf sheds its sheep's clothing and surged up to tangle with hers. He maneuvered them double time into her bedroom and banged the door shut on her curious pets. Pressing her up against the closed portal, he kissed her right to the raw edge of insanity.

Seconds or maybe eons later, he ripped his mouth away and leaned back from the waist. The movement ground the solid length of his penis against her stomach, and immediately he bent his legs to adjust their disparate heights, dragging his erection down to press hard between her legs.

Dear God. It had been so long since she'd participated in any kind of sexual interaction and it felt so good. A needy little moan escaped her lips.

"I want to see you," he said, running his hands up her hips to grasp the hem of her gauzy little top. "Now."

It was evident by the command in his voice that he didn't expect a refusal. Since she couldn't think of a single good reason to do so, anyhow, she simply raised her arms for him to pull the top off over her head.

Dropping it to the floor, he gazed for a long, silent moment at the practical shorts and anything-but-practical nude-shades-of-pink demi bra that remained. Then he slowly raised his right hand and watched his forefinger as it outlined the striped bra's perimeter and fiddled with the tiny ornate buckles on its shimmery straps.

The juxtaposition of his slightly scratchy fingertip against the satin-and-gossamer construction made muscles deep in Carly's body draw tight.

Wolf gazed at his handiwork through heavy-lidded eyes. "Soft," he said in a rough voice. "Like the whipping cream on one of my mother's cakes." His gaze abruptly lifted and the intense heat in his eyes soldered her feet to the floor. Then he slowly lowered his head until his breath washed over her ear, his lips a hairbreadth away. "I'm going to lick you all over," he said, his voice a dark, sexual promise that rasped its way down the delicate whorls.

Goose bumps cropped up all along her side and she responded to the underlying subtext of *I'm-the-master-and-you-are-mine-to-do-with-as-I-wish* with a sharp rush of arousal. It wasn't the most liberated reaction in the world, but all the same, his unflinching arrogance just flat did it for her. It was ironic when she considered the way the same take-charge attitude had ignited her temper in their earlier encounters and how it very well might tick her off again come tomorrow.

But for tonight, it was sexy as hell.

What a damn shame it was, then, that she couldn't let him get away with it—or at least not entirely. If she let him start ordering her around, she had a feeling she'd be setting a precedent she wouldn't be able to live with. This encounter could well turn out to be nothing more than a one-night stand. But if they did decide on an encore performance, she couldn't afford to leave any openings for him to take the inch she was prepared to give and stretch it into the proverbial mile. Reaching out, she tugged his shirttails free of his khakis.

"No licking," she said firmly, slipping the bottom button from its hole. "At least not before you display some of the goods yourself." Slowly she unfastened her way up the placket, exposing a stripe of blond hair that swirled around his navel before disappearing beneath the waistband of his pants, uncovering a slice of smooth, muscular abdomen, then the powerful, gently curved planes of his chest. Spreading the sides of his shirt wide, she examined the body she'd lusted over yesterday but had only allowed herself to look at in snatches. It appeared even sexier than it had then.

She hadn't thought that possible.

Her mouth watered and she realized she wouldn't mind doing a little licking of her own. Being pinned to her bedroom door from the pelvis down, however, didn't give her a lot of wiggle room. So, rubbing her hands across his pectorals, her palms flat and her fingers spread wide, she had to content herself with licking her lips instead. It wasn't nearly as satisfying.

Wolf seemed to like it, though, for he sucked in a sharp breath and his fingers clenched her hips. Then he bent his head and rocked his mouth over hers again, and this time his kiss wasn't the least bit gentle. She felt his teeth behind his lips, and his tongue pushed with give-it-to-me aggression past the slick inner lining of her lower lip to lay claim to hers. Skimming his hands up her sides, he kept her pinned in place with his erection while his fingers unhooked her bra. He peeled the loosened cups away from her breasts, but her upraised arms caused the bra to promptly ride up, its under-wiring turning on end to form a barrier between them. Wolf's growl of frustration made her release her hold from around his neck so he could peel the garment off entirely. He stuffed it in his back pocket, then slapped his hands flat against the door on either side of her head. Straight-arming himself back, he stared down at the curves he'd exposed.

"God." His tone rendered the word more benediction than blasphemy. He lifted one hand from the panel and stroked his fingers from her earlobe to her shoulder, then lightly trailed his fingertips down her sternum. Tenderly he cupped the full lower curve of her left breast, pressing it slightly upward. "I feel like I ought to be lighting candles in tribute."

When he bent his head, Carly fully expected him to use his mouth on her captured breast. It was the first place most men headed, but Wolfgang merely kissed her eyelids closed. A second later he moved lower and kissed her neck beneath the angle of her chin, his lips a brand that seared her with their confidence and heat. With a small moan, she bared more of her throat to his ministrations, and he strung kisses down its side.

Then he raised his head and stepped away. She blinked at him uncertainly, but before she could focus, he snatched her up off her feet.

With a soft shriek, she clung to his shoulders, which made Wolf laugh under his breath and toss her a couple of inches into the air. He caught her in his arms, only to immediately toss her up and catch her again.

She clutched him harder as he strode across the room. "What are you doing?"

"Playing."

"Playing what? Let's bounce Carly?"

"Sure. No. I don't know." His wide shoulders rolled beneath her grip. "Maybe I'm showing off. Big strong man sweeps beautiful woman off her feet."

He thought she was beautiful? Before she could start to preen, however, he added, "Of course, it's hard to give you the whole show when you're clinging to me like a barnacle to a rock."

Stung, she whipped her arms away from his neck. He promptly tossed her even higher than before, and the next thing she knew she was falling through the air.

She landed on the bed with a bounce and he knelt on the mattress beside her. Hunching over, he framed her cheeks with his thumbs, his long fingers splayed to cup the back of her head. She stared up into his green eyes, which were suddenly, mesmerizingly, an inch away, and her breath labored in her lungs.

"That pride of yours makes you easy to manipulate," he

said matter-of-factly, then essayed the equivalent of a facial shrug. "But it takes one to know one, I guess." His gaze locked on her mouth and his eyelids grew heavy. "I've kissed you," he said huskily. "Now you kiss me."

Oh, yeah. She started to reach for him before remembering her vow not to let him have everything his way. "Well, I don't know," she drawled. Planting both hands against his shoulders, she gave a little shove, delighted when he flopped over onto his back. A smile fought to break free, but she frowned with mock concern instead. "Dangerous things happen when I allow myself to kiss a guy without making sure there are restrictions in place." She rolled onto her knees and looked down at Wolf propped up on his elbows, his open shirt pulled off one shoulder. He stared back up at her, and she swung a leg over his midsection and came up onto her feet, her hands on her widespread knees and her hips lowered to crouch over him without quite touching. "Men have been known to go blind when I really let myself go."

"I'll take that chance. Because you letting go is exactly what I want. So kiss me, Carly. Full out, no foot on the brakes. And don't worry about me going blind." He gave her a faint smile. "I'm a responsible adult. I'll call a halt when it gets to the point where I need glasses."

She had to bite her lip to keep from laughing aloud. Oh, God, he had a sense of humor, after all. How was a girl supposed to resist that? Feigning boredom, she crossed her arms in the air over her head and looked down the length of her nose at him, watching his gaze track the way her boobs lifted. "Well, maybe if you sign a waiver first. I have to cover my assets, you know. Because truly, toots, I'm so good you'll probably be paralyzed for life. And I don't intend to spend the rest of mine tied up in court because you insisted you could resist my charms even after repeated warnings."

"So far I hear you talking a good game." He reached up to touch the underside of her left breast, seemingly fascinated by its texture and weight against his fingertips. "But you know what they say. Those who can, do. Those who can't—" his gaze flashed up to capture hers "—chat."

She gave her head a sad shake. Heaved a sigh. "Very well. But don't say I didn't warn you." And grabbing him by his shirt plackets, she yanked, shifting her center of gravity backward.

Going with the flow, he came to a seated position with an easy contraction of his abs. Carly slid onto his lap and wrapped her legs around his hips. Just as she crossed her ankles behind him, Wolf spread his thighs and they slipped together like two pieces of a puzzle. The hard thrust of his erection met the soft notch between her legs, with only a few thin layers of material separating the two. They both froze, their gazes locking.

Framing his face in her hands, she massaged her palms over the faint prickle of blond stubble along his jaw and tilted her head to one side. Then, aligning their lips, she locked her mouth over his.

The fire between them, which had been temporarily banked but by no means extinguished, flared back to life, the newly revived flames threatening to burn them alive.

Carly lost all desire for teasing. A desperation she hadn't anticipated licked along her nerve endings and she poured its energy back into her kiss. Releasing Wolf's face, she wrapped her arms in a stranglehold around his neck, moaning when his shirt parted and for the first time they touched bare skin to bare skin. She stroked her breasts against his chest and rocked against the steely erection pressing authoritatively between her legs, shifting in search of the most sensation.

Just as she felt his erection bump her sweet spot, sending all her senses circling down to that one small ultrasensitive realm, Wolf lifted her off his lap and tipped her backward to lay on the bed. Before her skin cooled from the sudden loss of body heat, however, his weight crushed down on top of her, pressing her deeper into the mattress. He kissed his way down her throat while inserting a hand between their bodies to fumble with the waistband of her shorts.

Then he lifted his head to stare down at her. "I want you naked," he said in his don't-even-argue-with-me voice. "Naked and under me with those legs wrapped around my waist." When she didn't immediately hop to, he added peremptorily, *"Now."*

"Take your shirt off," she countered.

He pushed back to sit on his heels and removed the already half-off shirt. Tossing it aside, he pointed a long, blunt finger at her shorts. "Now you. Lose those."

She shucked out of them, enjoying the way his eyelids drooped when he saw the tiny V-string panties that were all that stood between her and total nudity. Seeing his hand reach out to touch her, she shook her head at him. "Uh-uh-uh. Your turn." Her gaze was glued to his hands as they went to his waistband.

He unbuckled a brown leather belt and finessed the khakis' riveted button through its buttonhole. Then he fingered the zipper tab and stared down at her. "Untie your panties."

She reached for one of the ribbons that held the two V-shaped scraps of satin together. Pulled its bow undone. "I'll do the other side when I see that zipper come down."

He lowered it an inch, two inches, revealing a flat expanse of abdomen that was graced with the blond stripe of hair she'd noticed earlier. As the V of his fly widened, so did her eyes. Man, he either had on the world's tiniest briefs or—

"Oh, my God," she whooped. "You're going commando." She *never* would have pegged him for the kind of guy to forgo his underwear.

He indicated her undies. "The other side, Carly." But he didn't make her wait before tugging the zipper all the way down.

She untied the remaining ribbon just as his erection sprang free of the constricting khakis. It was long and thick, and as she stared at it jutting out at her, she knew her mouth was hanging open. She couldn't bring herself to care. "That is so—" *Stupendous. Amazing. Gorgeous.* She couldn't narrow it down and waved a hand. "Wow. Words fail me."

He grinned at her, an honest-to-God big, broad smile such as she'd only seen once before on Monday night when she and Treena were escorting the card cheat into the ladies' room. It suited his normally taciturn face surprisingly well, and she couldn't help but grin back. As he kicked free of his sagging pants, she realized she'd never before noticed just how strong and white his teeth were.

Then he leaned down, snagged the front V of her panties and pulled them off of her. The rear V's ribbons, caught between the comforter and her bottom, whisked a satin caress against her cheeks as he whipped the undies away.

His grin dissolved and he swallowed hard enough for her to watch his Adam's apple slide up and down his throat. "God." Licking his bottom lip, he tore his gaze away to look up into her eyes. "You are so pretty. All over." Lying alongside her, he lowered his head and whispered in her ear, "Pretty eyes." He kissed the side of her neck. "Pretty lips." He pressed a here-and-gone kiss on her mouth. "Pretty legs." He hooked his ankle around hers and jerked them apart. "Pretty—"

Cutting himself off, he looked down at her in confusion. "I'm sorry, I don't know what to call this." His gaze returned to her newly revealed sex. "You'd probably find what I was going to say insulting, but vagina is such a clinical, hard-sounding word." Propping his head in his left palm, he trailed his right hand down her chest, circled her breasts, then continued down her rib cage to her stomach. He brushed all four fingers down her abdomen until they reached the rise of her mons. Then, stroking his forefinger along the narrow stripe of blond curls that graced the apex of her legs, he inserted its tip between slippery folds of feminine flesh.

Inhaling sharply, he stared down at his hand between her legs with a gaze rapidly going dark with passion. "Pretty *Muschi*," he whispered. His touch slipped and slid, and his finger and thumb caught first one silken plump lip between them, then the other. "So slick and wet." He moved his hand lower and eased his long middle finger into her.

"Oh, God, Wolf." She bit her lip and only half swallowed the moan his teasing touch dredged up from the depths of her lungs. "I don't care what terminology you use. Just touch me."

"Like this?" He glided his finger in and out, then pressed a second one in to join it. "Or like this?" Lowering his head, he caught her nearest nipple between his lips and drew on it strongly at the same time that his thumb rose to nudge the straining bead of her clitoris.

Carly exploded in a hard, fast orgasm that arched her back up off the bed. She rode it, her head thrown back in a silent scream as sweet, satisfying contractions commandeered her senses. When the last one had passed, she collapsed in a boneless heap against her counterpane. "Damn," she whispered.

"No fooling," Wolf agreed in a husky voice. "I don't think I've ever seen a woman come quite like that."

She cracked one eye open and saw him still propped up alongside her, staring down at her with hot-eyed intensity. "Give me a minute to catch my breath," she said with a languid smile. "And we'll see about you."

"Oh, we've got plenty of time to take care of me," he replied, still lazily circling his thumb around her clitoris. "I'm not finished with you yet."

Carly's other eye popped open. "Uh, maybe we'd better take turns. I'm still vibrating like a tuning fork. I'm not sure I can handle more right now."

Wolf could feel the Jones wild streak threatening to slip its leash and knew he ought to rein it in. The smart money argued for doing what she said, taking his turn, then getting the hell out of there.

Instead, he heard himself saying, "Sure you can. I bet you could come all night long."

The snug, silken sheath still hugging his fingers clamped around them with surprising force, and he gave her a fierce smile. "Ah, you like that idea, don't you? Me, too." Slipping his fingers free, he rolled on top of her, pushing up onto his forearms and straddling her legs with his own. Carly's outer thighs felt strong and sleek where the inner contours of his own rubbed along them, and he closed his eyes for a moment in sheer appreciation. His lids felt heavy even after he opened them to gaze down at her again.

She lay there staring back at him, her hair mussed, her cheeks flushed and her lips swollen from his kisses. He didn't think he'd ever seen a prettier sight. Afraid that the wet, sucking sound in his head was him getting drawn deeper and deeper into the quicksand of her spell, he stiffened, a frisson of unease crawling up his spine.

Then pride reared up to stomp it flat. He was firmly on top

of the situation. Literally. There was no need to feel edgy. "Seems to me I promised to lick you all over," he said silkily, and the helpless arousal in her eyes restored his tenuous control. "A man is only as good as his word, after all."

"Omigawd," she said faintly.

"No deities involved, Beauty. Just you and me." And he slipped downward, licking the lobe of her ear, then the shallow dent in her chin. Moving lower yet, he lapped at her throat and pressed his tongue flat against the rapid pulse beating in its hollow. He kissed the delicate arch of her collarbones and down the smooth-skinned plane of her chest. When he reached her breasts, he framed the heavy globes in his hands, pressing them against his cheeks as he tongued the resultant cleavage. He alternately licked and blew on her nipples, and when they drew into tight, straining beads, he grasped them between his thumbs and index fingers and gently tugged.

Carly moaned and her head dropped back.

He felt that moan clear down to his toes and had to shove his cock against the mattress to keep from thrusting it inside of her. Staving off temptation, he licked lazy figure eights down the smooth skin of her diaphragm. Pausing when he reached her navel, he lightly rimmed the deep indentation. Then he raised his head to gaze at his ultimate goal.

He'd never seen a woman as denuded of hair as Carly. He understood the reasoning behind it, since a showgirl's costumes weren't exactly known for their excess of material. But the narrow stripe of pale hair and bare feminine lips still struck him as so erotically charged that his eyes nearly crossed just trying to take it all in.

"Like what you see?"

He looked up to see Carly pushed up on her elbows, staring

down at him with languorous eyes. "Very much." He'd intended to skip past the main attraction to kiss his way down to her toes, but there was just something about her that brought out a latent need to dominate, and peeling the delicate lips of her labia open with his thumbs, he lowered his head.

Then, his gaze still locked with hers, he lapped the flat of his tongue along the revealed furrow from stem to stern.

She screamed his name and fisted her fingers in his hair, dragging his head back. "No more teasing," she panted. "I'm not kidding, Wolfgang. I want you inside me, right now. Don't make me hurt you."

"Right," he scoffed. "I'll probably lose a lot of sleep worrying about that."

In a sudden flurry of long legs she slid out from under him. They rolled to face each other, and even as he reached for her, she grabbed his cock and looked him in the eye. "Inside me, Jones. Now." Her fist tightened around him in implicit threat.

"You're the boss," he said, conceding the dominant position without a qualm. But as he turned to pull her atop him, he suddenly stopped and swore.

"Now what?" she demanded impatiently. "You want to be on top? Fine. But for heaven's sake—"

"No condom," he said. "I didn't plan on this and I don't have a goddamn condom!" He sure as hell wouldn't have teased himself into one big grievous hard-on if he'd remembered *that* little detail sooner.

She grinned at him. "Not to worry. I've got it covered. They might be a little on the old side, but we're not talking dangerously so." Climbing over him, she dove face-first to the far side of the bed, where she pulled open the nightstand drawer.

Her left foot was braced against his calf, and he looked at her sprawled out on her stomach with one arm outstretched and buried to the wrist in the compartment. "This is a view I haven't seen before." He ran his hand up the silky skin of her calf. "I like it."

"Yeah, my butt's almost as nice as yours." Pulling a dented box of condoms out of the drawer, she slithered back to a more stable position on the mattress and started to roll over.

Wolf grabbed her ankles and tugged her back to the middle of the bed, then climbed to his knees behind her. "I like this view a *lot*." He slid his fingers between her legs.

"Oh, God." Pushing up on all fours, she grabbed the box, shook a condom free and tossed it back to him. "Hurry."

He rolled on the protection, then lined himself up behind her. Air hissed through his teeth as he eased the head of his cock into her. "*Gott*. You are so creamy. So tight."

"More," she urged, lowering onto her elbows and pushing back against him, and he watched another inch disappear. "Please," she added, an unapologetic supplicant. "It feels so good."

Gripping her lush cheeks in his hands, he worked his hard-on into her until he was buried to the hilt. Then he pulled out until once again only the head remained inside of her.

And thrust back in.

She cried his name.

A feeling of power exploded in his chest, and instigating a rhythm, he stared down at her. Her knees were wide and her rump beneath his gripping fingers was high, lunging back to meet each thrust. The long, supple line of her back angled downward and her arms stretched flat from elbow to wrist, her hands gripping fistfuls of the comforter overhead. He could see the sides of her breasts where they were crushed against the mattress. Tightening his grip on her, he gritted his teeth against the drag of her swollen inner tissues as he withdrew once again. Then he drove back in and she was right there to meet him. The melodious moans that purled out of her throat and the escalating sound of their bodies slapping in rhythm was the tune he moved by. He could tell that she was close, but he feared he was closer.

"I want you to come for me, Beauty," he said. "Can you do that for me? You're so pretty like this, all flushed and turned on and out of control. I want to feel you coming all over me. I want to feel this sweet, little puss— Ah, Jesus, Carly!" His brain shorted out as her inner muscles began to spasm around him, clamping down like hot, wet fingers. He retracted his hips to pull out one final time, then slammed back in and ground against her, holding himself deep. The top of his head blew off, and groaning her name through clenched teeth, he came.

And came.

And came.

Until stunned, exhausted and quite possibly ruined for life, he toppled on her like a felled tree.

Sixteen

"I think we made decent progress tonight," Niklaus said as he and Natalie returned their pile of reference books to the biology stacks. He studied the pretty teenager from the corner of his eye.

"I know!" She shoved the last book onto the shelf and twisted toward him, her face alight. "Our project is gonna rock!"

She enthused over the enterprise while they gathered their book bags, then chatted about it the entire time it took them to reach the first floor of the starkly modern library and push through the entrance doors out onto the pale stone plaza. Finding himself effortlessly sucked into the conversation, Niklaus admitted he really liked that he never had to rack his brain to come up with clever stuff to say when he was with her.

Once they reached her car, however, she suddenly fell silent and stared at him over its roof. Staring back, he swallowed a lump in his throat and braced himself for the big brush-off. She was probably dying to dump him on his doorstep so she could go meet up with her friends.

She cleared her throat. "Would you mind terribly if we stopped at Burger King before I drop you off?" she asked. "I'm starving and my parents never have anything worth eating at home. They're into this totally disgusting macrobiotic crap."

Pleasure suffused him that she didn't intend to burn rubber to unload him as quickly as possible. "No, that sounds good."

They piled into the car and roared out of the parking lot. "I'm telling you," she said as she took a left onto West Sahara, "when your uncle offered me some of your Chinese food, I nearly dove headfirst into one of the cartons."

"No shit? You should have fixed yourself a plate."

"I was afraid I'd take one bite, lose control entirely and start stuffing it into my mouth as fast as I could until every last carton was emptied." She grinned over at him. "That might have been kind of hard to explain."

They pulled into the burger joint's parking lot a moment later and went inside. "Whoa," he said when their orders arrived. "You weren't kidding about that starving thing. Fries *and* onion rings?"

"So what's your excuse?" she demanded, nodding at his full tray as they wound through the tables to an empty booth in back. "At least I only got one Whopper."

"I'm a growing boy, I gotta keep up my energy." Sliding into the vacant booth, he watched her unload her meal onto the table across from him. "I got like two bites of Chinese food, and those burned off an hour ago. At least you probably got some brown rice or something else that sticks to your ribs."

"Why did you only have two bites when you had all those cartons of food?"

"We were supposed to eat earlier, but Carly was late getting there." Unwrapping the first of his burgers, he took a big bite and groaned ecstatically. "Now, this hits the spot. Great idea, Natalie."

"I know, doesn't it tastes wonderful?" Dabbing a French fry in the pool of ketchup she'd squeezed out onto her burger wrapper, she studied him. "So, about Carly," she said casually. "Is she a showgirl?"

"How'd you know that? Is that one of those women's intuition things, where you, like, get a flash or something?"

"That would be handy, wouldn't it?" A faint flush painted her cheeks pink. "But I heard you telling Kev Fitzpatrick and David Owens one day about having dinner with an Avventurato showgirl, so when your uncle introduced us tonight, I figured she must be the same one. She sure looks like a showgirl."

"Yeah, she's hot."

Popping the fry in her mouth, she drew patterns in the ketchup with a fresh one for a moment before glancing up at him through her lashes. "Is she your girlfriend?"

He barely avoided spewing Coke all over the table. Setting his cup carefully back on the tabletop, he swiped his mouth with a paper napkin. "Uh, no. We're just regular friends. I'm sort of hoping she and Uncle Wolf will click so he'll want to stick around Vegas." When Natalie gave him a questioning look, he shrugged. "I'm sick of moving every few months." Of course, changing residences might not be his primary problem if Wolf moved on and left him behind, but he didn't feel a pressing need to share that. "What made you think she was my girl?"

It was Natalie's turn to shrug. "I don't know. Something about the way you talked about her to your friends. As if you really, you know, loved her."

"I do. But mainly because she feeds me all the time and

never talks to me like I'm some stupid kid. Plus, she's got all these really great pets she's rescued from different places. She's got two cats, one who's only got three legs, and these two smokin' dogs—Buster, who's the goofiest-looking mutt you've ever seen, and Rufus—" He stopped, suddenly remembering. "No, only one dog now, I guess. She gave Rufus to some kid today."

"She *gave away* her dog?"

Part of him appreciated the incredulousness in Natalie's voice. Clearly she agreed with his opinion that relinquishing Rufus was just plain wrong.

A larger part, however, decided that only he got to criticize Carly. "Yeah, but to this little boy with cancer who was going home today after having been in the hospital for months." He related what he knew about the pet-therapy program. "That's why she was late, apparently. She was crying and stuff about giving up Rufus and forgot all about our dinner until Uncle Wolf went and got her." He shook his head. "But let's not talk about her. I want to know about you. Tell me about this macrobiotic thing."

She grimaced. "Trust me, you don't want to know. Let's talk about moving around a lot instead. How many places have you lived?"

He hitched a shoulder. "You got me. I lost track by the time I was about eight."

"Just hit some of the highlights, then."

He ate a fry and took another sip of Coke while he thought about it. "I've lived in every state except Nebraska, Oklahoma, Alaska, Hawaii and Iowa. Oh, yeah, and Florida. Then we spent about three months in Belgium and another—"

"You and your uncle?" She planted her chin in her palm and stared at him as if he were some globe-trotting rock star.

"No, me and my mom. This is the first time I've lived with Uncle Wolf."

"That's such a totally cool name. I have an Uncle *Bill*."

"It's short for Wolfgang. My mother is Katarina." He gave it its proper German pronunciation.

"And you pronounce yours Niklaus, instead of Nicolas. That's so much more exotic than the usual Brandon or Peter that we hear around here."

He shrugged as if it were no big deal. "Grandma's Bavarian and Mom carried on the tradition of German names," he said in an offhand tone. Inside, however, he was giving himself high fives. She could have used any number of names, but she'd said Peter, and he was pleased to hear himself come out on the favorable end of any comparison with Asshole Rushman.

She stared at him with bright, interested eyes. "How about other foreign countries? Have you lived anywhere besides Belgium?"

"Yeah, we spent another couple of months in Amsterdam. My grandfather has worked for a bunch of embassies, and since my mom is the biggest flake in the universe, I've lived with him and Grandma in Santiago, Botswana and Latvia. They're in Bolivia right now. I haven't actually lived there, but I spent last Christmas with them."

"God. That is so cool! I've never been *anywhere*. I lived my entire life in Armpit, South Dakota, until my dad decided to move us here for the weather and the golf. And even if your mother's a flake, I bet she at least lets you eat regular food. My folks have made a lifestyle out of trying to stay young— and not much else. Your people see the world and represent the country."

"But not like the ambassador does, or anything," he felt compelled to admit. "Grandpa's just a supply clerk."

"Still. *Santiago*. Geography's not exactly my strong suit, so while I know that's in South or maybe Central America, I'm not sure precisely where. But it just sounds like it's somewhere tropical."

"It's the capital of Chile. On the west coast of South America." He'd never considered his nomadic existence the way Natalie appeared to see it, as a "lifestyle" that other people would find interesting and exciting. He'd simply hated the loneliness of never-ending uprootings and detested the insecurity of his mother's skewed idea of fiscal responsibility, which pretty much consisted of an indifferent shrug and a careless "Don't you worry, baby, something will come along."

Yet the prettiest girl he'd ever clapped eyes on appeared fascinated by his experiences.

He watched her as he finished his first burger and reached for the second. She acted almost as if she liked him or something, and for a moment he contemplated finding out if that were so—or at least asking point-blank what the story was between her and Superjerk. He couldn't figure out if they were dating or what. But if they weren't, maybe *he* and Natalie—

Then he quit fantasizing and got real.

What difference did it make? She might think he was intriguing as all get-out because he'd lived all over the world. Hell, she might even think he was the hottest stud to ever hit Silverado High. But other than a gratifying stroke to his ego, where would that get him?

Probably shipped off to yet another school in yet another state before he even got the chance to kiss her. Or even worse, it would turn out she actually did like him and he'd finally get the girl of his dreams for his very own. *Then* he'd be shipped off to Timbuktu.

His mood turned black. What the hell was he doing letting himself get all invested in friendships with *anyone* at this school? You'd think he'd know better than that by now. Because sooner or later Uncle Wolf would leave and he'd be left scrambling for a place to call home. Or Mom would show up and yank him out of here to go set up digs with her in some city halfway across the continent. Any way he looked at it, putting everything he had on the line was a dangerous proposition. It was just asking to be knifed in the gut when things fell apart on him—which they would. And as bad as things had been in the past, at least he hadn't had any kind of meaningful relationship to lose. No, this was bound to be way more painful than usual.

He'd be smarter all around to step back while he still had the chance.

Throwing his half-eaten burger onto its paper wrapper, he slid out of the booth. "You about done there?" he demanded when Natalie gaped up at him, her drink suspended halfway to her lips. Picking up his tray, he jutted his chin toward the door. "'Cause I've still got a ton of homework left to do tonight and I gotta get going."

The janitor felt restless and at loose ends as he headed to the hotel lobby to begin his shift. Last week he'd discovered that Wednesday was one of his darling Carly's nights off, so now an entire evening stretched ahead of him without hope of seeing her. No wonder he felt jittery. He'd gone more than forty-eight hours without a glimpse of her.

It was clearly time to find out where his showgirl lived so he could quit suffering through these cheerless, Carlyless days. And once they were an official couple…well, he would simply have to talk to her about quitting her job. Not that he expected any in-depth dialogue on the subject. She needed to be more accessible when he wished for her company.

There were days when he longed for a confidant with whom he could discuss her. It would be nice to talk about his woman the way he heard the other guys around the locker room talking about theirs. Unfortunately there wasn't anyone with whom he shared that kind of relationship. Oh, *he* could always talk to Dr. Asher, but he would merely start throwing around shrink expressions like *harassment* and *unrealistic goals*.

Garbage, in other words. He wasn't harassing anyone. And what was so unrealistic about expecting the woman you adored to adore you in return?

Seventeen

Wolf was having a great dream. A fragrant woman was snuggled against him, and he felt satiated and mellow and better than he ever remembered feeling in his life. A shapely butt spooned into his lap, a warm back pressed against his front. His arm was a diagonal bar wrapped around the woman in his embrace, and groggily he lifted his hand to cup the full breast grazing his knuckles. It was both firm and giving beneath his palm and his fingers tightened possessively. A satisfied growl rumbled in his throat.

Hearing it made him realize this was no dream and he pried his eyes open. What the hell? For a disoriented moment all he could comprehend was that he was in a dark room and indeed in bed with a soft-skinned, firm-bodied female.

Then the lingering fog of sleep dissipated and he remembered everything. Finding Carly crying. Dinner. The most-out-of-control, mind-boggling sex he'd ever known. No wonder he felt as if a thief had stolen in and appropriated every bone in his body. Hell, who needed a skeletal system, anyway? As long as blood flowed to the proper organ, they were in business. Carly could always supply the motion. She was incredibly flexible. Very fit.

As he was contentedly mulling over the most effective way he could wake her up already primed and in the mood, a flash of Niklaus as he'd looked escorting his pretty lab partner out of the apartment darted across his mind's eye. "Shit!" Whipping his arm free, he rolled for the side of the bed.

"What's wrong?" Carly's voice, husky with sleep, was an almost inaudible mumble from the darkness at his back. She cleared her throat. "Wolf?"

"What time is it?" he demanded. "Dammit, I can't tell what time it is!" The stygian surroundings prevented him from making out the face of his stainless-steel tank watch, so it could be anywhere from the middle of the night to close to dawn. For all he knew, Niklaus had been left alone next door the entire night.

The bedclothes rustled, then her voice, closer and more alert than it had been an instant ago, said, "Relax. My alarm clock says it's nine-thirty, and considering how dark it is in here, that's got to be p.m. I think we've only been asleep about an hour."

Tension released its steely grip on his shoulders. "All right, good. That's good." But his mellow mood was destroyed. "Where is the light?"

"There's a lamp on the nightstand."

Locating it, he snapped it on. Then he turned to face her.

She was propped on one elbow, the sheet pulled snug over the thrust of her breasts. Her hair was flattened on one side and sticking up on the other, her eyes had smudges of mascara beneath them and her lips were slightly puffy.

He desperately wanted to pull her under him and take up where they'd left off.

Muscles beneath his skin twitched at the strength of that desire, and he said flatly, "We can't do this again." He'd taught himself a long time ago to step back from any emotion that included too much need.

Something passed across her expression but was gone before he could interpret it, and when her gaze met his, her blue eyes were steady and self-possessed. She inclined her head. "All right."

That was it? *All right?* Instead of feeling grateful that she wasn't making a fuss, he found himself irritated. "I've got a plan for my life," he said, as if she'd argued with him. "And this—" he indicated the two of them with blunt stabs of his forefinger "—is not part of it."

"Yes, you've mentioned that before." She climbed from the other side of the bed with a complete lack of concern for her nudity and bent to scoop her discarded panties off the floor. Tying their side ribbons into floppy bows, she glanced over at him and raised her eyebrows inquiringly. "Would you care to share what your plan is?" Stepping into the delicate underwear, she pulled them up her long legs.

The sight of her—tight little butt, high, full breasts, messy hair and bee-stung lips—made him want to grind his teeth and howl. "I'm going to head security in a corporation somewhere far away from the glitzy craziness of Vegas." He hesitated, then, deciding to put temptation beyond his reach once and for all, he looked her in the eye and added, "Then when I'm reasonably established, I'm going to find someone who fits into the corporate milieu and marry her."

"Good for you," she said, looking around for something, then shrugging and pulling her gauzy top on over her head. "I wish you luck with that. Personally, I can't think of anything more stifling than being a good little corporate wife, but then, that's just me. My lifetime goal has pretty much been to avoid marriage entirely."

"Why?" He was truly shocked, and perhaps a little nettled by her attitude. "I thought all women wanted to get married."

"Please." She made a face that broadcast *get real* loud and clear even if it wasn't verbalized. "The prince who takes the poor hardworking girl 'away from it all' is a crock. There is no life of leisure. One way or another, all women pay a price for their upkeep. If marriage is the compensation most want in return, more power to them. It's just never been my dream to be the princess in some guy's ivory tower. I'd rather be queen of my own little abode, modest though it may be. Because while I might not have help paying the bills, I alone get to decide what goes on within these four walls."

She regarded him without apparent rancor. "So in that spirit, know that I chose to sleep with you tonight. It was great and I loved it. But you're probably right. When it comes right down to it, you and I are two very different people. We had our fling, scratched our itch, and now we're agreed. No hard feelings and no more sex. Right?"

Biting back an instinctive protest, he nodded crisply. "Right."

She gave him a decisive little dip of her own chin in return. "It's definitely better to stop while we're ahead." Circling the bed, she halted in front of where he still sat on the edge of the mattress and leaned down to give him a quick, soft kiss on the mouth. The thin cloth of her top whispered over her bare breasts as she straightened. "Thanks for one of the hottest nights of my life," she whispered, and turned away to walk toward the bathroom. Pausing at the door, she looked back at him. "Do me a favor and lock the front door on your way out, will you?"

The latch catching was an audible snick in the silent room as she firmly shut the door between them. Wolf stayed where he was for a frozen moment, wondering if he'd just side-stepped a lethal pitfall on his meticulously mapped road to the future.

Or if he'd detoured from a path to somewhere less well planned but infinitely more interesting.

No. Absolutely not. He surged to his feet and looked around for his pants. Locating them at the foot of the bed, he jerked them on. Of course he hadn't. He'd set his course years ago, and he was getting closer to achieving his goals all the time. Incredible sex simply wasn't reason enough to jettison everything he'd been working for since he was sixteen years old.

Unearthing his shirt from beneath the comforter that had slid off Carly's side of the bed, he yanked it on but didn't bother buttoning it. When the shirttail hung up in back, he reached behind him to untangle it. His hand brushed something both cobweb soft and rigidly structured, and he pulled her bra out of his back pocket. For one long moment as he stood staring down at the garment of subtly striped satin, underwire shaping and brass-buckled shimmering straps, flashes of the two of them up against the door and on the bed accelerated across his mental screen with strobe-light rapidity.

Then he shook the memories aside, carefully smoothed the bra flat and laid it atop the nearest chest of drawers. Letting himself out of her bedroom, he headed for the door.

Putting an end to this now was the best solution for both of them.

Eighteen

Carly arrived at Treena's apartment first thing the following morning. She was so focused on getting to her friend that she blinked when Jax answered her urgent rap on the door.

"Well, hey there," he said, stepping back to admit her. "Who would've guessed it was you on our doorstep?" Flashing her a sideways glance, he gave her a crooked smile. "I didn't realize you even knew how to knock."

"Try to keep up, Gallagher," she advised, breezing past him into the small entryway. "I always assumed a hotshot like you made your killing on the poker circuit by paying attention to the details. Apparently not, or you would've noticed that I quit letting myself in the day I walked in to find you all over my best friend on the credenza. That was more education than I ever cared to get, thank you very much." She headed straight for the living room, but Treena wasn't there. She whirled back to face the big man ambling in her wake. "Don't tell me Treen hasn't rousted her butt out of bed yet."

"Hey," her pal called from down the short hallway. "I'll have you know I've been up for hours."

"Or a good fifteen minutes, anyhow," Jax murmured.

"I heard that, bud. Carly, c'mon back."

She strode down the hall, pausing in the bedroom doorway to stare at Treena on her hands and knees in her closet—or more accurately at her friend's Levi's-clad calves and bare feet, since that was the sum total that was visible. Over the rustle of the other woman's activity inside the confined space, she demanded, "What are you doing?"

"Looking for my other Mephisto." Treena thrust her hand around the slider door to wag a thong-style, rosette-adorned red leather sandal. "It's gotta be in here somewhere. The damn thing didn't just up and walk away."

"Well, look for it later. I need to talk."

"Uh-oh." The furious activity within the closet ceased. "That's your serious voice." Treena backed out, her pale red curls absorbing the light as she came under the overhead fixture. "What's up?"

Now that she had her friend's undivided attention, Carly wasn't quite sure where to start. "I had an…eventful day yesterday."

"Eventful how?"

"Well, first of all, Iago Hernandez was finally released from the hospital, so I took the babies down to give him a proper send-off. And somehow in all the festivities—" she cleared her throat "—I ended up giving him Rufus."

"What?" Treena shot to her feet and crossed the room to tug Carly over to her bed. They sat side by side on the edge as the redhead carefully scrutinized her. "Are you all right?"

Carly conducted a quick but thorough soul search and realized she was at least more acclimated to the decision this morning. "Yeah, I am. Or I will be, anyhow. It was the right thing to do." Working to project a confidence that was, in all honesty, on shaky ground, she explained the circumstances that had led to relinquishing Rufus to the recovering child.

"Still," Treena said when she'd finished. "I know how crazy you were about that mutt. It had to be a blow to turn him over to the kid, no matter how well they hit it off."

"It hurt like crazy," she confessed. "I was such a mess by the time I got home yesterday afternoon that I had a major meltdown and forgot all about Niklaus having invited me for dinner until Wolfgang came roaring over to get me. And that's the other thing, Treen. It was clear he hadn't had any previous warning that I'd even been invited, but when he saw the shape I was in, he was amazingly gentle and nice. So when Nik not only stuck him with paying for a delivered meal but then turned around and skipped out on dinner himself to go to the library with a cute girl from school, I responded in kind by trying to bow out."

"Whoa." Treena stared at her. "That's so adult of the two of you it's almost scary."

"I know. And it gets even more adult. Because Wolf wouldn't hear of me leaving without eating, and we actually had a really nice dinner together. He has a sense of humor, Treena, which I never would have guessed. He walked me home after dinner and even said something nice about Rufus. Then he kissed me and the next thing I knew we were doing the hootchie-kootch. And it was so freaking intense we both fell asleep afterward out of sheer exhaustion and—"

"Whoa, whoa, whoa, *whoa!* Back up there, cowgirl. You had *sex* with Wolfgang Jones?"

"Yeah." She smiled reminiscently. "Head-banging, burn-up-the-sheets sex."

"Good God." Treena simply stared at her for a moment, then her mouth ticked up on one side. "So, the Carly

Jacobsen dry spell is officially over. That's a good thing, right?"

"It was a fabulous thing…until he woke up all in a lather saying we couldn't do it again because it didn't fit into his plan." She turned her head to look at her friend. "What he meant was *I* didn't fit into his plan."

"Excuse me?" Treena demanded indignantly. "Who the hell does he think he is? If the man has some big, mysterious agenda whose criteria you don't fit, why doesn't he stop putting his hands all over you?"

"Excellent question. Although I did discover what his goal is, so that's no longer a mystery." She told Treena about Wolfgang's desire to be head of security somewhere other than Vegas.

"Okay." Treena nodded. "Vegas isn't for everyone. But what does that have to do with you and him doing the hootchie-kootch until he leaves?"

"Apparently he's afraid I'll get ideas about a more permanent relationship." Succinctly she outlined his intention to find the perfect corporate wife once his first objective was accomplished.

"He's looking for a *Stepford* wife?" Treena stared at her. "Lord. He has so got the wrong woman."

Carly snorted her agreement. "Which is why I wished him well and generally gave him the bum's rush out of my apartment. Considering my first impulse involved a shallow grave deep in the desert, I'm thinking he got off easy. I mean, the sex was beyond good, but no man gets to enjoy a piece of me then turn around and virtually tell me that while I'm good enough to screw six ways from Sunday, I'm not good enough for his stinking plans for the future."

She refused to acknowledge that, somewhere deep inside, hurt was a splinter lodged in her psyche. Doing so would churn up far too many older memories of being told she didn't measure up and she'd said "No" a long time ago to ever being that vulnerable again. So, insisting to herself that it was merely wounded pride she felt, she added acerbically, "As if I were thinking of picking out my frigging silver pattern, anyway."

This time it was Treena who snorted. But her eyes narrowed in outrage when she said, "Jax knows someone with a nail gun who's not afraid to use it. Want us to give the guy a call?"

Her heart lightening at Treena's ferocious indignation on her behalf, Carly gave her a slight smile and leaned in to butt shoulders. "Thanks for the offer, but really, the hell with Jones. It's not like I expected this to last more than a night or two, anyway. Frankly, with anything as hot and out of control as what we generated last night, we were bound to burn out pretty fast, so I probably didn't miss out on much. I wouldn't have minded a few more sessions before then, but easy come, easy go."

"So to speak."

Her smile grew marginally wider. "Yeah, no pun intended. Anyhow, from now on, toots, I intend to stay so far away from the man he's gonna think we live on two different continents."

"What about Niklaus?"

"Oh, I won't let him down," she promptly vowed, surprised at how quickly the teen had forged a place in her heart. "I'll just have to see him when his plan-happy uncle is somewhere else." When another stab of hurt attacked out of the blue, she once again assigned it a different name and shoved it to the farthest recesses of her mind.

Yet Treena, who saw past her defenses as if she had X-ray vision, slung an arm around her and gave her a fierce squeeze.

"I'm sorry," she said softly. "You want to hang out with us until it's time to leave for work?"

Carly loved her to pieces for the invitation, but the last thing she thought she could handle today was being odd woman out in her friend's blindingly successful relationship. "No. Thanks. I appreciate it, but I mostly just needed to vent a while." She took comfort in the other woman's embrace for an instant longer, then straightened. "I have a load of laundry I plan on sneaking down to the exercise room to dry, then I think I'll take Buster out for a walk."

"Why not use your own dryer?"

"Because the damn thing up and quit on me last night."

"My God, poor baby! You did have an eventful time of it, didn't you?"

"Yeah." Coming on top of everything else that had happened yesterday, the dryer's sudden failure had pretty much been the last straw. "Mack said he'll take a look at it, but he probably won't be able to get to it until tomorrow at the soonest. Meanwhile I've got a soggy load of towels that I washed last night in lieu of hurling dishes at the wall."

"Bring them over here."

"Aw, Treen, I adore you for offering, but I've still got a heap of leftover aggression I need to work off. That's why I plan on throwing the towels in the gym dryer and doing a circuit or two on the weight machines while they cook. But *thank you* for being here. I don't know what I'd do if I didn't have you to run to." As she rose to her feet, a slice of red leather peeking out from beneath the nightstand caught her eye.

"If I'm not mistaken," she said, happy to direct her friend's attention to something other than her pitiful problems, "there's your missing shoe."

* * *

Forty-five minutes later, ensconced in the well-equipped exercise room, she finally began feeling more like herself again. For the past half hour she'd gone from one weight machine to the next, monitoring herself in the mirror for proper form as she worked each set, and sweating out her ire to the homey accompaniment of the appliance tumbling her towels dry in the little utility room to the rear of the gym. When the exterior door suddenly opened behind her, she was busy counting down the final reps on her last set of squats and didn't bother checking to see who had come in.

Then the unnatural silence where the clatter of another exerciser selecting weights should have been made the short hairs on her nape abruptly stand on end. Pushing erect, she slowly raised her gaze to look beyond her own posture in the wall of mirrors directly in front of her.

Wolf's reflection stared back at her, and her heart contracted so tightly it felt as if it might never pump normally again. Seeing him standing in the doorway made all the pain she'd been busy denying wash over her in an unstoppable wave.

Her gaze snapping back to her own reflection, she resumed her squats on the Smith machine, even though it was an additional set she didn't need. But he was *not* going to drive her off. It would be a frigid day in hell before she'd let Mr. I've-got-a-plan Jones know he'd hurt her.

In fact...

Don't get mad. Get even. Eyes narrowing, she shot him another glance. What the big jerk needed was a taste of his own medicine—and she was just the woman to administer it. Surging upright for the last time, she braked the bar, then stepped away from the machine.

"Hello, Wolfgang," she said coolly as she reached for the

hem of her crop top. Peeling it off over her head, she used it to pat her face dry, then hung it from the end of the bar where she'd ordinarily add or subtract the weight plates. The air-conditioning immediately cooled the film of sweat she'd worked up, and its sudden chill against her overheated skin caused her nipples to harden behind the damp, thin material of her orange sports bra. "Just couldn't stay away from me, huh?"

His gaze zeroed in on her breasts for a moment before jerking up to her face. He scowled at her. "I am not following you. I had no idea you were even in here."

"Ah. I guess it's simply a case of great minds thinking alike, then. Well, why not? It's a good day for a workout."

He gave her a curt nod but didn't otherwise respond, and that very retreat back into his previous antisocial terseness was all the spark of encouragement Carly needed. She and Wolf had some extreme, volatile chemistry percolating between them. She'd give a bundle to deny its existence, but that train had come and gone. So, fine. If she couldn't declare their chemistry untrue, she could at least use it to her advantage. Despite what he'd implied last night, Wolfgang clearly wasn't any more immune to her than she was to him.

Without bothering to lower the bar on the Smith machine from its present shoulder-height position, she raised her left leg and hooked her heel over it. Leaning forward, she skimmed her hands along the outside of her knee to her calf to her ankle, until she was loosely cupping the bottom of her flexed foot in both hands while pressing her upper body flat against her thigh. The stretch felt good, and for just a moment she forgot all about Wolf. Then movement, caught from out of the corner of her eye, recalled her to the matter at hand.

He was seated astride a padded bench several feet away doing biceps curls. But his attention was riveted on her.

Good. Because she planned on getting him all hot and bothered, then walking away. And if there was a God in heaven, Wolfgang Jones would be left with a raging case of blue balls so severe he wouldn't walk upright for days. *That* would go a long way toward ameliorating her bruised…well, not heart—she refused to admit he'd wounded her heart— but her bruised feelings. Yes. It would placate the emotions he hadn't thought twice about stomping into paste last night. In fact, payback might even be amusing.

She applied the same stretch to her other leg, then turned to face Wolf directly. Balancing on her right foot, knees together, she bent her left foot up behind her, reaching back with both hands to grasp her instep and pull it toward her torso until her heel pressed against her butt. The position pulled her shoulders back and thrust her breasts out, and she gazed down at him impassively as if she didn't know exactly the effect the quad stretch had on her posture.

Then her eyebrows furrowed and she released her clasped foot and switched legs. He looked really good, damn him. He was wearing a gray muscle shirt and those disreputable cutoffs that just turned her to jelly, and he looked fit and sexy and ready to rumble. It didn't help that he kept his green-eyed gaze raised to stare at her as he leaned forward with his right elbow pressed against the long, hard inner muscle of a wide-spread thigh, his biceps straining beneath the heavy weight that he slowly curled up to his chest before straightening toward the floor again. A mist of sweat began to sheen his skin.

The idiocy of her so-called plan hit her like a wrecking ball out of the blue. Good God, what was she thinking? This was just plain stupid, like carelessly swinging a double-edged sword when it was just as likely to slice her to ribbons as it was to inflict any lasting damage on him.

It was time to concede defeat and get the hell out of here while she still had a modicum of dignity intact.

Dropping her foot, she shook out her hands and legs, then turned away from Wolf to fold forward into a simple palms-on-the-floor yoga stretch. There was nothing provocative about the movement, it was merely a good basic hamstring stretch with which to end a workout.

For Wolf, however, it was the final straw. Slamming down the twenty-five-pound dumbbell, he surged to his feet. "That does it!" he snarled, beside himself with frustration. He'd imposed an iron grip on the Jones wild streak when it had begun straining at its leash the moment he'd walked in and seen Carly, but enough was enough.

When she whirled to face him, the look on her face sent a lifetime of careful control slamming up against his emotional boundaries. It hesitated for less than a second before hurling itself over the edge like a lemming into the sea. "Don't give me that innocent-eyed look! You know damn well what you're doing, waving your tight little ass in front of my face."

Something hot and furious flashed across her expression, but almost immediately she gave him a haughty stare so frigid he nearly froze in his tracks. "According to you, champ, you're *through* with my tight little ass."

"Because of my plan!" Not because he'd *wanted* to be, that was for damn sure—and admitting it made him edgier still.

"Well, excuse the hell out of me if I think your plan sucks!" Taking an enraged step forward, she got right in his face. "You all but told me I'm good enough for a quick fuck but not for anything long term. Like I ever wanted to marry your sorry ass in the first place!" Then she stepped back, and with a look that said clearer than words that she didn't consider him worth wasting further breath on, she whirled and marched with long-legged strides toward the back of the gym.

He followed hard on her heels. He'd said that? That's not the way he'd meant it, although with her punk-rocker hair, showgirl body and say-whatever-the-hell-popped-into-her-mind mouth she wasn't even close to the type of woman he envisioned as his future helpmate. Still, he opened his mouth to let her know it wasn't because he thought she wasn't good enough, but rather that he didn't see her as a woman who'd be happy with the order of business he had in mind. Instead, he was appalled to hear himself demand, "Why wouldn't you marry me?"

"Was I talking to myself yesterday?"she snapped without turning to look at him. "I told you I don't intend to tie myself to anyone, let alone to someone so tight-assed there's no room in his life for anything that doesn't conform with his stupid plan." She stalked into a small utility room in the back, where she started hauling towels from the dryer and tossing them into a basket.

He grabbed her forearm and swung her around to face him. "My plan is not stupid! It's the only thing that kept me going when my dad's job dragged me from one fucking elitist embassy to the next. It's the goal I've worked toward my entire adult life!"

"Bully for you." She twisted her arm free but didn't retreat an inch. Thrusting her nose up beneath his, she said flatly, "That doesn't make it any less cold-blooded and soulless."

"As opposed to what? Your chaos theory approach to life? How is that working out for you?"

"Very well, thank you. Unlike you, I've got my friends and my babies and…oh yeah, a little hot blood running through my veins to keep me from freezing to death beneath the weight of a nuclear-winter personality."

A red mist obscured everything but the infuriating, exciting woman in front of him. "You want hot-blooded, *Liebling?* I'll show you hot-blooded!" Operating purely on instinct, he speared his fingers through her short blond hair and slammed his mouth down on hers.

Carly's ill-conceived I'm-gonna-make-him-hot-then-leave-him-flat project went up in flames at the first blistering touch of Wolfgang's lips. Snaking her arms around his neck, she opened her mouth beneath the rough demand of his and moaned when his tongue made immediate, aggressive inroads into the territory she'd conceded. A corresponding groan rumbled in Wolf's chest and his long fingers tightened against her scalp.

Endless minutes later he ripped his mouth free. They stared at each other, their breath sawing loudly in and out of their lungs.

"Dammit," he muttered hoarsely, kicking the utility room door shut. "I can't get enough of you." Grasping her hips, he lifted her onto the washing machine and stepped between her knees when she promptly widened them to make room.

Wrapping her legs around his waist, she crossed her ankles behind his butt and yanked him close. His erection smacked up against the soft, giving notch at the apex of her thighs and they both sucked in air. Then Wolf went into a flurry of activity, pushing her sports bra up until it bunched beneath her armpits, bending his head to suck a straining nipple into his mouth and divesting her of her spandex shorts and panties. An instant later, he freed himself from his cutoffs and thrust into her welcoming heat. Her head dropped back as he stretched up inside of her and she whispered a fervent "Oh, my God."

Five minutes later, sinking her fingernails into the firm

skin on either side of his waist to anchor herself, she screamed the same words. A moment after that, Wolf started doing some pretty powerful praying of his own. Then his hands released their iron-fingered grip on her butt and slapped down on the washer lid on either side of her hips as his forehead thunked down on hers.

Another instant went by before he stiffened and snarled, "Aw, *shit!*"

Her heart sank. If he mentioned his damn plan and how she didn't fit into it again, she was going to seriously hurt him. "What?" she demanded, bracing herself.

"I forgot a condom." Pulling out of her, he pulled up his jeans. "God, I am so sorry, Carly, but—"

"Crap!" She scrambled upright, frantically counting back. Then she relaxed. "No, we're okay. I think we're okay."

He looked down at her, his beautifully shaped eyebrows furrowed over the strong thrust of his nose as he watched her wrestle down her sports bra and reach for her discarded undies. "But if we're not—"

"We'll deal with it then. I'm generally regular as a Swiss clock, though, so I'm almost positive we dodged the bullet."

"Good." He gazed at her in silence for a second. Then he said, "I promise you it won't happen again."

She kept her face impassive, even as a knot began to form in her stomach. "What won't happen? Making love without protection or making love at all?"

A sarcastic bark of laughter escaped him. "I think you just got a firsthand demonstration of how well I stay away from you."

"That's true, you're not doing so hot," she agreed, the knot slowly unraveling. "You really ought to take a lesson from me because I'm so much better at keeping my distance."

A crooked smile played at the corners of his lips. "So, no

more going at it like minks without the proper protection, agreed? I'm having enough trouble parenting Nik."

"Agreed." She studied him a minute, then cleared her throat. "I want you to know," she said, pulling on her panties and climbing down from the washing machine to tug her shorts up her legs, "that you really don't have to worry about me making demands on you in the matrimonial department. Watching my mother go from rich to even richer husbands in a carefully plotted campaign that Alexander the Great would have envied taught me that marriage is the last thing I want in my own life. I meant it when I told you I get my kicks from being responsible for myself."

"So what do you suggest, then? That we be lovers for a while?"

"Yes. I like Vegas, you don't. You have an agenda for your future that doesn't include me, and that suits me right down to the ground. Obviously even if we were interested, we're not cut out for the long term." She laid her right hand in the center of his chest, smiling with pleasure at the tactile feel of tough muscle and smooth skin beneath her fingertips. "We definitely share a flammable chemistry, though. So I propose we indulge it until we burn the damn thing out. Then once we do, or when your dream opportunity comes through—whichever happens first—we say goodbye like adults. No recriminations and no regrets." She pressed a quick kiss into the hollow of his throat, then raised her gaze to his. "Do we have a deal?"

He gazed back down at her, his face impassive. He opened his mouth as if to say something, then closed it without speaking. He opened it once more, then closed it again.

Finally he nodded. "Deal," he agreed.

"Good," she said, relieved beyond measure that he'd

agreed. That made her feel the need to compensate, so she made her voice extra detached and efficient when she said, "Then, here are a few rules I propose we follow."

Still poker-faced, he heard her out. He only had one rule of his own to add. "What happens here stays here," he said coolly. "We keep our sex life separate from work."

Of course, she thought with a trace of bitterness. Heaven forbid anything should interfere with his precious job.

Then she gave herself a mental smack. He was hardly asking a big concession from her. Keeping their relationship out of the workplace was, in fact, in the spirit of what she'd proposed. And it wasn't as if she had some huge desire to spread their relationship around the casino. "Agreed," she said.

He stared down at her a moment, then nodded firmly. "Right," he said without inflection. "Agreed." And leaning down, he cupped her face in his long hands and sealed their arrangement with a kiss that blew all the rules to oblivion, if only for that moment.

Nineteen

Dr. Gloom was whistling. Freaking *whistling*. Niklaus glowered at Wolfgang's back as his uncle grilled a couple of cheese sandwiches in the kitchen. What did he have to be so damn cheerful about?

As if he could read Nik's mind, Wolf glanced over his shoulder. "Move your stuff," he said, indicating the work that Nik had spread across the breakfast bar so he could figure out what he needed to take with him to the library after dinner. His uncle slipped the spatula beneath one of the sandwiches and checked its golden underside before lifting it from the frying pan onto a plate. "These are done to perfection, if I do say so myself. You want milk?"

"Yeah, whatever." Stuffing everything back into his pack, he shoved the bag out of the way.

Wolf set his plate in front of him, then grabbed a shallow bowl out of the fridge and slapped it onto the counter between their usual places. "Look at this. Apples!" He turned away to grab his own plate and glass of milk.

"Yeah, you're a regular goddamn Harry Homemaker." Nik plucked a slice out of the bowl and consumed half of it in one bite.

"I know. Scary, isn't it?" Wolf rounded the end of the breakfast bar and climbed onto his stool. Picking up his sandwich, he gave Niklaus a sideways glance. "Carly said you need more fruit and vegetables in your diet." He bit into his grilled cheese.

For just a second the bleak mood that had been hovering over Nik's head like his own personal thundercloud lightened. Maybe his plan to throw Uncle Wolf and Carly together was panning out, after all. Maybe things actually would work out the way he wanted them to.

Yeah, and maybe pigs would frigging fly. He stuffed the fruitless hope into a far, dark corner of his mind where it couldn't raise painful expectations.

"So, you're going to the library with Natalie again tonight?" Wolf asked, half rising off the stool to reach over the bar for the napkins on the shelf below. Settling back into his seat, he handed one to Nik.

"Yeah."

"How is your project coming along?"

He shrugged and started eating faster. "It's coming."

Wolf studied him for a minute, and Nik half expected to get an earful for his lack of cooperation in holding up his end of the conversation. He geared himself up for a confrontation, but his uncle merely said, "What time do you plan to be home?"

Part of him wanted to say something civil, but the mood riding him, fueled by tar-black anger, made him snap, "I don't know. It's Friday. I'll be home by curfew."

His uncle gave him a level-eyed look that had him squirming in his seat until Wolf finally turned back to his meal without further comment. They ate in silence for several moments.

Then Wolf wiped his mouth on his napkin. "Natalie seems very nice," he commented neutrally.

Nik grunted.

"Pretty, too."

His gut knotting up, he kept his attention focused on his dwindling dinner.

"She dating anyone special?"

There was the million-dollar question. "Dunno."

"She's working on a project with you on a Friday night, so my guess would be not?" Wolf turned to face him, his eyebrows raised. "Are you two—"

"What is it with the thousand and one questions?" Tossing down his napkin, he pushed back from the breakfast bar. "You a goddamn Las Vegas gossip columnist now or something? Well, here's the entire scoop—you got your notebook? Because you might want to write this down. Natalie's a cheerleader and she's gotta be at the stadium by eight-thirty. So we're meeting early. To work. I don't know who she's dating. I don't know what her plans are for after the football game. And what the hell do you care, anyway, about any of it? What's it to you how my project is going or who Natalie is dating?"

Wolf swiveled to face him. "Nik—"

"I've gotta go." Refusing to feel guilty about the baffled look on his uncle's face, he snatched his bag off the end of the counter and headed for the door. "I've got a bus to catch, since someone I know won't even discuss lending me his car."

Wolf followed him into the foyer. "I'd be happy to give you a ride. I have to get to work myself."

"Don't do me any frigging favors, okay? I can take care of

myself just fine." Furious and not really certain why, he ripped open the door and barreled through it, taking a grim satisfaction in slamming it in his uncle's face.

He nursed his anger all the way to the library. But when he walked upstairs and saw Natalie's smile when she spotted him walking across the room toward her, something inside of him brightened.

Thinking back to what Uncle Wolf had said about her being at the library with him on a Friday night when she could be out getting I'm-too-cool-for-the-rest-of-you-fools Rushman all pumped up for the game, he felt even better. Then he gave himself a stern talking-to. Because even if a miracle should happen and it turned out that she somehow liked him more than Rushman, so what? The same reasons to avoid getting too close to her applied every bit as much tonight as they had on Wednesday. And he was *damned* if he would ever willingly put himself in a position where any girl had the power to rip his heart from his chest by its roots.

He'd watched his mom do exactly that too many times to want to experience it himself.

So fine, he had his head on straight, then. He was cool. He knew exactly what level his association with Natalie Fremont belonged on, and it was superficial with a capital Supe. One project partner to another.

And not one goddamn thing else.

He blessed the fact that she was wearing her little burgundy-and-white cheerleader outfit tonight. *That* ought to help keep their wildly divergent statuses front and center. It was almost as good as posting a sign that read: *I'm with the In crowd. You're not.*

Yes sir, the assignment was what mattered, and that's what he planned to concentrate on. Buckle down, do a great job of it, and the resulting grade would bring him that much closer to a scholarship. No personal stuff from now on for this kid. No way, no how. Screw a social life, he was strictly about the work.

He strode up to the library table, dumped his book bag on the floor next to it and flopped down in a chair across from the brunette cheerleader. "So, what's the deal between you and Asshole Rushman?"

Her big brown eyes did the impossible and grew larger yet. "What?"

Oh, man, did he actually say that out loud? "Sorry, I shouldn't have called him that. I suppose he's your boyfriend, huh? Peter, I mean. Just forget I asked, okay? It's not like it's any of my business anywa—"

"He's not my boyfriend."

He stopped scrambling to retract the question and stared at her across the table. She looked so pretty, with her flushed cheeks and wide eyes as she looked back at him. "He isn't?"

"No. And I know he can be a real jerk sometimes, but I think maybe it's his way of being in control."

"Of what? Those no-neck guys he runs with?"

Natalie smiled. "Of everything. If you think he's an ass, you oughtta see his father. I heard Mr. Rushman berating Peter over by the field bleachers one day when I was late coming to cheerleading practice. It wasn't pretty, Niklaus. He called Peter names and said things to him that nobody should have to hear from his dad."

"Like what?"

She told him and he winced. "Yeah, that sucks. I still think Rushman's a jerk, but it's gotta bite to have your own father treat you like crap."

"Yeah. So I make allowances for him. But he's not, like,

my boyfriend, or anything. I'm not going out with anybody right now."

Sweet. Holy frigging sweet, he thought the instant before he remembered it didn't really matter to him one way or the other. Frowning—was he acting like a freakazoid, or what?— he leaned down and started pulling papers out of his bag. Slapping them onto the table, he said briskly, "So, where did we leave off on Wednesday?"

Natalie gave him a long, perplexed look. Then she shrugged and reached for a book.

They focused on work, and it was a good forty-five minutes later when Natalie suddenly stretched her leg out beneath the table and poked him with the toe of her sneaker. "Hey, I just remembered. Your first soccer game is coming up."

"Yep. Monday afternoon."

"Are you totally psyched?"

"I'm getting pretty excited. We're ready." He thought about that for an instant, then said enthusiastically, "No, we're beyond ready. We're gonna kick some serious ass." Tossing his pen down, he angled his legs away from her, stretched them out beneath the table and crossed his arms over his chest. For the first time in nearly an hour he allowed himself to really look at her. "That reminds me. What's the story with the cheerleaders and the soccer team? How come you never show up to do your stuff for any of our games?"

"I don't know. This is my first year on the team, but from everything I've heard we only cheer for football and basketball."

"That's what I heard, too, and I gotta tell you that's just skewed. Silverado's soccer team has won the state championship four years in a row. *Four years.* What the hell have the other teams ever done? I haven't seen the basketball team play, but the Miners are, what, two-for-seven so far this season?"

"I'm not saying it's fair, Nik. I'm just saying that's the way it's apparently always been done." Then in an obvious bid to change the subject, she said, "Is your uncle Wolf coming to your game? I bet he's totally revved to watch you play."

Pain stabbed so sharp and suddenly he half expected to hear the shower scene music from *Psycho* start to play. He managed to shrug, though, and kept his tone casual when he replied, "Nah, he'll probably have to work."

"Oh, that's too bad."

"Yeah." He didn't tell her that he hadn't bothered posting the season schedule on the refrigerator. When he'd been a kid, he used to do that as soon as the coach passed them out, until he'd finally accepted it was a huge waste of energy, since his mom had never once shown an iota of interest in his soccer games.

He had no reason to believe it would be any different with Uncle Wolf.

So why set himself up for a fall? He'd learned the hard way that false hopes were ten times worse than no hope at all.

He directed Natalie's attention back to the project and congratulated himself when they finally packed it in for the night with no more personal information exchanged.

But when they reached the main door on their way out, Natalie turned to him with those big brown eyes and said, "You want a ride over to the stadium?"

"No. That is, thanks, but I'm not going to the game."

"Sure, I understand. It's not your thing. I just thought you might, you know, like to see me cheer or something. I'm not half bad."

"Oh. Hey. I bet you're beyond great. And I would like that. Only I've, uh, got plans already. With the guys." Okay, it was a big fat lie, since he'd been avoiding them almost as assiduously as he'd been trying to keep his distance from her. Still, he'd just as soon she not think he was a total loser, which having zero Friday night plans aside from a homework assignment surely made him.

"At least let me drop you somewhere," she said, and he didn't have the heart to say no to her again. So he had her drop him off at the Fremont Street Experience downtown, then had to go looking for a bus to catch back home once she drove away.

Damn, it had been a long night.

He dragged himself into the condo almost an hour later and was parked in front of the tube watching some loser Friday night crap when the doorbell suddenly rang. Figuring the way his luck had been running it could only be someone anxious to convert him to their religion, he ignored it. But it rang again.

And yet again.

"Shit." Muting the TV, he climbed to his feet and went to answer it. Aggressively ripping the door open, he was primed for a fight, ready and willing to give his unwelcome visitors a piece of his mind.

Only it wasn't Jehovah's Witnesses. It was Paddy, Josh and David.

"Hey, good, you're home," Paddy said, and Niklaus had to fall back as his teammates surged into the entryway, trailing the scent of pepperoni and hot tomato sauce in their wake. "We were about ready to give up. You've been mighty elusive lately, Jones."

"Yeah, well." He shrugged. "I've had my nose to the grindstone working on my advanced biology class project."

Paddy spun around to stare at him. "Dude, I know you're serious about your grades. But on a Friday night?"

"I know. It's pitiful. What can I say? Some of us have no social life." And that was the way he wanted it, right?

"The hell you don't. You have us, and we come bearing pizza. We tried to score some beer to go with it, but that was a big, fat no-go."

His teammates headed into the heart of the apartment and he had no choice but to close the door behind them and follow. In truth, he felt his mood lighten with every step he took. He was really glad to see them. Going back to being a loner after making friends with guys he actually shared some common interests with had been a lot harder than he'd thought it would be. And what was the point, anyway? It was going to hurt when he had to move on, either way. He might as well enjoy his friends while he had the chance.

Josh was already in the kitchen with his head in the fridge by the time Nik reached the living room. "Hey, you've got beer in here! Think your uncle would notice if we helped ourselves to a couple?"

"Dog, the man is Mr. Security at one of the biggest casinos on the Strip," David said as he opened the pizza box and separated a slice from the pie inside. "What do *you* think?"

"Yeah, he's probably got 'em inventoried," Josh agreed glumly. Then he cheered up. "What the fuck, there's Coke in here." He pulled out four cans.

Nik grabbed a roll of paper towels and they took the pizza box over to the small dining room table, where they flopped it down in the middle. Pulling out chairs, they sat, ripped towels off the roll to use as plates, passed around the cans of soda and dug in.

He was working on his second slice when Paddy said, "So, you done with that biology project yet?"

"Not quite. We've got some research left to do before we

start putting it all together. We came close to finishing that part tonight but Natalie had to quit early because of the game."

David lowered the slice he'd raised to his mouth to stare at him. "Natalie Fremont?"

"Uh-huh." Cheese strung out from his slice as he took a big bite. Hooking it around his finger, he shoveled it into his mouth.

"Natalie *Fremont* is your partner?"

"Yeah."

"She's hot," Josh said. "And totally, completely wasted on Asshole Rushman."

"She's not. That is, she *would* be if he was her boyfriend, but she told me he's not. She says she's not dating anyone."

Now all three of his friends were staring at him. *"Dawg,"* David said reverently.

Josh whooped.

"She told you that?" Paddy asked. "Personally?"

"Sure." He shifted beneath the weight of his redheaded friend's sudden regard. "What are you looking at?"

"Dude, a babe like her only makes a point of telling a guy she's not dating anyone when she's interested."

"She wants you, man," Josh said.

"You da *man*, Jones," David agreed.

He grinned and reached for another slice of pizza. He didn't tell them it didn't really matter if Natalie was interested in him or not, since he didn't plan on letting her get any closer than he already had. It was one thing to let the guys back into his life. It would be something else entirely to allow Natalie to get a foot in the door.

Still, it was cool to be thought of as "da man." That wasn't something that came his way every day.

Then Josh said something that made them all laugh. The timing couldn't have been better because it covered the great big guffaw that had already begun erupting up his throat. But, whattaya know?

He grinned at his friends.

He'd been telling the truth, after all, when he'd told Natalie he had plans with the guys tonight.

Twenty

"Wolf, hold up!"

Looking around, Wolfgang spotted Dan McAster striding across the casino toward him. He waited for his boss to catch up, refusing to allow the curse that crowded his throat to escape. But it had been a very long night, and he wanted nothing more than to head home.

Apparently that wasn't going to happen immediately, so he did what he always did when matters didn't go exactly the way he might have wished. He sucked it up and adjusted his attitude.

Dan wove between the gamblers crowding the floor. Reaching Wolf's side, he leaned in to be heard over the clang and clatter of the slots and the poker machines. "Let me buy you a cup of coffee," he said. Without waiting for an answer, he steered Wolf in a different direction than the one in which he'd been headed. "I've got something I'd like to run by you."

A few minutes later they grabbed seats at a small table in the open-air coffee shop, cups of aromatic java steaming in front of them. "Good job with that drunk," Dan commented, lifting his mug to his lips.

Wolf merely shook his head. "For a while there I thought we were going to have a debacle of monster proportions on our hands. But in the end I got the situation under control with the minimum of scars." He meant that quite literally, but didn't make a point of drawing Dan's attention to the claw marks he'd gained in the scuffle. Instead he shrugged. "Give me a belligerent man over a pissed-off woman any day of the week."

"Yeah, women will try to rip your hair out by the roots and skin your hide from your bones in the most painful manner possible. Your drunk sure as hell did a number on you." Dan looked at the raw lacerations crisscrossing the back of Wolf's hand. "Jesus, that's ugly. You probably oughtta stop by the first aid station and get some antibiotic cream put on it. Damn talons looked to be an inch long on the screens in the control room. There's no telling what might have been breeding under nails like that."

"Great, thanks for planting that idea in my head." The confrontation with the furious woman had merely been the capper in a night filled with irritations, starting with Niklaus's anger before he'd even left for work. What the hell had that been about? He'd asked the kid a few harmless questions and Nik had blown sky-high.

But he shoved the nagging worry aside to concentrate on what Dan wanted from him now. Attempting to figure out how to deal with his nephew just kept getting more difficult, and for what remained of tonight at least, he didn't see the percentage in even trying. He was off the clock, and thinking longingly of going home and burning off this restless discontent in Carly's arms, he eyed his boss across the table. "So, what did you want to talk about?"

Dan laughed. "Damn, Jones, you gotta stop wasting every-one's time with all this incessant small talk." Still smiling, he shook his head. "Actually, your people skills is one of the things I'd like to discuss."

Perfect. Another dissatisfied customer to round out my night. Wolf braced himself for a rehash of all he was doing wrong in that arena.

Instead, Dan gave him a nod of approval. "You apparently took our last conversation to heart, because your ability has improved quite a bit in the past couple of weeks. I've heard more than one good report about your new approachability."

The tightly wound spring in his gut loosened. "You have?"

"Yes. And in light of that, I'd like to tell you about an in-teresting conversation I had earlier this evening."

Wolf blew on his still-too-hot coffee and gazed across the table at his boss.

"An old friend of mine called me," Dan said. "His name is Oscar Freeling and he's the head of security at a place called OHS Industries outside of Cleveland. He's getting ready to retire and wanted to know if I had any suggestions for a replacement once he collects his gold watch." He gave Wolf a level look. "I recommended you."

"What?" Wolf straightened in his seat. "Are you serious?"

"As a heart attack, son. I know you've been chomping at the bit to head up your own division, and I think this is right up your alley."

"I don't know what to say." Surprisingly, he wasn't nearly as jazzed as he should be, given that this was precisely the goal he'd been working toward for as long as he could remember. He chalked it up to tiredness, however, and met his boss's gaze. "Thank you. I appreciate your vote of confidence."

"You've earned it. I'll tell you the truth, Wolf, I'm going

to miss you when you move on. You're one of the best workers I've ever had in S & S, and frankly, given your instincts for casino surveillance in particular, I think your skills will be wasted in corporate America. Still, I understand ambition, and this is a decent opportunity." He shook his head. "No, it's better than decent."

As if anticipating the questions beginning to form in Wolf's mind, Dan shrugged and added, "Not that there's much I can tell you about the job, aside from the company's name and where it's located. But Oscar said he'd fly out sometime within the next couple of weeks to meet with you, so he can answer any questions you have then." Tossing back the rest of his coffee, he set the mug down and slapped the tabletop with the flats of his hands. "But for now," he instructed briskly, "go home. Get some rest. You look beat."

He *felt* beat, Wolf admitted as he thanked Dan again, left his coffee untouched and headed for the parking garage. That *had* to be the reason for his lack of excitement over the opportunity he'd just been offered. Nothing else made sense.

By rights he should be dancing in the streets.

He decided during the drive home that he'd go straight to bed the minute he arrived. Maybe if he caught up on his sleep, matters would look brighter in the morning than they inexplicably felt tonight.

Apparently Nik had had friends in while he was at work, for Wolf walked into his apartment to find an abandoned grease-stained pizza box on the table and soiled paper towels and empty soda cans scattered across the counters. In direct contrast to the mess, his nephew was nowhere to be seen. Still, Niklaus had left the required note saying he'd gone with the guys to Neonopolis at the Fremont Street Experience. So shrugging off his irritation, Wolf handled KP duty himself.

When he ran hot water over the sponge, it made the mangled skin on the back of his hand sting like the devil. But he gritted his teeth, wiped down the counters and the table, then tossed the sponge next to the sink and reached for a clean dish towel. Patting his injuries dry, he called it good. He was too damn tired to deal with anything more strenuous tonight.

As he was walking into the master suite he heard Carly arrive next door. And just like that his fatigue disappeared. His stride went from drag-ass exhausted to energetic as he loped into the bathroom to brush his teeth.

Two minutes later he was knocking on Carly's front door. "Come in," her warmly welcoming voice called. "It's open."

He let himself in and marched straight through the living room. Buster trotted out to greet him, but for once the cats didn't accompany him. Wolf discovered why when he paused in the kitchen entryway and saw them stropping themselves around Carly's ankles.

The instant she glanced over at him he said sternly, "You do not tell people to enter your house before you even know who's on the other side of the door. You're supposed to keep the damn thing latched. Although, come to think of it, your locks are a joke. I'll replace those tomorrow."

"Good morrow to you, too, Wolfgang," she said serenely, and lithely dodged the felines twining between her feet to cross the short distance that separated them. Going up onto her bare toes, she gave him a soft-lipped kiss.

As usual when she was within touching range, his libido went haywire. When she slowly separated her mouth from his, stepped back and returned to feeding the cats, he had to think for a second before he could recall what they'd been talking about. "Good morrow?"

"It's a John Donne poem I read in college and I've always loved the expression. 'And now good morrow to our waking souls, which watch not one another out of fear.'" She grinned and picked up the two cat bowls. "How pretty is that?"

"You went to college?"

She paused mid-bend, looking up at him through narrowed lashes. "Careful there. You might want to watch that incredulous tone." She set the cats' bowls on the floor and straightened, reaching for the dog food.

"Sorry. That didn't come out right." He rubbed his hand over his lower face. "College is simply not the kind of surroundings I associate with a dancer, I guess."

"Okay, that's fair." She poured kibble into Buster's bowl and ruffled the dog's topknot when he promptly dug in. "I'd planned to be a teacher but discovered that it wasn't really my thing."

He thought he'd be wise never to underestimate this woman. Stepping around her pets, he leaned down and kissed her gently, taking care to only touch her with his lips. When he lifted his head a moment later, he brushed a soft wisp of hair off her forehead. "Good morrow, Carly."

"Aw, man. Just when I'm sure that hooking up with you is probably the craziest idea I've ever had, you go and do something to blow me away. What am I supposed to do with you?" Then she leaped into his arms, her own locking around his neck, her legs encircling his waist. "Oh, wait. I know." And she kissed him as if it had been an age since she'd tasted him and was starved for his flavors.

The next thing Wolf knew they were sprawled out on the postage-stamp-size dining room floor with their pants down around their ankles. While he fumbled in his crumpled slacks in search of the pocket containing his wallet with its emergency condom, she shoved down her camisole straps and extracted her arms. His progress slowed even further when her pretty breasts suddenly emerged from the purple lace.

Then, every bit as abruptly as she'd jumped him, she shoved him away. Scrambling out from between his widespread knees, she crouched in front of him, snatching up his wrist in both her hands. "Oh, my God!" she exclaimed, bending her head to examine him. "What *happened* to you?"

For half a heartbeat he didn't know what she was talking about. Then he saw that her attention was locked on the raw skin striping the back of his hand. And the injured area, which he hadn't even given a single thought to since entering Carly's home, suddenly started to smart like hell. Keeping his explanation brief, he told her about the woman who'd fought the staff's efforts to eject her from the casino floor, and how she'd gone postal when the pit boss had summoned him. "I had to physically pick her up and pack her out kicking and screaming," he concluded, and looked at his hand. "She did this before I ejected her."

"That skanky bitch!" Surging to her feet in one supple move, she tugged at the wrist she still grasped. "Come with me."

He looked up at her towering over him like some Valkyrie warrior queen, clad in nothing but a boyish pair of boxers and that cobweb-fine lace camisole puddled around her middle. The top's fabric hung up where her waist indented on her left side, but draped at an angle across her flat stomach and right hip. Her breasts rose above the rumpled lingerie, all pale, proud curves and soft pink nipples.

Kicking free of his slacks, he rose to his own feet but turned back at the last instant to snatch his wallet from the back pocket.

"Where are we going?" he demanded as she tugged him

down the short hallway. To the bedroom, he sincerely hoped. Because buck naked, with his cock leading the way, anything else was inconceivable. Clearly he was only fit for one activity. In fact, give him a pair of skates and shift her grip to a different body part and he could pass as a damn oversize, triple X pull-toy.

They entered her bedroom, but it was into the attached bath that she guided him. Flipping down the toilet seat, she pointed an autocratic finger. "Sit." She released his hand and began rummaging through the medicine cabinet.

Watching her, he did as she directed. "What are you doing?"

"Just grabbing a few things to fix you up," she said, pulling items from the cabinet and setting them on the vanity next to the sink. "I can't believe the casino let you leave before doing something about your hand. Considering the damage the woman did, she must have had nails like a griffin." She shook her head in disgust. "People-inflicted wounds are nasty enough. But if your drunk was playing the machines with real coins, her hands were probably filthy to boot."

"She wasn't playing the machines," he informed her, a queer feeling tugging at his heart at her determination to take care of him. "She was shooting craps before she started shooting off her mouth at the croupier and the other players at the table."

"Still." Without an ounce of visible self-consciousness, she untwisted her camisole to cover her bare breasts, but didn't bother pulling the garment's straps up over her shoulders. Then she opened the bottle of hydrogen peroxide and poured some into the cap. "Anything that's been handled by a hundred people over the course of an evening is not likely to be much cleaner." Holding his hand over the sink, she dribbled the antiseptic over his abraded skin, grimacing in sympathy when he sucked in a sharp breath. "I'm sorry, I'm sorry. I know it stings." She fanned it with her fingers, but determining that that wasn't particularly effective, she bent her head and blew on the raw flesh.

Aw, hell. Fisting his fingers through her hair, he tugged to bring her head up, wanting, *needing* to eradicate the funny little twist her insistent mothering put in his gut. Startled blue eyes met his for a second before he leaned forward to clamp his mouth over hers.

She promptly returned his kiss with reciprocal hunger, then pulled back, laughing. "No, wait…*wait!* We have to fix you up first." Grabbing a tube of triple antibiotic, she squirted a squiggle onto a two-by-two white gauze pad. Dodging his hand as it slid from her hair to her throat to her shoulder, she gently placed the bandage, doctored side down, upon his injured flesh. "Will you *wait?*" she demanded when he tugged on her camisole, nearly exposing one breast. Placing one hand on his chest to hold him back, she pulled the top back into place, then reached with the other for the adhesive tape on the counter next to her. She thrust the roll out at him. "Here. Make yourself useful. Rip me off four strips."

Ignoring it, he pinched her camisole between two fingers and started to draw it downward once more.

She yanked it away. "Don't make me hurt you, Wolfgang."

"I want you to pull it back down around your waist," he said. He needed to put this encounter back on a sexual level. There was just something about Carly when she was on a nurturing streak that made him crazy-weak inside.

And he didn't do weak. He'd made up his mind about that eons ago.

"You want to see my boobs?" Hooking her thumbs in the

hem of her camisole, she pulled it up to reveal her breasts and performed a little shimmy-shake. But it was more flash than full-out exposure, and covering herself once again, she nodded at the tape in his suddenly lax hand. "Show me those strips and I'll bare these babies for you once and for all."

He ripped off four strips in short order, handing them to her one by one as she taped the bandage in place. The instant the last one was applied, he stood, swooped her up in his arms and packed her into the bedroom. Crossing to the bed, he dropped his laughing bundle onto the spread-covered mattress and lowered himself beside her. "I've been patient."

Carly snorted. As if she'd ever seen that particular virtue from this man.

"Lose the top."

"Ooh." She pushed the fragile garment down over her hips and kicked free from it. "I love it when you're all dictatorial."

"Then you're going to like this a lot," he said, stripping her out of her boxers. "Because I've got all sorts of instructions in mind for you." Rolling to lie on his back, he crossed his arms behind his head.

"Cool." But instead of waiting to find out what Wolf's wishes might be, she knelt beside him. Reaching out, she wrapped her hand around the iron-hard, velvet-skinned shaft jutting up at her. It was solid and hot in her hand and she squeezed.

"*Hah!*" Breath exploding out of his lungs, he arched his back up off the bed, shoving his penis deeper into her grip.

A drop of fluid appeared on its tip and, pulling her gaze away from her thumb spreading its moisture around the blunt head that thrust demandingly through her fist, she grinned up at him. "You are *so* under my power, Jones."

An odd, edgy expression crossed his face. Then it disappeared and he wrapped his hand around hers to demonstrate a harder rhythm. Their eyes met and he nodded. "So it would appear. Lucky me."

Carly collapsed atop Wolf a short while later, warm and damp-skinned and satiated. "Whoa," she murmured. "I always feel so relaxed after doing the hootchie-kootch with you."

"Tell me about it." He stroked the nape of her neck. "In fact, that paralyzed-for-life thing you warned me that you do to men? I may have scoffed at the time, Beauty, but I'm a believer now."

She laughed and wiggled against the part of him still buried inside of her. "I think there's a little action left in you yet."

Then a matter she'd been thinking about earlier popped into her head and she said, "This is more than just sex, though, right?" Feeling him stiffen slightly beneath her, she propped her chin upon her stacked hands on his chest and looked at him. "I'm not talking about the lifelong-commitment kind of 'more.' But you and I are friends as well as lovers, right? We're…what's that catchphrase everyone's using these days? Friends with benefits?"

He relaxed again. "Yes. We're absolutely friends." He smiled and murmured, "With benefits. I like that."

"Good. Then how would you like to go to the survivors' picnic with me tomorrow?"

"All right." He was silent for a second, then said, "What's the survivors' picnic?"

"It's an annual get-together for cancer survivors. I always take—"

The room suddenly whirled as Wolf tipped her onto her back on the comforter. She looked up at him braced on his palms over her, their bodies no longer connected but still pressed together below the waist. He stared back at her from beneath furrowed brows.

"You've had cancer?" he demanded. Lifting a hand, he skimmed his long fingers over her as if they could magically discern the place where a malignancy might have grown.

"No, no, not me," she rushed to assure him, since he looked genuinely concerned. "But remember the pet-therapy program I told you about? Because of my work with them I always get an invitation." Enthusiasm suffused her. "I love this picnic, Wolf. It's uplifting and life-affirming and it's my one chance each year to see the kids I knew who were released from long-term hospital care."

"It sounds nice," he agreed, stroking a fingertip along her hairline.

"It is. It's just stupen—"

His sudden start cut her off mid-word. "Jesus!" he exclaimed. "What the hell is that?" He reached behind him. "Is that a *cat?*"

"Come down here, let me see." When he lowered himself onto his elbows above her, she peered over his shoulder. And grinned. "It's Tripod," she told him, looking at the cat who had curled himself into a ball in the small of Wolf's back. "I do believe he likes you."

He muttered something dark in German.

"What does that mean? Don't you know it's rude to speak a foreign language to someone who doesn't understand a word of it?" She narrowed her eyes at him. "Is that cursing?"

"Of course not," he retorted austerely. "I merely said that I guess I can sleep well tonight now. Knowing that your cat likes me."

"Ah. Sarcasm." Her relationship with this man always seemed to be two steps forward and one step back, and she gave him an austere look of her own. "I should probably warn you, I'll be taking Buster to the picnic tomorrow. In case you want to change your mind."

His thick blond eyebrows snapped together. "I am not changing my mind. I'm just not used to pets. Especially pets with claws who stake out a bed on my bare skin."

"Well, look on the bright side, toots. If you're buck naked Tripod can't shed all over your pretty clothes."

The cat began to purr loudly.

"There is that." Wolf's lips curved upward. "Plus he's warm and soft and a big talker. He obviously takes after you."

Aw, *man*. Every damn time she thought she had him pigeonholed as a humorless prig he managed to surprise her. Plus his faint smile was surprisingly sweet, and she felt herself melting like a Hershey square on a campfire S'more.

"You should have stopped while you were ahead," she said, poking him in the shoulder. "You had me in the palm of your hand with the soft-and-warm part." She kept her tone light, as if this were all simply one great big joke.

But inside she wasn't laughing. Because she had an uneasy feeling that she was one short step from walking off an unseen ledge and dropping into a bottomless pool.

One that would find her so far over her head with the complex Mr. Jones she just might sink without a trace.

Twenty-One

"Hi, Buster! Hi, Carly!"

Greetings and squeals of delight rent the air the instant Wolf and Carly stepped foot in the picnic area of the park. Wolf watched in amazement as children of every size, age and ethnicity imaginable swarmed like locusts toward Carly and her mutt. Even as he absorbed the sheer number of them, they bumped him aside to encircle Carly, vying for her attention and fussing over Buster. The dog seemed quite content to plop his wide rear on the ground and let the children ruffle his topknot and scratch his ears, focusing on whoever was currently in front of him with what looked like a big happy grin, his long pink tongue dangling out one side of his mouth. And Carly was all big white smiles, looking as though she were in her natural element as she hugged or touched every child who came within reach.

Which pretty much meant all of them.

"Marguerite, you've grown a foot since last year!" she exclaimed, and gave a little girl her complete attention for a moment before she turned to a boy of about eleven. "Jacob! Oh, my God—is that you? Look at your beautiful hair." Laughing, she tousled the mop of brunette curls in question, then reached through the mob surrounding her to grasp Wolf's forearm and pull him into the circle. She flashed him a radiant smile and, touching the youth's hair again, explained what he'd already figured out for himself. "The last time I saw Jacob here he was bald as a billiard ball."

She turned back to the children. "This is my friend Wolfgang," she informed them. "You'll have to move back a scooch and give him some breathing room. His nephew lives with him, so it's not like he doesn't know kids. But he's not used to being around this many all at once." As they obligingly widened the circle by a whopping two inches, she proceeded to introduce each boy and girl to him by name, mentioning something personal about every last one of them.

By the time the kids raced off with Buster in tow a short while later, Wolf had gained a whole fresh perspective on Carly. He watched with new respect as she dragged him from group to group, laughing and talking to parents and to the children who'd been too shy to approach her with the pack. Left to his own devices, he would have been perfectly content to remain on the periphery as she chatted with what seemed like dozens of people, but she insisted on drawing him into every group, including him in every conversation. And in truth it was pretty painless because the focus was all on her. The only thing he had to do was exchange a few pleasantries and she handled the rest.

Or the families she conversed with did. They made it easy and simple, just the way he liked his social obligations. Because while they acknowledged him, talking to him with friendly openness, it was Carly they were hot to see, Carly they plainly wanted to visit and fuss over. Even without several parents singing her praises to him about how she and her pets had entertained this child or that child during the sickest, most frightening period of his or her young life, he would have seen how much they admired her. How much they adored her.

While he, in all his wisdom, had accused her on more than one occasion of being irresponsible.

An hour or so later he was watching her laugh and listening to her talk between bites of an everything-on-it hot dog when a woman suddenly shouted out her name from the other side of the picnic area. People had been calling out to her since they'd arrived, so although he made note of the greeting, he was prepared to just as immediately forget it.

But Carly's head snapped up and swiveled in the direction of the voice. For a fleeting instant, sadness chased pleasure across her face, expressions so at odds with each other that his internal radar immediately went on alert. Then she shoved her half-eaten hot dog into his hands, excused herself from the group and strode over to meet the woman making her way through the crush of chatting, laughing people.

The two women shared a fierce embrace for a long, silent moment. Then the older woman pulled away and grasped Carly just above her elbows, holding her at arm's length to examine her. They exchanged words that Wolf was too far away to make out before they hugged again. This time when they stepped back, Carly murmured something to the other woman, then took her by the hand and led her over to him.

He swallowed the last of Carly's hot dog, which he'd been absentmindedly munching, and surreptitiously checked his hands for mustard stains.

"Marilyn, I'd like you to meet Wolfgang Jones. Wolf, this

is Marilyn Bradley. Her son David was the very first child I
ever visited when I joined the pet-therapy program a little
over four years ago."

Failing to see a kid lurking in the vicinity, he looked at
Carly. "Is he one of the boys running with the pack that
greeted you and Buster when we first got here?"

The subtly stricken look on her face let him know he'd
stepped in it even before Marilyn said, "No, he died three and
a half years ago."

"Oh, Christ. I'm sorry." He stared at the woman help-
lessly. "I shouldn't have jumped to conclusions—that was
insensitive."

"No, don't apologize," she said. "You came to a survivors'
picnic, you certainly had every reason to expect that's who
you'd be meeting here. I just drop in for a few minutes each
year to see Carly." She patted the tall blonde's hand, but kept
her gaze on him. "Her weekly visits with Rags and Buster
meant the world to David. They were the bright spots in a
dreary, pain-filled world. I hate to think how much bleaker
my son's last months would have been without them."
Stepping closer, she touched his forearm and said fervently,
"Your wife is a wonder. You must be incredibly proud of her."

His *wife*?

"Oh, Wolf and I aren't married," Carly said.

"You're not?" The woman turned to look at her in surprise.
"But I thought you—"

"No, *no*." Carly laughed as if the very idea were the most
absurd notion she'd ever heard. "Trust me."

The word *wife* in conjunction with Carly had thrown him,
but her big fat rush to correct Marilyn's erroneous impression
seriously pissed him off. Since there was no good reason
behind his irritation, he shrugged the feeling aside and merely

said, "We are extremely good...friends however. And I am proud of her. She's really something with the kids."

"She certainly is." The older woman studied his face for a moment before she turned to Carly. "Did I hear Wolfgang mention that Buster is here?"

"Yes. Somewhere. He's being spoiled by the kids."

"May I see him for a few minutes before I leave?"

"Of course you can." Carly slid her arm around Marilyn's shoulders and turned her toward the playground, where she'd last seen her dog loping happily with a gang of screaming, laughing children. She glanced over at Wolf, and for some inexplicable reason her heart began to beat a ragged rhythm in her throat. "Coming?"

"Sure." Hands in his pockets, he fell into step beside her, where he'd been all afternoon.

Where she had very much enjoyed having him.

She gave him a little sideways glance as they crossed the park. Marilyn mistaking him for her husband hadn't sent him running for the hills. That was probably a good thing. She couldn't prevent a little wince, though, because she didn't doubt for a minute where that particular misunderstanding had come from.

It was her own fault. Not only had she been affected by seeing Marilyn again, but she'd been feeling almost giddy with the happiness of seeing all the no-longer-ill children and sharing in their families' joy. And when the two disparate emotions had collided, it had somehow led her to invite the other woman to "Come meet my Wolf."

She had *no* idea where that had come from. She certainly didn't think of him as hers.

Did she?

No, of course not. It was merely the adrenaline high she

was riding. It was knowing that Wolfgang's quiet strength had been available the entire afternoon, a support for which she had been grateful because it helped to keep her grounded when rampant sentimentality threatened to swamp her usual common sense. And it no doubt also had something to do with the incredible sex the two of them had been sharing the past several days.

But that was it. She'd just gotten a little carried away there for a minute. She now had herself well in hand, though.

She located Buster and was in the midst of extricating him from his gang of new friends when she suddenly spotted Rufus racing toward her across the park. "Oh, my God." She laughed as a heretofore unrecognized small dark hollow in her heart filled with light. "Look who's here." Rufus hurtled through the playground like an arrow shot from a bow, and she laughed in delight as he sped straight toward her. She dropped to her haunches to greet him.

The pup she'd rescued and loved like a mother blew right past her to leap up on Wolf.

His expression blank, he stared down at her, then turned his attention to Rufus as the dog danced on his back legs and drummed his front paws against Wolf's thighs, staring up at him in rapt adoration. He detached the canine from his jeans. "You disloyal little shit," he said without inflection. "I see there's been no improvement in your intelligence."

She tried not to be crushed, she truly did. Giving in to hurt feelings would be too absurd, especially considering she'd already relinquished all rights to the dog. Rufus's first allegiance was to Iago now, so what did it matter if the silly mutt singled out Wolf for a moment's attention rather than her? Some dogs simply responded more strongly to one gender than the other. No one knew that better than she.

Shaking off the treacherous pinch of jealousy, she efficiently reintroduced Marilyn to Buster and smiled at Iago and his mother when they caught up with their errant dog a few minutes later. She was not going to duplicate the embarrassing falling apart she'd done the day she'd given Rufus away. And really, it wasn't that difficult to avoid because boy and dog were clearly thriving together. So everything was fine. Hunky-dory in fact.

Funny how exhausted she suddenly felt, though.

Wolf draped his arm around her shoulders and leaned his head close to hers. "We should probably be taking off." He rubbed his chin against her temple for a second before pressing his lips to the same spot in a quick now-you-feel-it-now-it's-gone caress.

She felt such a strong surge of…well, affection surely, that it nearly brought tears to her eyes, and she looked up at him in gratitude. "Yes. Yes, we should."

The people around them immediately protested, but Wolf gave them the impersonal smile he was so good at—the one that was at once eminently civil and a great big No Trespassing sign. "Much as we'd love to stay, both Carly and I have to work this evening. I'm sure you all understand what that's like." Then his smile widened into something wryly, genuinely friendly. "Or maybe you don't. I sometimes forget that not everyone works the same bizarre hours we do."

After she exchanged one last round of hugs, Wolf firmly pulled her away from the group, escorted her across the park to the parking lot and settled her in the front seat of his antique street rod. Minutes later they were cruising down the wide arterial with the radio playing softly and Buster snuffling happily behind her as he thrust his head out the window, his ears and tongue blowing in the wind. She and Wolf barely exchanged two words, but it was an easy companionable silence.

They were less than a mile from home when he suddenly swerved into one of Las Vegas's ubiquitous strip malls. Startled out of her reverie, she looked at him in surprise. "What are you doing?"

He pulled into a parking spot in front of a small adobe restaurant, cut the engine and set the brake. His left wrist still draped over the steering wheel, he turned to look at her. "I'm going to feed you. All you've had to eat all day is half a hot dog."

"I had a banana for breakfast."

"Oh, well, in that case, forget it. Why would anyone require more than five hundred calories a day? It's not like you need energy to dance or anything." He reached for the keys still in the ignition.

She laughed and stayed his hand. "Okay, I admit it, I'm starving. An early dinner would be great."

Several minutes later they were settled in a booth. As the waitress flipped closed her pad and walked away with their orders, Carly settled in. A contented sigh escaped her and she smiled at Wolf. "This is nice."

He didn't return her smile. "I owe you an apology," he said with his usual straightforwardness.

She cocked an eyebrow at him. "Toots, you owe me a dozen apologies. What's this one for?"

"I said several snide things to you about your lack of responsibility. I was out of line, not to mention completely off base."

Ooh. Sweet vindication. She liked this. Resting her chin in her palm, she contemplated his serious green eyes, the sober slant to his mouth, and gave him a sad, forgiving smile. "You did do that. It hurt my feelings a lot."

His eyes narrowed. "You are mocking me."

"Get out. Would I do that?"

"Hell, yes. My attitude pissed you off. It made you shove back and it probably contributed to the way you forever seem to be laughing in my face. I doubt it hurt your feelings, though. I can't imagine doing that a little, let alone a lot."

She thought of the way she'd felt when he'd inferred she wasn't good enough for his stupid plan, then shoved it aside. "Well, it would have, if I were a different sort of woman. You might think about that the next time you're tempted to jump to conclusions."

He studied her for a moment, then his chin dipped in a brisk nod. "I'll do that." He slid one long-fingered hand across the table and touched her forearm. "How did you ever make yourself go back to the hospital when Marilyn's son died?"

"Ah, man, good question." It was, in fact, an excellent I-care-about-your-feelings kind of question, and she leaned intently toward him, her hands and forearms pressed flat against the cool smooth wood of the tabletop. "It was hard, Wolf. David was so sick, and every time I went back it was plain to see he was getting worse. But I could also see that the babies helped, if only for the half hour or so that we were there. It was just Buster and Rags at the time—I hadn't found Tripod or Rufus yet. But those two would climb right up on the bed with him and you could literally see the pain recede for a while as he petted and talked to them. Kids with serious or terminal illnesses sacrifice so much, not the least of which is the carefree sort of play other kids take for granted. But I have the means to bring them a warm furry body, a cat or a dog to entertain them or simply snuggle up with them for a while. And amazingly that helps. So although it hurts like crazycakes when one of them dies, I can't bring myself to quit. The joy far outweighs the sorrow."

"How many others have died during the time you visited them?"

"Four." And she vividly remembered each one. "Maria, Edgar, Jamie and Trish. But you saw for yourself today all the children who survived. And nothing beats the feeling of knowing that you helped them a little, and that now they get to go home and be regular kids. That's all any of them want, you know. Just to be regular kids."

The waitress delivered their meals and conversation was shelved as they both dug in hungrily. When the meal was done and they were waiting for the waitress to come back with their coffee, Carly gazed across the table at Wolf.

"Can I ask you something?"

"Sure."

"Nik mentioned that you lived in embassies all over the world when you were growing up, and that your parents are still at one in Bolivia. To an outsider that sounds very exciting, very glamorous. Yet you said something that day in the gym about how your plan kept you going when your dad dragged you from embassy to embassy. I think your exact words, in fact, were fucking elitist embassies. So can you tell me a little bit about that?"

Wolf swore to himself because he would rather poke needles in his eyes than talk about those years. Still, Carly had just shared something she'd probably rather not talk about as well, so he supposed he needed to reciprocate.

But things sure were simpler before Dan had demanded he improve his social skills.

"I was about a year younger than Nik when my dad retired from the army," he said slowly. "By the time he mustered out, we'd lived in three or four different countries and maybe eight or nine different states. I had been waiting for that day to arrive for what felt like forever, because all I ever wanted was a permanent home where we didn't have to pack up every damn time I finally got settled."

The waitress delivered their coffee and he waited for her to walk away before he looked over to see Carly, her chin resting in her palm, nodding at him as if she not only understood but fully agreed.

That seemed unlikely, though, and he shook the impression aside. "Instead of settling down somewhere permanent, though, Dad signed on as supply clerk for an embassy in Rangoon."

"Forgive my ignorance, but geography was never my strong suit. Where is Rangoon?"

"In Burma." She still looked blank, so he said, "Southeast Asia."

"Ah." She nodded. "So the moving from place to place continued. That's rough. I can see why you'd have a beef with it."

He looked at her in surprise. "You can?"

"Absolutely. I didn't move anywhere near as often as you did, but do you recall me mentioning that my mother was a marital social climber?" When he nodded, she said, "Well, every time she got upwardly mobile on the matrimonial front, I got uprooted from the home I'd barely had time to get used to from the *last* time she'd gotten married. And once again I was hauled off to the next bigger, more impressive mansion in the next bigger, more impressive neighborhood. Why do you think I've been in my condo so long?"

He grinned at her because she never ceased to surprise him and for some reason that tickled him.

She grinned back. "So what is the elitist part of the embassies?"

His smile faded. "That was just me venting," he said evenly, and hoped she would let it go at that.

He should have known better. She leveled a look on him. "Wolfgang."

"Look, it's ancient history. There are divisions and social strata everywhere. That's just a fact of life. Hell, all the time we were in the army, I bet I knew maybe one of the brass's kids. They just didn't hang out with the non-com kids."

"And yet here you are, still bitter over something about that time all these years later." She regarded him with those big tell-me-everything blue eyes, and he swallowed a sigh of defeat.

"Yeah, well, I thought I was used to the social divisions." He hated the way learning otherwise had sandbagged him, but he rolled his shoulders in a show of indifference. "When we got to Rangoon, though, it was different at first. Nicer. There were only a few kids my age attached to the embassy and the language barrier with the locals hindered opportunities for making friends outside of it, so we all banded together. The ones who were there before I arrived naturally knew one another better, but they were friendly enough." He fell silent for a moment, recalling what a pleasant surprise that had been. The daughter of the administrative aid to the ambassador in particular, a pretty girl named Mariah, had made the hours fly by in a haze of hormone-driven contentment.

Carly reached out to touch soft fingertips to his bandaged hand, which he hadn't even realized until then was gripping his coffee cup with excessive force. "So what happened to change that?"

"Are you sure you're interested in this?"

She met his gaze head on. "I'm positive."

He thought about it for a few moments, then blew out a breath. "We'd been there maybe two months when there was a formal dinner for a visiting dignitary. As the hired help, so to speak, my family wasn't invited to it. I didn't particularly care, but I thought it would be sort of cool to see, since I'd never been around anything like that. Plus, it was a golden opportunity to make some money, a commodity I always had in short supply. So I signed on to be a glorified gofer for the night. My job was to see to it that the hors d'oeuvres trays were kept full and to ferry the courses from the kitchen to the servers during the sit-down event, as well as to fetch silverware or napkins or whatever else might need replacing."

For a second he could see Mariah in her flouncy white dress, see her brother, Kevin, and some of the others whose names he could no longer recall in their custom-fit, tropical-weight formal wear. "The kids I thought were my friends were all there as guests. I tried to catch their eyes. I had some dumb notion of making faces behind the dignitaries' backs, I think. But they wouldn't even look at me."

She patted his fingers. "Maybe they were afraid to rock the boat in front of their parents."

"Yes. Maybe they were. But they weren't afraid to drop their silverware to the floor on a regular basis. And they certainly weren't the least bit apprehensive about knocking over their water glasses or somehow losing their napkins from their laps."

She straightened. "They deliberately made extra work to keep you running?" she demanded indignantly.

"The whole frigging night. Then they'd watched me out of the corners of their eyes to see my reaction, which I was damned if I'd give them the satisfaction of showing. The next day I called them on it, but they said to grow up, that it was an initiation of sorts. And we went back to normal—except I didn't feel as open with them as I had before."

"And did it turn out to be merely an initiation?"

He laughed shortly. "What do you think?"

"I'm guessing not."

"You'd be correct. The next event was a rerun of the first one." He could feel his face harden but was helpless to prevent it. "That was pretty much the end of my friendship with that bunch." Looking at her gazing back at him, he said defensively, "I know what you're thinking, that it was one group of cliquish teenagers."

"I don'—"

"But it was like that at every damn embassy we went to. I swear, there must have been a course taught at all the boarding schools the ambassadors' kids attended—Class Distinctions 101 or something. Because if you came from the wrong side of the service door, you were good enough to hang out with when there was nothing better to do. But you sure as hell weren't good enough to speak to in public. I played nice for as long as I could take it, but after a few more set downs I gave up trying to fit in." And God, it had been lonely. He had never been the most outgoing boy in the world, but he'd sure never known what it was like to feel that alone. He'd hated it, but he hadn't seen that there was a hell of a lot he could do to change his circumstances. His dad had been busy doing his thing as usual, his sister had already begun to run wild even then. And while he hadn't doubted for a moment that his mother loved him, he'd also known that Rick was her number one priority. He'd always felt as if he came a distance second or third, and there was no goddamn sense crying over it since it wasn't about to change.

Then he'd gotten used to it and discovered that being alone wasn't so bad. It was preferable, in fact. No one could screw you over if you didn't let them get close in the first place.

Carly rubbed her fingers on his wrist. "I'm so sorry," she said softly. "That must have been incredibly tough."

Oh, shit. He didn't want her pity, so he shrugged as if it were no big deal. Which it wasn't anymore, and she needed to know that. "It was a long time ago. And it helped me set my sights on what I wanted out of life."

Her hand slid away as she sat back. "Which would be your Big Plan?"

"Yes." His skin where she'd been touching him suddenly felt cold, but he pretended not to notice.

"I take it you intend to be on the other side of that service door."

He knew there was a criticism in there somewhere, and his jaw set. "That's exactly what I intend."

"But you've accomplished that already, right? So why don't you seem happier?"

"Jesus, you sound like my mother." He started looking around for the waitress. Spotting her, he signaled for the check. Then he turned back to Carly and said flatly, "I am happy. I'll just be happier when the rest of my plan falls into place."

She held her hands out in surrender. "Okay," she said. "I hope that happens for you soon." Her voice was perfectly pleasant and her expression conveyed nothing but goodwill.

His defensiveness faded, yet uneasiness remained.

Because he couldn't shake the impression that she was sorely disappointed in him. And for some reason the knowledge grated.

Twenty-Two

"I've decided to dial back on my relationship with Wolfgang," Carly told Treena in the dressing room following the last show that evening. She finished glopping on the deep cleansing oil she used to remove her greasepaint, massaged it in and reached for a handful of cotton balls to wipe it off. "The man's got baggage up the whazoo."

"Sounds reasonable to me," Treena said, leaning into the mirror to peel off her false eyelashes. She glanced over at Carly and, beneath the chatter of the other dancers changing into their street clothes, added wryly, "Not the baggage up the whazoo part. I'd just as soon not think too closely about the logistics of that. But the dialing-back part does. I'm still amazed you let him anywhere near you after that 'you're-not-good-enough-for-my-almighty-plan' crap he pulled on you Wednesday night." Yanking off the skullcap that kept her hair confined under the swingy brunette jazz-baby wig, she burrowed her fingertips into the flattened mass and rubbed vigorously. Red curls began swelling and springing away from her scalp, growing in volume. "So what'd the big jerk do this time?"

"Hey!" She whirled to face her friend. "He's not a jerk. How would you like it if I'd called Jax that when you found out he'd been lying through his teeth to you about who he was?"

"As opposed to calling him a bastard and offering to castrate him for me, you mean?"

"Oh. Yeah." Throwing the wad of makeup-stained cotton balls into the wastebasket, she flashed Treena a sheepish smile. "I guess I did do that, didn't I?"

"Yes, you did. But I apologize all the same, because when I found out what Jax was up to, it seemed perfectly okay for me to call him every name in the book, but I still didn't like hearing anyone else do it."

"Not that they're really comparable situations," Carly backtracked. "You were in love, so that's a whole different ball game."

Treena gave her a skeptical look. "Are you saying that you feel nothing for Wolf but good old-fashioned lust?"

"Well, I like him."

"Uh-huh." Her friend's look delved deep. "And I'm supposed to believe that's it?"

"Yes. He can be amazingly sweet sometimes, and tough as it is to believe after our rocky start, we're actually friends. But he can be a moody devil, too. I'm not sure even the best sex in the world is worth the uncertainty of never knowing which way those moods are going to swing." His hot-and-cold behavior at the restaurant this afternoon was a case in point. Then she flapped her hand. "It's not like I'm dumping him, or anything. I just think it's a good idea to maybe step back and take a good hard look at what I'm doing."

"Hey, you two." Eve sauntered over, putting an end to their low-voiced conversation. "Who's up for a drink?"

"Me," Carly promptly declared. She turned to Treena.

"How about it, toots? You think Jax will live if we take an extra half hour or so before we head home?"

"I imagine he'll muddle through somehow." Treena applied her lipstick, stood back to inspect the overall transformation in the mirror, then shrugged. "Good enough." She grabbed her purse. "Let me just call home so he knows where I am, then we can go."

Michelle had also joined them by the time Treena finished her call, and the dancers headed out the door.

Chatting and laughing, they were almost to their favorite little open-air lounge in the middle of the casino when Carly felt a warm sensation start to vibrate in her breast. Looking across the vast, loud, brightly lit room, she spotted Wolf over by the ten-dollar roulette wheel. He had turned his back on a man who was obviously still talking to him and was staring holes through her. Even from here she could feel the heat of his gaze, and her feet stuttered to a halt as, heart pounding, she stared back at him.

"Holy shit," Michelle muttered. "You could toast marshmallows off those two. If I'd known I was gonna run into a big old blistering bonfire, I'd have packed provisions for the occasion."

"Yeah," Eve agreed. "Hard to roast up those wienies and marshmallows without a pointy-ended stick."

"So much for dialing back," Treena murmured.

The buzz of her friends' voices penetrated Carly's haze and she pulled her gaze away from Wolf's to blink at them. "Huh? Did somebody say something?"

"Don't mind us," Michelle said. "We're just talking to hear ourselves speak."

"Okay, good." Taking her at her word, Carly's attention drifted back to the tall blonde still watching her. Maybe she should go over and say hi.

"Dial back, my ass," Eve said. "I'll believe that when I see it with my own eyes."

"Yeah, that was pretty much my thought, too," Treena agreed.

Vaguely Carly heard her friends laughing.

The janitor across the room stood stock-still. She was looking at him! He'd always known the day would come when Carly would suddenly turn that *exact* look on him—and that day had finally arrived.

God, her eyes were filled with such sexuality, such *love*. He felt as if every second of his every waking moment up until now had been slowly building toward this precise instant. Building toward this moment when his life finally—finally!—aligned the way it was always intended to do and became perfection itself. Standing tall, he skimmed his hand down the chest of his uniform—and realized that he still wore his janitorial clothing.

Dissatisfaction immediately scratched for attention, but he shoved it firmly aside. Because clearly it made no difference to Carly what he wore. Anyone who looked at a man the way she was staring at him obviously didn't care whether his clothing was the sophisticated street apparel she'd first seen him in or the uniform that proclaimed to the world what his job was.

She was the *best*. Beautiful, smart and sexy as hell, not to mention discriminating. He was a handsome man either way, but not every woman could—or would—distinguish between the clothes and the man.

She was definitely worthy of him.

Someone jostled him and he moved out of the way, shooting Carly a jaunty grin in the expectation of her gaze following him.

Only it didn't.

She continued to direct that look—that perfect you're-the-only-man-in-the-world-for-me look—toward the spot where he'd been standing just a moment ago. Slowly, his absolute contentment beginning to fade, he turned his head to follow her gaze.

And jerked in shock to see the tall blond security guy who thought he was such hot shit staring back at her with a look even more incendiary than the one she was leveling on him.

Rage roared up his spine and he swung back to stare at Carly. That *bitch!* This was unacceptable. *Unacceptable!* She'd betrayed him. *His* woman did not do such a thing. Yet here she was for everyone to see, behaving like some slutty little cat in heat, making a mockery of the gift he'd made to her of his heart.

She had to be punished. And who better than he, the man she'd just cruelly betrayed, to deliver the comeuppance she so richly deserved?

Twenty-Three

This wasn't the way things were supposed to be. Wolf ran his hand through his hair as he stared at the apartment door in front of him. He had a dozen things he should be doing right now, not the least of which was spending some time getting his thoughts together for his meeting with Dan's security friend from OHS, who was scheduled to arrive any day now. So why wasn't he doing so?

Because Carly's turning out to be more addictive than methamphetamine, that's why. And I can't seem to leave her alone.

That wasn't a problem by itself, since both of them had already agreed to this affair. But it bothered the hell out of him that he couldn't say with any real authority that, given half a chance, he wouldn't have made a spectacle of them both last night. The magnetic pull had been damn near irresistible, even with an entire section of blackjack tables separating them. If she had come to him the way he'd started mentally commanding her to do from the instant he'd seen her—well, he just didn't know what sort of public display might have resulted.

He couldn't keep hanging around her all the time. Less than an hour ago he'd had a solid plan to drop Nik off at his friend's house, then head straight to work to catch up on his backlogged paperwork until he had to pick the kid up again. Between all the hours he'd expended recently trying to make sure his nephew didn't spend any more time than necessary on his own, and the minutes and sometimes hours he'd stolen to be with Carly, his accumulation of half-written reports had multiplied like rabbits.

Yet was he headed to the casino right now, all geared up to diligently whittle down the multitude of files that were starting to overtake his hard drive? Oh, no. He was standing outside Carly's door like some lovesick fool, craving her company more than he wanted to advance his plan. And that was just plain screwed up.

All right, he'd made a mistake coming here, but it ended now. It was past time to get his priorities back on track—and Priority Number One was to head to work while he actually had a couple of hours open to write his reports. And that's precisely what he was going to do. Squaring his shoulders, he took a firm step back.

Then wrecked his good intentions by reaching out and rapping on the door.

"*Shit!*" The immediate outbreak of barking on the other side drowned out his harshly whispered expletive. But what the *hell* was he thinking? And what had happened to the self-control he prided himself on maintaining?

He drew in a deep breath and exhaled. Okay. He was thinking he owed it to Carly to tell her about his new job prospect. Yes. That was the reason he hadn't walked away when he'd had the opportunity.

Then the door opened and all thought fled as he looked down at her.

For a single suspended moment she stood with one hand on the doorknob, gazing back at him. Then sliding her fingers from the handle, she tucked her hand in the back pocket of her orange capris and said a soft "Hi."

He simply said "Hi" back. Buster muscled past her and stepped out into the hallway to greet him. Head craned back to stare up the length of Wolf's body, the dog leaned heavily against his leg. Wolf bent, without taking his gaze off Carly, to scratch the mutt's ears. She looked casual and relaxed in those bright pants, white tank top and bare feet, and suddenly he felt relaxed, too, as if every tight muscle in his body had abruptly released the tension they'd been carrying.

It occurred to him that telling her about his possible job opportunity might be a bit precipitous on his part. After all, it wasn't a done deal. So why rush to broadcast an offer he hadn't even received yet? Plenty of time to do that after he actually met with Oscar Freeling.

Feeling unaccountably cheered, he straightened and reached out to smooth his thumb over her left cheekbone. "You sure look pretty today."

"You think?" Shooting him a sweetly lopsided smile, she stepped back. "Now, those are words a girl likes to hear. Come on in, you can tell me more."

He followed her into the living room. The Sunday paper was scattered across the hardwood floor and strewn over chairs, and used dishes littered the coffee table. "Did I interrupt you at something?" he inquired dryly. "Like picking through the rubble from the bomb that hit this place, maybe?"

"Cute, Jones, but no. The babies and I were just chilling. Something you could stand to do more often." She cleared off a chintz-covered chair and waved him into it. "Have you had a chance to read the paper yet?"

"No. I pretty much rolled out of bed, then ran Nik to his friend's house for some pool party."

She nodded. "Oh, sure. At Kev Fitzpatrick's." Thrusting into his hands the short stack of newspaper sections she'd swept off the chair, she used her foot to nudge an ottoman in front of him. "Here you go. Put your feet up and catch up on what's happening." She flopped down onto the couch opposite him.

"Wait a minute." He frowned at her. "Kev? That's not who he said was hosting it." Pausing in the midst of setting down all but the front section of the *Review-Journal*, he gazed at her, a sick feeling starting to make itself felt in the pit of his stomach. "Great. I've just sent him off to someone I've never even heard of."

"You've heard of him, toots. He's the one they call Paddy."

Dropping the newspapers in his lap, he reached up to rub his forehead between his thumb and index finger and simply stared at her. "How do you know these things?"

She shrugged. "I'm a woman. I demand details. For instance, I bet you didn't meet Kev's parents when you dropped Nik off, did you?"

"No. I just let him out in front of their house." When she rolled her eyes, he said defensively, "Hey, at least I took him to the door. For a while there I was sure that he was going to suggest I drop him at the mouth of the cul-de-sac."

She gave him a pitying smile. "A woman never would have let him attend the party in the first place without checking out the household and meeting the parents."

"Ha. Obviously you've never met Nik's mother."

She stilled for a moment, then nodded. "That's true, I haven't. And I am generalizing, which is never a great idea. You want a cup of coffee?"

"That would be nice." Picking up the front page, he rattled it busily. But he didn't take his eyes off her as she gathered the cups and plates off the coffee table and walked into the kitchen.

She busied herself out of his line of vision for a moment, then drifted back into view to pull a mug from the cupboard. Slapping its door closed, she bent to look at him across the breakfast bar. "Are you picking him up after the party?"

"Yes."

"Good. Go in and introduce yourself to Kev's folks."

"I'll do that. The truth is," he admitted, "I haven't even met Kev—or any one else in that group that Nik calls 'the guys.' They never seem to be around when I am and vice versa."

"They're nice boys." She carried out a mug of steaming coffee and a small plate that held a toasted bagel spread with cream cheese. "Here. I bet you haven't eaten yet today, either."

"Thanks." Unable to remember the last time someone had gone out of their way for him, and warmed by her thoughtfulness, he took a bite out of the bagel and looked at her while he chewed. After he swallowed, he said, "I guess you've heard Nik's birthday is coming up."

She smiled crookedly. "He may have mentioned it once or twice."

"I've been thinking of getting him a car. You want to help me look for one?" When she merely stared at him, he twitched his shoulders defensively. "What? You don't think it's a good idea?"

"No. That is, I think it's a—" She shook her head. "Wow. A very generous gift. He's going to flip."

"Yeah." He grinned at her. "A guy should have his own wheels."

She flopped down on the couch again and studied him over the feet she'd propped up on the coffee table. "What kind of vehicle do you have in mind? A first car beater?"

"No. Something nice. Not brand-new or anything. But nothing he'd be embarrassed to drive to school, either. I heard him say once that half the kids who attend Silverado drive cars worth more than my sister makes in a year." And no snobby little rich kid was going to look down his or her nose at his nephew. Not over the kid's ride, at any rate.

"Yes, he told me the same thing."

He felt no burning compulsion to tell her his own information had come from that evening when he'd overheard Niklaus talking to her out on her balcony. God knew his nephew never bothered to share anything with him. "I want something sturdy for him," he said instead. "Something built with a lot of steel. Maybe I should get him a classic ride like mine. He appears to like it, and an early fifties-era Buick might be a decent choice. They have a reputation for being built like Sherman tanks."

"You've obviously put some thought into this."

"A bit, yes. But I haven't definitely decided which direction I want to go in, so if you've got any suggestions, I'd love to hear them."

She laughed. "Honey, what I know about cars you could write on the head of a pin. But if you need help selecting a color, I'm your girl."

His girl. That sounded just a little too appealing and he determinedly got back to the subject at hand. "I already know what color you'd pick," he said dryly. "Candy-apple red, right?"

"You've gotta admit that would be a sweet choice."

Rags jumped up onto the arm of the chair and butted his

head against Wolf's biceps. Then, stropping Wolf's upper arm with a graceful full-body rub, the feline turned and stared down at his lap before delicately extending one paw toward it. When he put his full weight on the newspapers, however, they made an audible rustle and Rags pulled his paw back, fixing an imperious stare on Wolf—who inexplicably found himself clearing his lap. The instant the sections hit the opposite arm of Wolf's chair, the cat stepped regally onto his lap and circled twice before collapsing along the length of his thigh. A second later he began to purr.

Wolf stared down at him. "How did he do that?" He glanced over at Carly, baffled. "I had no intention of making room for him. Yet all the papers are out of his way, and there he is right where he intended to be."

She smiled at him. "Welcome to the wonderful world of cats. If they aren't meowing you to death to get their own way, they're practicing their telepathy skills. They're obviously strong broadcasters, too, because nine times out of ten they seem to get exactly what they want."

He had to admit the heat and slight vibration of the cat draped over his thigh was sort of soothing, and tentatively he stroked Rags's soft fur. The animal's rumbling purr kicked up a notch.

"So how did you handle your schedule for Nik's first game tomorrow?" Carly asked. "Did you arrange to go in to work a little late or are you leaning more toward the it's-bound-to-be-over-by-five-so-I-bet-I-can-make-work-in-a-timely-manner school of thought? The latter is the only option open to me, unfortunately, but knowing your penchant for crossing your t's and dotting your i's, I'm guessing that you lean more toward the former. Am I right?"

An icy ball lodged in his gut and his hand stilled on Rags's back. "Nik's got a soccer game?"

"Yes." She stared at him. "Didn't he tell you?"

"No."

"Oh. Well, he only mentioned it to me once, in passing."

"He didn't mention it to me at all." And even though he knew it shouldn't, that hurt.

"Could it be—" She hesitated, then met his gaze squarely. "Maybe he thought you wouldn't be interested?"

"I'm interested," he said flatly. His hand tightened in the cat's fur, and hissing in displeasure, Rags leaped to the floor where he lifted a disdainful leg and proceeded to lick his rear. Wolf didn't take issue with the cat's message, for he agreed. "Clearly I'm a bust as a parent because he never tells me a damn thing."

"Aw, toots, he's a sixteen-year-old boy." She climbed up off the couch and crossed over to sit in his lap. "Don't take it so hard. Sometimes teenagers just don't communicate all that great with the adults in charge of them. And I think boys are more apt to feel competitive with their dad—or in your case, uncle. Or maybe Niklaus is just afraid of being disappointed."

Some of the tension flowed out of his shoulders. "With good reason. He has a long history of disappointments in just about every other aspect of his life, and I sure can't see my sister attending many of his games. Hell, I'd be surprised if she bothered to show up at any of them."

Carly shifted her weight, as if getting comfortable, then looped her arms around his neck. "But you're different, right?"

"Yes. I'm different. What time is the game?"

"Three."

"Then you were right to choose option number one. I do like to cross my t's. I'll call Dan and tell him I'm going to be late tomorrow."

"Ooh." She wiggled in his lap and pressed a kiss to the underside of his jaw. "Who knew such rigid attention to detail could be so sexy?"

A slight smile tugged the corner of his lips. "You like it unbending? How very fortunate because my attention to detail is not the only thing that's rigid."

Oscillating her hips, she rubbed against his burgeoning hard-on. "So I've noticed."

He merely stared at her for a moment, taking in the flush on her cheekbones and the lambent light in her eyes, feeling the heat and weight of her in his lap. Then he bent his head to kiss her.

And nothing more was said.

Blowing out an inner sigh of relief, Carly waved Wolf goodbye and firmly shut the door. Thank God he was gone because she was about to have a nervous breakdown. Turning, she pressed her back against the solid panels and slid slowly down the door until she was sitting on the cool tile floor, her knees wavering in front of her. She hugged them to her chest. "Omigawd, omigawd," she whispered. "What have I done?"

The question was rhetorical, of course, because she knew darn well what she had done.

Dear Lord.

At some point between Wolf lounging on her chair with her cat draped over his lap and his final drugging kiss, she'd gone and fallen in love.

She squeezed her eyes shut.

No, no, she *couldn't* have. She hadn't known Wolf that long and most of that time she hadn't even liked him. Plus, face it, she'd never been in love before, and she wasn't sure that she even believed in the emotion—at least when applied to her. So, how likely was it that she should suddenly find herself staring it in the face?

Try one hundred percent, said a knowing voice in her head. Groaning, she ground her forehead against her kneecaps because, likely or not, *like* it or not, she was eyeball deep in love.

She'd gotten her first inkling as she'd listened to Wolf's enthusiastic plans to buy Nik a car for his birthday. Then he'd hammered the final nail in her coffin with that flash of hurt she'd glimpsed when he'd realized Niklaus's first soccer game was tomorrow and the teen hadn't even bothered to mention it to him. She'd been so sure Robo Guy was Wolfgang's middle name, but with every day that passed, it became more evident that he cared deeply about his nephew's welfare. And in truth, he'd made considerable changes in his life in order to accommodate Niklaus's needs.

Okay, so he had proven himself to be definite love-worthy material. So what? She absolutely did not want to feel this way! They'd had the perfect setup and now it was all messed up. An hour ago she probably could have watched him walk out of her life without a qualm. She might have regretted it, but she could have stored away the memories to appreciate at a later date, then gotten on with her life.

Now, though, she just knew that when he rode off into the sunset, chasing after his dream job, it was going to hurt like hell.

At five minutes to five, Wolf parked in front of the Fitzpatricks' house and climbed out of his car. He hadn't really checked out the area when he'd dropped Nik off earlier, but he looked around now with appreciative eyes as he strode up the walk to the white stucco house. It was a nice older neighborhood with comfortable-looking homes that appeared prosperous without being ostentatious. The Fitzpatricks' was single-storied with an attached double garage and three fruit trees adorning the small front yard. Their leaves were turning gold and russet in the mild autumn weather, and Wolf admired them as he rang the bell.

A stocky redheaded man in his early forties answered it. "Hey," he said with a friendly smile. "You must be Nik's uncle."

"Wolfgang Jones." He offered his hand.

The man firmly shook it. "I'm Joe Fitzpatrick, Kev's dad." He pushed open the screen door. "Come in."

Wolf stepped inside and gave the place a quick comprehensive glance. "You've got a great house here." It was elegant but warm and welcoming, too, the kind of place he'd often dreamed of as a kid.

"Thanks, we call it home. Come on back to the kitchen," Joe invited. "The boys are finishing up a game of water polo, so you have time to have a beer with me."

"Would you mind making that a club soda or soft drink, instead?" Wolf followed his host through a spacious living room to the kitchen. "I'm due at work in about half an hour." Light streamed into the room through the glass slider and the sound of teenage boys shouting, laughing and splashing in the pool on the other side of the tiled patio drew his attention. Picking out Niklaus, he watched him for a moment and smiled. He'd never seen such a big grin on his nephew's face.

Joe handed him a can of club soda and followed his gaze. "You've got a great kid there. In fact, that's the only thing that keeps me from hating your guts."

He froze mid-sip and slowly lowered the can as he turned to stare at Joe. "Excuse me?"

"Your nephew talks nonstop about your hot car, and the other kids are practically orgasmic over your cool job.

Between that and the equally hot showgirl who I understand lives next door, you're making the rest of us parents look old and dull."

The redheaded man had an easy way about him and Wolf relaxed, shooting him a game smile in return. "Good to know it's just my job and my proximity to a beautiful blonde that generates your hatred. You had me worried there for a minute. I've been told I can piss people off, but it usually takes me longer than a minute and a half to totally alienate someone."

Joe threw back his head and laughed. "You're okay, Jones. And because you've got a sense of humor, I'm going to let it slide that you dress sharp on top of everything else, even though that's adding insult to injury."

Glancing from his pin-striped suit to Joe's raggedy cutoffs and stretched-out T-shirt, he shrugged. "Work clothes. What do you do for a living?" He took a pull from his can of club soda.

"I'm a thoracic surgeon."

Wolf choked on the icy liquid sliding down his throat. Swiping the back of his hand across his mouth, he gave the other man a solemn nod. "I can see why someone with your lack of skills would be intimidated by a security wizard like me, then." He looked around the sunny kitchen with its cozy clutter of a party in progress, glanced out at the boys horsing around in the pool, then back at his host again. He raised his eyebrows. "It's a beautiful Sunday afternoon. Shouldn't you be out on the links?"

"The wife beat me to it." Joe grinned. "She's the golfer in the family. Truth is, I'm not all that crazy about the sport." He leveled a stern look on Wolf. "Information I expect you to keep under your hat."

"I can see why. That's probably grounds for expulsion from the AMA." Both pleased and amazed at the immediate rapport he felt with the other man, he was opening his mouth to give Joe further grief when the gang of boys barreled through the door.

There were about a dozen of them, and after meeting them all, he spent a few additional minutes talking to the ones he'd heard Nik mention most often: Paddy, Josh and David. And he was happy to note that Carly's assessment of them was correct—they were nice boys.

Niklaus insisted on showing them all Wolf's car, and the teens spent ten minutes enthusiastically crawling through and around it. Finally Wolf glanced at his watch. "I'm sorry to cut this short, Nik, but we've got to get going if I'm going to get you home and still get to work on time."

"Aw, *man*." Nik looked at the other kids still partying full blast, then sighed in resignation. "I'll go get my bag." He started trudging toward the house, disappointment rounding his shoulders.

"Look," Joe said, "why doesn't he stay here? Clearly the kids aren't ready to shut down the party yet, and there's no reason why he should be the only one to miss out. I'll take him home after dinner."

Nik loped back to them, his face alight. "Oh, wow! Can I, Uncle Wolf?"

"Do you have homework?"

"Just some German, and I can do that in my sleep."

Wolf grinned and said the equivalent of *damn straight* in the language under discussion. Then he nodded. "All right, then."

"Yes!" Nik gave him a spontaneous high five before he turned to Joe. "Thanks, Dr. Fitzpatrick!" He trotted off to join his teammates.

The warmth of his nephew's rare unguarded approval lingered as Wolf turned to Joe. "Yes, thank you. You just elevated my standing in his eyes, and this really is above and beyond the call of duty after an entire afternoon spent with a dozen teenage boys running wild in your house and backyard."

"I'm happy to do it. Nik is probably the most appreciative of all of Paddy's friends."

"He hasn't caught a lot of breaks in his life," he agreed. "My sister isn't the most responsible parent in the world."

"I'm guessing you are, though."

"Me?" Wolf laughed shortly. "No, I'm mostly just stumbling around in the dark."

"Hey, we all do that," Joe said. "The difference is, most of us at least get to start out with the dawn. The teenage years can hit some pretty bleak patches, yet you're hanging in there, searching for the matches to cast a little illumination. I'd say that's responsible parenting."

He stared at the redheaded man in silence for a minute before giving him a slow smile. Then he reached out to shake Joe's hand. "Those are quite possibly the most encouraging words I've heard since Niklaus moved in with me," he said fervently. "Thank you. You've just made my entire week."

Twenty-Four

Wolf's shades weren't equal to the strong glare as he and Carly crossed the soccer field directly into the sun the next afternoon. He could make out a group of boys milling about in the bright golden light, but had no idea if it was Nik's team or the other school's. As they approached the nearest bleachers, however, their angle shifted just enough to pick out the Silverado uniforms of burgundy shorts, white jerseys with V-neck stripes and raglan sleeves to match the shorts and long burgundy socks with white stripes. A second later he spotted Niklaus, laughing with Paddy and David as he bounced a soccer ball from his foot to his knee and back again. As goalkeeper, he wore a uniform that was distinguished from the rest of the team's by its reverse color scheme and a mesh vest he wore in place of his jersey.

"Oh, good, they saved us a place," Carly said, pulling his attention away from his nephew. He looked up the bleachers and saw Treena, Jax, Ellen and Mack seated on the top riser.

"I didn't realize everyone was coming."

"It's Nik's first game, we figured that called for an extra show of support." She started up the narrow steps at the northern end of the risers. Ascending the stairs behind her, he admired the metronome cadence of her hips as she climbed to the top.

Carly's friends all stood as they approached, and Treena pointed to the free bench space on the other side of Ellen, who was farthest from the stairs. "We saved you a spot."

"And you're going to make us climb over every last one of you instead of shifting down a couple of feet to make this easier for us, aren't you?" Carly asked.

"Yep. I test-sat every inch of these bleachers, and this is the best spot by far." The pretty redhead's lips crooked up in a little one-sided smile. "Hey, you gotta get here early if you want the premium seats."

Blowing her a raspberry, Carly started inching past her friend.

Wolfgang followed in her wake, but when Treena reached out to halt him with a cool-skinned hand on his forearm, he stopped in front of her. He bent his head accommodatingly closer when she crooked a finger at him.

"You hurt Carly," she warned him in a low voice, catching him in the crosshairs of a hard-eyed gaze, "and I'll make your life a living hell."

He blinked in surprise, but gave her a clipped nod and moved on. Where had *that* come from? Then he rolled his shoulders in a quick shrug. Never mind. The sun's warmth was a pleasant weight on his back, his nephew was playing his first game of the year and his tall blonde chose that exact moment to turn and flash him a big, warm smile. He shoved the mini confrontation aside to contemplate later.

But apparently he was the only one here willing to defer

this argument, for as he passed in front of Jax, the other man murmured, "I've come to admire Carly a great deal. So, mess her up and—"

"You'll make my life a living hell," he interrupted in an equally low voice. "I've heard it already."

"You haven't heard the worst, though, pal. Because I plan to stand back and let the women handle you." Jax shot him a feral smile. "And you can trust me when I say they can do damage that you and I would never even dream of doing."

Well...shit. These two sure knew how to take the fun out of an afternoon. He'd be damned though if he'd let the other man see that. Shrugging, he murmured in a bored voice, "Tough crowd." Then he looked Jax straight in the eye. "Relax, Gallagher. I'm just here to watch a soccer game. I thought I'd wait until at least tomorrow before I mess with Carly."

He was prepared when he got to Mack. As the older man opened his mouth, Wolf snapped sotto voce, "Yeah, yeah, hurt her, I die. I *get* it already." Then he braced himself for Ellen, knowing that her condemnation would hurt worst of all because, out of Carly's friends, he liked her best.

When she patted his arm as he passed in front of her, however, it was accompanied by a gentle smile. "How's your mother, darling?" she asked. "Still baking her cakes? Now, I'm probably not in her league, but I did bring some cookies this afternoon. I remembered you like them."

He stopped dead and stared at her. Then, without even stopping to think about it, he snaked his arm around her waist, dipped her backward over his forearm and planted a firm kiss on her mouth.

When he set her back on her feet and turned her loose a second later, she blinked up at him, all big eyes, round mouth and flushed cheeks. "Oh, m-my," she stuttered. "Oh…my…gracious."

"Thank you for the warm welcome," he said over Mack's sputtering and Carly's whoop of startled laughter. "I appreciate it more than I can say." Sliding a hand beneath her elbow, he eased her down to the bench and took his own seat next to her.

Carly leaned forward to stare at her other three friends. "Your welcomes weren't nearly as warm and fuzzy, I take it," she said.

"Hey, don't look at me," Mack said righteously. "I didn't say a word." But he didn't quite meet her gaze.

"We're just looking out for your interests, Carly," Jax added.

"Uh-huh. And you don't see the irony in that?" Subjecting him to an unwavering glare, she said coolly, "*Wolf* isn't the man on this bench who lied about who he is or what his intentions are, Jackson. So do me a favor and let me look out for my own interests. And you," she said, giving Treena a stern look. "You're supposed to be my best friend. What are you doing talking to everyone about a relationship I discussed with you in private? I might have offered to castrate Jax when he hurt you, but you didn't see me running around discussing the way he'd played you with everyone. So why don't you extend me the same courtesy?"

Wolf barely had time to wonder just what she had told her friend when Treena declared indignantly, "I didn't tell anyone except Jax!" She turned to her fiancé. "You told *Mack?*"

But Jax had clearly fixated on one word and wasn't paying attention to anything else. "Castrate?" he demanded, and hunched in on himself protectively.

So Mack took up the slack. "Now, sweetheart," he said to the redhead. "Don't blame Jax. He was just concerned for Carly."

"Concerned about putting Wolfgang in the hot seat with you in order to take the heat off himself more like," Treena muttered. She bent forward to look down the bench at Wolf. "I apologize if I misread the situation," she said. "And in that spirit, I'll only geld you if you hurt her."

"Oh, for God's sake," Carly muttered at the same time a junior-high-age boy on the bench in front of them let out a snorting laugh.

Treena merely shrugged. "Hey, you asked me to extend the same courtesy."

"Darling," Ellen suddenly said in a clear voice, leaning around Wolf to look at Carly. "I don't care what *any* of them say. I'd hang on to your young man if I were you. Anyone who can kiss like he does is definitely worth fighting for."

With a shout of laughter, Wolf leaned into the petite older woman, giving her shoulder a companionable nudge with the side of his arm.

She reached over and patted his hand.

Then the soccer teams jogged out and took their positions on the field, and Wolf turned his attention to the ref as he tossed a coin to choose the goals. The other team won the toss and chose the north net, and he watched Nik lope down to the south line. Once the goalies were in position, the Silverado team took the kickoff to start the match.

Nik's friend Paddy, as center forward, took command of the ball and raced it up the field toward the north goal. But as he was passing it to his wing forward up near the penalty area, the other team's striker intercepted it and passed it to his fullback down the field. Running with the ball, the fullback kicked it long and high toward his goal.

It looked as though it was going to sail right over Nik's head, but as if he had wings on his heels, he soared up off the ground and snatched it out of the air with both hands. Taking two strides out of the net, he dropped the ball to the grass, dribbled it outside the penalty area and kicked it to the Silverado midfielder.

With a roar of approval, Wolf leaped to his feet. "Did you see that?" he demanded, grinning at Carly, who was also on her feet screaming. In fact, their entire row was standing and cheering, and he grinned at all of them, their earlier encounter forgotten. The parents and friends dotting the rest of the bleachers yelled their approval as well, and Wolf nudged the teen seated in front of him. "That's my nephew," he informed him when the kid turned around. Down on the strip of grass between the risers and the touchline, Niklaus's friend Natalie and three other cheerleaders commenced a hip-rocking, high-kicking, pom-pom-shaking routine.

By the halftime break, the score was three to zip in Silverado's favor, and Wolf, who had practically yelled himself hoarse during the first half of the match, volunteered to buy everyone a drink. As he descended the bleachers and walked toward the little food shack situated forty feet away, he was conscious of the comforting autumn warmth on his shoulders. He'd been planning to leave Vegas since practically the first minute he'd rolled into town, but he had to admit he was going to miss the sunshine if—no, *when*—he moved to Ohio.

To his surprise, Joe Fitzpatrick was working the shack. The stocky redhead handed the woman in front of Wolf a hot dog and a Coke, said "Thanks, Mary," then turned his attention to Wolf.

"Well, hello there, stranger," he said with his easy grin. "Long time no see."

With a wry smile of acknowledgment, Wolf replied, "I didn't expect to see you behind the counter."

Joe shrugged. "What can I say? The head of our booster club is real good at her job, and somehow I find myself manning the refreshment stand several times a season. Speaking of which, what can I get you?"

"Three Cokes, a diet Coke, a 7-Up and a root beer."

"Thirsty boy."

Digging his wallet out of his hip pocket, he shot the other man a smile. "I'm parched, but only the root beer is mine. The rest are for friends." And weird as that word sounded coming from his mouth, the group who had come here to support Niklaus today actually felt as if they could be friends.

"I don't suppose there're any showgirls among your friends?"

Wolf held up two fingers.

"Ah, be still my beating heart. Hey!" His face lighting up with enthusiasm, Joe grabbed a plastic grocery bag and slid the six icy cans of soda into it, then passed the bundle across the counter to Wolf. "You'll have to lend us a hand in the booster club next year. I'm mostly surrounded by mothers and I could really use another male." He grinned. "For guy talk, if nothing else."

"Or a session of scratching and spitting, maybe," Wolf said. "That's a good, time-honored tradition among men."

"And always a fun way to pass the time."

"Only…maybe not around the food."

Joe laughed and Wolf grinned back at him, feeling mellow and content about his day. If a guy had to be in a booster club—and that was something he could honestly say he'd never really considered before today—Doc Fitzpatrick would no doubt be an entertaining man to share the duties with.

Then it hit him that he would probably never find that out. He would be somewhere else next year. If for some reason

he didn't get the Ohio job, he'd likely accept a position somewhere else in the near future. One way or the other, his time
was coming.

Collecting his change, he bid Joe farewell and headed
back to the bleachers. But his smile faded as he walked away.

Pumped up not only on the way the first half of the game
had gone, but from simply playing competitively again,
Niklaus mopped the back of his arm across his forehead, ran
his fingers through his hair and hoped he didn't look like a
total freakazoid. Giving his pits a surreptitious sniff, he snick-
ered in relief. At least his deodorant was holding, even if he
had been sweating like a pig. Peeling off his knee and elbow
pads, he tucked them under his arm. Then, deciding there
was only so much a guy could do in the middle of a match,
he rolled his shoulders, blew out a breath and strode across
the field.

Straight for Natalie.

He had to fight the smile that wanted to pull his mouth
into a big goofy grin, and instead slapped into place a slight
quirk of the lips such as the one he'd seen on Uncle Wolf's
face once or twice. That had to look cooler than having his
mouth stretched into an idiot clown smile.

But he sure had something to smile about! He still couldn't
believe she'd shown up with a couple of the other cheerleaders in tow and performed their routines for his game. You
could have knocked him over with a feather when he'd heard
the chant of a pep-rally cheer and looked over to see her and
her friends jumping and kicking on the sidelines. Good thing
the ball had been in play up beyond the halfway line at the
time or God only knew how many balls would have gotten
past him.

He could feel that cowboy-on-peyote grin gaining control again and he slowed to wrestle it into submission. When he stopped in front of her a moment later, however, he wouldn't have put money down on how well he'd done.

"Hey," he said. Man, she looked pretty, with those brown eyes and white teeth, the sun shining on her silky dark hair and teasing out hints of red.

"Hi!" Reaching over, she gave him a swift hug, then turned him loose almost as swiftly and stepped back, laughing. "Surprised?"

"I'll say." He looked at her friends, a fine-boned black girl whose name he thought was Sondra and a petite blonde named Tiffany, then back at Natalie. "Thank you. All of you. This is really great." That damn smile started taking possession of his face again, but with a mental shrug he let it. "I didn't think anyone was going to be here to cheer me on at all, and now—"

"Not only does he have an entire row of spectators, but his very own cheer squad, too," David said, walking up to him. He handed Nik a sports drink and turned to Sondra. "Hi, I'm David. This was really nice of y'all."

She eyed him with interest even as she essayed a nonchalant shrug. "You probably shouldn't plan on getting used to it. We don't intend to do this for every game."

"No? I'm real sorry to hear th—"

"What do you mean an entire row of spectators?" Nik demanded.

"Your fans," David said. Without looking up from flirting with Sondra he waved a long, narrow, big-knuckled hand at the bleachers. "Up there."

Niklaus turned and looked up the bleachers. "Whoa."

The minute they caught his eye, Carly and Treena went

nuts, cheering and jiving and calling out to him as if he were a bigger star than David Beckham. Jax, Mack and Ellen waved. His face heating in pleasure and embarrassment, he lifted an arm in acknowledgment. Everyone he knew was here. Everyone except—

"Didn't you hear them screaming your name?" Natalie asked. "Man, they went crazy when you blocked that goal. Your uncle—"

"Nik."

He slowly pivoted, and there in the sun, holding a Smith's grocery bag in one hand, stood Uncle Wolf. The older man gave him the slight smile he'd been trying to conscript for his own, and it suddenly hit Nik why he liked it so much. It wasn't merely that it made a guy look cool. It was more that, subtle as the smile was, it conveyed genuine pleasure.

"Your grandmother told me you were a good player," Wolfgang said. "But I had no idea just how good until I saw for myself." He reached out as if to touch Nik, but dropped his hand before it reached his shoulder. "You were amazing out there."

Oh, man, oh, man. Emotion so raw and explosive went off inside of him that for one shaky second he wasn't sure if he was going to burst with pride or burst into tears. Twisting the top off his Gatorade, he chugged down half the bottle. He didn't lower it again until he had himself back under control. "Thanks."

Wolf shrugged that aside. "I'm in awe of your talent." He nodded to Natalie. "Miss Fremont. It's good to see you again. I enjoyed watching your cheerleading routines."

She beamed up at him. "Thank you. We don't usually cheer for the soccer team, so it was a surprise for Niklaus."

"And one I don't doubt for an instant that he appreciates

immensely." Glancing back and forth between the teens, he cleared his throat and hefted the bag in his hand. "Well, I'd better get these sodas up to the crew before they get rowdy." He smiled wryly. "Rowdier. I've never heard Carly and Treena yell the way they've done this afternoon. You made their day, kid." Then, turning on his heel, he eschewed the stairs to climb the risers, weaving between the seated spectators.

"You made his, too," Natalie said. "He was yelling louder than everyone else combined."

Coach called the team together a short while later, and when halftime ended not long after that, Niklaus hiked to the north goal line in a haze of happiness. This had been such a great afternoon! And it continued in the same vein when his team shut out the other school's in the second half with a final score of seven to zero.

After the post-game congratulatory walk, where the two teams passed each other single file in opposite directions while slapping hands and saying, "good job," he found Uncle Wolf and Paddy's dad waiting for them.

"You kids want to go for pizza?" Mr. Fitzpatrick asked. "Wolf and I are buying."

His uncle tipped his chin toward the girls. "The cheerleaders are welcome, too, of course."

The idea was met with enthusiasm and Nik grinned. He'd never, *ever* had family participate in the after-game pizza party and it was all he could do to keep from laughing like an escapee from the psyche ward. Then Carly and Treena descended on him, insisting that he pose with them for pictures that Mack took on his digital camera. When that was done, they demanded Mack take one of him and Uncle Wolf, one of him and Natalie, one of him with all three cheerleaders and another of his entire team. Then they commandeered the camera to snap a couple of shots of him with Mack and Ellen, and another of him with Jax, all the while giving one another a bad time when one perceived the other to have allowed her finger or the camera strap into the picture. They teased and cajoled smiles from everyone, whether manning the camera or giving advice from the sidelines, and although he thought he should probably be embarrassed by the huge fuss they made, all he truly felt was proud.

Besides, his friends already thought it was completely righteous that he knew real live showgirls, and here the two of them were going out of their way to express their friendship. What was embarrassing about that?

Everyone caravanned to the designated pizza joint where the seating arrangements fell into natural divisions of age. Pitchers of soda made the rounds at the team's table, and the noise level within the parlor's small back room grew louder as players relived aspects of the game, blowing off steam and generally showing off for the girls.

Things quieted down temporarily when the first of the pizzas hit their table, and before it could gear up again to its pre-food noise level, Carly and Treena came over and stooped down on either side of his chair.

"I'm sorry, toots," Carly said, "but we have to get going if we're going to make our first show with enough time to get into costume and makeup. They don't give dancers permission to go in late the way they do the security mucky-mucks."

"Let's have a little respect here," Wolf said from the next table. "That's *Mister* Mucky-muck to you two."

"Yeah, yeah, yeah," she said with a dismissive wave of her hand.

Treena ignored the byplay to tell Niklaus, "We just wanted to say one last time how great you were today. All of you," she added, including the rest of the team and the cheerleaders in her praise.

"Yes, you guys totally rocked," Carly agreed. Then she kissed him on one cheek while Treena kissed him on the other. "See you later."

He grinned as every teammate on his side of the table turned to watch them walk away.

"The redhead told your uncle she'd castrate him if he hurt the one who called you toots," said a youth down the table.

Nik leaned forward to see who had spoken. It was Jimmy Caswell's kid brother. "What?"

"Before the game everyone except the lady with the cookies was giving your uncle a rash and the blonde said for them to stay out of her relationship with him. So then the redhead apologized to your uncle, but said if he hurt the blonde she'd do the same thing the blonde had offered to do to *her* boyfriend and castrate him. I thought that was pretty cool."

So Uncle Wolf and Carly *did* have a relationship going? He twisted around to glance over at the grown-up's table, where his uncle was laughing at something Paddy's dad had said.

Yes! Turning back, he mentally rubbed his hands together. Now maybe his uncle wouldn't be in such a big hurry to chase that dream job of his.

Jax, Mack and Ellen left a while later, and about twenty minutes after they had stopped by to say their goodbyes, Uncle Wolf came over to his table. "I have to leave for work, too. Do you want a ride home or—"

"I can take him, Mr. Jones," Natalie offered.

His uncle turned to look at her. "Call me Wolf," he said. "And thank you. Drive carefully." Wolf turned back to him. "Be home in time to get your homework done," he said, and rose to his feet. Then he cupped his palm over the curve of Nik's shoulder and gave it a brief squeeze. "You did great out there today." He turned away to settle the bill with Mr. Fitzpatrick.

"Your people are so much cooler than mine," Natalie sighed. "If my folks were here they'd have bored everyone to tears with a lecture on the evils of pizza and sugared—or, God forbid, chemically sweetened—soft drinks. Plus, my mother would have had a plastic container of macrobiotic garbage in her tote that she'd expect me to eat instead. Tif, pass the pizza." When Nik snorted, she poked her elbow into his ribs. "Hey, you laugh, but I've gotta eat while I can."

The party started breaking up a short while later and Natalie and Nik walked out to her car. They talked nonstop as she drove him home.

When they arrived at the condo complex, he turned in his seat and looked at her. He didn't want the evening to end, but he hesitated to ask her in for fear she'd think he only had one thing on his mind.

And even if that was starting to be true, he didn't want her to think it. "You wanna go hang out by the pool for a while, or do you have a bunch of homework waiting for you at home?"

"No, I did it earlier. Hanging by the pool sounds great."

Sitting on the side of the pool, they dangled their feet in the water and continued talking about everything under the sun. "What college are you going to attend?" he asked at one point. He didn't ask whether she planned to go to college because he didn't doubt for a moment that she did.

"I'm thinking of Berkeley, but a lot will depend on what kind of scholarships I can get."

"Yeah, me, too. What do you think you'll major in?"

"I don't know! I envy kids who have a burning desire to be something. Take Sondra. She's known since she was about twelve that she wanted to be a doctor. But I don't have a clue what I want to do for the rest of my life. How about you? What do you want to be?"

"Rich."

"That's it?" She laughed skeptically. "Just rich? You don't think that's a little...shallow?"

"Spoken like someone who's never had to worry about money," he said without heat, and shrugged. "I have, and I don't want to scrabble for pennies the rest of my life. So I'm not planning to major in anything like liberal arts. Whatever I decide on is going to be marketable." He tangled his ankle around hers beneath the water. "And hopefully something I'll really enjoy, as well. But like you, I'm not quite sure yet what that will be."

At ten forty-five, Natalie reluctantly climbed to her feet. "I have to be in by eleven," she said.

Nik walked her to her car. At the driver's door he hesitated, then took a deep breath and lowered his head to kiss her.

Her lips were soft and warm and she stepped closer and wound her arms around his neck. He groaned and kissed her until he was dizzy.

Finally, he forced himself to raise his head and step back. "I'll see you tomorrow, okay?"

"Oh, yes." Opening the door, she slid into the driver's seat and smiled up at him. "See you tomorrow."

He watched her drive away, not even blinking until her headlights disappeared. Then, grinning like a fool, he turned toward his building.

No contest. This had been the best day of his whole life.

Twenty-Five

"So what was all that about with Wolfgang earlier?" Carly demanded of Treena as they removed their wigs and shed their costumes in the backstage dressing room between acts later that evening. The wardrobe mistress passed by and, collecting their headpieces for the new number, Carly handed Treena hers. Her friend accepted it without looking up from wrestling her G-string up her legs and Carly dropped her own on the mannequin head she'd nailed to the corner of her station.

Then Treena finished untangling the twisted beads from her new costume bottom and straightened to meet Carly's gaze head-on. "I merely warned him that he'd have to deal with me if he hurt you." She shrugged her bare shoulders. "Swear to God I didn't know it was going to turn into a serial bash."

"But why feel the need to warn him at all? It's not like he's some sleazy porn king trying to lure a kid fresh off the bus into the sex trade. I made a conscious decision about this relationship. I walked into it with my eyes wide open."

"But you're not your usual love-'em-and-leave-'em self with him. You keep making noises about dumping him, and you seem pretty adamant about it, too, until the next time the two of you clap eyes on each other. Then, bam! You're superglued together all over again."

"Yeah, I know. It's a little tough to explain even to myself. I mean, he's not the easiest man in the world to get along with, so you'd think it would be a piece of cake to walk away from our arrangement. But, God, Treen, there's just something about him. Every time I think I've got him pegged as this sort of guy or that sort of guy, he goes and does something that turns everything I thought I knew about him upside down."

"Like laying that hot one on Ellen," Treena agreed with a solemn nod. Then a laugh escaped her. "Lord, did you see the look on her face? That must have been one smokin' kiss. I gotta admit his panache bowled me over."

"That's an excellent way of putting it. Because when he does something like that, 'bowled over' is exactly how I feel. Suddenly our arrangement is no longer just an arrangement, it's an honest-to-God relationship." Her lips turned up in a wry smile. "And I can personally testify to how well the boy can kiss."

Treena sobered. "I just don't want to see you hurt."

"I don't want to see me hurt, either. But I don't know how you go about preventing something like that. It's not like you can simply stop taking chances. That might keep you out of harm's way, but at what cost if the price turns out to be total boredom?" She picked up the aqua-and-seafoam-green plumed headpiece and anchored it in place, then leaned into the mirror to check her theatrical makeup. "One thing I can say about Wolf, I'm never the least bit bored when I'm with him. Seems to me the dynamics between men and women are a crapshoot at the best of times. But while there's always the possibility you'll get your teeth kicked down your throat, you might also get something really wonderful that you never even anticipated." Deciding she looked a little lopsided, she added a bit more blush to the apple of her left cheek, then set the brush down atop a vellum envelope on her station.

And smiled dreamily.

"Oh, my God," Treena said slowly.

Carly turned to her friend, who gawked at her while efficiently twisting her curly hair into a bun atop her head. Peering at the redhead as she ruthlessly pinned the mass in place, Carly said encouragingly, "And?"

When Treena merely stared back at her for a second, she gave her a *c'mon, c'mon* twirl of her hand. "You said, Oh, my God. Do you have something to add to that?"

"You're in love with him."

"*What?*" She laughed incredulously. "Don't be ridicu—" Unable to force the words of the denial up her throat, she instead gave her chin a tiny dip of acknowledgment. "Maybe," she admitted. Straightening her shoulders, she looked Treena in the eye. "Maybe I am."

And, oh, what a tight little corner she'd painted herself into if that were true.

Treena lifted the tall headpiece onto her head. "Are you going to tell him?"

"One-minute warning, ladies!" Julie-Ann barked.

Ignoring the question, Carly focused instead on the envelope she'd just noticed on her station. "What is this?" she demanded. Easing it out from beneath her makeup brushes, she turned it over and was about to work a finger beneath the glued-down flap when Treena's impatient reply halted her.

"A freaking card, probably from some horny Stage Door

Romeo, that's been there since last night. It's waited this long already, so put it down and answer my question. Are you going to tell Wolfgang that you love him?"

"*No.*" She dropped the envelope back on the countertop. "Are you crazy? At this point I'm not really positive that I do love him, and I sure as hell have no intention of burdening him with a bunch of messed-up emotions that aren't even clear in my own mind."

"I think maybe you should."

"Well, that's quite the little turnaround, considering two hours ago you were threatening to cut off his pride and joy."

"Thirty seconds!"

Carly looked over at her friend as they headed for the wings. "What's suddenly changed between then and now?"

"Your feelings for him."

"Yes, well, that remains to be seen, doesn't it? *I* don't think I should say a word until I know for sure what I'm talking about. And since this is my life, my wishes supersede yours." Exhaling gustily, she gave a helpless shrug. "Treena, I agreed to a no-strings fling with the man." She laughed wildly. "No, I didn't do anything so passive as agree, I *insisted* on no strings, going out of my way to lay down an entire list of rules. So I can hardly take it back to the table now, demanding new negotiations."

"I disagree," Treena said quietly as they lined up with the other dancers in the wings. "This isn't some insignificant decision that won't impact your future one way or the other. This is your chance for happiness we're talking about. Take it from someone who's been there, it ain't over 'til the fat lady sings. And until that happens, honey, you can do any damn thing you want."

Julie-Ann, who had been counting down the last ten seconds, lapsed into silence just then and began using her fingers to count down the final five. When she hit zero, she thrust her arm toward the stage, finger pointing.

Shoving every other consideration aside, they slapped smiles on their faces and two-stepped out into the light.

Carly really had to focus on keeping in step with the rest of the dancers for the remaining numbers. Her thoughts kept jumbling up in her mind, where they played over and over again like an ancient film strip stuck in an endless loop. *Was she in love with Wolf? And if she were, all other considerations aside, how did she feel about that? If she hadn't agreed to a no-strings arrangement and if she didn't know that Wolf was dying to take off for greener pastures on the employment front, how would she feel about falling in love with him then?* She thought about it long and hard until she finally came to two independent conclusions.

One: she was pretty damn sure what she was feeling was the real deal. And two: she wasn't nearly as rattled by the idea as she thought she would be.

"And isn't that the craziest damn thing," she murmured at the end of the first show, when she could finally quit worrying that her wandering thoughts would sabotage her in the middle of a routine and instead start putting all her resources into the issue that had been distracting her.

So did she love Wolf?

She'd loved watching him this afternoon. He'd been no-holds-barred happy to be at a high school soccer game. He'd also been funny and touchingly sweet in his unabashed bias toward Nik's efforts. Clearly he was proud as punch of the teen's accomplishments, though she had the feeling that he would have cheered just as loudly, would have proclaimed his relationship with the boy to everyone around them just as proudly, if Nik had been a total loss at defending his goal.

All the same, observing her mother's series of upwardly mobile unions hadn't exactly reinforced the one-man-for-one-woman concept in her head. And as she'd once told Wolfgang with perfect honesty, she much preferred the idea of taking care of herself to having a man do it for her.

Yet the idea of living day in and day out with Wolf didn't feel wrong.

Not that she could wrap her mind around the concept of actual marriage. Little alarms went off in her head at the mere word. It was simply too large a step, not to mention putting the cart so far ahead of the horse it was ludicrous. Wolf had no desire to marry her. He wanted to move to bore-your-pants-off Middle America and marry some nice docile woman who would never give him a moment's grief. A sweet young thing whose only conversation would be, "*Yes*, Wolfgang, *no*, Wolfgang…whatever you say, Wolfgang."

She made a rude noise. That would never be her, so why was she wasting her time even contemplating this stuff? Plainly it was making her crazy. Looking around a bit frantically, she sought a distraction.

Treena was laughing with Eve, Michelle and Jerrilyn at the latter's station across the room, and although joining them would no doubt help take her mind off all this pointless what-iffing, she simply didn't feel like it. Her costumes had been returned to the wardrobe mistress and her station was actually in pretty good shape, so there was nothing there to deflect her racing thoughts. She could always go plunk a few bucks into a slot machine, she supposed, except that didn't appeal to her, either.

Then her gaze caught on the vellum envelope she'd

noticed earlier and she eagerly snatched it up off the counter, sending makeup brushes rolling in three different directions. Gathering them up, she reflected that the probability was high that Treena was right, it was most likely an invitation or a proposition from a Stage Door Johnnie who'd caught their show and taken a shine to the shape of her boobs or the length of her legs. But beggars couldn't be choosers. She was desperate for a diversion, so this would have to do.

Setting the brushes in a jar, she slid her thumb beneath the glued flap, broke the seal and pulled out the card inside. She flipped it open and read its message.

Then she set it down again.

"Well, shit," she whispered. "This is not a good thing."

"Wolf." Beck walked up to him in the hotel lobby, where he stood listening to the bell captain's report of a guest's suspicious behavior. "The boss is looking for you."

"Okay. Take over for me here, will you? The head valet reported a guest who arrived in a taxi with an especially heavy suitcase that he didn't want anyone to handle. Miller here ran into the same problem with the man."

"He set it down just inside the door, so I assumed he wanted it carried up to his room," the bell captain explained. "But when I went to lift it onto the trolley, I barely had time to realize the thing weighed a ton before the guest snatched it away. I talked to Duval and both he and I thought the same thing—the suitcase weighed a helluva lot more than the usual guest's and that there was something a little hinky about the guy's determination to keep anyone else from lifting it."

"You get a room number?" Beck asked, and knowing he was leaving the problem in good hands, Wolf thanked Miller

for bringing the issue to his attention and headed for the
S & S command center.

He found Dan in front of the north wall of surveillance
screens, pointing out various forms of suspicious behavior to
a heavyset man with a receding hairline. After a few seconds
spent watching to see if it was appropriate to approach, he
walked up to them.

"Sorry to interrupt, but Beck said you were looking for me?"

"Yes. Wolf, I'd like you to meet Oscar Freeling. Oscar, this
is Wolfgang Jones, my second in command I've been telling
you about."

Wolf's gut produced a sudden rush of acid at the realiza-
tion this was the OHS man he'd been waiting to meet, and
his heartbeat picked up its pace. But he'd been working
toward this moment for far too long to let his sudden nervous-
ness show. Smiling with pleasant professionalism, he stuck his
hand out, firmly shaking the older man's when it was offered.
"It's good to meet you, sir."

"Good to meet you, too, son. Dan here's been telling me
nothing but good things about you." Freeling studied him for
a silent moment, then nodded as if he'd come to a decision.
"How about I buy you a cup of coffee and we have a little talk?"

"That would be great." He looked at Dan. "With your
permission?"

"Absolutely. Take your time." He smiled wryly. "We'll
muddle through somehow."

Wolf directed Freeling to the hotel coffee shop, where the
older man bought them both a Danish and a cup of coffee.
They exchanged pleasantries for a few minutes, then Freeling
got down to business. He talked at length about OHS Industries, what they did and what the head-of-security position
entailed.

It sounded like the very job Wolf had been searching for. Maybe a little dull after three years of nonstop action at the Avventurato, but the perfect opportunity to finally be in charge.

As if reading his mind, Freeling suddenly said, "Dan's given me a pretty detailed rundown of the duties you've performed and the creative thinking you've applied to various problems that have arisen. Why would you want to leave an exciting job in a big casino for one in corporate security?"

I don't know.

He gave himself a mental shake. Where the hell had that come from? Of course, he knew. "Because I thrive on responsibility, and the province for this company's security would be all mine. I've been preparing for the opportunity to head my own division for as long as I can remember."

He may as well have said nothing at all, for Freeling no longer appeared to be listening. He was staring over Wolf's shoulder with slightly glazed eyes, and even as he turned in his chair Wolf was pretty sure what—if not exactly whom—he would see.

Yet his heart still gave a solid kick against the wall of his chest when he saw Carly standing a few feet away. Her expression, as their eyes met, was noncommital, and he wondered if she'd overheard his conversation with the other man. The thought caused his heartbeat to double its pace with unspecified guilt.

But that was an emotion that had no place in his life, and he straightened in his seat. "May I help you, Miss Jacobsen?"

"I'm sorry to interrupt...Mr. Jones...but I think I've got a problem with a fan and I need to talk to someone about it before the ten o'clock show starts. If this is a bad time for you, though, I can take it to someone else in S & S."

Someone was giving her trouble? Every other consideration emptied out of his mind. "What kind of problem?" he
demanded, at the same time Oscar Freeling assured her that
her timing was just fine.

The older man rose to his feet to pull out a chair for her
at the table. "You just sit right down," he instructed gently.
"Can I get you a cup of coffee? Or perhaps you'd prefer I take
a walk, so you can talk in private."

"No, you're welcome to stay. I wouldn't mind that coffee,
though." She turned to Wolf as the heavyset man hailed a
waitress. "I think I might have a stalker."

The hell you say! But he shoved aside his incredulous indignation and slapped his professional face in place. Pulling
a small notebook out of his inside breast pocket, he flipped
it to a clean page, set it on the table in front of him and
clicked down the ballpoint of his pen. "What makes you
think so?"

"It started a few weeks ago when I received some flowers
from an anonymous admirer." She went on to tell him about
the two flower arrangements that had shown up at her station
in the showgirls' dressing room and the unease they'd
inspired. Asking questions when he needed clarification, he
took notes.

"Then things settled down," she said, "and I thought
maybe I'd overreacted. But tonight this was on my station,
and now I'm freaked out all over again." She pushed an
envelope across the table toward him.

He picked it up and pulled out the card inside. Flipping it
over to read the manufacturer's mark on the back, he saw it
was a generic blank card that could have been bought in any
drugstore or hotel gift shop in the city. He turned it right side
up again and opened it.

"I saw you watching that man like a bitch in heat," Wolf read. "You must stop if you want to regain my respect." He looked up from the card. "And you're convinced no one you know might have sent it as a joke?"

"Yes. I don't know anyone who would consider this funny."

"It sounds a little obsessive," he agreed. "Any ideas on who he thought you were watching?"

She gave him an Are-you-kidding-me? look and he thought, *oh, shit*, then reluctantly answered his own question. "Me."

"Yes. A few of my things had piled up on top of the envelope at my station and I didn't notice it until tonight. Treena said she saw it yesterday, though, so I'm thinking it's maybe in regard to Saturday night down on the casino floor—"

Where they'd exchanged a look so hot that he would have cleared off the nearest gaming table and laid her out on top of it if she'd come within touching distance. He glanced at Freeling, but didn't have time to feel embarrassed over a potential employer hearing hints of his lack of professionalism, because years of security training were kicking into high gear.

"First thing I do is talk to the florist," he said firmly. "Maybe we can find out who ordered the—" Carly was shaking her head, and he chopped himself off mid-word. "No? Why not?"

"I did that. I went and talked to the florist."

"When? And who did you talk to?"

"It must have been—I don't know, maybe two weeks ago? Something like that. I talked to a man named Mr. Beezer or Mr. Belzer, who wasn't very cooperative, and a nice young woman named Lisa, who was much more helpful. But the upshot was they have no record of a delivery to the dressing room, and Lisa said that while they might not have records of the sale if it was paid for by cash, they always have records of deliveries."

"Unless the buyer took the arrangement with him."

"But even if that were true, how did he get it into the dancers' dressing room?"

"Good question. The time frame between receiving the first batch of flowers and tonight's card is a bit longer than three weeks, am I correct?" He glanced up from his notes, and when she nodded an affirmative he continued, "Then your admirer's actions span a little less than a month, during which time his gifts to you have turned up in a backstage dressing room that the average tourist wouldn't even know how to locate, let alone have the nerve to breach. And his comments in this card refer to an exchange that happened on the casino floor at about—what?—midnight?"

"Somewhere around that time."

"So, using that as a jumping-off point, let's narrow his window of opportunity down to the wee hours, since that would be his best bet for getting in and out of the backstage area without detection." He scribbled a few notations in his notebook, then looked up at her. "It's not beyond the realm of possibility that we're dealing with a local who spends a lot of time at the Avventurato. But the dressing room deliveries in particular suggest someone who can blend in, so it strikes me as more likely that it's one of our own employees—and most likely one on the swing or graveyard shift."

Tossing down his pen, he promised, "I'm going to look into this, Car—uh, Ms. Jacobsen. But while this gives me a starting point, I can't predict how long it will take to track down who's responsible." He focused his stern regard on her because he wanted her full and undivided attention in order that she heed his next instructions. "In the meantime, I want you to take a few basic steps to protect yourself. That means not getting onto any of the elevators here if the only other occupant is a single man. It means always having someone with you when you go to and from your car, especially in the parking garage, which can be pretty deserted in the early morning hours. I assume that in most instances your friend Ms. McCall will be your companion. But if she should have a different night off from yours—"

"I'll catch a ride with my next door neighbor," she interrupted. "He works pretty much the same shift that I do, and while he's not the most gregarious personality in the world, he is a big, strong guy."

Smart-ass. A smile wanted to tug up the corner of his mouth, but he bit it back. "He sounds like just the ticket." Glancing at his watch, he rose to his feet, then studied her as she, too, stood. She looked strong and confident in her showgirl regalia and dramatic makeup, but he knew she had to be nervous about her unwanted admirer to have brought it to his attention. "Are you heading back to the dressing room for the second show?"

"Yes."

"Then allow me to accompany you." He turned to Freeling, who had been quietly listening to their exchange. "I'm sorry, sir, but I'm going to have to postpone our talk. I need to get started on this."

Freeling also climbed to his feet. "Of course you do," he said briskly, then turned to Carly. "I'm sorry about your troubles, miss," he said gently. "But if you don't mind, I'll just tag along to see how Jones handles the matter."

She stared at Wolf for several silent seconds before switching her attention to the older man. Finally she shrugged. "Sure. Why not?" she said. "The more the merrier, I suppose."

Twenty-Six

Carly arrived home from work jumpy and unsettled. She fed the babies, took Buster for his evening constitutional around the grounds and devoted a little time and attention to the cats, but even then she wasn't unwound enough to go to bed. Pouring herself a glass of wine, she went out onto the lanai, where she lit the candles on her little mosaic table, plopped her butt in a comfortable chair and propped her feet up on the table's edge. Both cats leaped into her lap and Buster came over to rest his chin on her knee.

Little by little she began to decompress.

She was starting to make definite progress when the slider next door opened. A moment later, Wolf vaulted the half wall that divided their balconies. She watched as he crossed the small lanai and dropped down onto the chair beside her.

"I thought I might find you still up," he said softly, swinging his feet up onto the table next to hers. Tripod jumped down from her lap and hopped up into his, and Wolf massaged his hand deep into the cat's fur as he looked over at her in the flickering candlelight. "You still too rattled over receiving that note to sleep?"

"Yes. Did anyone suspicious pop up when you went back to S & S?"

"Not yet. But I've got the tech wizards running employee records for any complaints that are even remotely similar, so that may kick something loose soon."

There didn't appear to be any point badgering him with questions that he hadn't had time to find answers for, so she nodded and offered him a glass of wine.

When he turned it down but said he wouldn't say no to a beer, she got up to grab him one. Then they sat beneath the desert moon sipping their drinks in companionable silence for a while.

It didn't take long, however, before she began to grow less comfortable and started feeling increasingly more agitated instead. Tension built within her until she finally heard herself blurt, "So, Mr. Freeling seems like a nice man. Is he here to talk to you about that dream-position-somewhere-other-than-Vegas you've been waiting for?"

The words had no sooner left her lips than she could have ripped out her tongue. Dammit, she had promised herself she wouldn't go there once she'd begun to suspect the reason behind Freeling's intense interest in Wolf's performance earlier this evening. Yet here she was, desperate to know if her suspicions were valid and incapable of preventing herself from asking.

Wolf stilled, his beer bottle suspended mid-tilt. Then he took a sip, lowered the bottle and turned to look at her, his eyes hooded in the candlelight. "Yes."

Her heart jumped as if he'd given her a zap with a stun gun. And that was precisely how she felt—stunned and miserable.

But what could she say? She'd walked into this relationship with her eyes wide open. She could hardly kick up a fuss now that Wolfgang was prepared to do as he'd planned all along and take a job he'd been waiting half his lifetime to be offered. Clearing her throat she said huskily, "Congratulations, Wolf. I'm…happy for you."

"You are?" He looked at her closely. "You think I should take the job, then, if he offers it to me?"

What are you, crazy? Of course I don't! I think you should stay right here with me.

But she couldn't say that. They had both agreed theirs was to be a short-term arrangement, and if it was about to end far sooner than she could bear to think about—well, she would simply have to suck it up and take it like a woman. "If you feel that strongly about sinking roots anywhere but here, then…yes. I suppose you should."

Dumping Tripod onto the deck, he rose to his feet and stuffed his hands in his slacks pockets, rocking back on his heels as he stared down at her. "Yeah. I suppose I should."

She must have looked as unconvinced as she felt, however, because all of a sudden he dropped to a squat in front of her and reached to scoop her out of her chair. Her heart tripping, she emitted an embarrassingly mouselike squeak as he surged upright before swiveling to reclaim his seat.

Clutching him as she sprawled off center across his thighs, she drew up her legs, which were sliding helter-skelter down his and threatening to dump her off his lap onto the floor.

He tucked her more securely against him and stroked a soothing hand down her back. "I suppose in the end I probably will take the job," he reiterated. Then he regarded her with a serious gaze. "But not before I find out who's messing with you. I'm not going anywhere, Beauty, until I've put a stop to this bullshit. You can take that to the bank."

The ringing telephone awakened Wolf around eight-thirty. It had been after three before he'd gotten to bed last night, but this was the beginning of his Tuesday-Wednesday weekend, so he'd thought he could catch up on his sleep this morning.

Apparently that wasn't in the cards, however, and groggily he patted the nightstand, fumbling across its smooth cherry surface until he located the phone. Thumbing the button that mercifully cut short its annoying ring, he brought the receiver to his ear. "H'lo?"

"Wolfgang? Oscar Freeling here."

"Um." Pushing himself up in bed, he rubbed a hand over the morning stubble prickling his jaw as he sought a little clarity from his slumber-clogged brain. "What can I do for you, sir?"

"I realize I probably woke you up and I apologize for that, but something's come up at OHS and I have to leave for the airport in a few minutes. I just wanted to tell you how much I enjoyed being able to talk to you and watch you work last night. And I want to officially offer you the position of head of security at OHS before I leave."

"Oh." His mind went blank. "Ah…"

"I know it's sudden. You don't have to give me an answer right this minute. I'm sure you have questions, so just think about it and I'll give you a call later this week. Okay?"

"Yes. Certainly. I mean, thanks. I will. Think about it, that is." Christ. Could he *sound* any more imbecilic? Gathering his wits, he said with all the dignity he could muster, "Thank you, sir. I'll give your offer my full consideration."

"Excellent. Talk to you soon." And before Wolf could say "Have a safe flight," the older man had disconnected.

Leaning back against the headboard, he blew out a breath. He stared out into the middle distance and attempted to clear his wits. Only one thought lightened the fog hazing his brain, however. He'd gotten the job.

Holy shit. *He'd gotten the job!*

He always figured he'd be a lot more excited when the day finally came.

"*Congratulations, Wolf,*" he heard Carly's voice whisper in his mind. "*I'm happy for you.*"

Digging his elbow into his raised kneecap, he brought his hand up to squeeze the spot between his eyebrows where a headache was starting to brew. Offering felicitations for achieving a goal he'd longed for years to attain had been a nice gesture on her part. So why had he felt as if she'd just given him a swift kick to the crotch instead?

Pinching the bridge of his nose tighter, he sighed. Maybe because he was being offered everything he'd ever thought he wanted out of life—and he wasn't sure if he wanted it still. Or maybe because being with Carly made him happier than he could ever remember being.

But who knew how long that would last? He sure as hell didn't have a clue whether Carly suffered from any of the conflicted feelings that had his gut in an uproar. Maybe she truly was happy for him and would be just as content to see him go.

Sliding down to lie flat on the mattress, he pulled the pillow over his head and crossed his arms atop it, mashing it into his face.

What was he thinking? There was no question he still wanted the job. It was just— He'd lived in Vegas for three years now, and for as long as he'd been here he had been making plans to get the hell out and live somewhere more real. Yet somehow in the past couple of weeks, between Carly, her strays and her overprotective friends, and Nik, with his determination and athletic skills and *his* new group of buddies, and meeting Joe, a guy who felt like a friend despite the fact he'd only known the man for a total of maybe an *hour*, Wolf had started to feel as if he had roots in the community. He'd come to realize that Sin City wasn't merely flash and glitter, that there were actually nice people in nice neighborhoods who made good lives for themselves here.

And maybe in a far-off corner of his mind he'd even begun to think that perhaps he could make a life here, too.

Now, if *that* didn't fly in the face of his all-important plan, he didn't know what did. He was grateful he had a couple of days to think things through, because he didn't have the first idea how this sudden turnabout to his usual way of thinking would hold up beneath the weight of all his long-held beliefs.

Flinging the pillow aside, he stumbled to his feet. The condo was quiet when he entered the short hallway and he padded toward the kitchen in search of a cup of coffee. Pleased to discover that the morning pot Nik always made before he left for school still had coffee in it, Wolf poured himself a cup and stuck it in the microwave to heat. The timer had just sounded and he was reaching into the oven for the reheated brew when the phone rang for the second time that morning. Grabbing the mug, he took a scalding sip as he reached for the receiver on the breakfast bar. "Jones."

"Wolfgang, this is Fred at Security and Surveillance. I'm sorry to bother you on your day off, but—"

"You've got someone for me to look at?" Wolf interrupted, snapping to complete attention at the sound of the computer tech's voice.

"Yeah. That is, some preliminary data's kicked loose. I've got one possibility and two less likely prospects that I thought you might like to take a look at. You want me to read you the information I've collected so far?"

"No. See if you can get any of the suspects under surveillance. I'm coming in." The tech was still protesting he hadn't meant to pull him away from his weekend when Wolf hung up.

He was halfway to his car when a sudden thought struck him, and he stopped to gaze back at his building as he considered its viability. Then, shaking his head, he right-faced toward the garage once more. He took several additional steps before halting again.

Finally he cursed, blew out an exasperated breath and loped back to the condo. A minute later he knocked on Carly's door.

When she answered it, she looked about as alert as he'd felt when Freeling's call had awakened him, all blurry eyes and finger-in-the-socket electrified bed head. Gazing at the flowered cotton boxers and orange tank top she slept in and the pillowcase crease in her cheek, he grimaced apologetically.

"Damn. I'm sorry, I should have looked at the time."

"Whatcha want, Wolf?" A huge yawn cracked her jaw as she blinked up at him with sleepy blue eyes.

"I'm going in to work for a while to look over profiles of the men my tech pulled up as possible suspects for your stalker. I thought maybe you'd like to go with me." He couldn't decide if including her was a new low in professionalism for him or a smart way to expedite the process. But if she recognized any of the men Fred had culled from the employee files, it could cut through a lot of crap. And that would at least give them a place to start.

On the other hand, he could be totally off track. He never knew what his true motives were concerning her anymore.

Luckily she cried, "Yes!" and leaped into his arms before he had a chance to second-guess himself yet again. Wrapping her legs around his waist, she plastered herself against his chest to press an enthusiastic smacking kiss to his lips. Then before he could grab onto her butt to hold her in place, she'd disengaged herself and was back on her feet in front of him. "*Thank* you," she said, apparently wide-awake now. "It will only take me a minute to pull myself together."

"Wear something conservative, if you own any such clothing," he said as she headed toward the hall.

"Yessir, Mr. Jones, sir. You're the boss."

"Excuse me?" He stuck the tip of his little finger in his ear and wiggled it. "Would you mind repeating that?"

"Oh, honey, don't you wish." Laughing, she disappeared down the hall to her bedroom.

Figuring it would be a while, he turned his attention to the babies to help kill the time. When Carly entered the living room ten minutes later, he was crouched in front of her red chintz couch rubbing Buster's exposed belly while Tripod stropped himself against the side of his leg. Hearing her footsteps on the hardwood floor, he looked up.

And did a double take. Then, giving her a slow, intent perusal to be sure his eyes weren't deceiving him, he climbed to his feet.

She was clad in khaki pants and a designer blazer with a white t-shirt beneath, and she'd done something to her hair that made it look casually tousled instead of her usual don't-mess-with-me spikes. Except for her scarlet toenail polish, she looked eerily like the idealized kindergarten teacher he'd fantasized about for so long.

Which, while a little surreal, ought to be a good thing. So why did it make him feel so dissatisfied instead? "Whoa," he said softly. "That is quite a change."

"You said conservative, toots." She looked down at her outfit, a flash of something both sad and kiss-my-ass rebellious crossing her face. "These are part of my Junior Leaguer duds that I keep specifically for visits with my mother."

"You make yourself over completely for your mom?"

Only if I want her approval, Carly thought. But she wasn't about to admit she'd never entirely outgrown the need for that. She was over thirty, for God's sake, she ought to be beyond such things by now. So she merely shrugged and said nonchalantly, "Pretty much. It's either that or listen to a litany of my shortcomings."

"Well, you look very…nice."

She couldn't prevent the trace of bitterness that edged her laugh. "Yeah, I thought you'd probably like it."

To her surprise, he shook his head and said, "To tell you the truth, Carly, I'm not sure that I do."

"No kidding?" Genuine amusement replaced the jaundiced laugh of a second ago. "There may be hope for you yet, Jones. By rights, this outfit oughtta be right up your alley." Modeling it, she turned in a slow circle in front of him. "What don't you like about it?"

"The fact that you don't look anything like you." He slung an arm around her shoulders and turned her toward the foyer. "But it might come in handy as stalker bait, so I guess I'll just have to live with it."

"So I'm to be the sacrificial goat?" she inquired dryly as he ushered her out the door. She watched as he nudged Rags back inside her apartment with the side of his foot and gently closed the door on Buster's inquisitive face. "Good to know you find me useful."

He looked down at her with sober eyes. "You might be surprised what all I find you."

What was that supposed to mean? That he had feelings for her? That he found her—what?—attractive? Competent? Worthy of his *love?* Maybe even all of the above? That would all be very nice, but what she'd really like to know was, if by some miracle the latter should be true, would he leave to take that damn job in Wherever Middle America anyhow?

And when the hell had she turned into such a chicken-shit that she was afraid to even ask?

She chewed over her newly acquired yellow streak as they drove toward the Avventurato. No matter how she approached it, she was no closer to discovering a resolution by the time they walked into the Security and Surveillance department than she'd been when she'd first started gnawing on the subject.

Guiding her with a firm hand under her elbow, Wolf made a beeline across the room to a young man with a shock of dark hair and largish ears. "Show me what you've got, Fred," he commanded before the poor guy had a chance to do more than blink up at them.

She gave the computer tech a smile. "*Please*, he meant to add," she said, remembering the young man from the night she and Treena had helped catch the card cheat. "How are you, Fred? It's nice to see you again."

His Adam's apple rode the length of his throat as he swallowed hard. "I'm good, Ms. Jacobsen."

She waved aside the formality. "Please. Call me Carly."

His ears began to glow red from the dull flush climbing his face. "Okay, sure. Thanks, Car—"

"Do you two mind?" Wolf's snarled. "This isn't a goddamn ice-cream social." But visibly collecting himself, he turned to Fred and said with exaggerated politeness, "Show me what you've found, *please*."

When Fred promptly reached for a folder on his desk, Wolf turned to snag a rolling office chair and demonstrated his civility by politely seating her in it. For just a second after she'd settled herself, he continued to smooth his thumb over the shoulder of her jacket. Then, stepping back, he rolled another chair over for himself.

"As I mentioned on the phone," Fred said, clearing off a space on the long lab-style table next to him and laying out the contents of his folder in three slender piles, "I came up with one guy who seems like a real possibility and two who seem less likely, but who I still didn't feel comfortable just blowing off."

He pointed to the first one. "This is Jeff Evans. He seems our most likely bet. Do you remember this guy, Wolf?"

"The name sounds familiar." He reached for the paperwork. "That's not the guy from Catering who was put on probation for bothering a couple of female guests and one of the girls from the spa, is it?"

"Yep."

"As I recall—" Wolfgang turned his head to give Carly a considering look "—the women he targeted were all blondes."

She'd been leaning into him trying to read the report in his hand, but the angle was wrong so she sat back again. A second later Wolf passed her the top sheet from the two-or-three-page stack he held, and her gaze went directly to the employee ID photo in the top right-hand corner.

"Do you recognize him?"

She studied the picture intently, but her shoulders finally slumped and she was forced to shake her head as she handed it back to him. "No. He doesn't look familiar at all."

"There's no guarantee that you would have actually seen

your stalker. But since he seems to believe the two of you have a relationship, I'm betting you have come face-to-face with him at some point." He turned to Fred. "Who's next?"

Fred passed him the next report. "This was a classic case of he said, she said, so I don't know how plausible he is as a suspect. But I included him because the allegation made against him is similar in tone to Carly's case."

Wolf glanced down at the report. "His name is Brian Hyde?"

"Yes. He works in Janitorial-Housekeeping. Last year a guest filled out a complaint to the effect that when she came up to her suite to get a sweater, she found Hyde making himself at home in her room. She claimed he was harassing her. *He* claimed that he'd been sent to clean up her bathroom, which Maintenance had made a mess of while fixing a stuck drain in the tub. She said—and this was the thing that struck me—that he talked to her as if they were a couple in an ongoing relationship and refused to hear her suggestion that he didn't even know her, let alone have a relationship with her. He said he had no idea what she was talking about. Maintenance backed him up insofar as they had been sent to that room to fix the drain, and since Hyde had no other complaints lodged against him, we ended up comping the woman her room and making note of the allegation without taking action against the employee."

Once again, Wolfgang passed the top sheet to her and she studied the picture. Something niggled at her this time and she glanced up at Wolf. "He looks familiar, but I can't remember where I've seen him."

"Sometimes still photos don't jog the memory because of the lack of animation." Gesturing toward the wall of security monitors, Wolf glanced at Fred. "Did you get any of our suspects on a security cam?"

"No. Hyde doesn't come in until three, Evans is involved in catering a rehearsal party brunch in the Piccola Room and we don't have cameras in the kitchen they're using. It should be over by one or so. Sikes—" Fred handed Wolf the final report "—has the day off."

"What's the story on him?"

"He's been served with restraining orders that prohibit him from coming within fifty feet of two separate women."

"That sounds promising," Wolf said.

"Yeah, except they were sworn out by his ex-wife and ex-girlfriend."

"Women he actually knows, in other words," Wolf said.

"Exactly."

"And we know this how? You have a source in Metro you haven't told us about?"

Fred laughed. "No, his file was flagged when the ex-wife garnisheed his wages for back child support. She was both bitter and talkative, and the information went in his record."

"You did good work here, Fred. Very good work. I want to put Carly within sight of all three men to see what kind of reaction we get. Since Sikes sounds the least likely at this time, we can wait until he's back at work. We have grounds to summon Evans for questioning if he's broken his probation with the hotel, so I'd like you to call him up here as soon as possible. And I want to know the instant you see Hyde so we can set Carly up where he'll see her. You've got my cell phone number—call me as soon as you know something about either man."

Then he turned to Carly. "As for you," he said. "We're going to get out of here for a while. I pulled you out of your house pretty damn abruptly this morning. So come on. Let me buy you a proper breakfast."

Twenty-Seven

"So here I sit, dressed as requested," Carly said as they waited for their post-breakfast coffee to arrive in a Spring Valley neighborhood restaurant. The sun suddenly crested the piñon pines across the lot and poured through the window, flooding their table with light. She fanned herself with her fingers. "Wow, that certainly warmed things up in a hurry." Removing her lightweight wool blazer, she stood to hang it from the back of her chair. Then reseating herself, she pinned Wolf in place with her blue-eyed gaze and picked up the conversational thread she'd interrupted. "So *why* did having me dress in PTA duds sound like a good idea to you again?"

He stared at the skimpy white tank top her jacket's removal had revealed. "Whoa. *Now* you look like you. Are you wearing a bra under that thing? You're not, are you?"

She didn't reply, merely gave her shoulders a subtle shimmy and wagged her eyebrows at him.

"Hell, you're not. Is that the way you get around your

mother? By wearing the furthest thing from conservative you can find under the clothing she sees?"

"Yep. You like?"

"Oh, I do." He thought his tongue might be hanging out, he liked it so well. Shaking his head to clear it, he tried to get back on track. "What did you ask me?"

"Why you wanted me to dress like this."

But he still wasn't focusing. "What are you wearing under the khakis?"

"Well, unlike you," she replied serenely, "I don't go commando. I've got on a nice little red lace thong. The emphasis, of course, being on little."

"Holy shit." He swallowed hard. "So, uh…where were we again?"

"Why you wanted me to dress like this."

"You've said that before, haven't you?"

"Yes, I have." A satisfied gleam in her eyes, she gave him a smile that promptly fired his engine and sent it revving into high gear. "But for you, toots, I don't mind repeating myself."

"Okay, now you're just messing with me." His competitive streak belatedly kicking in, he straightened in his chair. For about two seconds he considered retaliating in kind. Given the chemistry between them, he didn't doubt for a minute that he could get her just as worked up as she'd gotten him. But recalling his professionalism—an attribute that *used* to be his number one priority—he reluctantly abandoned the idea.

"I wanted you to wear something conservative," he replied instead with cool-voiced authority, "because, as I told Fred, I intend to put you within sight of all three men to see what kind of reaction we get. But our top concern is your safety, and given the tone of last night's note, I thought putting you in soccer mom clothing might help dial back the inflammatory factor a little. Anyone who throws around terms like 'bitch in heat' and 'regain my trust' obviously has a problem with your sexuality."

"Not to mention his own grasp on reality."

He nodded his agreement. "That pretty much goes without saying."

"So the plan is to attract his attention without pissing him off?"

"Exactly. Our goal is to glean the maximum information with the minimum exacerbation."

"Ooh." Gazing into his eyes, she ran the tip of her tongue with exaggerated sexuality along her upper lip. "Do you have any idea how hot it makes me when you use those ten-dollar words?"

He frowned. "This is serious, Carly."

Her sexy facade promptly fractured. "I know." Blowing out a breath, she pushed aside her plate with its remains of ham-and-scram, hash browns and toast and propped her elbows on the table, leaning toward him. "I'm sorry, I do know it's serious. I'm just a little nervous about being the focus of some perv's attention. And when I'm nervous I tend to get flippant. Just ask my mother."

He snorted. "Forgive me for saying so, but your mother sounds like a royal pain in the ass. I doubt I'd ask her for a glass of water if my hair were on fire."

That earned him a laugh that was pure Carly—spontaneous, warm and genuine. "And that's without even having met her," she said wryly. "Count yourself fortunate, toots. Because unless you're rich and influential, she doesn't improve upon acquaintance."

The coffee arrived at the same time his cell phone rang. Pulling the unit from his pocket, he saw it was his work number. He excused himself, brought it to his ear and punched the talk button. "Jones."

"Wolf, it's Fred. I just got off the phone with Evans. The good news is I set up an interview with him. The bad news is it's in twenty minutes."

"We'll be right in." He started to disconnect, then hesitated. "Thanks, Fred. You've been a lot of help today." Pocketing the phone, he called the waitress back and asked for the check and their coffees to go. He looked across the table at Carly, who was already on her feet, reaching for her jacket once more. "You're ready, I see," he said softly. "Good. It's almost showtime."

Despite harboring high hopes for a quick resolution, Wolf was certain within the first five minutes of his interview with the employee from Catering that Evans wasn't their stalker. It only took being face-to-face with the man to remember his previous dealings with him. And the last time they'd met, Evans had been a belligerent, bellicose loudmouth.

Today, however, even though Wolf kept his allegations vague when the man had every right to know the name of his accuser, Evans was soft-spoken and cooperative.

Wolf used the turnabout as a wedge, hoping to find a fissure he could crack open. "This is quite a flip-flop for you," he said with flat-voiced skepticism. "The last time you and I had a little chat about your habit of bothering blondes, you were all mouth."

"I know," Evans agreed. "And I apologize for that. But since then I've joined AA. I've found Jesus."

"Uh-huh."

"It's true." Earnestly, Evans leaned forward in his chair, meeting Wolf's cynical gaze with level eyes. "I've been sober six months, two weeks and four days. And you can check with the pastor at Beautiful Savior down the Strip. Ask him if I haven't been there every Sunday for that same time period."

Wolf signaled unobtrusively to Beck and watched as his co-worker kicked over his wastebasket. It made a clamor rolling across the floor, and swearing under his breath, Beck rose to his feet to right it. He was bent over scooping up papers that had spilled out onto the floor when the department door opened and Carly walked in.

She stopped to look around, then headed straight for Beck's desk, which was conveniently located within a few feet of his own. "I need to talk to Mr. Jones when he gets a minute," she said softly.

"As you can see, he's tied up right now," Beck replied. "Perhaps I could help you instead?"

"I'd rather wait for him, if you don't mind. It's regarding a note I received last night, and I think it might concern him, as well."

Wolf kept an eagle eye on Evans, but although the man looked over at Carly, he didn't seem particularly interested in her or her problem and soon turned his attention back to his own concerns. Rocking up onto one hip, he fished his wallet out of his back pocket and thumbed through the contents until he found a couple of well-worn cards. He passed them across the desk, and Wolf saw that they were business cards for man named Bagley at a local engineering firm and the church Evans had just mentioned.

"The top one belongs to my AA sponsor and the bottom one is the pastor I told you about. Call them," Evans urged. "I haven't broken my probation, Mr. Jones. I'm a changed man—I swear it."

"I hope that's true, Mr. Evans. For your sake, I honestly

do." He rose to his feet, nodding dismissal to the other man. "Thank you for coming in to help clear this up. You can return to work now."

The minute Evans cleared the door, Wolf crossed over to Beck's desk. "Well?"

"Not our man," Beck said.

Carly nodded her accord. "I didn't feel so much as a spark of interest from him."

"That was my take, too. Which is probably just as well, since I'm seriously rethinking the whole idea of you and me in the same room with your admirer. That's probably not the brightest idea I've ever had. Seeing us together could too easily backfire by pushing the guy in directions we're not prepared to handle." Reading the strain around Carly's eyes, he reached out to run his thumb down the smooth curve of her cheek. "What do you say we take another break away from here?"

Her eyes immediately lost half the shadows clouding them. "*Could* we?"

"Sure. Fred said Hyde's shift doesn't start until three, so we're free to disappear until at least two." He racked his brain for an activity she'd like that they could do in the time allowed. "Let's go visit the local pet shelter."

The incandescent smile she sent him warmed him from the inside out, and she launched herself at him, winding her arms around his neck in a fierce, strangling hug. "Oh, my God, Wolf," she breathed, "I love, love, *love* you to death." She set him loose again and turned away to collect her purse.

Wolf stood poleaxed. Okay, he knew she didn't mean she actually *loved* him loved him. She meant she appreciated him doing something thoughtful. Nothing, at any rate, for him to be standing here with his heart beating like a kettledrum over. He was providing her with a brief reprieve from a stressful day and she was grateful. That was all. He shook himself.

All the same, Wolf knew in that moment that something monumental had just changed. Given the effect her innocent words had had on him, he was kidding himself if he thought all he wanted from her was sex. He might not know where the hell this thing between them was going—or even if it was headed anywhere at all.

But he knew he wouldn't be taking the OHS job when Freeling called to discuss it.

Carly was pretty sure Wolf assumed she couldn't do much damage in the short amount of time they had to poke around the pet shelter. As it happened, in this instance he was correct. None of the animals they saw were in dire need of rescuing, nor did one in particular simply grab her by the heart and refuse to let go—her usual gold standard for adopting a pet.

But something even better happened. She got to watch big, bad Wolfgang Jones fall in love with a three-year-old boxer named Jasper.

The dog spared her little more than a glance when she strolled by his cage, but when Wolf appeared, he trotted up to the front of his pen as if he were a contender for best in show at the annual Westminster Kennel Club competition. Plopping down on his butt, he politely offered up a white-stockinged paw.

"Hey." Wolf sank to sit on his haunches in front of the wire-front pen. "Aren't you the friendly, handsome fellow." Presenting the back of his right hand for the dog to sniff, he then eased his fore and index fingers through the chain link to gently support the paw that was once again proffered.

She leaned over his shoulder to inspect the pup. "He is a beauty, isn't he?" Muscular and sturdy, the dog had a sleek caramel-brown coat with the standard black mask from eyebrows to muzzle, broken only by the white blaze that ran down the center of his face. His throat, chest and stomach were also white, as were all four feet.

Jasper didn't seem to care one way or the other if she found him appealing. His attention was strictly for Wolf. And for the man squatting outside his cage, he was all limpid brown eyes and an endearingly wrinkled forehead.

Wolf ate it up. As clearly as if a cartoon conversation bubble came from his mouth, Carly read his urge to take the dog home with him.

Encouraging pet adoption was programmed in her genes, and she could see that Wolf needed only the barest of nudges to do what he was dying to do already. Opening her mouth to urge him to follow his inclination, she found herself in the unfamiliar position of snapping it closed again.

The words she'd left unspoken clamored deafeningly inside her mind. But she was a firm believer in owner responsibility, and she couldn't in all conscience urge him to take on a new dog when he'd very likely soon be moving halfway across the country to a job that would eat up his every waking hour.

All the same, she tried to convince herself that having a dog to love would at least help take the sting out of the move for Niklaus. But the truth was, there was no guarantee the dog would even bond with the teen. In all likelihood he would. Yet if he turned out to be a dog of the one-master-only variety, then there would be one miserable boy *and* an unhappy dog.

She moved away, walking slowly down the alley between the kennels to look at the other dogs before continuing on to the cat area. Wolf remained with Jasper until it was time to go.

Neither of them spoke much on the drive back to the Avventurato.

Feeling grim and impatient with herself, she was grateful for a moment of privacy to get her head together when Wolfgang's co-workers converged on him the instant they entered the Surveillance control room. While the men requested his opinion on a situation brewing in the casino, she chose a chair as far away from the action as she could get. Sitting, she crossed her arms over her chest and glumly stared at a shoe scuff that marred the otherwise pristine linoleum floor.

What was the matter with her? She'd known going into this affair that Wolf would likely be offered his dream job sooner rather than later. Yet somehow that nebulous some-time-in-the-future possibility kept catching her by surprise every time she realized anew the future was fast approaching. It sent her mood spiraling into a tailspin faster than she could say centrifugal force.

She had to quit allowing that to happen.

Putting a stop to it called for something—*anything*—to divert her attention from a head full of constantly circling thoughts. Climbing to her feet, she approached Wolf once again and tapped him on the shoulder.

"I'm sorry to interrupt, but I'm gonna go buy myself a magazine at the mall newsstand," she said as soon as he turned to her.

Wolf glanced at his watch, then back at Carly's face, hating the tension that once again stamped her features. The trip to the pet shelter clearly hadn't been as successful as he'd hoped it would be. For either of them.

He pushed aside the memory of the dog that, against every instinct, he had left in that bare, sterile cage and forced himself to concentrate on what was happening now. "Try to make it quick," he advised. "We don't know if Hyde is the kind of employee who doesn't give his job a minute more than he has to, or one of those guys who likes to arrive early to ease into his shift."

"I'll be back before you even know I'm gone."

He doubted that, but after she left he quickly hammered out a solution to the situation his co-workers had brought him. Then, tracking Carly's movements through the cameras he'd instructed Fred to activate, he sat down in front of the bank of screens to keep an eye on her. As he watched her enter the main casino and head for the elevators that led to the basement level shopping mall, he went back to brooding over the subject he'd been worrying about since leaving the pet shelter—why he'd left behind a great dog to face a future that was uncertain at best.

He'd never experienced the immediate connection with an animal that he'd felt with Jasper, and didn't know why he simply hadn't told the people in charge that he wanted to adopt the dog. Yes, it would be a huge departure from his usual nobody-to-care-for-but-me lifestyle, but hell, he'd pretty much abandoned that way of living the day he'd agreed to be Niklaus's guardian. Not to mention he had every confidence that the teen would be thrilled to have a dog. And considering he'd already decided against taking the OHS offer, it wasn't as though the upheaval of a move and breaking in a new job were unscalable obstacles standing in his way.

So why hadn't he taken the plunge?

He'd like nothing better than to claim force of habit. After all, he wasn't a man who made rash, impulsive decisions.

He had a bad feeling, however, that the truth had less to do with the need to think things through than it did with the fact that he didn't know how to tell Carly he was going to refuse the OHS offer. It galled him to admit that he didn't know how he'd handle it if she acted disappointed he was staying. After all, she was the one who'd come up with the blueprint for this affair. She was the one who scoffed at marriage.

Not that he'd been thinking along those lines himself. But if he *had* occasionally thought of something that eventually might be more permanent, and he was ever foolish enough to tell her about it and she laughed in his face, what would he do then? Rather than find out, he'd left Jasper behind.

It bit deep that the dog was looking at the business end of an euthanasia needle because its potential owner feared a woman's reaction to the news that he didn't plan to leave town after all.

Wolf scowled as he watched Carly walk up to the mall newsstand and select a couple of magazines. Okay, that might be a bit melodramatic. The card on Jasper's pen had said he was scheduled to be put down next Saturday if he wasn't adopted by then. Wolf still had a few days to make a decision; it wasn't as if they planned to drag the dog to the Chamber of Death today because he'd failed to snatch him up.

He was still stewing about it a minute later, however, as he watched Carly step into an empty elevator. The lift doors were closing, slowly obliterating her from view on screen twelve, when a man suddenly slid between them into her car.

"Shit!" He jackknifed upright in his chair. "Activate the camera in elevator six in the mall bank," he ordered. "Now, Fred!" he snapped when results weren't immediately forthcoming. "We've got an intruder who made it on just before the doors closed."

A second later the elevator interior came up on the same screen he'd been watching. He and Fred both cursed.

But it was the young tech who said, "Son of a bitch," and stared at Wolf. "It's Hyde."

Twenty-Eight

Brian Hyde felt the faint swish of air as the elevator doors slid smoothly closed at his back and smiled exultantly. Finally he was alone with Carly. This was the moment they'd both been waiting for.

Their relationship had hit some snags lately, but now, finally, it was back on track. Clearly they were meant to be, for it was sheer chance that he'd seen her entering the casino elevator at the same time he'd been coming in to work. Recognizing destiny when it kicked him in the shins, he'd raced down the nearest stairwell and tumbled into the mall corridor in time to see her paying for a couple of magazines at the newsstand. A moment later she was at the elevator.

And so was he.

"Casino level?" she asked with sweet concern, and punched the corresponding button on the panel before he could reply. The car began to glide upward.

No! They needed more time than they could possibly get from a lousy one-floor ride. Struggling to curb his pounding heart, he sidled closer to the control panel. "Actually, I think it's time we finally talk. Don't you, darling?" Reaching past her, his hand brushing deliciously against her warm smooth-skinned arm, he hit the red stop button. The car shuddered to a halt and he turned to face her.

"What the—"

"Shhh." She smelled wonderful and he was so proud that she was his. He took a step nearer. "You look beautiful today."

A spark of something came and went on her face so quickly he wasn't even certain he could trust the veracity of his own eyes. Especially when all she said was a pleasant, "Thank you."

"It's much more appropriate than the usual things you wear."

Just for a moment her blue eyes flashed. Then her lashes lowered, disguising her expression. "Pardon me?"

"Now, dear, I know you're a showgirl, so of course you're required to wear skimpy costumes. And don't mistake me, you look gorgeous in them. But this—" he indicated her expensive, conservative jacket and khakis, her suburban hairdo "—is much more suitable for my future bride."

Her head reared back and a look of utter repugnance flashed across her face. Almost immediately it morphed into an expression of tranquil acceptance.

But he knew what he had seen and, insulted to the bone, he took an incensed step forward. Adding to his affront was a sudden flashback of the faithless way she'd looked at another man. Rage, never far from the surface, surged in a blistering tide through his veins, and he clenched his fists. "You don't even know who the hell I am, do you?"

Oh, man, you've really stepped in it this time, sister. Carly liked to think she'd been holding it together pretty well since her stalker had slithered onto the elevator. She hadn't screamed. She'd kept her expression mostly neutral. And in the face of extreme provocation, she'd spoken in a calm, rational manner.

Altogether, she'd been pretty damn cool, calm and collected, if she did say so herself.

But that "suitable attire for my future bride" crack had slipped beneath her guard and sent the needle on the incredulity meter leaning hard to the right. And before she'd been able to monitor herself, her knee-jerk reaction had stamped her feelings across her face.

A very big mistake. "Of course I know who you are, Brian," she said with all the equanimity she could muster and watched his hands relax. The guy might be a freaking nutcase, but she had to maintain better control if she wanted to get out of this mess without finding herself beat into a viscous little puddle. She couldn't afford to send Hyde plunging off the deep end. Not when she didn't know if Wolf had the first idea where she was or if someone might come soon to check on the stalled elevator.

For the moment at least, she was on her own. Even if Wolf knew precisely where she was and had deployed the entire security department like a television SWAT team to the rescue, there was still the matter of being stuck between floors in a sealed five-by-five-by-nine-foot box.

The last thing she needed was for this raging psycho, standing between her and the control panel, to go off on her. Never in her life had she been threatened with physical violence, so seeing the fury shimmering off him like a heat mirage off the highway was unnerving enough. But it was the expression on Hyde's face that really gave her the jitters.

Because clearly the guy wasn't playing with a full deck. She met his gaze squarely, however, and said, "We met the night I twisted my ankle in the casino." It had taken her a moment but she remembered him now. He was the nice-looking man who'd offered his help when she'd taken that graceless tumble down the stairs. And looking past his natty clothing, she realized she'd also seen him several times around the hotel and casino in his janitorial uniform.

"Exactly." He smiled at her as though they were sitting in a coffee shop chatting about their day. "So what are you reading, darling?"

His ping-ponging moods kept her off balance and she gaped at him blankly. "Huh?"

He nodded at the magazines she held clutched to her breast.

"Oh." She showed him. "*Dog & Kennel* and *Cat Fancy*." Okay, this was good. Weird and scary, but good. If she could keep him talking, maybe Wolf would have time to send a commando rappelling down the shaft to enter the car through the trap in the roof. And if S & S didn't have such an employee, then he'd do it himself—she didn't doubt that for a moment.

Fastidious disdain pulled down the corners of Hyde's mouth. "I don't care for animals."

Didn't care for…? She couldn't allow herself to follow through on such blasphemy and still continue holding it together. The guy was starting to seriously hack her off, but she said neutrally, "I'm sorry to hear that. I love them. I have two cats, Rags and Tripod, and a dog named Buster. I used to have two dogs, but I gave my pup Rufus to a boy named Iago who—"

"You'll have to give the others away, as well."

I will see you rot in hell before that happens, you sick-ass son of a bitch.

She had to bite her tongue nearly in two, but she managed

not to say the words out loud. Where her babies were concerned, keeping her opinion to herself was anathema to all she believed in, and every last cell in her body screamed an enraged protest over the necessity to do so now. But she wasn't stupid. Only an idiot tweaked the tail of a madman.

Something must have given her away, though, because the next thing she knew Hyde's face was twisting in fury, and with a motion that was just a fast blur coming at her he backhanded her across the face.

Pain exploded in her cheek and, stunned, she fell back against the rear wall. Tears welled involuntarily as she assimilated the fact that she had actually been struck. Then anger, hot and empowering, began to pump through her veins. This was all wrong! She'd done everything she possibly could to avoid this kind of violence and he'd hit her anyhow.

He looked almost as stunned as she felt as he stepped back and stared at her. But he soon roused himself.

"You shouldn't have made me do that," he said defensively, legs akimbo and his fists propped on his hips. "Don't think I liked it, because I didn't. I'm not a violent man and it hurts me more than it hurt you to be forced to hit you."

Usually when she was in a temper, she was all reaction and insufficient thought—a character flaw that had caused her to say words she'd come to regret more times than she cared to remember. At this moment, however, her mind burned with an ice-cold clarity. She brought her hand up to gingerly touch the flesh she could feel beginning to swell in her cheek. But it was more to distract his attention while she coolly judged the distance between them than it was to assure herself that he hadn't broken the skin and drawn blood.

"No...darling...I have to respectfully disagree," she said with a tremor in her voice she didn't have to fake as Hyde's gaze followed her assessing hand. "*This* is going to hurt you more than it does me."

And executing one of the most precise high kicks she'd ever performed, she brought her foot up squarely between his legs.

With a wet, gurgling "Ulp," Brian Hyde dropped like a felled tree to the floor of the elevator.

Carly stepped over him and reached for the stop button on the control panel. Her hand shook so badly it took her three tries to disengage it and select the casino floor. Then, keeping an eagle eye on the man curled in a tight fetal ball with both hands protectively cupped over his crotch, she pressed herself into the corner farthest away from him as the car began its smooth ascent.

It was the longest short ride of her life. All she could think of was Wolf. She just needed to hold it all together for a few seconds longer and he'd be there. If he wasn't waiting, he'd soon arrive—she knew that for a fact. Then everything would be okay.

Her chin wobbled but she firmed it up. Her muscles twitched with unspent adrenaline, but she hugged herself against the encroaching shimmy-shakes. She would not cry, she vowed fiercely. She would not fall apart.

And she would not throw herself into Wolf's arms the minute she saw him and embarrass him in front of his co-workers. Not when the only stipulation he'd ever made in this affair of theirs was that they keep it out of the workplace. But, God, she needed to see him.

She just needed to see him. Then everything would be okay.

Wolf ignored the bustle of gamblers and guests flowing around him as he paced in front of the door to car six in the casino elevator bank. Fred's excited voice kept up a running commentary in his earpiece as it had been doing since he'd left the tech monitoring the screen with orders to keep him apprised of the activity within Carly's elevator.

Fred had followed his orders with blow-by-blow descriptions that had tied Wolf's guts into knots of helpless fury when the situation had degenerated faster than he had any hope of alleviating.

"Holy shit, Wolf," Fred crowed now. "She must have kicked his balls clear up between his shoulder blades. There's one guy who won't be producing little Hydes any time soon."

"Did you call Metro?" he interrupted as a chime sounded and the light above the car came on. He'd just had the scare of his life and was in no condition to hear the risk Carly took dissected again, even if it had done what he'd been unable to do and freed her from that obsessive freak's hands. Besides, this was a police matter now. And a good thing, too, in his opinion, because he sure as hell didn't trust himself around the man who'd dared to hit her.

"Yeah," Fred said soberly. "Detectives are on their way. And so is Beck. He should be there any second to take Hyde into custody until Metro gets here. All you need to do is take care of Carly."

"Good." Then the elevator doors opened and he disconnected.

He braced himself for Carly to hurl herself into his arms. What he didn't count on was the stampede of guests making for the elevator. Before he could do more than take a quick look into the interior, he was forced to pull his security badge from his pocket and bark at the four women and two men trying to push past him to back off, that this car was temporarily closed for business.

Beck walked up at that moment, and for the first time in

his life Wolf resented the need to put his job ahead of all other considerations. Both he and Beck asked Carly how she was doing, and although she claimed she was fine, he noticed that she stuck close to them while they hauled Hyde to his feet. The janitor sagged within their less-than-gentle grip, mumbling complaints about being misunderstood.

"I'll give you misunderstood, you sick monkey," Carly muttered with furious disdain. She looked at Wolf. "I don't suppose you'd let me kick him again?"

"No, sorry," he said with real regret, then in a rough voice commanded Beck, "Get him out of here before I give into temptation and break every bone in his body."

A moment later he was alone with Carly in the temporarily deserted elevator alcove. She didn't throw herself in his arms so he moved in close to her instead. Her left cheek sported a contusion that was already turning color, and he didn't even try to resist the need to reach out and gently examine it with his fingers. "Are you really all right?"

"Yes," she said. "So much for needing a guy to ride to the rescue, huh?" She thumped herself on the breast. "I am Woman. Hear me roar."

Her cockiness made him overlook the signs of strain tightening the corners of her eyes and lips and allowed him to forget that this sudden nobody-messes-with-*me* attitude failed to match her every action since she'd emerged from the elevator. Instead, his eyebrows slammed together as he took her words at face value.

He'd been worried to the point of nausea, and she hadn't even thought for one goddamn minute that she might have some small need of his help? Soul-sucking anxiety abruptly transformed into hot anger. Reaching out to grab her shoulders, he dropped his hands to his side before they could touch her. He didn't trust himself to be gentle, and whether she needed him or not, she'd suffered enough abuse at the hands of a man today. But his voice held all the harshness of his emotions when he demanded, "What's the matter with you, Carly? You don't engage in hand-to-hand combat with a madman! What the hell were you thinking?"

Her mouth dropped open. Snapping it shut, she narrowed her eyes at him. "I was *thinking* I needed to get myself out of that little box on a string before he beat me senseless."

"And it never occurred to you to hang on until I could get to you?"

She suddenly grew an inch taller as her spine snapped straight. "Ex*cuse* me?"

"It never occurred to you," he bit out furiously, "that he could have had a gun or a knife? That he might have blocked your kick and then been so enraged at you for fighting him that he wouldn't be satisfied with a single blow? He could have beaten the bloody hell out of you before I had a goddamn chance to help!"

"I didn't know if you even knew where I was!"

"I knew *exactly* where you were every minute you were gone, and I was working to get you out," he said, his voice rising with each word he spoke. "That's what I do for a living. Among other things, some people actually depend on me."

She thrust her nose up beneath his, and her cheeks that had been unnaturally pale were suddenly suffused with color. "Don't you yell at me, Wolfgang Jones!"

"I fucking well will yell at you. *Mein Gott!* You acted like a rash teenager with nothing but cotton between her ears where her brains were supposed to be!"

He was sorry for the words the instant they left his mouth.

He didn't mean them. They weren't true, and God knew they were the worst kind of unfair. But still feeling too raw, he neither took them back nor apologized. Instead he watched in misery as her eyes iced over and she did the impossible by drawing herself even more fully erect than she'd stood a moment ago.

"Well," she said with chilling politeness, taking a stiff-legged step away from him. "Don't let me keep you. I'm sure a big, important, *intelligent* man such as yourself has much to do. God forbid I should inflict my brainless presence on you any further."

Aw, shit. He'd hurt her—he could see it in her eyes. He was an oversensitive idiot to have let his ego be so easily bruised, and he took a contrite step forward, prepared to tell her so. "Carly, listen—"

Her frosty dignity splintered. "No, you listen! I got myself out of an awful situation the best way I knew how. So screw you, Wolfgang, if my methods weren't up to your exalted standards. Now, if you'll excuse me, I've had a perfectly lousy day and I want to go home. I don't need this crap." The look she leveled on him froze him in his tracks. "And I don't need *you,* either."

Wolf stood stock-still, a jangling mass of stripped-raw nerve endings. Through lips that felt starched he said, "You can't go home yet. You have to give your report to the police and probably go down to the station to file a complaint against Hyde."

"Fine," she said coldly. "But I want you to stay the hell away from me."

Something hard settled in his chest, but stiff-necked pride brought his head up. She wanted him to stay away from her? Well, that was just fine by him. He wasn't begging for any woman's attention. He gave her an abrupt nod of assent. "You got it."

Then he followed behind her as she headed across the casino to his department.

Twenty-Nine

Niklaus couldn't remember a time when he'd felt this consistently great. Not even by diligently searching his memory could he bring up more than a handful of truly wonderful moments in his life—nothing like the several weeks' worth he'd been treated to lately. For the first time in forever, he harbored a little spark of hope for the future. He knew that wasn't the brightest leap of faith to take, since he'd learned the hard way that hope could be a dangerous thing. But what the hell.

Sometimes a guy just had to live on the edge.

Slowly lifting his head, he looked down into the flushed face of the girl he'd been kissing. "You taste so good," he said, brushing a dark wisp of Natalie's hair away from the corner of her swollen lips. Then, still riding this uncharacteristic wave of optimism, he decided it was time to take a giant leap outside his safety zone. "Would you go out with me Friday night?"

She scooted upright on the backseat of her car and looked

out through the windshield at the vast empty desert for a second before turning her attention back to him. "You mean like a date? A real date?"

"Yeah." Would she think he was too anxious? Too…needy for words, maybe? They'd been kissing up a storm since last night, but it wasn't like they'd declared themselves a couple or anything.

"That would be really nice."

He grinned in relief. "Yeah, that's what I was thinkin'." *Damn* he liked her! "Maybe I can even get Uncle Wolf to lend me his car. Not that he's ever let me drive it, but who knows? Maybe for a special date…"

"If not, there's always mine." She nudged her shoulder companionably against his. "Although I gotta admit, his street rod is way hotter than my safe little sedan." She looked at her watch. "Oh, damn! I have to get home. I told Mrs. Owens I'd babysit Cassie and Katie tonight and I'm supposed to be there by five. I know it's only four but I don't wanna get hung up in traffic and have to bite my nails worrying I'll make it in time. But first—" She threw her arms around his neck and tugged him down on the seat for another slow, deep, drugging kiss.

Five minutes later they climbed over the front seat and headed back to the city.

They made record time and exchanged one long last kiss before he finally tore himself away. Watching her drive away, he mused that if he died right this minute, it would probably take the undertaker three days to erase the big-ass grin from his face.

Letting himself into the apartment a moment later, he headed straight for the kitchen to assemble an oversize roast beef, cheese, pickle and tomato sandwich for a snack. While he built it he fantasized about getting to first base with Natalie this coming Friday night. He probably wouldn't achieve bare tittie or anything, he acknowledged as he slapped his sandwich on a plate and slid it across the breakfast bar. But a quick feel of those perfect breasts through her clothing might be a possibility.

Or not. He'd have to play it by ear, because he sure as hell didn't want to wreck what they already had. Grabbing the milk out of the fridge, he carried the carton around the bar and pulled up a stool to eat. The red light was blinking on the message machine, and taking a huge bite out of his sandwich, he pulled over the tablet and pencil that always sat next to the phone, then punched the play button.

"Dude," Paddy's voice said. "Your cell phone's turned off. I left a voice mail, but in case you don't check it tonight I just wanted to let you know we're thinking 'bout going to the Century Suncoast Saturday night to catch a movie. Or maybe the Crown 14 at Neonopolis so David can try out that rap song he's been practicing on the open mike at the food court. Haven't nailed down that part yet, but I'll catch you at school tomorrow and we'll hammer out the details. Later."

"All right," he murmured, and bit off another monster bite of his sandwich. It looked like he had plans for both nights this weekend.

The second call was a reminder from Uncle Wolf's dentist that he was due for a cleaning. He wrote the message down on the tablet, then swigged milk from the carton.

The third was another voice he didn't recognize, but it, too, was for Uncle Wolf, so he wrote down Oscar Freeling and OHS, then waited for the man to recite a call-back number.

"…and I think you'll like living in Cleveland. Anyhow, I

look forward to discussing the details of the offer I made you, so call me at your earliest convenience at area code 216—"

His newly embraced hope detonated like a tripped landmine. Moving? Uncle Wolf was *moving?*

Shit. Numbly he stared down at the half-eaten sandwich in his hand, the consumed portion a sudden anvil in his gut.

As if *that* were a big fucking surprise. Leaden stomachs were only the beginning of what a guy could expect when his life turned to crap.

Well, this day had sure as hell turned to crap. Wolf took the condo stairs two at a time. It had started out so promising, too. Despite the reason for going into work on his day off, he had truly enjoyed the mellow twenty minutes spent combining two of his preferred things, tooling along in his beloved car and spending time with his belov—favorite woman.

Wolf slowed his pace as he passed Carly's apartment. If she was inside, she was too quiet to hear, and with a growl of self-disgust he continued on next door. She'd left work about fifteen minutes ahead of him. She hadn't had her car with her, of course, but rather than wait a few minutes to ride with him, she'd elected to catch a cab.

Between talking to the police, having the medics check out Carly's cheek and answering questions that were eventually converted into reams of paperwork that they'd then had to initial or sign, they'd been tied up for hours. His part had been covered more swiftly than hers. But he'd stayed with her the entire time, even though she would neither look at nor talk to him. Now he was hot, tired and about two shaky seconds away from implosion. All he wanted was a cold beer, several aspirin and twenty minutes in a dark, quiet room.

Letting himself into the apartment, he tossed his keys in the pottery bowl on the half-moon-shaped table in the foyer and headed for the living room.

"It's about time you got home, you goddamn shit!"

His head snapping up, he dropped his hand from where he'd been trying to rub the knots out of the base of his skull. "Nik?"

His nephew emerged from the lanai, a dark silhouette against the brilliant sunshine pouring through the open sliders. His long-legged strides ate up the space that separated them, and Wolf only had a moment to register the fury on his nephew's face before the teen barreled up and gave him a hard shove to the chest with both hands.

"Hey!" His savage mood had been seeking an outlet and instinctively he cocked back a fist. It took everything he had to recall that this was a boy he was dealing with, not a man upon whom he could pound out his aggressions. He dropped his hand, shoving it into his pants pocket.

"You goddamn shit!" Niklaus reiterated. "I hate you!"

The words had unexpected wounding power, but damned if he'd let the kid know he'd scored a direct hit. "I can't say I'm particularly fond of you at the moment, either. Look, can we do this some other time? I've had a lousy day."

"You think *you've* had a lousy day? *You* have? Oh, God, that's rich." Nik couldn't prevent the loud laugh with its bitter dearth of humor that exploded out of his chest. When it started to slide dangerously near hysteria, however, he abruptly cut it off. "You don't have the first idea about lousy," he said flatly. "Hell, you've been offered your goddamn dream job. How crappy can that be?" Without waiting for an answer, he said categorically, "Well, you can't take it."

"You dare to dictate what I can and cannot do?"

A touch of fear wove its way through Nik's misery as, for

the first time since he'd moved in with his uncle, he saw real temper flare in Wolf's eyes. He'd had enough experience with a couple of his mother's "friends" to step beyond reach of those long arms, but recklessly he thrust his chin up. "Yes," he said with all the force he could muster. "I forbid it."

Something dangerous detonated in the icy-green gaze pinning him in place. "You don't get to forbid me to do anything," Wolfgang roared. "I've worked too long and too hard for some snot-nosed kid to tell me he won't 'allow' me to attain my goals."

"What about *me?*" Nik yelled, hating that the question came out sounding like the wail of a lost child. On the other hand, how fucking fitting considering that was exactly how he felt—like a powerless, scared, abandoned child. "What about *my* goals, huh? You just gonna up and walk away, leaving me to fend for myself?"

His uncle's brows drew together and his eyes grew icier yet. "Is that what you honestly think? Jesus. You've lived with me for a month now and you still don't know the first goddamn thing about me, do you?" Wolf dug his fingers into the muscles at the back of his neck. "Well, I'm tired of knocking myself out for you, so read my lips, kid, because I'm only going to say this once. Where I go, you go. Your home is with me."

That sentiment would have been music to Nik's ears when he'd first arrived here. But that was before he'd discovered what it was like to feel as if he really belonged somewhere. Now that glorious feeling was going to be ripped away from him and it wasn't fair. He'd started to feel safe with Wolf as his guardian, but it was nothing but a frigging illusion. And somehow that was ten times worse than if his uncle had simply deserted him. "Yeah, well, maybe I don't wanna go!"

"And maybe you don't get a vote!"

Resentment warred with impotent fury. "I *hate* you! You've ruined everything!" Then he ran from the room before Uncle Wolf could see he'd started to cry like a baby.

"Nik!" Wolf bellowed. "Get your butt back here. We are not finished!"

Yes, they were. They were *so* finished.

Blurred vision robbed him of his usual adroitness and he careened off the little table in the entryway, sending its contents rocking. Quick reflexes rescued the shallow free-form pottery bowl on the table, but the keys in it bounced out onto the floor. Sweeping them up, he saw they were Uncle Wolf's.

He blinked back fresh tears. There wasn't a hope in hell his uncle would ever lend him his car now.

Well, screw him. He pocketed the keys. Everything else had turned to shit today, he might as well have one good memory of driving that sweet car. What could his uncle do? Banish him to Bumfuck, Ohio, where he'd be forced to start over at another strange school yet *again*?

Apparently that was gonna happen anyhow.

Hearing the front door slam, Wolf swore. Could this day *get* any worse? Flexing the fist he was tempted to put through the nearest wall, he stalked into the kitchen to wash down three aspirin with a huge glass of water. The room seemed to close in around him and he felt as if he were suffocating. With a curse, he crossed the room and stepped out onto the lanai. Bracing his hands against the warm stucco balustrade, his arms stiff and his head bent, he pulled air deep into his lungs.

"Maybe you don't get a vote!" The words he'd yelled at his nephew haunted him. He couldn't have handled that worse if he'd tried. Instead of telling Niklaus he'd decided against

taking the job in Ohio, he'd let the kid's attitude put him on the defensive. He'd blustered and issued orders and hadn't once attempted to put the teen's fears to rest. As a result, he had come off sounding like…oh, shit, he'd come off sounding exactly like…

Sonovabitch. His father.

He'd sounded just like Rick, who he'd always despised for dragging him around without caring whether or not he wanted to go. Who had never given a damn if his latest job disrupted Wolf's life or not. As long as Rick got to do what *he* wanted to do, he'd assumed it would work out just fine for everyone else, as well.

Lowering his elbows to the balustrade, he clutched his throbbing head in both hands. "Way to go, champ." The only bright spot in this mess was that once a man messed things up as badly as he'd done today, there was damn little damage left to be done. So, really, things could only get better.

"Way to go indeed," Carly said acerbically from the other side of the wall that divided their balconies. She watched as Wolf straightened from his exhausted-looking slouch against the balustrade and turned to face her.

For just a moment something inside of her softened at the bleak expression on his face. Then she hardened her heart. Rather than make her presence known, she should have gone inside while she'd had the chance. But from the first day she'd met this irritating man, she'd found it impossible to walk away from him. And even knowing that she had more to lose emotionally than he—that any confrontation between them was likely to end up with her clutching the short end of the stick—well, some things never changed.

"Eavesdropping, Carly?"

His cool voice interrupted her musings and she gave him

an insouciant half smile in return. "It's hardly eavesdropping when you're bellowing like a wounded bull, pal."

"Perfect," he muttered, taking a step in her direction. His eyebrows drew together over the strong thrust of his nose. "You haven't had two words to say to me for the past—what? three and a half hours? But *now* you suddenly want to visit?"

She shrugged. "What was there to say? You were busy being Mr. Important Professional—you didn't need my input."

Stepping closer yet, he shook his head in disgust. "Figures it would somehow turn out to be my fault."

"Hey, if the stuffed shirt fits—"

"I was being Mr. Professional—I object to the *Important* assignation—because that was all you left me."

"*Excuse* me?" Incensed that he had turned this around on her, she strode forward until nothing but four inches of waist-high stucco prevented them from standing toe-to-toe.

"You are Woman, hear you roar, remember?" he said without inflection. "You made it crystal clear you didn't need me in any other capacity. What was it you said, 'So much for needing a guy to ride to the rescue'?" He hitched a muscular shoulder. "Far be it for me to stand between a woman and her liberation."

Oh. Oh! She wanted to scratch his face off. She'd needed him so desperately when she'd stepped off that elevator, and he'd *reprimanded* her for saving her own neck. Now he dared treat her as though she'd been some bra-burning libber spouting the party rhetoric? "I was following the rules you laid down," she said hotly, thinking back to the day they'd defined the parameters of their relationship. "So if you have a problem with that, blame yourself! *You* were the one who came up with the 'What happens at home *stays* at home' part of our bargain. If you recall, you said we were to keep our private lives out of the workplace."

"Because, once again, that's all you left me!" he roared. "You were so goddamn busy laying down the groundwork to define our relationship that I felt I'd better contribute something."

"Do I look like a freaking mind reader to you?" She slapped the balustrade. "Don't you dare fault me for taking you at your word! You said keep it out of the workplace. I kept it out of the workplace."

"Oh, that's good. That's beautiful." A harsh laugh escaped him. Cutting it off, he bent his head until their noses almost touched. "If you think no one at work realizes you and I've got something hot and heavy going on, then you haven't been paying attention," he said flatly. "The guys in S & S sure as hell know. In case you haven't noticed, I can't keep my hands to myself where you're concerned. Offhand, I can think of at least one instance where I touched you in a manner that's inappropriate for co-workers."

"What?" She shook her head. "No, you haven't."

"Sure, I have. And so have you. I've done this—" he ran his thumb down her cheek "—in the middle of my department. You hugged me in the same spot. Hell, from a single look we exchanged on the casino floor, even your *stalker* knew we had something going on! So don't tell me we've left our relationship out of the workplace."

It all came boiling out then, all the resentment and hurt overflowing the place where she'd tamped it down. "You treated me like an idiot! I kept thinking I just had to hang on a few seconds more, then you'd be there and everything would be all right. I knew I wasn't allowed to throw myself in your arms because we had that rule. I *thought* we had that rule. But I clung to the idea that you'd be proud of me for extricating myself from Hyde's clutches. And were you?" She laughed bitterly. "Oh, no."

"Carly—" He reached out to touch her.

She jerked out of his way. "You yelled at me, freaking *chastised* me for protecting myself, and pretty much called me brainless. And from what I overheard between you and Nik, I'm guessing you gave him the same treatment. Given your exalted people skills, it's no wonder he hates your guts."

The shock of hearing her own words reverberated through her bones. A flash of indescribable hurt crossed his face and she leaped back to the wall. "*No,*" she denied fiercely, gripping the stucco ledge so tightly her fingertips turned white. "I didn't mean that, Wolf. Niklaus doesn't hate you. I was so wrong to say that he does. Completely, low-down-lying-*bitch* wrong. He's just hurt and confused right now. But he knows you love him." She reached out imploring fingers, but this time he stepped out of range.

"How? How does he know that? From my swell parenting skills? No. The truth hurts, but that doesn't make it any less the truth."

"It is *not* the truth! It was just me feeling hurt and striking back."

Thrusting all ten fingers through his hair, his fingers gripping his skull, his elbows pointing skyward, he stared at her. "How the hell did we get to this point, Carly? How did I go from being happier than I can ever remember being, to screwing it all up and alienating everyone I care about?"

Pain splintered a great gaping hole in her chest, yet her heart continued to beat. It pounded, in fact, with soul-destroying shame. "Oh, God, Wolf, don't let my words make you doubt yourself. I am so sorry. I was angry and I just said the first awful thing I could think of."

He shrugged. "It doesn't matter. Anyhow, I know all about saying hurtful things, don't I? I didn't mean it, either, when I made that crack about you acting like a teenager with cotton between her ears. You did great in that elevator today. I was just jealous that it wasn't me who rescued you."

His weary voice and the growing distance in his eyes terrified her and she clambered over the wall.

He took an equal number of steps backward, keeping an invisible bulwark between them. She wasn't certain why panic kept choking her breath off. It wasn't as if he were calling her a faithless bitch and ordering her to never darken his doorstep again. But this defeated, exhausted lack of animation, this total absence of his usual competitiveness, struck her as somehow worse. She knew how to deal with his anger. This weary indifference was scaring her to death.

"Well, listen," he said, "I've got some puppies to kick and I know how much you like dogs. So you'd better go home now."

"Stop it!" she said. "Just stop it right this minute. Let's sit down and—"

"Go home, *Liebling*. You've got so much to offer and I— Hell, I couldn't even dredge up an 'I'm sorry' after I hurt you, not when it might have meant putting my ego on the line. You're twice the person I'll ever be, Carly. So go home. There's nothing for you here."

"There's *you*." *Please, please. There's you.*

A small huff of unamused laugher escaped him. "Like I said." His cell phone rang and he pulled it from his pocket. "Go home," he reiterated. Then, turning away, he punched the talk button and brought the phone up to his ear. "Jones."

Wolf was right, of course. She should go home. She wasn't hardwired to cling to some guy's heels if he didn't feel for her what she felt for him. So she'd climb back over the wall, start putting her life back together. Pretend she'd never even known, much less fallen in love with, a man named Wolfgang.

He wasn't going to be around much longer, anyhow. She trudged over to the stucco barrier.

"*What?*"

The anguish in his voice sent her whirling back around.

"Where?" he demanded. Taking a giant stride forward, he clamped hard fingers around her wrist with punishing force. But his attention was riveted on his conversation. "Yes...yes. I'm on my way. In the meantime you have my permission to do whatever's needed."

Dread played havoc with her nerve endings as he disconnected. "What?" she demanded. "Is it Niklaus? Is he all right?"

"Yes. No." He shook his head. "Christ, I don't know." His face had turned a faintly greenish tint. "That was Desert Springs Hospital. Nik's been in a car accident."

Thirty

"Where are my car keys?" Squatting down to look beneath the little foyer table, Wolf felt his trademark coolheadedness start to disintegrate. "*Where are the fucking keys?* I left them right here in the bowl!"

Carly's hand closed over his shoulder, calming him. "Do you have another set?"

"Yes." Drawing in a stabilizing breath, he rose to his feet. "Yes, of course. Good idea. I'll get them." With a purpose to steady him, to divert his imagination from all the awful possibilities awaiting him at the hospital, he strode into the bedroom and grabbed his spare key.

Moments later they stopped before the garage, where he punched in the security code. Holding tightly to Carly's hand, he stared blankly when the rising door exposed an empty garage. "Oh, sweet Jesus," he breathed as comprehension dawned. He looked at her in horror. "That's why the keys weren't where they were supposed to be. Nik must have taken the car."

"Come on." She steered him toward the parking lot. "We'll take mine. You probably shouldn't be driving right now anyhow."

It seemed like forever before they reached the hospital, but in reality it probably only took fifteen or twenty minutes. Upon arriving at the E.R., he strode straight up to the counter with Carly in tow as she had been since he'd first heard the news. Holding on to her helped to anchor him.

He gave his name to the woman manning the desk. "I got a call that Niklaus Jones was brought in from a car accident. What can you tell me about his condition?" *Tell me he's fine. Please, God, just tell me that.*

"I'm afraid I'm not authorized to give out that information, Mr. Jones, but let me just page Dr. Merriweather. If you and your wife will take a seat for a few minutes, the doctor will be right out to talk to you."

He wanted to argue, to force the woman to tell him about Nik, but Carly squeezed his hand and led him over to a bank of chairs. Sitting, he continued to hold tightly to her long, strong fingers, his free hand balled into a fist on his knee as he stared down at the floor between his widespread thighs. "What if he's not okay?" he demanded in a low voice. "*Gott*, Carly, what if? It will be all my fault."

"No." She stroked their joined fingers. "It won't be."

"You don't understand. I had the chance and didn't take it to tell him that I wasn't going to accept—"

"Mr. Jones? I'm Jennifer Merriweather, the doctor in charge of your nephew's case."

A tired-looking fortysomething woman with pale skin and nondescript hair color stood before him. He surged to his feet, Carly rising right behind him. "How is he?" he demanded. "Is he all right?"

"Niklaus is currently stable but I'd like to run an additional test."

"Okay, sure." She was the doctor. If she felt that was necessary, then it was fine by him. All the same, concern made him ask, "Why?"

"Well, the good news is we've patched up everything that was visible to the naked eye. Niklaus was in shock when he came in, but we got him stabilized. He had a head laceration that turned out to look worse than it actually was, which we've stitched and cleaned. We're concerned about splenic trauma, but his blood test, urinalysis and rectal exam have all come back within acceptable limits."

When she paused to draw a breath, Wolf was too worried to sweat his manners. "So what's the bad news?" he demanded.

"Maybe nothing. We hope nothing. But while he hasn't complained of abdominal pain, it was clear upon palpation that that's a very tender area. Is Niklaus a fairly stoic kid?"

"Yes," Carly said, and Wolf nodded his agreement.

"In every way," he added. "And he's an athlete, so he probably wouldn't complain."

"That's why I'd like to do a CAT scan to rule out the possibility of a ruptured spleen. It's a common injury for kids who've received blunt abdominal trauma and a leading cause of internal bleeding."

Shards of ice slicing through his gut, he gave the doctor a curt nod. "Do what you need to do. Can I see him?"

"Yes. It will take a few minutes to get someone up here to take him to Radiology. You can talk to him until then." She signaled to a woman standing a few yards away. "Mary will take you and your wife to his room."

That was the second time someone had mistaken Carly for

his wife and for the second time they ignored it. Hell, they were together, clutching hands and no doubt looking equally worried to the outside observer. It was a logical assumption and not worth correcting.

Not to mention that it eliminated any possible arguments about Carly's right to see Nik at this stage of his treatment. Having her by his side comforted Wolf in a way he couldn't even begin to quantify, and as far as he was concerned, where he went, she went. So he merely thanked the doctor for her care of his nephew and shook her hand.

But it occurred to him as they followed Mary that the real reason he hadn't corrected the misconception was because he *liked* it. No. Liked was such a pallid word—he loved it. And wasn't that a kick in the head? If someone had suggested three months ago that the idea of being married to a mouthy, messy showgirl would fulfill every need he'd ever dreamed of, he would have laughed in their face. But not only did the notion appeal to him, it struck him as the very best of all possible worlds. Carly was bighearted, passionate in everything she did and the most nurturing person he'd ever met. As for messy—big deal. He knew how to run a vacuum cleaner. And mouthy? She might be way too emotional in her convictions, but he'd rather argue opposing points of view with her than have any other woman in the world validate his every opinion. He could no longer remember why an anemic yes-woman had seemed like such an ideal choice. He should be so lucky to have someone like Carly for his mate.

Too bad he'd screwed everything up between them.

Eventually Mary came to a halt in front of one of the closed doors lining the corridor, gave it a rap with her knuckles, then opened it and poked her head into the room. "I've brought you some company, Niklaus," she said cheerfully, then stepped aside and held the door open for him and Carly to enter.

Wolf barely noticed when she pulled it closed behind them. Neither did he pay heed to the nurse who smiled a greeting from over by the sink. He had eyes only for Nik, who was struggling up onto one elbow from where he was stretched out on his back atop a gurney. His nephew's face, where someone had swabbed it clean, was whiter than paper, with not a drop of blood left in it.

The teen's entire blood supply instead appeared to be clotted in his hair, smeared down his neck and arms and soaked into his T-shirt. Wolfgang felt his heart stop and knew Carly was equally shocked when she squeezed his hand hard enough to stop his own blood flow. But a quick glance showed that her face was as composed as he was fighting to keep his own. Still, the sight of Niklaus covered in blood, with fresh stitches bristling in a shaved spot above his left temple, kept him frozen in place for a long, interminable moment.

"It looks much worse than it is," the nurse informed them gently. "Head wounds bleed like the devil."

Pure relief had filled Nik upon hearing Wolf was here. Oh, thank God, thank God, he was no longer alone. But finally propping himself upright, he took one look at his uncle's stern, expressionless face and knew he was toast. The tight control over his emotions that had gotten him this far started to crumble.

"I'm sorry, Uncle Wolf," he said. He was genuinely ashamed his rash decision had brought them to this point. But that didn't stop him from feeling mortified at the quaver in his voice when he said, "I know you must h-hate me because I totaled your car and—"

"Screw the car."

"Huh?" Sure he must have misunderstood, he watched mutely as his uncle released Carly's hand and crossed the space that separated them in two huge ground-eating strides.

Reaching out, Wolf picked up his hand. Folding it in both his own, he sank down onto the stool that the nurse rolled up. "I can replace the frigging car," he said gruffly. "There's no replacing you."

That was the last thing he'd expected. God, he hadn't expected to hear that at all. Tears began to stream down his face. "This m-monster truck just came out of nowhere," he tried to explain, certain, despite his uncle's words, that he had to be wondering what had happened to his beloved street rod. "One minute the road was clear and the next thing I knew I was being T-boned." He wobbled atop his braced elbow and was aware of an increased beeping coming from one of the machines they'd hooked him up to.

"Lie back," Wolf urged, and helped him lie flat on his back again. "I want you to take some slow, deep breaths and try not to think about that right now, okay? The car's not important, Nik. Getting you better is." Reaching behind him, he tugged Carly forward. "Look who else is here to see you."

Nik closed his eyes for an instant when her fresh girl scent briefly replaced the odor of Betadine and blood surrounding him as she leaned to press her lips to his forehead. When she pulled back, he opened his eyes to see her smiling down at him.

"Hey, toots. I'm so glad you're okay." Her smile went crooked. "And God knows Wolf is relieved. You've never seen such a frantic guy in your life as this one when he heard you'd been hurt."

"Yeah?" He couldn't imagine that; Dr. Gloom didn't get frantic. Yet he found the idea of it somehow comforting. He drew in some deep breaths as instructed and didn't know if it was that or having concerned adults at his side that made the beeping of the machine slow down again. Either way, he felt a lot better than he had five minutes ago.

His cheeks felt cold, though, and he swiped his free hand across them. Staring blankly at the mixture of tears and diluted blood that soaked his fingers, he murmured, "Shit, I'm crying." Embarrassment flooded him and he looked up at his uncle and Carly. "You must think I'm nothing but a big baby."

"No," Wolf said as Carly brushed back a hank of hair that had flopped over his eye. "We think you're probably feeling a little weak from blood loss and one hell of a traumatic experience. You've had a day to make anyone feel like crying."

No shit. He'd destroyed the greatest car in the world, been hurt, scared and alone, and a lady doctor had stuck her finger up his butt. The humiliations just kept piling up. "Can we go home now?"

"Not quite yet. Your stomach's a little sore, right?"

Fear flashed through his gut and he shook his head. The doctor had kept trying to get him to say it hurt, too. But he hadn't because he'd known if he admitted that it felt sore, something terrible would turn out to be wrong with him. "Nah, it's fine." As long as he denied it, everything would be okay.

"Nik."

There was something about that stern, level-eyed look that made lying impossible. "Okay, it's a little uncomfortable. But nothing major."

"That's for the doctor to determine. She wants to run a scan to make sure there's no damage to your spleen."

"There *isn't*." God, don't let there be.

"I'm sure you're right," his uncle agreed, and his no-nonsense demeanor alone made Nik feel safer, not so scared. Especially when Wolf gently cupped a warm palm over his forehead and met his eyes with a serious nothing-up-my-sleeve gaze. "But even if there is, the sooner they find it the sooner they fix it. So if the doc says you need a scan, you get a scan. She's the one who put eight years into her medical training, not you or me."

"But—"

"No buts. It's painless and it's the smart thing to do—and you don't get those great grades by being stupid."

"Okay. But you'll take me home as soon as the test is done?" That was all he wanted right this moment, to go home with Uncle Wolf.

"If the doctor says I can. And no matter what, kid, Carly and I aren't going anywhere until you're ready to go with us." Wolf rolled his stool closer and bent his head to Nik's ear. "And about earlier," he said in a low voice, "I'm sorry. I should have told you then that I'm not taking—"

"Somebody in here call for an electric Kool-Aid acid test?" A young man, with a collage of tattoos that covered his arms from his wrists to where his biceps disappeared beneath the sleeves of his scrubs, strolled into the room. Stopping alongside the gurney opposite Wolf and Carly, he leaned down to release the brake. Nik stared at the disks stretching holes the size of dimes in the tech's earlobes. That didn't look like the most comfortable fashion statement in the world.

Straightening, the guy gestured grandiosely. "Let me introduce myself. My name is Mike. I'm your guide to the universe today. You ready, dude?" Moving around to the head of the gurney, he started rolling it down the room.

Every inch of Nik ached, but he twisted to look at his uncle as the tech wheeled him toward the door. "You'll still be here when I get back, right?"

"Absolutely," Wolf said with a seriousness that alleviated

Nik's last lurking fear of returning to find himself all alone once again.

He blew out a breath. "Okay, then." Until a few minutes ago, Nik hadn't realized just how much Wolf had come to mean to him over these past weeks. But he did—he meant the world. His uncle was steady and decent and always *there*, and Nik knew he could depend on him to do what he said.

He didn't have the first idea how to verbalize all that, however, and he sure didn't know how to apologize adequately for all the things he'd done wrong today—for stealing Wolf's car, then wrecking it, for saying he hated him when that was the furthest thing from the truth. So he merely met Uncle Wolf's gaze squarely as the friendly tattooed tech rolled him out into the hallway. He still detested the thought of leaving Las Vegas. But all the same—

"Maybe it won't completely suck, living in Ohio," he said as the door started to whoosh closed between them. "At least you'll be there."

Then the door clicked shut and he went limp on his back again. He looked up at the tech. "Let's get this over with. I wanna go home."

"Aw, damn, Carly. Damn."

Seeing Wolfgang stare at the closed portal, Carly thought the look on his face—the shock, the helpless love and hope—might just break her heart. She moved up behind him as he buried his head in his hands and reached out to rub his shoulders.

"See?" she said softly, digging her thumbs into the bunched muscles at the base of his neck. "He loves you." Nik's reminder that Wolf—that *both* the Jones men—would soon be leaving was a splintery stake in her heart, but she ignored the pain as best she could. "I don't ever want to hear you say again that you're a lousy parent, do you hear me?"

The nurse picked up some boxed supplies and headed for the door. "There's a buzzer on the end of the counter if you need help when your nephew returns," she said, then paused at the door to look back at them. "For what it's worth, 'Uncle Wolf,' I've seen my share of lousy parents around here. Trust me, you're nothing like them." She let herself out of the room.

"There you go," Carly said. "I rest my case."

Even as she watched, Wolf collected himself. He dropped his hands, squared his shoulders and straightened, swiveling around to face her. But instead of addressing the subject under discussion, he said crisply, "I suppose, if my rod is as totaled as Nik seems to think it is, I'd better start looking for two cars."

She blinked. "You're still going to buy him one?"

"Of course. It's still going to be his birthday in a couple of weeks." A wrinkle formed between his eyebrows as he looked up at her. "Why would you think I'd change my mind?"

"I don't know. Some might see it as rewarding him for bad behavior."

He snorted. "Like anyone's ever rewarded that kid for *good* behavior. He's been given damn little in his life, Carly. Aside from my mom, he hasn't had anyone or anything he could count on, and if you ask me, he could stand to be gifted with something that will be his alone. He screwed up today. But Nik is a great kid who turned out a hell of a lot better than any of us deserve, given the lack of support he's received all his life. I'm giving him the frigging car," he stated flatly. "And if that's rewarding him inappropriately, so be it."

"God, I love you."

He froze and so did she. She hadn't meant to say that out loud. It had just slipped out, had just—

Then she stood tall. She *did* love him and she was tired of holding it in like some shameful family secret that had to be kept tightly under wraps. It felt good finally to say the words aloud.

"*What?*" he croaked, slowly rising to his feet in front of her.

"I love you," she said serenely. "And before you say anything, I know we have an agreement, so don't worry that I expect this to change anything between us. I realize you're still going to Ohio, but I just wanted you to kn—"

His mouth cut off her words as he kissed her with a hot, hard intensity that left her leaning against him limply by the time he raised his head once again.

He stared down at her. "I'm not."

"What?" This time it was her voice that cracked. Stepping back, she licked her lips, still tasting him. "You're…?"

"Not going to Ohio. I'm turning the job down." A small, crooked smile tugged at his lips, and reaching out, he ran his palms down her bare arms.

"Since when?"

"Since this morning at work when you said you loved me." He stepped closer still, bending his knees to bring their faces level until she was staring directly into his eyes. "I knew then that even if you only said it because I offered to take you to the pet shelter, I couldn't leave."

Her heart started tapping out a thunderous tattoo. "So you're staying here for…me?"

He kissed the side of her neck. "Yes," he breathed in her ear. "For you and for Nik."

She tipped her head back to look at him. "But…if you weren't planning on taking the job offer, what were you guys fighting over?"

He sighed. "I didn't tell him I was turning the job down. I should have said something right away, but he started yelling

at me the minute I cleared the door. It got my back up. So I
suppose all of this—" he indicated the hospital diagnostic
room "—is really my fault."

"No. It's not." She leaned back from the waist in order to
level her sternest look at him. "Niklaus made choices, and
he has to accept responsibility for them. Perhaps you could
have handled things better, but you're not accountable for his
actions."

In a voice quiet but filled with conviction, he said, "I love
you, Carly."

She stared at him, her mouth agape. Snapping it closed,
she whispered, "Excuse me?" But deep inside warmth started
to bloom.

"You heard me. I love you. Somehow you've become the
most important person in my life."

Even as joy mushroomed in her chest she regarded him
skeptically. "That's quite a change of heart. I'm a far cry from
the *Stepford* wife you said you were looking for."

"That's a fact. And I find myself thanking God for it."

"Good answer." It earned him the biggest, brightest smile
in her arsenal. "So what happened to your big plan?"

"Oh, it's still there, it's just been tweaked a little and is no
longer the be-all and end-all that it used to be."

Wrapping his long hands around her hips, he picked her
up and gently set her on the counter. He nudged her legs apart
and stepped between them. "I was sixteen years old when I
first forged that dream," he said, rubbing his hands up and
down her khaki-clad thighs. "An unhappy, ambitious kid
with nothing else in his life. Hell, I'm still ambitious, and I'm
warning you right now that's probably never going to change.
I just know now that there's more to life than work, and I no
longer believe that I have to move to Middle America in

order to carry out my master plan. I've learned in the past few weeks that a guy can actually live a pretty decent life right here in Las Vegas."

Hope was a shining talisman floating up through the ether. "So you're willing to stay here after all?"

"Yes. At least until Nik gets through high school, and possibly even beyond. The truth is, working security for the big resorts is a major rush. I can't think of another job where I'd get to do so many different things in one shift. I've risen about as far as I can at the Avventurato, since Dan's not going to retire any time soon. But there are a lot of other casinos out there."

Wolf bent his head to give Carly a long, leisurely kiss, suffused with a happiness he'd never expected to feel this side of fulfilling his lifelong plan. Her lips were soft and pliable, and for a few sweet minutes he got lost in her taste, forgetting where they were and everything else that didn't have to do with having her in his arms again. Finally, he raised his head and said, "What about you? What do *you* want to do when it's time to stop dancing?" There was so much he wanted to know about her, so much that the parameters of their arrangement had prevented him from discovering.

"I don't know for sure. Something to do with animals, I suspect." Smiling softly, she reached up to cup his jaw in her hands. "Say it again."

"I love you." The emotion filled him to overflowing, lodging in his heart, occupying the very air he breathed, spilling through his bloodstream like a champagne fountain.

Her face glowed. "Oh, God, Wolf, I never knew I could love anyone the way I love you."

"That's what I like to hear." In fact, she couldn't say the words often enough to suit him. "So when do you want to get married?"

"Whoa." Her hands slid from his face and she scooted back an inch. "Let's not get carried away here."

For just a second his ego felt the sting of rejection. Then an empathy that was new to him took over. "It's called commitment, Beauty," he corrected gently. "That's a fair distance from getting carried away."

"You know my opinion on marriage."

"I also know how you came to hold that opinion. But you aren't your mother."

She drew in a breath, then slowly eased it out. "I know that, but I'm sure not ready to talk about getting hitched. Let me just have this moment of discovering that you love me, Wolf. Let that be enough for now, okay? Please."

He wanted it all, but he looked at her, sitting there with her flushed cheeks, her eyes filled with all the love that five minutes ago he hadn't even dared to expect. And he nodded. "Okay. It's enough. For today." Tomorrow, however, he planned to launch a brand-new campaign.

He saw the moment she realized it, too, for her eyes narrowed. "Resistance on my part just fires up your competitive juices, doesn't it?"

"Yep."

The light of battle began to flicker in the depths of her blue eyes. "And you think this is an argument you can actually win?"

"When the prize is living happily ever after with you?" Tightening his grip around her hips, he jerked her forward, eliminating the tiny space she'd put between them. Feeling her ankles hook behind his thighs, he gave her a smile that was all teeth. "Oh, yeah. So you might as well give in right now. Because *this*, my tall, beautiful blonde, is one battle I don't intend to lose."

Epilogue

"I now pronounce you man and wife."

Turning from the altar with a joyous smile, Carly gazed straight at Wolf.

He stabbed a blunt finger between the two of them. *You and me. Soon,* he mouthed from his seat in the third pew as she and Treena trooped behind Ellen and Mack, who had started down the aisle.

She grinned wider. He'd been relentless in his push for marriage for the past several weeks now, and she had to admit she was weakening.

Still—

"Don't start," she said a short while later when he asked her what kind of flowers she wanted for *her* wedding. They stood in the church parking lot loading Mack and Ellen's arrangements into the backseat of Niklaus's car. The sun was warm on her shoulders, the late afternoon sky a vast blue canopy overhead.

"You oughtta just marry him and put him out of his

misery," Nik chimed in. "I mean, when are you gonna make him stop sneaking back and forth every night? Not getting to actually sleep with you is making him cranky."

Carly raised her eyebrows at the youngster. "And this is different from his normal personality how?" she asked, then turned a stern look on Wolf. "You're enlisting *children* in your campaign now?"

He shrugged broad shoulders. "All's fair in love and—"

"So, Natalie," she said, ruthlessly cutting him off. Turning to the pretty brunette climbing into the front seat of the car, determined that she would change the subject, she said pleasantly, "How do you like Nik's new ride?"

"Omigawd!" The girl closed the door but lowered the window to beam at them as Nik started up the 1952 Buick Roadmaster his uncle had given him for his birthday last week. "Isn't this just the sweetest car *ever*?"

"Purrs like a kitten," Wolf said approvingly. Thumping the flat of his palm against the roof, he leaned down to look at Nik. "Drive safely."

"Like I have any other option," the teen replied cheekily, "with you right on my tail."

"Smart-ass kid," Wolf grumbled without heat as he and Carly climbed into the 1940 Ford coupe he'd chosen to replace his car, the same model as the one that had been totaled.

"And you love it." She flashed him an understanding smile, knowing how relieved he was that Niklaus had no lingering health issues from his accident. His spleen had only been bruised, and his biggest problem these days appeared to be whether or not he should eventually paint flames on the Buick's dark green fenders. He was definitely leaning in that direction, while Wolf declared it overkill, given the Roadmaster's myriad chrome features.

It was a short drive from the church back to the condo, where they met up with the kids to unload the flowers and carry them to the clubhouse Ellen and Mack had reserved for their reception.

Jax relieved Carly of her arrangement at the clubhouse door. "I have strict instructions where to place this," the tall man informed her. He gave her a quick once-over. "Did I tell you how pretty you look in your bridesmaid dress? Damn near as good as Treena—and that's saying something."

"Yes, we clean up pretty good," she agreed, performing a little tap and twirl in her peacock-blue satin slip dress. Materializing at her side in a matching daffodil-colored dress, Treena fell into step, and what had begun as showcasing her dress turned into an abbreviated impromptu dance.

They brought it to a halt, laughing, when it began to fall apart on them. But enthusiastic clapping greeted their efforts, and Carly looked over to find Ellen beaming at them from within the drape of Mack's beefy arm, her face alive with delight.

"Why, Mr. and Mrs. Brody!" Taking Treena's hand, Carly strode over to the newlyweds.

Ellen smiled radiantly, her face aglow with happiness. "Oh, my darlings, it's been a while since I've seen you dance! What an absolutely lovely wedding present."

"And dirt cheap, too," Carly said with a grin. "I guess we can take back the restaurant-quality cookie sheets we got you."

Treena gave her a slap on the hip before turning her attention back to Ellen. "Speaking of lovely as usual, you were a beautiful bride," she said, and bent down to kiss the petite woman. Her cloud of red curls drifted forward to brush against the shoulder of Ellen's periwinkle gown.

Carly followed suit, then both dancers turned and simultaneously bussed Mack on either cheek. "You treat her right," Treena admonished lightly when they pulled back.

"Aw, he will," Carly said, and gave Mack an additional kiss. "Mack's no dummy. He knows a good thing when he sees it, dontcha?"

"Darn tootin'." Wrapping his arms around his new bride's waist, he snuggled her back against his tuxedo-clad chest.

She smiled at the pure happiness that stamped the older couple's expressions. "Congratulations both of you. If *I* feel like you've been working toward this day forever, I can't even imagine how thrilled you must be that it's finally arrived." She glanced around. "Where are your girls, Mack?"

"Cracking the whip over the caterer." Mack chuckled. "Mags is her mother's daughter."

Guests started filtering in, coming over to offer their congratulations to the bride and groom. Carly and Treena drifted over to the bar to each get a glass of wine. Gazing at her friend over the rim of her glass, Carly said, "Are you ready to burst with excitement over your trip yet? Only a little over a week to go now."

"Oh, God." Treena laughed. "I'm already packed, which even I know is absurd. But, Paris! I am so pumped I can barely stand it." She took a sip of her Chardonnay and moved closer. "Jax and I have been doing a lot of talking lately and we've made some decisions about our future."

"Beyond quitting the troupe after this year?"

"Yes. We've decided I'm going to accompany him on his more exotically located tournaments for the next two or three years so I can see a little of the world. Then I'm going to open my own studio."

"Oh, Treen, I'm so happy for you!" Slipping an arm around her best friend's shoulders, she gave her a fierce hug. "Traveling is fantastic, but you've wanted your own dance studio for as long as I can remember."

"I know." Treena nearly hummed with contentment. "I am *so* excited. I never knew I could be this happy, Carly."

"No one deserves it more, toots."

Niklaus skidded to a halt in front of them, holding Natalie by the hand. "Hey, Nat and me are gonna go take Jasper for a walk. You want me to take Buster along, too?"

"That would be great! Let me just find where I put my purse and I'll get you my keys."

"No need," he said, racing off again. "We've got a spare at our place."

"Throw some kibble in the cats' bowls while you're at it," she called after him, and saw him wave a long-fingered hand in acknowledgment.

"You know he's dying to call you Aunt Carly," Wolf's voice murmured in her ear, and she tipped her head back to see him standing close behind her. "You really should put him out of his misery."

"Misery, my sweet fanny. I've never seen a kid so happy as that one is these days. I haven't seen him quit grinning since you gave him the car, although I personally believe that adopting the dog was probably the clincher."

"But then you think pet adoption is always the clincher."

"True. Still, the poor sucker actually believes you brought home Jasper for him, when you and I know you did it for yourself." And didn't she just love that impulse from a man not ordinarily given to impulsiveness.

He grinned sheepishly. "Yeah, well." Leaning around her, he gave Treena a smile. "So, you getting excited about your trip?"

Later in the evening, when the meal had been served, the toasts had been made and the lights were lowered while music filled the room, Wolf came up to Carly, where she was visiting with Ellen and her brother over by the bar. Claiming her for the next dance, he excused the two of them.

"You gonna let me lead?" she asked, tongue in cheek, as he led her onto the floor.

"Hell, no."

She gave him a wide-eyed look. "I am the professional."

"And I'm the big, strong man." He thumped his fist off his chest. "Trumps that professional crap every time."

"Ooh, caveman tactics." She slid into his arms. "That's always such a turn-on."

"I sure do like Ellen and Mack's choice of music tonight," he murmured as they swayed to Eva Cassidy's "Dark End of the Street." "Lots of slow numbers."

"Um-hmm." She felt the frenetic rush of the day fade away in Wolfgang's arms. "There is a definite upside to having mature friends."

They slow-danced for three consecutive songs. A Gary Moore blues number was about to come to an end when Wolf rubbed his jaw against her temple. "I love you, Carly Jacobsen," he said in a low voice. "I love you more than I ever knew it was possible to love a woman, and I want to bind you to me with every means at my disposal. Nik was right when he said I want to sleep the night by your side. I do. I want to fall asleep with you in my arms after we make love, not roll out of bed and sneak back over the balcony wall. I want to introduce you as my wife and have your picture on my desk at work. I want to grow old with you in a house full of animals. But you know what I want most of all?" He didn't wait for her to ask. "I want to knock you up."

She jerked, and a short laugh escaped him. "I know, it's a shocker. But I want a baby with you. Babies, if you're willing.

You'd be such a great mom. So, I'm asking you one more time—no competition, no one-upmanship involved. Will you marry me?"

"Ah, man." She turned her face into his throat and pressed her lips to the hot, damp skin beneath his jaw. Hearing him talk of lying in his arms at night and having his children had raised such a surge of longing in her that she knew it was time to quit saying no strictly for the fun of driving him nuts. "Okay."

He stopped dead. "Okay?" Leaning back, he stared down at her. "Okay, as in—"

"As in, yes, I'll marry you."

He whooped and swung her around, causing the other dancers on the floor nearest them to scramble out of range of her long legs.

"I take it she finally caved, huh?" Jax called from across the room as Mack and Treena echoed Wolfgang's ebullient hoot.

"Like a cheap paper plate." Wolf threw back his head and laughed, slowly grinding their mad twirl to a halt.

"Oh, very nice." Biting the inside of her cheek to keep from smiling at his delighted glee, she gave him a look of faux disgust. "Gloating is so attractive. I have to admit that was pretty good, though, sucking me in with the old romantic speech ploy."

"Make no mistake, *Liebling*, I meant every word I said. But you made me work harder for your slippery little hand than I ever anticipated. You gotta allow me a second or two to savor my victory."

"Savor it all night long, lover boy. I have the rest of my life to make you pay."

"Yeah." Hugging her close, he rested his forehead against hers and grinned. "I look forward to watching you try."